Fic
DeS   DeStefano, Sal
       The Methuselah gene

2/26

The Methuselah Gene

New Millennium Writers Series

The Methuselah Gene

A Science Fiction Adventure Thriller

By Sal DeStefano

BAINBRIDGEBOOKS
Philadelphia

Published March 2000
by **BainBridgeBooks**
a division of
Trans-Atlantic Publications Inc.
311 Bainbridge Street
Philadelphia PA USA 19147

Website address: http://www.transatlanticpub.com

ISBN: 1891696106

Library of Congress Cataloging-in-Publication Data:

DeStefano, Sal, 1956-
The Methuselah gene : a science fiction adventure thriller / by
    Sal DeStefano.
        p. cm. - - (New millennium writers series)
        ISBN 1-891696-10-6 (hardback)
        I. Title. II. Series
    PS3554.E846M47   1999
    813' .54—dc21

                                        99-34321
                                        CIP

To my beloved parents, Anthony and Gaetana,
and my good friend, Steven C. Schultz,
all snatched from me too soon by the scourge of cancer.

ACKNOWLEDGEMENTS

Many gave selflessly of their time to help mold The Methuselah Gene. Those who shared their unique professional expertise include Peter T. Amoroso, Third Mate, US Merchant Marine; Robert W. Fournier Jr., Director of Animal Husbandry for the New Jersey State Aquarium; and Lieutenant Erich G. Herkloz, Station Commander, New Jersey State Police, Point Pleasant Bay Station (now retired).

I particularly appreciate the contributions of Catherine Bansbach, Ph.D., Molecular Biology, who selflessly shared with me her broad and deep knowledge of bio-genetics.

For their assistance and inspiration, I am also thankful to Lee Greb, John A. Kiernan, Susan E. Light, William J. McDermott, James M. McKenna, Joseph A. Muresco, Stanton S. Roller, Jon and Kay Sontz, Mary Vines, and the entire staff of the Roxbury Township Public Library.

Perhaps my most ardent champions have been my wife, Doreen (my most candid editor), and my children Anthony, Rachel, and Sarah. I've been truly blessed to share life's journeys with these four wonderful people.

I am especially grateful to Ron Smolin of BainBridgeBooks, whose strong editorial leadership and belief in this story propelled my labor of love from dream to reality. Also at BainBridgeBooks, I thank W. Lane Startin, Anthony Notaro, and Peter Glaze for their insightful comments.

"... laboratory manipulations, both genetic and environmental, can lead to significant life extension ... it may be possible to develop methods for life extension in mammals, including humans ... these findings have tremendous implications for human society at large ..."

— Drs. Thomas E. Johnson and Shin Murakami
    Institute for Behavioral Genetics
    University of Colorado
    Journal of Gerontology: Biological Sciences

" ... at some point, almost every human disease will be treated in one form or another by gene transfer."

— Dr. Paul D. Robbins, molecular geneticist
    University of Pittsburgh School of Medicine
    BioScience

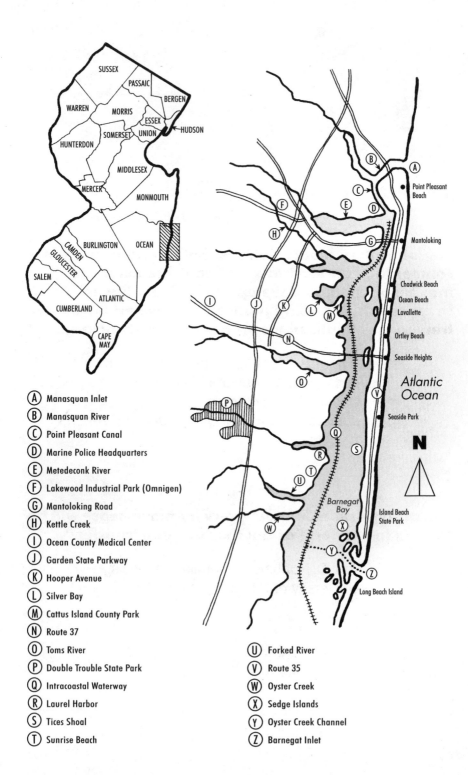

A Manasquan Inlet
B Manasquan River
C Point Pleasant Canal
D Marine Police Headquarters
E Metedeconk River
F Lakewood Industrial Park (Omnigen)
G Mantoloking Road
H Kettle Creek
I Ocean County Medical Center
J Garden State Parkway
K Hooper Avenue
L Silver Bay
M Cattus Island County Park
N Route 37
O Toms River
P Double Trouble State Park
Q Intracoastal Waterway
R Laurel Harbor
S Tices Shoal
T Sunrise Beach

U Forked River
V Route 35
W Oyster Creek
X Sedge Islands
Y Oyster Creek Channel
Z Barnegat Inlet

Prologue

Dr. Brian Byrne peered into the trinocular microscope at the same slide he'd gazed at countless times during the past two hours. He couldn't believe he had isolated the cause.

"Come quick, they're here." Ramanathan Patel, his second year graduate assistant, called from outside the tent.

At that moment, Dr. Byrne heard the muffled beat of distant rotors. He shot one last glance at the slide under the microscope, turned, and charged through the tent's door flap.

Rama pointed toward an immense orange ball looming low on the horizon, the sun sliding behind a vast expanse of rippling desert dunes. The spinning blades grew louder, but Dr. Byrne, blinded by the bright orange disk, could barely make out the approaching helicopter.

Rama glanced at his wristwatch. "Right on time."

Dr. Byrne chuckled. "I knew old man Andrews wouldn't let me down."

"Not after he read your report."

Dr. Byrne's archaeological team, consisting of himself and six graduate students, had struggled five weeks in the searing Western Desert to verify the truth behind hieroglyphics etched on 18 stone coffins unearthed in a burial chamber beneath a crumbling Egyptian temple 80 miles southwest of Damanhur. The symbols inscribed on each sarcophagus suggested the subterranean chamber held the remains of the eldest citizens of the ancient city, Saqqara, their ages at death ranging from 145 to 200 years.

Relying on the usual indicators of human aging when skeletal fragments were the only available evidence, such as size and number of teeth, tooth wear, and bone structure, Dr. Byrne, who had led archaeological expeditions in the Middle East for two decades, could accurately guess age at death to within five years. His team had exhumed the skeleton of an ancient Saqqaran woman, and according to the hieroglyphics engraved on her crypt, she had endured 160 arid

Egyptian summers. Dubbing her "Dusty Donna," Dr. Byrne's painstaking examination of her bones confirmed that the ornate picture symbols spoke the truth: she had indeed lived more than four decades longer than the generally accepted upper limit for human longevity.

Tapping his expertise in DNA profiling — the same technique used by police technicians to identify criminals — Dr. Byrne set out to learn why these fortunate few had lived such exceptionally long lives. He extracted cell samples taken from Dusty Donna's femur and made a startling discovery. The length of her Chromosome 16 was two-thirds shorter than that found in normal humans. Dusty Donna's genetic deformity had provided a critical starting point in Dr. Byrne's probe to determine the cause of her extraordinary life span.

Under a broiling sun amidst the desert dunes, he toiled with his six students inside a makeshift laboratory housed in a tent the size of a two-car garage. After seven days of intense effort, Dr. Byrne was sure he'd found the answer.

To confirm his hypothesis, he needed to perform another battery of DNA sequencing tests. Exhausting his supply of gel-forming reagents, he had e-mailed Dr. Henry Andrews, Southwestern University's Biology Department chair, requesting that five additional mini vertical gel systems, a dozen auto-radiography cassettes, and a drum of Acetonitrile be delivered to the dig site. Last night, Dr. Byrne received a reply. All the supplies he requested would be flown in from the American University in Cairo by 7:00 tomorrow evening.

Squinting at the blazing orange ball slung low on the horizon, Dr. Byrne could now pick out the head-on outline of a helicopter, about a mile away, coming straight at them.

He turned to Rama. "When Dr. Andrews saw the mutant L-2 sequence for himself, his eyes must've popped. Somewhere between those lines of DNA codons, you bet he read 10 more years of guaranteed federal funding."

"Let's hope the Southern blottings of Donna's L-2 hold up on retrial."

Rama was referring to the process by which geneticists compared two or more radioactively tagged DNA fragments. When DNA taken from a criminal suspect matched DNA taken from the crime scene, the probability the police had nabbed the wrong man fell to a scant one in 70 billion. Using similar technology, normal genes could be matched against those showing a mutation to pinpoint the exact location of the defect on the tainted gene.

The mutation Dr. Byrne and his students detected in Dusty Donna's L-genes, the mutation they hoped to confirm when re-supplied with gel systems and Acetonitrile, would explain why these 18 lucky Egyptians lived to such advanced ages.

The chopper's swelling silhouette, low in the sky, blocked the waning sun. Its engines roared so loudly Dr. Byrne was forced to shout. "I feel good about our initial results. Either way, by sunrise tomorrow, we'll know if we can break out the Dom Perignon."

Soaring to within 50 yards of the encampment, the helicopter hesitated, then hovered 20 feet over a landing pad the graduate students had leveled off in the sand. The brilliant red glow of the dying sun bathed the chopper from behind and prevented Dr. Byrne from discerning the big bird's color. Its shape, however, was plainly visible, and what he saw twisted his gut.

The helicopter swung sideways and descended. Its screaming rotor and jet thrusters kicked up sand and dust all around. Behind him, Dr. Byrne heard the walls of the tent flap wildly, like a flag battered by the winds of a hurricane.

Rama turned away, covering his face with the crook of his arm.

Dr. Byrne grabbed his student's elbow, and shouted, "That's no civilian transport."

Shielding his eyes with one hand, Rama looked back. "What are those things attached to the bottom?"

From the chopper's belly hung four cylinders, their fronts tapered to rounded points, their backs, blunted. Fins protruded from three sides. "Missiles. But why would the university send a military helicopter?"

The chopper's twin flat-bottomed runners touched the sand, and the roar of its engines softened to a steady whine.

Dr. Byrne squinted through the tawny cloud whipped up by the helicopter. He read five white block letters painted on the tail: BHERT.

The spinning blade above the chopper's main cabin slowed, and the sand began to settle. Before the rotor came to a stop, a wide door in the passenger cabin rolled open.

Dr. Byrne gasped. "What the hell?"

In quick succession, eight soldiers leaped through the door and dropped to the ground, their heavy black boots kicking up a storm of tiny dust clouds.

Rama stepped back, behind his teacher. "Who are they?"

Dr. Byrne counted five men and three women, all clad in solid beige battle fatigues, sprinting toward the tent. Each gripped a semi-automatic rifle. For a split second, Dr. Byrne thought about running, but from the looks of this bunch, running now might only get him killed.

In seconds, the eight combat-ready invaders formed a perfect half-circle around Rama and Dr. Byrne, trapping them against the tent.

Dr. Byrne tried not to stare at the eight muzzles aimed at the ground. He noticed stitched on the chest of each soldier's uniform a round blue patch displaying the same five letters he'd seen on the helicopter's tail.

From behind, Rama blurted, "Who are you? What do you want?"

One of the female soldiers, a tall brunette with emerald eyes, stepped forward, and hollered, "Speak only when told to."

In the threshold of the chopper's cabin door appeared a large, burly man wearing the same beige uniform as the others. Dark sunglasses hid his eyes.

Peering through the settling dust, Dr. Byrne couldn't be sure, but the big man looked African-American. He confirmed his hunch when the husky soldier hopped off the platform and sauntered closer.

"Dr. Byrne, I presume."

Dr. Byrne loathed conversing through sunglasses, but with those eight formidable weapons so close he squelched his impulse to demand the stranger remove them. "That's right. And who, may I ask, are you?"

"Major Charles F. Clayton, Ph.D. I'm with the United States government."

"Are you affiliated with the American University in Cairo?"

"Not exactly." The big man took a step closer. "And I'm the one who asks the questions. Is it true you requested five vertical gel systems, twelve auto-radiography cassettes, and a canister of Acetonitrile from Dr. Henry Andrews, Biology Department chairperson, Southwestern University?"

"Yes, but how could you know? My transmission was coded. Who are you people?"

"Isn't it a little odd an archaeologist would send a coded message to request supplies and equipment for gel electrophoresis?"

"Not if he's a bio-archaeologist, and DNA sequencing is routinely performed by his field team. And what business is it of yours, anyway?"

"If you use gel electrophoresis routinely, why the need for encryption?"

Dr. Byrne wasn't about to share the most important archaeological find of the decade, maybe the century, with some military hotshot barging in as if he owned the place. "I'm not saying another word. You haven't told me who you are, where you're from, or what you want. Unless you give me answers, you can take your guns and goons, and get lost."

Clayton flashed a smug grin. "So you want answers, do you?" He un-zippered a chest pocket on his desert fatigues, pulled out a blue document, folded in quarters, and thrust it in Dr. Byrne's face.

Dr. Byrne snatched the paper and began reading. At first glance he thought it was a prank conceived in poor taste by Dr. Andrews. Scanning to the bottom, Dr. Byrne realized not only wasn't this a joke, but the future of his project was in imminent danger. His eyes lingered on the signature and embossed seal at the lower right-hand corner. "What does the President of the United States want with me?"

Without a word, Clayton walked past him, yanked open the tent's door flap, and waved both him and Rama inside. He pointed to the emerald-eyed female soldier and a blue-eyed male corporal to follow.

Inside the tent, the green-eyed soldier positioned herself a few feet to Rama's right. The male soldier stood a yard to Dr. Byrne's left. Both warriors clutched their weapons, aiming them toward the floor.

Clayton spoke with hushed intensity, as if disclosing top-secret military information. "Now, Dr. Byrne, tell me exactly what your preliminary sequencing tests revealed."

The federal search warrant shoved at him by Clayton convinced the archaeologist he'd best cooperate. "I'll tell you. But it's a little technical. So try to ..."

"I have more training and experience in bio-genetics than you'll see in a lifetime, so don't dumb it down. You advised Dr. Andrews that you isolated a mutation in Chromosome 16 of the remains entombed at the burial site. On what gene?"

The L-genes. They're the genes that ..."

"I know damn well what L-genes do. Give me specifics."

"A guanine base replaced a cytosine in the DNA sequence direct-ly upstream of the L-2 coding region. The mutation created a novel, dominant messenger RNA splice site, resulting in partial truncation of the L-2 repressor protein. The allele inhibits expression of ..."

"Methuselah!"

Confused by the intruder's reaction, Dr. Byrne said, "If you know so damn much about the mutation, why bother asking?"

Clayton ignored him and barked at the young woman, "Take these two outside. Have Childers and Ryan round up the other five students. They can't be far. We'll return them to the embassy for debriefing." His probing brown eyes scoured the tent. "Come back with Jacobs, Cho, and a dozen boxes. I want this place cleared out. When you're done packing, burn the tents."

Before Dr. Byrne could protest, Rama lunged toward the big man thundering the orders.

The green-eyed soldier guarding Rama's flank lifted her rifle and whacked the charging student across the belly

Rama doubled over, moaning. His legs folded and he collapsed to the ground.

"How dare you!" Dr. Byrne kept perfectly still. "You can't just barge into my camp, disrupt my work, and brutalize my students! I'll report this to the university. And the press."

"Once you've been debriefed, Dr. Byrne, you'll understand why you and your students, and the president and my team, are the only ones who'll ever know about my trip to the desert this evening."

"What about my work?"

The black intruder's hard brown eyes locked Dr. Byrne firm in their grip. "By executive order of the commander in chief, your work at Saqqara is done."

"When can I return?"

The big man's gaze held tight. "Never, Dr. Byrne. Never."

(Eighteen Months Later)

SUNDAY

JUNE 28

1

The fishing line jerked taut. A sandy-haired boy, no older than 10, wearing blue jean cut-offs and a white tank-top firmed his grip on the rod. He locked the spinner and glanced to the bow. "I got something big!"

On a padded bench seat in the fore section of the 15-foot bowrider, a muscular teenager lounged with his eyes shut. He dangled his own line in the bay under a steamy mid-morning sun. Lying perfectly still, he said, "Yeah right. Another patch of seaweed. Or the anchor again."

The black foam handle slipped from the younger boy's grip. He squeezed his fingers deeper into the black rubber, paling his knuckles. "No way. This time, I got a live one!"

A tug from directly beneath the boat yanked the line straight down, and dropped the boy to his knees. He gripped the rod even tighter. The boat, pulled down by the unseen force, listed left.

Not looking back, his older brother barked, "What are you doing, Joey, trying to sink us?"

Joey said nothing. His arms, bent at the elbows and pressed hard against the fiberglass wall, began to numb. Clutching the handle close to his face, his nostrils stung with the strong scent of salt-soaked line wrapped around the spool. The tip of his pole curved into a strained arc that touched the dark green surface. "Get up, Bobby! I need your help."

Bobby still ignored him.

Watching the pliant shaft of his fishing pole dip underwater, Joey groaned. He saw a submerged object beside the vessel, about two feet below the rod's tip. The size and shape of a rowboat, a shade of green darker than the sea, the underwater shadow moved closer to the boat and vanished under the hull, taking line with it. Joey grasped the rod even tighter, sure the line would snap, hoping it would, but the nylon held fast, tilting the small fiberglass craft 45 degrees to port.

"What are you doing on the floor?"

Joey shot a look to the bow and saw his big brother sitting up, gawking at him. "Can't you see I'm in trouble?"

Bobby dropped his rig on the bench seat and leaped into the boat's stern, straight to Joey's side.

"I can't ... can't let go of the pole. Take it, cut the line, do something."

"Take it easy," Bobby said. "Maybe it's a 10-pounder. I'll set down next to you and take the pole out of your hands. Whatever you do, don't let go 'till I tell you."

Joey's forearms, bent together at the elbows, rod stuck in between, had turned chalk white. "Like I could let go if I wanted to."

Bobby crouched beside his brother. He slipped his left palm around the foam handle above Joey's knuckles, the other around the rod below the spin reel.

As Bobby's grip firmed on the pole, relief came to Joey's fingers. His arms free, he sprang back, fell on his butt, and rolled to his side. Crumpled on the fiberglass floor, Joey's fists knotted into balls of pain snuggled close to his chest.

"I'll be damned," Bobby hollered, "We got us a tough guy. He don't know it yet, but I got a trick or two."

Knees tucked to his belly, Joey felt the boat pitch. He tried stretching his arms, but they wouldn't budge. Startled by clanging metal, he turned his head and watched a stainless steel socket roll past on the floor. The boat's tool kit had spilled its contents. He whiffed the stench of petroleum. Gasoline tinted blue with oil dribbled into the drain well. Knees throbbing, he looked down to find his kneecaps scraped raw. He fought the pain racking his arms, and extended his hands straight out.

Sensation returned to Joey's fingertips. He flipped onto his back and stared at blue sky, finally able to stretch his legs. Somewhere to his right, he heard Bobby swear.

He watched as his older brother stumbled backward, right toward him. No time to move, his knees bore the full impact of Bobby's rump.

Joey screamed. Bobby, clutching the rod, rolled right, and unpinned his brother's kneecaps, smeared with blood.

Joey pushed himself off the floor and collapsed onto a vinyl seat mounted to the transom. The brown bag that held their lunch skidded across the floor. Two sandwiches wrapped in deli paper tumbled out and softened into a pair of soggy purple masses saturated with salt water and gasoline. Repulsed by the smell, he looked up at his brother.

Bobby slanted the fishing pole down over the bowrider's port side. The nylon line ran straight into the water, pulled by whatever clung to the hook.

Bobby looked over his shoulder. "You okay, kiddo?"

Joey rubbed his forearms. "Sore as heck, but I'll live. "What do you think I snagged?"

"Maybe the biggest blue ever to pass this way. Could have wandered in through the inlet."

The nylon line slackened, wafting free in the breeze. "I'll be damned," Bobby said. He jerked the rod three times, then slowly turned the reel. "This bad boy's still on the hook, but his fight's gone. Too bad. I wanted a game."

Bobby released the spool lock.

Joey's belly turned. "Just reel him in and let's go home."

"Patience, little brother. You got to …"

The spinner whizzed like a swarm of angry bees. Twenty-pound test line whirled off the reel so fast that the spool smoked.

"That's better!" Bobby shouted.

The fish hadn't given up after all. "I hope you're happy."

As fast as it started, the reel stopped spinning. Bobby snapped lock the flywheel. "Do me a favor, Joey. Fetch me the net. I'll need a hand when I pull this baby in closer."

Limping to the bow, Joey heard the spinner click-click as Bobby took up line. Up front, Joey reached down for the net, arms tender, knees bleeding. Planting the net handle on the floor, he leaned on the pole. Joey glanced back and saw his older brother fiddle with the spin reel. Dreading the fight ahead, he lingered in the bow, scrutinizing the sky over the New Jersey Pine Barrens. On the western horizon he noticed a line of clouds. By the looks of their puffy white tops and slate gray bottoms, they'd have just enough time to reel in their catch and get back home.

"What are you waiting for? I got him real close."

Joey hobbled back to the stern, leaning on the net's shaft like a crutch. "Can you see him yet?"

"No, but he's right under us. Stay left of me and hold the net in the water. Remember, keep it close — real close. Soon as I pull him up, shove it under him."

Joey's adrenaline pumped. He gripped the handle and leaned over the side. Holding the pole inches above the surface, he looked down and saw only dark green water.

"Bring the net closer," Bobby said. "I got a feeling he's coming straight up."

Joey choked up on the handle and angled the rim down, close to the boat's hull. The netting floated limp on the calm surface, waiting to snare whatever lurked below.

Something beneath the vessel slammed hard against the fiberglass bottom.

Joey lurched forward, dropping the net. He grabbed the black rubrail to stop himself from tumbling overboard. The impact sent the bowrider bobbing out of control. Bent over, holding the side, Joey stared into the murky green and watched a surge of furious ripples circle out from under the wobbling craft.

The net began drifting away, and Joey reached out to grab its handle. His arm extended over the water. He saw the same submerged object he'd seen before move out from under the boat. A long oval, about six feet across, pointed at both tips, it lingered inches under the surface. The object's broad flat side, mostly olive green, was streaked with electric blue and copper red. One rounded edge of the ellipse appeared smooth and sharp, the other, serrated and sawtoothed, and its green surface, coarse and pitted. Joey recognized the shape, but its size was all wrong. "Is that what I think it is?"

"I don't know." Bobby's voice quaked. "Just forget the net, and pull your hand in."

Joey stared mesmerized. Eight or nine hinged spindles spoked out from under both sides of the elongated disk. Their length was a mystery, for the tips of the protrusions vanished into the depths of the muddy bay.

The oval shuddered, and the dangling protrusions flexed. Joey's neck tingled, for he understood the oval and the spindles moved with purpose. Before Joey could retract his outstretched arm, a giant claw shot up from the water and clenched tight.

Pain! Blinding pain! — as the claw tore through sinew and muscle. He shrieked, yanking his arm toward his body, but the huge claw, bright white and brilliant blue, held tight.

Then he saw its eyes, smoke gray bowling balls, set on the tips of green, fleshy stumps jutting from under the edge of the beast's jagged shell. The blank eyes stared past Joey, indifferent to his agony.

The pincer tightened its grip. Razor sharp teeth, like the ragged blade of a bow saw, pierced deep into Joey's flesh. Blood gushed from his arm and dripped to the sea. He heard a dull snap, his radius and ulna split by the talons of the massive beast.

Joey felt his chest, then waist, rake the top edge of the vessel's outer wall. The claw was pulling him over the side. From behind, Bobby's sturdy arm closed firm around his belly.

Hunched half out of the boat, Joey glimpsed sideways, and saw Bobby clutching a steel wrench. His brother pounded the tool against the green elliptical shell, but the creature seemed unfazed by the blows. Joey felt the arm slip from his waist. "Don't let go Bobby! Don't let go!"

A willowy wet whip, green and coarse, brushed Joey's neck. With his free hand, he slapped it away. From between the creature's eyes protruded some sort of antenna. The living wand sprang back against the side of Joey's head. Its rough surface probed his ear and cheek.

Centered beneath the two antennae radiating from the edge of the green oval, Joey saw a rectangular opening, a breach in the monster's shell. Remnants of brown seaweed clung to its razor sharp edges. The bone white plates, the creature's mouth, pulsated open and shut in measured mechanical motion, ready to devour their next meal. The vacant ashen eyes no longer gazed past Joey. They focused directly at him.

A rancid odor oozed from the creature. Shards of half-eaten marine matter dripped from bone white slits creasing the rim of the rectangle. Joey retched.

Tool in hand, Bobby reached over his younger brother's back taking aim at the claw's joint just above where it gripped Joey's arm. Each blow of the wrench pulsed Joey's arm with excruciating pain. Turning his head, he pinched his eyes shut.

After a flurry of whacks, Joey heard a sharp crack. The force tugging at his arm ceased. He felt nothing where his arm should be, and thought for sure it was gone. When he opened his eyes, he was amazed to find the blue and white claw, severed at the joint, attached to his elbow.

Cream-colored liquid spewed out from the jagged break in the pincer where Bobby hammered it off. Bobby hauled Joey into the boat. Joey, dazed and bewildered, collapsed face-up on the floor, the detached claw still clamped to his arm.

A high-pitched wail split Joey's ears. He looked over and saw another of the creature's claws latched across Bobby's chest.

Bobby clutched the wrench with one hand, the claw with the other. "Let go you son of a bitch!"

Boosting himself with his unfettered arm, Joey sat up. A putrid stink emanating from the animal filled his lungs and made him dizzy. His brother's shriek, steady and harsh, split his eardrums.

Through blurred vision, Joey saw Bobby's fingers grope in vain at the claw affixed to his torso. He heard the splash of the wrench as it dropped from his brother's hand into the sea.

Then Joey heard a loud snap, like a tree trunk split by lightning, as the claw sliced through Bobby's breast bone. Blood gushed from a gaping wound, tarnishing his golden tan. His arms flopped to his sides, and his bright blue eyes opened wide. He tried to speak, to scream, but said nothing. Without a fight, Bobby, in his blood-soaked blue jeans and muddy sneakers, disappeared over the side of the boat.

Too scared to move, too weak to cry, Joey sat mutely, gazing toward the distant swamps on Cattus Island, impervious to the oppressive humidity and stifling heat emanating from the fiery sun overhead. The serene slapping of shallow waves against the bowrider's hull was all he heard from Barnegat Bay.

2

At the austral tip of New Jersey's Barnegat Peninsula, surrounded on the east by the Atlantic Ocean, the west by Barnegat Bay, and the south by Barnegat Inlet, lies a nine-mile spit of salt marsh, beach plum, and sloping sand called Island Beach. Less than 1,000 feet wide along most its length, Island Beach stands as the last vestige of raw land on a barrier island confronted with suburban sprawl.

On a deserted path snaking through the park's bay side forest of oak, holly, pine, and ever present marsh grass, the 36-year-old father, wearing faded blue jeans and a crisp green sport shirt, hiked with his nine-year-old son.

David, eyes as brown as his father's, wore khaki cotton shorts and a white T-shirt emblazoned on front with two royal blue letters, "NY," the immortal logo of the New York Yankees. Perched on his head, an oversized Yankees cap, the same cap Allen had bought him two years earlier in Anaheim at an Angels double-header against the Bronx Bombers.

Sipping Cokes and munching franks under the California sun, Allen had explained to his son the fine distinction between tossing a curve and hurling heat. He would never have imagined that only two summers later, he'd care less about teaching David how to pitch a baseball than doing everything humanly possible to ease his son's agony. All conventional therapy had failed David, and the inoperable brain tumor kept growing. Now Allen faced his toughest task ever — instill in his son the will to live — though death must surely prevail.

David tugged the tip of a marsh stalk growing along the footpath until he could pull the blade no further, then snapped it free, like a slingshot. "I know why we're here, Dad."

Allen swallowed hard. "Since when do you read minds?"

David answered as blandly as he recited his multiplication tables. "You're gonna' tell me I'm not getting better."

David's neuro-oncologists used the term glioblastoma multi-forme, a type of brain stem glioma, to describe the silent invader killing David. Classified a Grade III astrocytoma because of its rapid growth, the expanding tumor exerted tremendous pressure on surrounding brain matter, damaging the healthy tissue, and producing all the terrible symptoms — vomiting, headaches, and dizziness — David endured with increasing severity and frequency. In time, the swelling mass would choke off his brain's ability to regulate the basic bodily functions necessary to sustain life. Chemotherapy had proven ineffective.

Radiation might extend David's life an extra month, maybe two. Long enough, perhaps, to allow Allen and his boy one last summer of early morning strolls along the surf, sifting for sea glass. Two more months, maybe, of building cities of sand at the edge of the sea, then watching the tide wash them away. By September, if David held out that long, the tumor in his head would drain what little strength was left, and his last days would be spent in a hospital bed. Allen prayed they could share this one last summer together.

They came to a place on the trail at the edge of the water where the dense marsh grass succumbed to an open vista of Barnegat Bay. Allen could see clear across the teal waves to the mainland, five miles west. He spotted the Bayville water tower, a pale blue cylinder rising high above the coastal plain.

The stiff breeze blowing at his back gave cool relief from the midday sun. A single pearl-colored osprey, gliding into the wind above the sea, cawed a lonely cry.

Allen squatted beside his son and looked squarely into his chestnut eyes. "Sometimes, no matter how hard parents try, they can't make their child better, and ..." Cowardice swelled. "... and you shouldn't worry, because your mom and I are doing everything we possibly can to —"

"Does it hurt when you die?"

Allen had not anticipated the question. "No one knows for sure. I believe your spirit, the invisible part of you that makes you special, goes to heaven. Your spirit lives with God and the angels and the spirits of all the people who died before you, the people who loved you when you lived on Earth."

Eyes shimmering, David said, "When I'm in heaven, will I still be able to give you and Mom hugs and kisses whenever I feel lonely?"

Allen's facade began to crack. He scooped David up, into his arms, and carried him, chest-to-chest, eyeball-to-eyeball. "Let's say you died first, before me or Mom. Even though we couldn't see you, your spirit would always be with us. Same thing if I died before you or Mom. You couldn't see me, but I'd be right there beside you, whenever you needed me. To know I was near, you'd just have to listen. Not with your ears, but with your heart."

David's eyes scoured Allen's. "When I die, please don't stop talking to me. Tell me stories at bedtime, like you do now. I'll miss them so much if you stop. I can't imagine what it would be like not to have you and Mom around — to tuck me in bed at night or take me to neat places or even yell at me when I do something bad. I don't ever want to leave you guys."

Allen could barely compose himself. "Don't worry about that, either. You'll be with us so long, I'll be telling you what to do when you grow up and have children of your own."

Secure in Allen's arms, David squeezed his father tight, as if he'd never let go.

At a clearing in the path along the bay, where the woods opened onto a vast field of crawling beach heather, Allen stopped. He turned his back on the meadow and looked out on the smooth rolling Barnegat.

David's tone betrayed no emotion. "If I'm gonna' be around so long, when will I start feeling better?"

Deserted by his courage, Allen answered, "Soon," but remembering why he was here, added, "The important thing is that you fight. Don't give in, and don't give up."

David pulled back in his father's arms, revealing a stern gaze and a new, dark mood. "I don't believe you. I know I'm gonna' die soon."

"What makes you so sure you're going to die before me or Mom? Nobody really knows when it's their time to go."

"I know how sick I really am. After you guys tuck me in bed at night, that's when I hear you and mom fight about my medicine. You say the doctors should try something new. Mom says something new could make me worse. Then Mom cries."

David's voice began to crack. "You always tell me everything's going to be all right. If everything's going to be all right, why does Mom cry so much?"

Allen's face burned, angry at his inability to restore his son's will to live. Left with only his heart, he answered, "The chemotherapy isn't working the way it should. We haven't told you because we're afraid you'll lose your will to fight. Your only chance to beat the tumor is if you believe you can."

David exploded, sobbing, "I knew you were lying! You should've told me the truth before. I'll never believe anything you say. Never!" David wriggled in Allen's arms. "Put me down!"

Allen released his son, who spun and raced down the path, disappearing behind a swathe of bayberry bushes at the far end of the meadow. Tears blurring his vision, Allen stared at the trodden sand, furious he could not tell David the truth without destroying his faith. He sat down, cursing his clumsiness. A few minutes passed, which seemed like hours.

From behind the bayberry shrubs he heard young male voices filled with scorn and mockery, then an anguished cry, David's cry.

He dug his heels in the spongy sand, and dashed toward the voices he heard on the opposite side of the thicket. Around the corner, the beach widened to about 50 feet.

Four boys ringed his son. The youngest looked no more than 10, the oldest, 15 or 16. The oldest boy, a gangly stick with a dangling brown pony tail, clutched David's Yankees cap. David stood in the middle of the pack, his scalp, ravaged by chemotherapy, laid bare for all to see.

David darted forward to retrieve his cap. The lanky boy jerked it away and tossed it to one of the younger boys, who jeered David. "What happened to your head? Get run over by a lawn mower?"

Through the taunts, David said nothing, but Allen read his tears. Intense fury rose within Allen. He darted straight at the largest youth, screaming, "You're brave when it's four on one. Let's see what you can do against me."

Four startled faces turned in unison. The long-limbed teenager, bug-eyed, pivoted and fled into the swamp grass beyond the beach. The boy clutching David's cap froze. He dropped the hat and bolted into the marsh, chasing his older cohort. The other two, abandoned on the beach, spun and fled.

Allen sputtered to a stop where the dark blue Yankees cap lay on the sand. He watched the last two scoundrels vanish into the willowy reeds like hunted deer. Allen cupped his hands to his mouth. "Assholes!"

He snatched his son's cap from the sand, smacked it against his leg to remove the sand, then handed David his cherished possession.

David stood silent, looking down. His bloodshot eyes belied his hurt. "Keep it," he said. "I don't want it."

"Don't let those jerks get the best of you. You're better than they are."

"I'm not better. They're better. They're gonna' live and I'm gonna' die. They can keep my stupid hat."

"You love this cap."

A single tear coursed David's cheek, lingering at the corner of his mouth. "I don't need a stupid hat if I'm gonna' die."

Allen knelt in front of David and clasped both his arms. "You think I'll let you go without a fight?"

His son's eyes glimmered. "You going to invent a new medicine for me?"

Allen wished his answer could be different. "You know I'm not the kind of doctor who heals people."

"You're a doctor. Doctors make sick people better."

"I study plants, not people."

"You work in a laboratory. Scientists invent things in laboratories. You could invent some kind of fruit that makes cancer go away."

If only it were that easy. Ten years ago, Allen had earned his Ph.D. at the University of Southern California, where he studied the use of recombinant DNA technology to increase nutritional yields in food crops. After graduating with honors, he pursued a postdoctoral fellowship under the tutelage of Dr. Milton Levy, perfecting state of the art gene engineering protocols to improve agronomic efficiency. Together, they genetically altered wheat seeds to produce crops resistant to toxic rust fungus.

"If I could invent a medicine in my lab to kill your tumor, I'd already have done it. But that's not what I do."

Plucking the Yankees cap from his father's hand, David covered his naked scalp. "I heard you tell mom about some experiments you did with rice. You changed the insides of rice plants so they could grow in the ocean. Couldn't you change the cancer inside my brain to make it go away?"

Last September, six months after David's diagnosis, Allen left California to accept a post as research manager for Omnigen, a nine-year-old biotech company with its single office in Lakewood, New

Jersey. His wife's family resided two hours away in Allentown, Pennsylvania, his own mother in Seaside Park on the barrier island. The job at Omnigen gave them both a chance to live closer to family during their time of crisis.

Omnigen's owner, Devon Maddox, betting on the future of agrogenetic manipulation, had hired Allen for the purpose of charting a new course for the company. At Omnigen, Allen devised a procedure using micro-injection to combine the genes of *Distochlis palmeri*, a species of saltgrass that flourishes in seawater, with genes in the germ cells of *Oryza sativa*, common paddy rice. The result: a halophytic strain of genetically enhanced rice seed capable of thriving in high-saline environments, such as saltwater bays and coastal estuaries.

Aquaculture, the science of raising animals and plants in water, had been practiced as long ago as the 17th Century, when the Japanese cultivated amanori, an edible red algae, at the edges of the ocean. Four-hundred years later, in a world where fresh water stores had grown more precious than ever, the integration of biotechnology and aquaculture had propelled geneticists to the brink of developing a broad array of salt-tolerant crops — a true "blue revolution" — promising abundant food supplies for the burgeoning global population.

USDA approval for commercial use of Allen's protocol was certain. By next spring, after a final battery of validating tests, Devon Maddox would be pitching Allen's recombinant DNA protocol to world markets.

An offshoot of Allen's research had led him to discover genes that when altered, improved the ability of tomatoes, corn, and soybeans to grow in high saline environments. He envisioned future generations of farmers cultivating entire crops under the Earth's oceans.

Allen remained painfully aware, however, his high-tech solutions for fending off starvation in less developed nations could not save his son. He locked eyes with David. "I can't make anything to destroy your cancer. I change plants to make them better. I don't invent cancer cures. Someday, other scientists —"

"I don't care about other scientists. I only care about what you can do. If you can't help me, nobody can."

David's words cut like a knife. Allen drew a long, slow breath. "Please David. Your mom and I love you more than anything. You can't give up."

"I can too." David whirled and strutted defiantly across the beach toward the marsh stalks.

Allen caught up. "Where do you think you're going?"

David faced him with a frown. "I don't feel like fighting any more. I'm tired of the headaches. I'm tired of throwing up. I'm tired of hospitals. I just want it to be over."

"Don't say that. You belong with mom and me. You give up, the tumor wins. You fight, maybe you have a chance." He searched his son's eyes for hope.

"But I'm not getting better, Dad. You can't help me, so I might as well be dead."

"David …"

"I made up my mind. I don't want any more needles or pills. I don't want to be hooked up to any more machines. I just want it to end."

"That's the worst thing you can —"

David covered his ears, squeezed his eyes shut, and screeched, "Don't say anything!"

Allen conceded and did not speak.

Lowering his hands from his ears, David opened his eyes. "I'm tired. I just wanna' go home."

On the same path that led them to the beach by the bay, father and son retreated, side-by-side, divided by a wrenching silence.

Allen had come to this magical place to revive hope, not deliver despair. He detested his inability to formulate a plan to beat David's tumor. In the past, meticulous attention to detail, rigid adherence to plan, these never failed. But against David's cancer, Allen could conceive no blueprint, no strategy to guarantee success. Defeat seemed inevitable.

Allen scanned the horizon over Barnegat Bay. Towering gray-bottomed clouds floated inexorably east toward the Atlantic, signaling the arrival of a storm front. The blue-green sea had begun to swell. A gloomy rain would soon drive out the sun.

At first glance, the bay appeared empty clear across to the mainland. Then Allen spotted two New Jersey State Police Marine Division rescue skiffs screaming one after the other, about a half mile offshore, headed for the upper bay. Allen's eyes followed the small, fast vessels until they disappeared behind a subtle bight at the north end of the park. They sure looked anxious to get somewhere.

Allen and David resumed their trek along the sandy trail that twisted inland into a thicket of red cedar, sassafras, and low pine. Allen's heart broke, watching David, his every step a labored effort. With diabolical efficiency, the cancer, chemicals, and radiation all sucked his energy. Allen would gladly have offered his shoulders, even insisted, but David disdained any reminder of his frailty. When his son wanted help, he would ask.

Strolling a few paces behind, giving David his distance, Allen again considered the medical options. Surgery, long ago ruled untenable, left only radiation therapy and chemotherapy. Both were tried and neither helped. The neuro-radiologist had recently suggested increasing the potency of David's radiotherapy. He warned, however, of severe neurological damage to David's healthy brain cells. And the time his son would gain was measurable in weeks. Weeks!

Clearly, Allen must try something else, something different, anything but sit back and watch his son die.

He glanced ahead. With each step, David's Yankees cap bounced up and down. Staring at the bobbing cap, David's earlier plea came back to him — could his father change the inside of his brain to make the cancer go away?

Three months earlier, David suffered a particularly virulent reaction to his bi-weekly chemotherapy session. He vomited all weekend, day and night, until his stomach ejected blood and mucous. Allen had planned to take his son to the Yankees home opener the following Monday, but the two hour car ride would have depleted David of all his energy. Instead, Monday morning, Allen returned to the lab as usual. Dr. Nathan Miles, Allen's senior colleague at Omnigen, sensed his dejection. Allen asked Miles what he thought about using gene therapy to fight David's glioblastoma, but his response was luke-warm.

An avid reader of *Nature Genetics* and *Science Age*, Allen knew well the incredible achievements of the legions of geneticists and biochemists who devoted their lives to the development of gene therapy protocols. By the dawn of the 21st Century, these leading-edge scientists had added recombinant DNA technology to the medical profession's arsenal in the war against many diseases, including cancer.

But precious few gene protocols for treating cancer had earned FDA approval for use as standard treatment, and administration of those required strict supervision by the recently revamped Recombinant DNA Administrative Council, known commonly as the RAC. The FDA's reluctance to grant wholesale approval was grounded in concerns about safety as well as the reality that remission rates using gene therapy exclusively to combat cancer had proved mixed at best.

Before surmounting the restrictions imposed by the RAC and the FDA, however, he must overcome the doubts of the most important person in his life, his wife, Jennifer. Fiercely protective of her son, she was torn between her willingness to do whatever she must to help her son live and her fear of the harm that could come to him from unproven treatments. She was particularly fearful that David might be turned into one more guinea pig for geneticists striving to perfect experimental cancer therapies.

But David's options were limited and time was running out. Backed in a corner, Allen's only chance to help David boiled down to a gene therapy plan that had once crossed his mind but promptly forgotten in the face of Jennifer's concerns. True, the untried recombinant DNA protocol he had contemplated involved risk, but offered no less hope than chemicals or radiation. Any logical plan, even an unproven one, was better than waiting idly by for death to steal his only child. First, though, he must persuade Jennifer that his plan for David would cause him no harm.

Father and son came to a two-lane asphalt ribbon running the length of Island Beach, dividing the ocean side on the east from the bay side on the west. Allen paused at the edge of the pavement, watching an exodus of cars, vans, and SUV's withdraw north in advance of the storm's arrival.

Smarting from David's words on the beach, Allen readied himself to act. Of course, actually conducting the gene replacement procedure meant risking his job at Omnigen, maybe his career as a scientist. But these seemed a paltry price to pay for a chance to save his son.

When they crossed the blacktop, Allen observed his metallic-blue Honda parked alone in the small lot beside the roadway. A low-lying sheet of heavy gray obscured the sun. Unlocking the front passenger door for David, Allen felt a raindrop spatter his cheek. He made sure David fastened his seat belt, then strode to the driver's side, imbued with renewed vigor.

As Allen opened his door, the silence of the surrounding sand collapsed under a deafening roar of mechanized rotors shrieking overhead. He glimpsed up. A single helicopter, its tail sporting the blue and gold triangle of the New Jersey State Police, barreled north with dogged urgency, vanishing quickly over the bayberry-covered dunes. That must have been some nasty accident in the upper bay.

3

New Jersey State Police Lieutenant Lawrence Bateman lingered on the top landing of the black wrought iron stairway hugging the rear outside wall of Point Pleasant Station, two stories of white concrete block overlooking Point Pleasant Canal. Built in 1926, the canal linked the Manasquan River with the head of Barnegat Bay, transforming Barnegat Peninsula, previously attached to the mainland at Point Pleasant, into a barrier island. On sunny Sundays between June and August, the two-mile canal bustled with activity – cabin cruisers, center consoles, motor yachts all returning from the Atlantic through the Manasquan. Today, the arrival of chilly temperatures and overcast skies had driven the Sunday sailors home early.

Bateman's freshly pressed blue-gray uniform fit just right. He stood a strapping six-foot-two, and his waist revealed only the slightest trace of a bulge. In preparation for the news conference, he had dutifully combed every black hair on his head into a flawless part. At 37, he was the youngest state trooper to earn the rank of regional commander in the history of the Marine Division.

Bateman had earned his triumph hard and early. Ten days out of the academy, during his second week of a six-month tour with the Urban Tactical Unit, Bateman found himself responding to a Newark bank robbery in progress. Entering an air conditioning duct from the elevator shaft, he shimmied his way into the hollow space above the square ceiling tiles. When Bateman crashed through to the tellers floor below, two astonished gunmen cramming fists of cash into burlap bags never knew what hit them. Bateman broke his right ankle and took a .38 slug in his thigh, but the perpetrators suffered a far worse fate. Today, both can be visited at Pineview Memorial Cemetery, Rows 2-B and 9-C respectively.

Bateman healed and then promptly transferred to the Marine Division. Growing up in Brick Township, 10 minutes from the Point

Pleasant Canal, he welcomed the opportunity to return home to the Jersey shore. His love of the sea and his job as a maritime law enforcer proved a perfect marriage.

Bateman gained a reputation for slamming the door in the face of trouble. He brought to its knees a ring of coke dealers based in Hoboken who used the Intracoastal Waterway as a supply route. He busted a syndicate of yacht thieves operating out of Marine Park in Brooklyn who targeted the Jersey coast. And he plucked from frigid December waters a young boy who fell through a thinly iced lagoon off Bay Head, all in his first four years of service. In his fifth, he collected his reward, promotion to buck sergeant, unheard of for a trooper less than 10 years on the force.

Today, a different kind of foe lay in wait, an enemy Bateman dreaded worse than any encountered during his 14 years of service to the state. These were the news reporters, assembled out front, who Bateman had summoned for a late afternoon news conference. He viewed this meeting as a necessary evil, hoping to douse wild rumors circulating among the local press corps about this morning's incident in Barnegat Bay.

Only two hours after it happened, stories of transplanted Loch Ness monsters and Peter Benchley sharks surfaced like dead fish in a barrel. Since 1 p.m., reporters from Ocean and Monmouth Counties had rung his phone off the hook. Although it was too soon to know the accident's cause, Bateman felt obliged to give the press a statement. Left to their imaginations — and desire to sell papers — the reporters would no doubt incite every half-cocked Captain Ahab in the state to hunt some non-existent, modern-day Hydra.

At today's gathering, Bateman expected the same faces he'd seen at other news conferences, the same reporters from *The Asbury Park Press* and *The Ocean County Observer* who grilled him two years ago about his alleged mistreatment of a crack dealer he arrested after a high-speed boat chase from Bay Head to Barnegat Inlet. Putting that fiend behind bars cut the legs off a major tri-state distribution channel. But the reporters hammered him for the strong motivational techniques he purportedly employed to encourage the crack peddler to spill his guts — a rope, a cinderblock, and the bay. The furor nearly cost Bateman his job. As usual, they had overreacted, for Bateman had hauled the scum out a good two minutes before the tide topped his chin.

Much as he despised the news hounds out front, he knew most were local folks, like himself, out to earn an honest living. Most, that is, except one. Just thinking the name — Brian Strasser — induced a wave of nausea Bateman associated with a three-day stomach virus.

Strasser was no reporter. Reporters impart information. Instead, Strasser oozed with the stench of rotting garbage. Bateman could count on his pinkie the number of times Strasser wrote the truth. Worse yet, the mealy slime bore a grudge against him — perhaps because Bateman made no secret of his view that Strasser plied a sleazy brand of yellow journalism for the *Toms River Chronicle* not worth the paper it was written on.

Strasser's deceptive methods of interrogation irked Bateman most of all. He lured his victims by confronting them publicly with a bald-faced lie, touting it as truth, then watching with sadistic satisfaction as his target twisted and turned, struggling to refute the statement's accuracy, pleading to clarify the record.

Today, Strasser would have a field day, because today, Bateman did not know the truth.

He gazed down the black metal stairway glistening from afternoon showers that had eased to a light drizzle. Descending the steps, he hesitated at the bottom, stealing a last glance at the canal. Maybe Strasser had missed his call. If he were really lucky, maybe Strasser was off on a hiking expedition — in the foothills of an active Mt. St. Helens!

Bateman ambled the concrete walk along the side of the building. When he reached the end, he unlatched the chain link gate and turned the corner.

"Bateman, why are you hiding the truth about what happened to those boys?"

The too-familiar drone gnawed his ears. Strasser stood front and center at the base of the white marble stairs cascading from the building's main entrance in a crowd Bateman estimated at 20. Strasser wore the same olive green corduroy leisure suit he wore at every news conference. The repulsive jacket fit his short frame and plump middle like the scaly skin of a lizard.

Bateman made his way to the portable podium his men set up for the conference. Through the volley of questions thrown at him, a single voice pierced the din.

"Isn't it true the kids' boat was destroyed by an animal with a giant claw?"

Bateman struggled to retain his composure. From the swarm of faces, which on second guess numbered over 30, he recognized only a dozen or so. "Ladies and gentlemen, thank you for taking time out of your busy schedules this afternoon."

A sea of hands shot up.

"I know you have lots of questions, so let's get started." Bateman spotted Peggy Mitchell, a veteran reporter for *The Asbury Park Press*. He always gave Peggy the privilege of first inquiry. Though tough, she never goaded or embarrassed anyone. "Peggy, your honors."

"Can you confirm reports that the boy injured in Barnegat Bay this morning was attacked by an animal? If so, what is his present condition?"

Bateman answered the easy question first. "We recovered a 10-year-old male from a 15-foot bowrider. He was admitted to Ocean County Medical Center at approximately one o'clock this afternoon. Because he's a minor, I can't release his name. The victim sustained severe trauma to his left arm resulting in significant blood loss. At the time of rescue, he was conscious, but in severe shock. I received word less than a half hour ago his condition was upgraded from serious to stable. He's expected to make a full recovery, but he's still despondent and hasn't been able to answer questions regarding the incident."

"You're begging the question." It was Strasser. "She asked if the boy was attacked by an animal."

Bateman addressed the group as if Strasser weren't there. "If you kind folks would give me a chance, I'll answer all your questions." Bateman paused. "We have yet to determine the cause of the accident, but we're confident the physical evidence collected from the scene will assist in reconstructing the events resulting in the child's injuries. To answer your other question, Peggy, the accident hasn't been ruled an animal attack, a collision, or anything else. I hope you, along with your colleagues, remember that fact when you write your stories."

A clutter of hands reached for the sky, a dozen voices barked in unison. Bateman picked out William Brennan of *The Ocean County Observer*. "Yes, Bill."

"Is it true a second boy was involved?"

"Yes, we believe a second male, the teenage brother of the boy we recovered, was also in the boat at the time of the incident. The parents gave a statement that the boys left their backyard dock at approximately 7 a.m. for a fishing trip in Barnegat Bay. We've initiated search and rescue operations to recover, to locate, the missing youth. We will continue —"

"Bateman, the people have a right to know the truth. First you call it an accident, then you call it an incident. What the hell really happened out there? What if I told you I took an exclusive with someone at the scene. Someone who actually saw that boy's arm nearly cut in two?" The throng broke into a loud buzz.

Bateman glared at Strasser. "You can't tell fact from fantasy."

"I'm glad that statement's for the record. I only wish I were a fly on the wall when you see my cover story in tomorrow's *Chronicle*."

Strasser must be lying. Who would have given him an eyewitness account? The first trooper on the scene, Officer O'Donnell, was a good man with good sense. Any leak wouldn't have come from him. "Okay, Strasser, where did you get your information?"

"My secret, and if you don't behave yourself, I just might print a certain picture in my possession, a photo of the victim, Joey Martin, with his arm drenched in blood, dangling off his little shoulder."

Bateman reeled. How did he get the boy's name? A picture too? Impossible. "Strasser, what are you talking about?"

"Oh boy, are you in for a surprise." Turning his back on Bateman, as if to exclude him from his own news conference, Strasser raised his arm and pointed south toward Barnegat Bay.

"Folks, there's something big out there. Something that maimed a little boy in our own backyard, probably killed his older brother too. Something that grew a claw as big as a man, a claw the police recovered from the boys' boat and brought back to this building. I'll defy Mr. Bateman to refute the word of the first person who arrived at the scene — a fisherman anchored only 500 feet from the attack, the same fisherman who radioed the police for help."

The horde erupted, swarming Strasser with a barrage of questions, disregarding Bateman.

So that was it! The vulture had gotten to Kurt Clemens, the fisherman who initially broadcast the call over Channel 16 to report a vessel in distress.

It wouldn't surprise him if a sportsman plying these waters kept a camera on board to back up his fish stories. Clemens had plenty of time to snap a few photos during the seven-minute interval between the time he radioed for help and the moment O'Donnell arrived at the scene. Strasser must have paid a bundle for those pictures.

The thought gave Bateman a headache. Splashed on the front page, a grisly photo of the Martin boy, his limp body covered in blood, mangled arm dangling off his shoulder. The gruesome image, along with Strasser's claim as to the cause, would entice yahoos of every ilk to hunt the bay for an unknown predator. Also certain, any army of weekend warriors converging on Barnegat Bay would suffer casualties, either by grounding up on the bay's expansive shallows, or colliding into each other's Wellfleets and Bayliners.

His primary duty, to ensure public safety, required that he warn these journalists to report this incident with discretion. Attempting to capture the attention of the babbling crowd, Bateman let out a sharp, hacking cough, as if to clear his throat. Eliciting no response, he tried again, this time louder. Still no reaction. Finally, he roared, "Excuuuse me! Excuuuuuuse me, folks!"

A hush fell over the assemblage. All heads turned to him. He seized the reins, narrowing his eyes and deepening his voice.

"Look, people. I called this conference to relate facts, not fairy tales. The facts lead this department to only one conclusion: late this morning, a young boy and his brother fishing in Barnegat Bay were involved in a life-threatening encounter. We know the nature of the boy's injuries. We know the location of the accident, incident, or whatever you choose to label it. We've recovered the vessel. As we speak, my men are combing it for evidence that could shed light on the cause.

"I can also tell you what we haven't concluded. We don't know for sure the boy's wounds were the result of an animal attack. Yes, that's one possibility under investigation, but until we analyze all the evidence, we can't say for sure. It would be irresponsible for me to stand here and tell you there's a sea monster loose in Barnegat Bay. And it would be reckless for you to report anything that could incite public hysteria. I went out of my way this afternoon to meet with you people so you could report fact, not fiction."

Strasser sneered. "You didn't come here to reveal facts, you came here to hide them. This time tomorrow, the citizens of New Jersey will know what really happened to Joey and Bobby Martin, no thanks to you."

Bateman restrained his instinct to leap those four steps and pound Strasser's greasy flesh to a pulp. How dare Strasser imply he had anything but the best interest of the public in mind? Obviously, he was wasting his time with these reporters, particularly with Strasser stirring them up like this. He addressed the group.

"Ladies and gentlemen. I assure you that our department is looking at every possibility regarding this unfortunate incident. When the investigation is completed, we will release all pertinent information and take any steps necessary to preserve public safety in the bay. Thank you."

With that he strode back into the building, oblivious to the cacophony of the press corps below him.

As he marched through the double-glass front doors, the state trooper gave the dilemma his total attention. What kind of animal grew a claw that large? The sooner he knew, the faster he could quash the media frenzy he sensed was about to explode, nourished on half-truths and blatant lies.

After assisting the paramedics load Joey Martin onto the rescue chopper, O'Donnell removed the claw from the bowrider and returned it immediately to headquarters. Bateman and O'Donnell measured the claw, then packed it on ice in the evidence lock-up on the lower level. An unearthly 52 inches from the tip of its pincer to the point where the shell had been broken or chopped off, something about the claw's shape and color appeared as common to Bateman as August flounder, but was something he couldn't put his finger on.

Bateman slipped into his office on the second floor. From behind his desk, he stared out the window at the Point Pleasant Canal trailing north in a straight line toward the Manasquan River. The drizzle had given way to steadier rain, casting a depressing shroud over the lonely waterway. He turned and glanced down at his desk to a five-by-seven photo of his wife, Judy, sunshine blonde hair and plucky grin, huddled with their three sons in the last car of the roller coaster at Seaside Heights. The thought one of his own children might be savaged like the Martin boys sent a shiver through his spine.

He knew the claw held the key. Police regulations governing the handling and storage of animal remains in a police investigation required he promptly deliver the claw to the state's forensic laboratory in Trenton. But his gut told him to hold off. The start of peak summer season, July Fourth, was less than a week away. If a dangerous animal stalked Barnegat Bay, Bateman needed to know exactly what he was dealing with, and he needed to know within the next 48 hours. Weeks could pass before the bureaucrats at state headquarters provided an answer. He needed a faster way to identify the beast.

First, he considered calling Joe Larson, a marine biologist at the New Jersey State Aquarium in Camden. Bateman's unit once helped Larson free a pair of dolphins stranded in the Navesink River. But Larson was too closely linked to the state police superintendent's office. He might try Barb Davis, an old girlfriend from Brick Township High School who worked her way up to operations manager at Jenkinson's Aquarium across town. The danger there, as with any aquarium, too many hands got involved. Inevitably, someone would leak information. He needed to find a knowledgeable scientist he trusted completely, someone with no ties to the state.

Bateman plopped into the brown leather chair at his desk and closed his eyes. Instantly, they snapped open. "Damn, why didn't I think of you sooner?" At the academy, an eloquent guest lecturer from the New Jersey Department of Environmental Protection instructed cadets on identifying marine plants and animals indigenous to the bays and estuaries of the Jersey shore. Love of fishing and a common interest in target shooting forged a camaraderie between student and teacher. Every other weekend, from April through October, they chased fluke and women. When both stopped biting, they honed their sharp-shooting skills at Shore Shot Pistol Range.

Ten years ago, his fishing partner relocated to southern California to pursue a doctorate in biology. Since then, Bateman rarely saw him, but they spoke on the telephone at least once a year. Last September, his friend returned east to accept a position with a local firm engaged in genetic research, bringing with him a lovely wife and adorable son, both of whom Bateman met last December. Bateman could trust this man — both his intelligence and discretion. And he hadn't worked for the state in a decade, another huge plus. Twirling his Rolodex, he stopped at 'J,' spotted 'home,' and punched in the number of Dr. Allen J. Johnson.

4

Jennifer looked Allen square in the eye. "I want what's best for David, too, but we're talking about his genes. Conjuring up salt water rice seed for Omnigen is one thing, meddling with our son's life, quite another."

Jennifer demanded complete honesty, especially when it came to David's illness. She insisted on understanding every detail of his treatment, from what triggered the side effects of his chemotherapy to how his doctors selected radiation dosages. Her thirst for truth, in fact, was what Allen loved most about her.

An hour earlier, Allen tucked David in for the night. Trying not to wake him, he kept his voice low. "Jenn, the chemo isn't working. It only makes him feel miserable. You and I both know we have to try something different."

In faded blue jeans, Jennifer sat on a blue plaid sofa beneath their living room picture window. Her shaggy chestnut hair poured over her shoulders, accenting large doe-like eyes, browner than coffee. Curved in all the right places, motherhood merely enhanced her graceful arcs. She gave the look of a girl in her mid-20's more likely to name the hottest Manhattan nightclubs than a well-schooled, 34-year-old mom who could rattle off the latest Caldecott Medal winners.

Allen desired her. But David's rigorous care left little time or energy for the sensual pleasures that complete a well-rounded marriage. Their son's illness, a darkening storm cloud, cast a shroud over their intimacy.

Behind Jennifer, open milk-white blinds exposed a vacuous night sky made darker still by steady showers that had drenched the streets of Lavallette all evening. Jennifer rose brusquely from the couch, averting Allen's gaze, and brushed past him. She shuffled through a pine-paneled arch leading into the kitchen, and dropped wearily onto a wood-frame cafe chair tucked under a rectangular table. He followed her, taking the seat directly across.

Her loose paisley pullover, white swirls on forest green, did little to mask the alluring curves of her breasts. Elbows planted on the white Formica, Jennifer set her chin in the cupped palms of her hands and dared him with simmering mahogany eyes. "You and I both know if there were a safer alternative to chemo, we'd already be doing it."

"But I'm not talking conventional —"

"I know damn well what you're talking about. Alternative therapies. We covered that ground months ago. First, we ruled out shark cartilage. Then we spoke to a slew of certified nutritionists about megavitamin therapies, macrobiotic diets, and nutrient supplements. We even talked to that Sudanese faith healer.

"We agreed from the start we wouldn't subject David to half-baked voodoo remedies. You told me yourself unorthodox treatments could actually accelerate cancer. Now, out of the blue you'll concoct some unproven DNA therapy, and expect me to say: 'OK, Allen, go ahead and do what you think is best, what I say doesn't matter anyway."

A lonely tear rolled down her cheek. "Well I've got news for you. He's my son too, and before you play God with his life, you'd better convince me you know what the hell you're doing."

The truth stung hard. The type of treatment Allen contemplated had achieved only mixed results in humans, and those limited successes were achieved by scientists who spent their entire professional lives experimenting with gene-based cancer cures. Allen's own experience was limited to DNA re-engineering of plants, occasionally animals, but never humans. But his colleague, Dr. Nathan Miles, had devoted most of his adult life developing recombinant DNA protocols to combat disease, including cancer. With help from Miles, Allen was convinced he could make gene therapy work for David. "As a weapon against cancer, gene manipulation is no half-baked voodoo remedy. I admit, the protocols aren't perfect, but we don't have a whole lot of time, do we? We wait for perfect and David will be dead. Then, who —?"

"That's not fair!"

"Let me finish!" Allen shot up and marched to the sink under a small solarium window blackened by the night sky. He turned to face Jennifer, who glared at him. Realizing he would lose her with angry lecture, Allen checked his frustration with a tone of gentle persuasion. "Even when the results start proving consistently effective, it'll be years before the FDA approves DNA treatment for cancer. At least I know the ins and outs of genetic engineering. With a little guidance from Nate, I could use that knowledge to help David. I can't sit back and watch him die. I have to do something, anything, to keep him alive."

Jennifer wiped her cheeks dry with the palm of her hand. "Do you think I enjoy sitting around watching our son waste away, a little each day? One minute he tells me how scared he is to die, the next, he gets so depressed, he won't speak to me for hours." Her dam burst, spewing a torrent of hurts. "I'm the one who holds his head when he vomits so hard he wishes God would take him. I'm the one who cradles him in my arms and sings to him when his head hurts so bad I have to stop him from pounding his skull against the wall. I live with it every day, so how dare you suggest I would sit back and do nothing if I knew there were some other way to help him?"

She shot up, shoved her chair backward, and stormed across the kitchen, stopping so close to him, their toes nearly touched. Her five-three frame forced her to look up. Indignation burned in her eyes. "You know perfectly well what's at stake for me. I'd give anything for a miracle cure, maybe more than you." She scowled. "Ever think what happens to our marriage if David dies?"

Then she said nothing. All at once, the tension in her body melted, and she stared straight ahead with a glazed, far-away look. Allen saw in her drooping shoulders and glassy brown eyes resignation and sorrow. She spoke in a frightened whisper, "I know David means everything to you. With all my heart, I love him, too. But I also love you, and there may come a time when we'll be alone again. Will you love me then? Will you still want me, even if ..." Her voice trailed to silence.

She was right. Allen hadn't given much thought to their lives without David. In one very important respect, Jennifer's stake was higher than his.

Two years after David was born, Jennifer experienced unusually painful menstruation accompanied by profuse bleeding. After the third month, she sought the help of her gynecologist. During her pelvic exam, Jennifer's doctor discovered abnormally firm tissue in her abdomen. Following laparoscopy, the diagnosis was swift and devastating. Jennifer suffered from progressive endometriosis, an aberrant growth of uterine mucous membrane in the pelvic cavity.

Jennifer's gynecologist hoped after six months Danazol would shrink the patches and Jennifer would conceive. The medication proved worthless. As a last resort, Jennifer opted for laser surgery to excise the hardened tissue. Two months passed, and she still hadn't conceived. Another exam showed the debilitating implants had returned. Six months and three professional opinions later, their choices were reduced to one. Shortly before Valentine's Day, less than two years after her symptoms appeared, she was forced to undergo a hysterectomy.

Allen understood why Jennifer questioned his love for her in a tomorrow without David. But Jennifer was wrong. His devotion to her transcended all, the tragedy of David's illness, and the certainty she would never bear another child. He had always cherished her and would cherish her always.

When they met at USC, Jennifer was pursuing her master's in computer science. From their moment of chance encounter in the campus library, strangers among the stacks, stalking the same poet, Emily Dickinson, he opened his heart to her. Though their intimacy had waned since David's awful disease, the fire of his yearning still burned bright. No matter what happened, even the loss of their cherished David, he would never leave her.

Her head hung low before him as she wept. He wrapped his arms around her and pulled her close. "Know one thing. I will never abandon you. I'll never stop loving you. David's death may leave a hole in my heart that never heals. But without you, that hole only gets deeper and wider until it swallows me up, and then I'm nowhere. I need you, Jennifer. I need you to keep that hole from getting bigger, to stop me from falling in."

Jennifer looked up. Fresh tears marred her perfect cheeks. "I love you so much, but if David dies, I'm afraid I'll lose you."

He would never be complete without her, and he must make her know that. "I won't leave you, no matter what. Remember what I said way back when. Good times and bad, forever."

They stared into each other's souls. Though no words passed, Allen read in her eyes that a prayer had been answered.

Clasping his fingers, she stepped back and seemed to study him. Her lips parted, as if to speak, then withdrew to a tight sliver.

"What is it?" Allen coaxed.

She hesitated. "I know chemotherapy won't save our son. But how can you do better than his own doctors?"

Convincing her to give him a shot at David's tumor with his own gene-based remedy would require all the powers of persuasion at his disposal. In her quest for truth, Jennifer demanded facts. Once she absorbed information, she based her decisions on sound reasoning and common sense.

She raised a valid point. How could some unproven procedure he might devise at Omnigen do more for David than the best oncologists and neuro-surgeons in the region? To sway his wife, Allen must appeal not only to her heart, but to her mind. Above all, he must be honest.

"I can't say for certain my plan will stop David's tumor. Some scientists spend their entire careers searching for DNA-based cancer cures, and come up empty. But not all have failed. Some of the brightest minds in the country are making important progress with gene therapy to battle cancer."

"But what can *you* do?"

"You know I have a solid background in genetic science, and maybe I can use it to help our son." Allen heard his own desperation. "This afternoon in the park, David begged me to help him. He doesn't understand why I'm a doctor and can't do anything. Well, maybe I can. He's not looking for guarantees, he just wants me to try." Allen closed his eyes, squeezing back the pain. "I'm only asking you to let me try."

Jennifer released Allen's hands and drifted to the kitchen table. Her back to him, she paused. The stance was familiar, She struck it whenever mulling a difficult decision. Finally, she turned. "If you want me to consider this crazy notion of yours, I need to know exactly what you intend to do and how you intend to do it. I'm no geneticist, but I need to understand. Remember, we're not talking about some silly grain of rice. We're talking about our son."

Jennifer had cracked the door open. He would either gain her undying support for his plan, or remove it forever from her thoughts. Since Jennifer based her decisions on fact and logic, his work was cut out. But he excelled at imparting knowledge to others, whether at USC, filling the minds of budding biochemists with nucleotide sequences, or in his own back yard, showing David the basics of riding a bike without training wheels. Invariably, the light of achievement emanated from the eyes of his students, and for Allen, that beam was its own reward.

Adrenaline pumping, he marched over to Jennifer, clasped her elbows, and slapped a kiss on her forehead. "Jenn, you're absolutely right. I wouldn't think of trying something like this on David unless you understood exactly what I was doing."

He grabbed the looped back of a kitchen chair and waved for Jennifer to sit. "Let me explain."

5

Jennifer's intense brown eyes never left his as she snuggled into the chair Allen offered her. Allen sat at the head of the table, close to her right. "Do you know what DNA is?"

She frowned, as if insulted at the mere suggestion of her ignorance. "How could I forget? Bio 101 was a required course at USC, and Dr. Nealy was my professor. He was so old, the kids took bets he wouldn't make it to the end of the semester."

Allen persisted, "What exactly do you remember about DNA?"

"It's the stuff life's made of. At least, that's how Dr. Nealy put it."

"Too vague. You need a clearer image in your mind. DNA isn't some amorphous notion. It has physical properties."

"Doesn't DNA have something to do with chromosomes?"

"Warm," Allen nodded. "But do you remember what DNA looks like?"

"I remember it has a special shape, a shape that lets it make copies of itself."

"Right. Let me show you." Allen stood and spun, pulling from the drawer behind him a white-lined legal pad and a yellow pencil. He sat back down, eager to strut his stuff for Jennifer. "Bear with me." For two minutes, Allen sketched feverishly, than slid a diagram in front of his wife.

"This is the famous 'double helix.' It's what deoxyribonucleic acid, commonly known as DNA, looks like inside the nucleus of every cell of every plant and animal alive. Of course, DNA isn't two-dimensional, like on the paper. It's really an intertwining spiral. Think of the double helix as a microscopically small, incredibly long rubber ladder twisted around from the tip of one end to the other. The cross rungs of the twisted ladder consist of molecules called nucleotides.

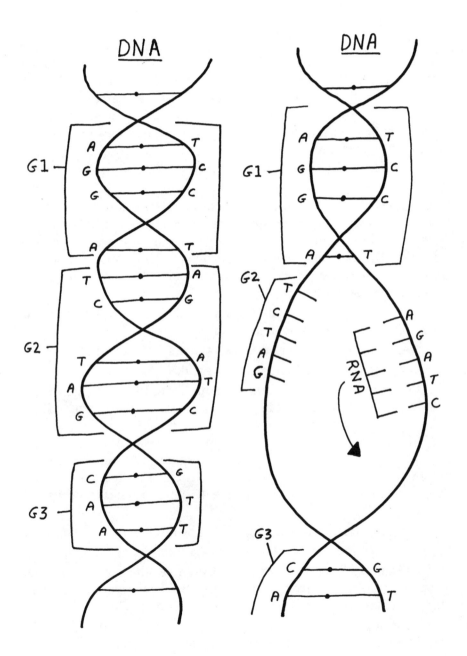

Nucleotides contain sugar, phosphate and one of four types of nitrogen molecules. The key ..."

"Not so fast. Give me the basics. What does DNA have to do with genes?"

"I was getting to that." Leaning over the table, Allen pointed to the sketch with his pencil. "The key to telling one gene from another lies in the nitrogen component of the nucleotide. Each half of each cross-rung in the DNA ladder can hold only one of four possible nitrogen bases: adenine, thymine, guanine, or cytosine. In the drawing, that's what the letters A, T, G, and C along both sides of the helix stand for." Allen paused, allowing Jennifer to digest.

"You only have the As connected to the Ts, and the Gs with the Cs."

Allen continued with boyish enthusiasm. "You're absolutely right. Because of their unique shapes, adenine can only bond with thymine, and guanine with cytosine. And that's the way it goes all along the DNA ladder. Each set of nitrogen bases is called a base pair. A gene is simply a specific group of base pairs along the sides of the DNA ladder. So —"

"Let me guess. The base pair you labeled 'G1' represents one gene, 'G2' a different gene, and so on."

Allen beamed. "You're the best student I've ever had."

"You're the best teacher I've ever had."

"Understand, my diagram is simplistic. In reality, genes are made up of thousands of pairs of nitrogen bases, not just two or three. The smallest genes contain over a thousand base pairs. The largest, 200 times that. A chromosome is simply a series of genes strung out on the winding DNA ladder. No two organisms contain the same sequence of nucleotide base pairs in their chromosomes, unless they're identical twins. Humans have 46 chromosomes in every cell, except —"

"Except for sperm and egg cells. They only have 23."

"I guess some of Dr. Nealy's lessons stuck."

Jennifer's lips curled into a devilish smile, and her eyes gleamed a naughty look he hadn't seen in months, "When we studied the chapter on human reproduction, you bet I was listening."

He lingered on her playful gaze, savoring its erotic flavor, so afraid it would recede before he was willing to let it go.

Jennifer prodded, "Let's get on with it."

Wistfully, he asked, "With the DNA story, or something more interesting?"

"So far, I haven't heard how you intend to help our son."

Her words shattered his brief lapse to fantasy, jerking him back to the task at hand. "I'm getting there."

She must have sensed his letdown. "Maybe we can save 'more interesting' for later. Right now, give me DNA."

Allen blinked, wide-eyed.

Jennifer's cheeks flushed. "I mean the stuff on the paper, not in your pants." Her delicious lips formed an inviting smile.

Lifted by her implied promise, Allen proceeded with renewed vigor. "When I talk about DNA, I'm really talking genes. That's where God's miracle of life begins. The genes inside each cell contain instructions for that cell's function. Genes direct some cells to form heart tissue and others to form blood platelets, and still others to reproduce themselves. You might ask how genes orchestrate such a complicated symphony of biological activity.

"The answer is proteins. Proteins perform different jobs inside a cell to keep the cell alive. Special types of proteins, called enzymes, act like catalysts to promote specific chemical reactions inside the cell. Like the Energizer Bunny, these enzyme-induced chemical reactions just keep on going and going, doing their job, whether to digest food, produce new blood cells, or whatever, until the organism dies. But we have a problem — the useful life of most proteins is only two days."

"That can't be. People use protein all their lives."

"They do, and that's why it's constantly manufactured inside our cells. The synthesis of protein lies at the very heart of life and," Allen paused to make sure she was with him, "the calculated manipulation of life." He fixed his eyes on Jennifer's to see if she had grasped the meaning of his statement.

She nodded, her lips a tight line of rumination.

"All those nucleotide base pairs I talked about before, strung together to form genes, which in turn make up chromosomes, are like libraries of information that instruct a cell what proteins to make, how to make them, and when they should be made. When a particular protein is produced, the section of the chromosome containing the recipe for that protein is unraveled by a special enzyme. That special enzyme causes the rungs of the DNA ladder to split apart, as I show in the diagram on the right. But it splits the ladder only along that length where the nucleotide bases are located which code for the desired protein. Follow?"

"So far. In your picture, 'G2' would be a gene that codes for a protein made up of five base pairs — TCTAG."

"Precisely. And the same special enzyme that disconnects the rungs of the DNA ladder also picks up free-floating nucleotides inside the cell. The enzyme takes these nucleotides and joins them in a string to form a single strand opposite the split DNA strand. The new single-strand entity created in this process is known as ribonucleic acid, or RNA, which is a template of the gene used to create the desired protein. When the RNA template is completely built, it doesn't attach back to the open DNA ladder. Instead, the severed rungs of the DNA ladder re-connect, and the RNA string leaves the cell's nucleus. Outside the nucleus, it goes about creating whatever protein it was coded to produce. Of course, it's more complicated than that, but essentially, that's the process."

"Inside David, where exactly do you plan on messing around with this neat little process?"

"That's *the* big question, because this neat little process and cancer are integrally related. David's cancer, like most cancer, is ultimately traceable to something that goes wrong when genes go about their normal business.

"So tumors start when cells make protein?"

"Sometimes. Mistakes leading to cancer also happen when a cell divides. And cells divide all the time, not only in children, but in adults. Before any cell splits, its entire set of chromosomes must be duplicated so that each new cell gets an exact copy of that person's unique genetic instructions. This duplication occurs when the chromosomes split open at their rungs along the entire length of the DNA ladder.

"Nucleotides floating around inside the cell attach to their corresponding nucleotide bases on both sides of the opened DNA strand, adenine to thymine and guanine to cytosine. You end up with two identical sets of chromosomes. But the process isn't always that tidy. In the genes of humans, you're talking about three billion base pairs — three billion! Something's bound to go wrong when DNA duplicates itself. During cell division, for example, a gene can spontaneously swing over to a chromosome where it doesn't belong, and actually become part of it. The DNA copying machinery itself is prone to some degree of error. When the DNA sequence changes, you have what's called a mutation."

"Is that the only time you get a mutation? When a cell divides?"

"No, they also occur in a resting cell if a DNA strand breaks and needs to be repaired. A single nucleotide might attach itself to the wrong partner, resulting in a deformed base pair, rendering the gene useless.

"That kind of mutation can prevent the cell from making a protein vital to its existence. Conversely, some mutations cause a cell to produce too much protein, or cause it to make some entirely unintended protein. But what's amazing, mutations happen all the time and you never know it. That's because of special helper genes whose only function is to manufacture proteins that travel around the cell to correct mistakes during DNA replication and repair. Problem is, not every mistake is caught. And even —"

"Back up. You mean David's cancer was caused by a mutation that started in his brain cells?"

"Yes."

"But what causes a mutation in the first place?"

"Just about anything. Environmental contamination, like cigarette smoke, radiation and pesticides, things you already know about. Other mutations are linked to viruses. And sometimes it's just pure chance. A gene jumps to the wrong chromosome for no apparent reason."

"But wouldn't the damage be limited to the one cell where the mutation occurred?"

"Only if it results in the death of the cell. But not all mutations are lethal. Some actually hasten cell reproduction by upsetting nature's intricate system of checks and balances. And uncontrolled cell growth is precisely what makes cancer such an efficient engine of destruction.

"Some of the special helper genes I started telling you about are called tumor-suppressor genes. One of the most important discovered to date is p53. When the p53 gene is activated, it produces a unique repair protein that blocks duplication of deformed cells. Without tumor-suppressor genes to stop them, mutated cells may grow into large, self-contained masses, like David's tumor, or they can spread to other organs in the body.

"I believe David's cancer occurred because of a mutation in a critical tumor-suppressor gene in his brain. Either that, or another gene was damaged in such a way that made his tumor-suppressor genes stop working."

"Is there some way to repair the tumor-suppressor genes, some way to get them working again?"

"That's what I hope to do for David."

"I'm listening."

"I can't be 100 percent certain the root cause of David's tumor is a defect in his p53, or any other gene in the tumor-suppressor family. I'll need a biopsy."

"Can you get that from Dr. Loman?"

"I'm not performing this procedure with the blessing of David's doctors, so I'll need to get the biopsy on my own. That's the first place Nate's expertise will come in handy. He's conducted hundreds of experiments dealing with cancer mutations in animals from mollusks to mammals. At least he did before I started at Omnigen. Nate will extract a few cells from David's tumor and then help me identify the presence of a p53 mutation. Even if we don't find a flaw in his p53's, gene therapy could still help. A defect in another gene might be blocking the production of his tumor-suppressor genes. Or maybe the tumor cells are growing so fast, they're overwhelming the therapeutic effect of the p53 proteins.

"Either way, if I inject enough p53 into David's tumor, I might reverse or overcome the mutation that's allowing the cancer cells to grow in the first place. Even if the suppressor genes don't kill the tumor already there, maybe they'll stop the mutated cells from dividing further. Maybe that'll be enough to save David's life." Allen paused, anticipating Jennifer's next question.

"Let's say you deliver enough of these healthy tumor-suppressor genes into his cancerous cells." She pointed to Allen's diagram, "How exactly do they fix his damaged chromosomes?"

"First, I'm going to extract a cluster of David's brain cells from an area that hasn't been affected by the tumor. These cells will have normal copies of the p53 genes. Then, I'll combine the normal p53's with a special enzyme made of RNA, called a ribozyme. The ribozymes act as a catalyst for opening the DNA ladder at specific points matching the nucleotide sequence of the gene they're combined with.

"I'll insert these hybrid genes into David's tumor cells. With a little luck, the hybrid gene will trick the chromosomes with defective or missing p53 genes into producing normal RNA templates coded for tumor-suppressor protein. I won't know for sure until I try, but my goal is to get the p53's to start expressing normally."

"Meaning what?"

"Meaning they'll start synthesizing the protein for which they were coded before the mutation occurred, namely, p53. If enough p53's start expressing properly, David's tumor might stop growing, and if we're really lucky, start shrinking."

"I'm pretty sure I understand."

"If it helps, think of the computer programming adage: garbage in, garbage out. A mutation causes garbage to be programmed into the RNA template for making the right protein. As a result, the output you get is all jumbled up. If you fix the instructions, you fix the output, and the program works exactly as it should."

Though she spoke not a word, the intensity in her eyes told Allen she was considering his plan. If Allen played his cards right, she would become an ardent supporter. If not, she would stop him dead in his tracks. Cautiously, he asked, "Do you understand, at least in theory, what I hope to accomplish?"

She seemed to ignore him, apparently lost in her own thoughts. Allen slouched against the back of his chair, never taking his eyes off her, giving her as much time as she needed to organize and process the data he had fed her.

As if her entire decision rested on his answer to one final query, she uttered her words slowly and deliberately. "Could your experiment hurt David in any way, under any circumstance?"

Allen had anticipated this question, but for him, the answer was obvious. Any action was better than no action.

True, his experiment involved inherent risk. If the gene hybrid he created using the ribozyme opened up the wrong series of nucleotides along the DNA double helix, the resulting RNA template could cause another mutation. Such mutated RNA, if expressed at all, might be without effect. On the other hand, it might accelerate the growth of David's tumor, causing him to die sooner. But taking no action spelled certain death for David, anyway. Moreover, standing idly by, his heart and mind would agonize every waking moment knowing it was within his grasp to have done something, but did nothing.

To insure Jennifer's approval, he need only remain silent about the hazard. Those lustrous brown eyes searched his for the truth. No matter how carefully Allen planned and plotted, they always found it.

He admitted, "There are some risks. But ultimately, my experiment could harm David no more than the tumor in his brain."

Elbows planted on the table, Jennifer buried her face in the palms of her hands. Allen wished he didn't have to heap such a terrible burden upon Jennifer. As it was, tending daily to David's physical and emotional needs stressed his wife to the breaking point.

She looked up and folded her hands on the table. Her glistening brown eyes shone like windows on her heart. She spoke not with weepy vacillation, but with the conviction of a woman hardened to final judgment.

"I'll agree to your plan on one condition. Nate must help you. You're good at what you do, and in California you performed lots of gene splicing experiments with animals, but your strength lies in plants, not people. I've lived with you long enough to know if you thought you could do this procedure without him, you would. But you keep mentioning how he can help, so you must need him pretty badly to pull this off. Sounds to me like you know exactly what you want to do, but I won't allow you to touch our son unless Nathan Miles stands behind you."

Allen leaned forward, smiling in spite of himself. His chance to toss aside impotence and take action lay within reach. "Miles will help me. I know he'll help. He likes me, he likes you, and he feels awful about David. I'm sure he won't refuse."

"You obviously place a great deal of confidence in your colleague. Remember the reason you got your job with Omnigen in the first place."

Working closely with Dr. Nathan Miles every day and many nights for the past 10 months, Allen observed in him a fluent command of theoretical concepts and a solid ability to apply them as well as any molecular biologist with whom he'd worked. But for reasons not clear to Allen, in the nearly 40 years Miles had conducted biogenetic experimentation, whether at an institution of higher education, or in private enterprise, he had not scored one significant breakthrough.

"Nate is competent and conscientious. He's just had some lousy breaks. Other than you and David, I spend more time with him than anyone else. I know he's good. If anyone can help me, he can."

"What about gene therapy for treating cancer? Does he know anything about it?"

"He was an early advocate of using gene engineering to treat cancer. He taught at Stevens Institute and performed hundreds of experiments altering mouse genes, first to induce tumors, then to shrink them. Then, when he worked for that biotech firm outside Philly, he conducted countless experiments manipulating DNA to treat disease. At Omnigen, before I was hired, I know for a fact he spent three years exploring the use of bacterial and viral vectors to repair the genetic codes of cancerous cells. I'm confident he knows what he's doing."

With the slightest hint of cynicism, Jennifer replied, "I'll see how impressed I am when I talk to him myself."

What Allen hadn't disclosed to Jennifer was Miles' lack of experimental models using human subjects. Though Miles had conducted numerous gene therapy studies using mammalian test subjects, including rhesus monkeys, he'd never attempted a single experiment on a human. Since the fundamentals of DNA recombination were identical across species, Allen considered this lack of experience a minor detail he need not bother Jennifer with. For now, he felt extremely pleased with himself for having won his wife's qualified approval.

Allen said, "I agree. You should speak with Nate yourself. Then you'll see why I put so much trust in the man."

Cool and calm, Jennifer stood, walked behind Allen's chair, and leaned over his shoulder. Her soft layered hair, dark chocolate, tickled his cheek. She wrapped her arms around his shoulders, locking her hands at his chest, and whispered, "You seem so sure ... but promise me you won't take any unnecessary chances."

Gently clasping her arm, he rose and turned to face her. He pulled her close and locked on to her irresistible eyes. With the tip of his finger, he caressed her lips. She responded instantly, eyes closed, head back, hair flowing. He whispered into her ear, "I give you my word, Jenn. I give you my word."

With his open hand he held the back of her head and gradually pulled her to him until their lips met. He kissed her, gently at first, and then, when she answered with probing tongue, the blind fervor of an impassioned lover. For many minutes they embraced, lost in torrid lust he hadn't felt since their first time together on Laguna Beach.

She pulled away, and with certainty of purpose, led him to the master bedroom. At that moment, nothing seemed more important than the desire to satisfy an insatiable craving. For one night, at least, the bitter despair of a dying son would give way to the instinctual carnal impulse that moves the human species inexorably toward eternal existence.

MONDAY
JUNE 29

6

The two concrete lanes directly ahead vanished into a veil of gray mist. Crossing the drawbridge that linked Mantoloking to the mainland, Allen looked out over the cement railing. Through the dense fog, he could not make out the headwater of Barnegat Bay below. Recalling the pleasures he shared with Jennifer last night, he hardly noticed the drone of his tires rolling over the bridge's metal grating.

Arriving on the mainland, he passed Hibberd Boat Works, where last autumn he purchased a vintage 17-foot Boston Whaler in the hope of sharing its thrills with his son. David was now too ill to handle the rough ride of a Whaler, so Allen had used the boat only twice in 10 months. Now the forgotten vessel sat on a trailer behind his house.

Approaching the red light at Hooper Avenue, Allen's thoughts turned to the man who would guide him through the maze of DNA recombination and surgical procedures he planned for his son.

When Allen joined Omnigen, Nathan Miles, toiling for Omnigen since the day it opened, remained the only scientist on a staff decimated by red ink. Silver-haired in his early sixties, Miles held a Ph.D. in biochemistry. Though Omnigen's owner, Devon Maddox, had more than once labeled Miles a first-rate eccentric, Allen considered him a true pioneer in the application of recombinant DNA technology. If not for Miles' expertise in genetic engineering, Maddox and his financial backers could not have launched Omnigen.

Allen viewed Maddox as a money-hungry entrepreneur blessed with the right connections to raise enough cash for a roll of the dice in the high-stakes biotech industry — and lucky enough to have found in Dr. Miles a skilled scientist willing to take the gamble with him.

Having shared the same lab with Miles for almost a year, Allen had come to know his colleague as a professional and a friend. Miles lived alone, never married, and spent most of his free weekends strolling the boardwalk at Point Pleasant, grabbing a drink or two on Saturday nights at Marty's Fish House. Last Thanksgiving, at Jennifer's suggestion, Allen invited Miles to their home to partake in roast turkey and cinnamon-apple stuffing. His tongue loose after three gin and tonics, Miles shared with Allen and Jennifer the triumphs and failures of a checkered career.

In a series of experiments at Stevens Institute in the mid-70s, Miles spliced DNA extracted from human cancer tissue into a mouse virus known to cause respiratory infection. The mouse virus carried only enough cancer DNA to encode one or two genes, but could express large amounts of human protein in the mice he deliberately infected. To Miles' amazement, over 20 percent of the infected mice developed lung cancer. He isolated the virus out of the tumors he induced in the mice, hoping to identify those human genes—known as oncogenes—that had initially caused the human cancer.

Rather than sequencing the human genes, which in those days was labor and time intensive, Miles planned to use the human DNA directly to create an antisense viral vector that would neutralize the activity of the cancer-inducing genes. If successful, this vector, introduced into cancer cells, would cause one of three possible effects: halt the growth of the cancer cells, shrink them to a harmless size, or wipe them out altogether.

He never got the chance. The year was 1977, not long after the watershed conference at Asilomar, California. Scientists, administrators, journalists, and lawyers had come together to discuss the dangers, both medical and ethical, associated with gene therapies and DNA experimentation. The conference spawned a strict set of guidelines governing gene research.

Having no tolerance for red tape, Miles viewed the Asilomar directives as bureaucratic chains binding his innovative hands. Without permission from the biology department chair, he attempted to splice anti-tumor DNA into a viral vector engineered to attack tumors, and infect cancerous tissue biopsies from human subjects.

A graduate student blew the whistle, and Miles was discretely asked to resign under threat of legal action. He chose not to contest and instead accepted a research post with Delta Therapeutics, a mid-sized pharmaceutical and bio-genetics company based in Willow Grove, Pennsylvania, about half an hour north of Philadelphia.

At Delta, Miles employed genetically altered retro-viruses as a vector to combine with, and destroy, tumor cells. His protocol achieved mixed results, shrinking benign tumors in 15 percent of test mice. Delta's CEO never allowed Miles to refine his protocol, squelching his foray into gene-based cancer therapies. The "pig-headed vixen," as Miles described her after a fourth gin and tonic, complained his digression into such speculative areas of gene design was inconsistent with Delta's long-term research and marketing objectives. Her disdain of his cutting-edge research led Miles to jump at Maddox's lucrative offer to help launch Omnigen.

Miles endured one miss after another at Omnigen, consistently falling short in a 10-year struggle to create a dependable gene-based cancer therapy for Maddox and his investors. FDA approval for even Phase II testing eluded Miles. His only success in the decade before Allen joined Omnigen involved species transference of genetically engineered growth-promoting genes. Miles extracted from hamsters the gene that encodes for growth-inducing protein, programmed it for high-level expression, and micro-injected it into the eggs of the common toad, causing the toads to grow to twice their adult size.

Turning left off Airport Road into Lakewood Industrial Park,, Allen felt confident in his own plan, and the skill of Nathan Miles to carry it out. Together, they might improve David's chances of survival. In the process, Miles might attain professional recognition that had eluded him throughout his career.

Allen pulled his Honda into Omnigen's empty rain-slicked parking lot. The first employee to arrive, he chose a spot close to the walk leading to the front entrance. The one-story square building was set back about 50 yards from Salem Street on a heavily wooded three-acre tract. The structure's facade, from foundation to roof, consisted of mirrored windows that reflected the lush canopy of pine and maple trees flanking Omnigen.

Allen hastened as he entered Omnigen's glass double-doors. The building's interior layout was simple, a modest front foyer ending at a T, and off the ends of the T, two corridors running the shape of a square inside and parallel to the square structure's outer walls. The hallway, in essence, formed a square within a square. Occupying the space between the inner square and the mirrored exterior, 14 offices for administrators and scientists, all but three now vacant, and a lunch room that barely fit a card table and two vending machines.

Within Omnigen's square core were three laboratories, labeled A, B, and C.

In the empty foyer, Allen paused to consider where he should meet with Miles to discuss the experimental DNA therapy he had conceived for his son. The last person Allen needed stumbling into their conversation was Devon Maddox, who thought nothing of barging in, unannounced, on anyone he pleased. Most prudent, Allen decided, to discuss his business with Miles in Laboratory C, the smallest and least used of the three labs.

Only two other employees worked for Omnigen: Ellen, a receptionist doubling as the firm's bookkeeper, who sat glued to her desk in Omnigen's foyer, and Claire, Maddox's secretary, who buried herself in a small office adjacent to Maddox's plush quarters at the front corner of the building. When Allen joined Omnigen, the firm had also employed two lab assistants and a medical transcriptionist. Last December, Maddox cut all three, a move, he told Allen, required to free up funds to pay down mounting corporate debt.

Allen rushed down the hall toward Laboratory C, thrilled at the prospect of putting his plan into action. After explaining to Miles his idea for creating a hybrid gene using ribozymes to implant healthy tumor-suppressor genes into David's brain tissue, he would begin by running computer verification models that very day. By the middle of the week, they could draw cell samples from David's cerebrum, and by Friday, assemble the hybrid genes and inject them into his tumor. He would invite Miles for supper that very evening to answer Jennifer's questions and allay her fears. His pulse racing, Allen could hardly wait to begin.

He reached into his pocket to retrieve the key to the lab, when he felt a folded sheet of paper, a reminder note he'd written himself last night. He'd almost forgotten about his telephone conversation yesterday with Larry Bateman, his old fishing buddy and pistol range partner. Larry asked if he could spare a few minutes Monday morning to take a look at some physical evidence his men recovered from the scene of an accident. Part of an animal, Larry said, that couldn't have come from local waters. Allen had agreed, requesting he stop by before lunch.

Allen would keep his word, and examine the evidence for his friend, but quickly, for nothing must delay his carefully conceived plan for David.

7

Dr. Nathan Miles leaned back against one of the two waist-high work benches in Laboratory C. The twin tables, 20 feet long and parallel, topped with smooth black granite, were completely barren but for a few empty test tube racks and a half dozen clear glass beakers. Bulbous hazel eyes and scraggly gray hair, receding to the crown, gave Miles the look of a mad scientist. "Honestly, A.J., you've already done everything you can for David."

Allen regarded Miles not as a mad scientist, but a neglected visionary. All the more reason he could not understand his colleague's hesitation, even after explaining in painstaking detail every meticulously planned step of the tumor-suppressor, ribozyme-delivered gene therapy he planned for David.

Miles continued, "You and Jennifer have consulted with the best oncologists and neurosurgeons in the region — Sloan Kettering in New York and Children's Hospital in Philadelphia. You can't do much better."

"We've tried chemo, it isn't working. Even if we increased his radiation dosage, what would it buy him? A month, maybe two? Let's be honest. The standard treatments aren't cutting it."

Miles shook his head. "I'm not entirely surprised you'd try tackling this thing yourself. You've never been one to sit on the sidelines. But you've got to accept your limitations."

Lurking close beneath the surface Allen knew he'd find a scientist as much the adventurer as he. "It's a good, viable strategy, and if anyone has the smarts to pull it off, you do."

Miles jerked forward off the edge of the table, his paunch jiggling like gelatin as he steadied his corpulent, five-foot-five frame. He wore an argyle jacket, gray and peach, with tan suede patches stitched on at the elbows. The jacket covered a plaid sport shirt, distended at the waist and unbuttoned at the collar. Wearing no necktie, donned in oversize white trousers, Miles hardly presented the image of a professional. But Allen wasn't looking for a man in touch with the latest fashions. He needed someone to cure his son.

Turning his back to Allen, Miles shuffled down the aisle between the two monolithic tables. "I've scrambled toad DNA to grow giant frogs. I've restructured defective beta-globin genes for sickle cell patients. I've even induced benign tumors in mice using re-engineered viruses. But I've never developed a reliable gene-based protocol for treating cancer. Truth is, no gene-based cancer treatment has proven 100 percent effective."

"I'm not looking for 100 percent. I'm looking for 60, 40, even 10. Any odds over zero are better than his chances now."

At the far end of the two tables, Miles turned, then paced back toward Allen. "Every one of my attempts has failed. I couldn't possibly be of help to you."

"I don't buy it." Allen raised his right hand, touching the ball of his thumb to the ball of his forefinger. "This close. You never let me forget how you've come this close to reaching your goal. My plan can work, and you can make it happen."

Halfway up the aisle, Miles hesitated, shaking his head. "I don't know."

"Look. Do you think I'd put David's life in the hands of a scientist I didn't trust?"

Miles didn't answer. He walked forward, stopping beside the table across from Allen.

Allen heard himself beg. "What do you say, Nate. Will you help me help my son?"

For a long time, Miles stared at the floor, as if the cream-speckled squares held his answer. When he looked up, he fixed his bulging hazel eyes on Allen. "You're not stupid, A.J. I'm sure you know if you get caught, your career is finished."

Allen had anticipated what he considered a valid objection. Four years earlier, stringent federal regulations had pulled the noose tight around the neck of the biotech industry. More than 200 firms had been choked out of existence since the effective date of the new statutes.

The squeeze began when researchers at BioMac, a biotech company in Denver, successfully cloned a human. The company's interest in people-cloning was based purely on scientific curiosity, so claimed the firm's board of directors. They were besieged by public interest lawsuits and called before a Senate subcommittee impaneled to probe their motives.

In response to BioMac's illegal experimentation, Congress bestowed upon the Recombinant DNA Advisory Council, established in the 1970s by the National Institutes of Health in response to growing public fear of genetic engineering, broad investigatory and enforcement powers. Prior to that, the RAC consisted of 25 scientists, ethicists, and legal professionals with limited authority to approve untried gene engineering protocols.

The committee's recommendations were merely that ultimate authority rested with the FDA. In 30 years, not one catastrophic accident had occurred arising out of gene manipulation research, no Andromeda Strain inadvertently created and released into the population threatening humanity's existence.

But the proliferation of advanced mammal cloning experiments transformed the federal government's attitude toward gene engineering from indifference to paranoia. In an about face, Congress broadened the committee's powers, changed its name to the Recombinant DNA Administrative Council, kept the acronym, and infused its rulings with legislative muscle. Designated a branch of the FDA, the RAC wielded the power to nix gene engineering experimentation it deemed "a direct or indirect threat to public safety, national security, or inimical to the best interests of the United States of America."

The reinvented RAC held life-or-death power over the biotech industry. The RAC required extensive background checks on principal shareholders of start-up firms. Anyone failing to pass muster was banned from holding an equity interest. Owners who incorporated prior to the effective date were exempt from this provision of the new law, and more than once, Miles opined that Devon Maddox could not have entered the biotech business today.

Under the new rules governing recombinant DNA research, violators paid a high price for non-compliance. Any institution subsidized by taxpayer dollars caught performing unauthorized genetic engineering had its funds pulled immediately and irrevocably. Private firms had their corporate charters permanently invalidated. Any shareholder owning 20 percent or more of the company's stock found themselves subject to prosecution under federal criminal law.

Miles had good reason to worry. But as usual, Allen had prepared an answer. "I'd never jeopardize your career. You're more than a colleague, you're my friend. I'll make sure there's no record of your involvement. I'll do all the modeling and verification under my own login. I'll perform the actual extraction and injection. I only need what's in your head. I need you to look over my shoulder."

Miles cracked a grin. "Leave it to you to think of everything." Just as quickly, his smile vanished. "What about your own career? You have too much to lose. You're closer than I ever was to turning a profit for this company. At least you'll make a name for yourself."

Allen shot back, "We're talking about my son. They can take my degree, they can take my house, and they can take the shirt off my back. I just want David to live."

"I'm going to ask you a hard question." Miles paused, as if measuring his words. "Don't you think ... don't David's physicians think the tumor has grown too large? Even if you stimulated his tumor-suppressors, isn't it too late to save David?"

"That's why there's no time to lose. That's why I'm not chancing DNA replacement using viral vectors. I need something that directly induces tumor-suppressor synthesis. Ribozymes are the fastest way I know."

"You're right about that. When speed is top priority, you need something that goes after messenger RNA."

"My plan uses ribozymes to repair defective messenger RNA generated by the mutant cancer-causing genes. Rehabilitating mRNA preserves the normal timing of protein production, which —"

"Increases the chances of faster p53 expression."

Allen smiled, "Then you're with me?"

No response. Instead, Miles dropped his head and trudged the aisle between the glistening black granite tables. Reaching the far end, he turned around. His eyes always shone greener under the harsh fluorescent light. "I think you're on the right track. Your idea might work, but I ... I just can't do it. I'd like to help you, but I can't."

Miles spun awkwardly, like a top losing momentum, and lumbered toward the door.

More hurt than angry, Allen bounded after him. Just as Miles turned the knob, Allen stretched out his arm and held the door shut. "I was counting on you, Nate. I know damn well you'd love to give it a try. I don't understand why you're just walking away. What do I tell Jennifer? You just won't do it?"

"I can't do it."

"Nate, I don't understand. This isn't like you at all. I know you want to help David. Why won't you? At least give me a reason."

Solemnly, Miles stepped back. "You want a reason? I'll give you one. But promise me you'll never bother me again about this experiment."

Allen withdrew his hand from the door.

Miles' hazel eyes bulged with resentment. "Ever wonder why I stick around this place? Especially after Maddox chopped 30 grand off my salary to hire you?"

"That's no secret. You knew Maddox couldn't afford both salaries. You said you'd sacrifice short-term gain, and hope as a team we could turn the company around. He also promised you a bonus when the company started showing black. Twice your pay cut, retroactive to when I started."

"He put it on paper," Miles added. "At least that's what he told me. But that's not the only reason I tolerate his crap."

"Why else?"

"Let's face it, A.J. Where am I going? I'm a has-been excuse of a scientist. I'm ..."

"That's not true."

"I'm pushing 65, I was bounced out of a university, and I haven't published in 15 years. No one would hire me, so I suck up to the corrupt son of a bitch to pay my rent."

"But your experience?"

"It's worthless ... and that's not the whole story."

"What do you mean?"

"It's not important, at least not to you."

"If it prevents you from helping me, then it's damn important."

"Forget it. I won't ... I can't talk about it."

"That's not good enough."

"Good enough? Do you know what Maddox would do if he caught me working on an experiment that could send us both to prison? I might as well throw in the towel. That should be good enough. Anything else Maddox has on me is only added fuel for the fire."

Allen studied Miles, whose expression bordered on anger and remorse. "What exactly does he have on you?"

"I said drop it."

Allen did, guessing that Miles would level with him in his own time. Right now, David's life was at stake, and somehow he must get through. "You may have your reasons, but my son is dying. If you help me, I'll take every precaution to protect you. We'll meet outside the lab, after-hours, someplace where Maddox won't find you. As I work on the procedure, I'll keep you informed. You advise me if I'm doing it right, and every once in a while, sort of accidentally peek in on me to make sure I'm still on track."

Miles' protruding green eyes turned hostile. "I know David is gravely ill. I understand you need to do something. But using your son's disease to pressure me into risking my job, my very freedom, is absolutely wrong." Miles jabbed his finger into Allen's chest. "Throw away your own career if you must, but I'd like to keep what's left of mine."

Miles grabbed the doorknob and swung the door so hard it froze open. Storming down the corridor, he left behind the clatter of angry heels.

No place to turn, no cause for hope, Allen stood alone in the bleak and barren laboratory. He needed Miles' guidance. Without it, he could not perform the delicate brain tissue extraction, synthesize the tumor-suppressor hybrid gene, and inject the therapeutic ribozyme into the base of David's skull.

Maybe Miles was right. Maybe the cancer in his little boy's head had spread too far even for gene therapy to help. Maybe it was better for David, Jennifer, and all concerned if Allen let nature take its course, let his son meet his maker in peace. How dare he be so arrogant to believe he could intercede against the will of God? David was to die and he could not stop it. As if his son's inevitable passing struck him for the first time, Allen shut the door, hung his head, and shuddered.

Four weeks of planning and preparation in the steamy equatorial jungle blanketing the heartland of South America had left Major Charles F. Clayton deaf to the chirps and shrieks of unseen insects hidden in the lush foliage outside his tent. He looked forward to the end of this mission, 26 hours from now, and knew the others in his team felt the same.

So little time left before the extraction team arrived, Clayton worried why the link-up with General Stanton was taking so long. He glared at the 17-inch monitor, glowing baby blue, flashing six amber words:

ACCESSING BHERT INTERACTIVE NETWORK /CODE FIVE

Drumming his fingers against the side of the keyboard, he noticed the flimsy particle board desk had begun to sag under the weight of the terminal. He doubted the fragile surface of compressed sawdust and resin could endure another week of the blistering humidity pervading his makeshift laboratory in the middle of Hades. Hopefully, he wouldn't have to stick around long enough to find out.

Preparing to disengage the scrambled radio signal that bounced uselessly from the dish outside his tent to BHERT's Anstat-2 communications satellite orbiting the earth 200 miles above, Clayton heard the terminal's built-in speakers crackle to life. The blinking amber words disappeared, replaced by five white block letters filling the screen: BHERT.

"Jungle Dragon, Jungle Dragon. Safe Harbor receiving your signal four-by-four. Harbor Master ready to engage."

"This is Jungle Dragon," Clayton answered. "Reading you four-by-four. Engage when ready."

Seconds later, General Stanton's deep sixty-something voice boomed over the speaker. "What's this I hear you're ready to wrap up Beta-5 Slayer tomorrow?"

Clayton leaned forward on his seat, and spoke into the inch-square grid at the base of the monitor. "Affirmative, Harbor Master. Surveillance indicates 50 acres harvested during the past 48 hours. Calculate targets will be ready to ship by 0900 tomorrow. We assume assault positions at 2100 hours."

"You'll need the support of special ops."

"Not my team. They're up, armed, and ready to rock."

The general paused, perhaps put off by Clayton's glib reply. "I've placed Wheaton's crew at RS-42 in Panama on stand-by. If you run into trouble, they'll be at your side in 90 minutes."

"With all due respect, I don't believe Captain Wheaton's services will be necessary."

"He's available if you need him."

Clayton swept his tongue over his lower lip. "The primary reason I called. Can I expect the extraction crew to arrive on time?"

"I've never stranded you before."

Except for those 12 hours in Havana, Clayton thought.

"They're set to depart Andrews at your command. I've assigned Sergeant Jacobs as team leader for the flight down."

"Thank you, sir."

General Stanton's tone lightened. "Before you sign off, how'd you like to hear the results of Cutler's dig at Tanta?"

Clayton recalled his own mission a year and half earlier in the Western Desert outside Damanhur. "Same as Saqqara?"

"Identical. Fourth site in 26 months showing evidence of Methuselah."

"Did Cutler encounter any overzealous profs from the States?"

"Not this time. BHERT took complete charge up front — identification, excavation, and recovery — with the full knowledge and consent of the Egyptian government, of course."

"Of course."

"Eighteen cadavers, like at Saqqara. All en route to Spokane."

Clayton chuckled. "Dusty Donna's getting plenty of company."

"They can throw a regular convention."

Clayton wondered how much longer the mutation could be kept classified. "You know, it's only a matter of time before Methuselah gets out."

"Not our decision to make."

"Don't I know."

"Well, Jungle Dragon, look forward to having you home."

During the past two years, Clayton had accumulated eight weeks vacation. He planned on using one after he returned to Washington. "Looking forward to coming home, sir."

After exchanging standard valediction protocols, Clayton hit the Control, F-2, and Escape keys, terminating the transmission.

He sat back and stared at the bright blue screen, void of data, surprised to hear the shrill din of those blasted jungle bugs screeching in his ears. He'd had enough of this God-forsaken place. He'd better enjoy every minute of his time off next week. After that, who knew what hellhole General Stanton would drop him into?

8

Allen looked up at the circular clock above the door in Laboratory C. Though it felt like hours, only minutes had passed since Miles deserted him. Allen shut off the lights and returned to his office.

Ignoring files piled high on his desk, he gazed out the window into the dense conifer forest behind the lab. He would miss David more than anyone he'd ever missed, even his own father. He turned to examine a collage hung on the wall beside him. A photo of Jennifer and David riding on the Pleasure Pier carousel captured an isolated fragment of joy he once shared with his family. Soon these snapshots would become a grim reminder of former happiness.

Allen sunk into the chair behind his desk. As he reached for the telephone to spill his heartache to Jennifer, the red intercom light flickered. "Dr. Johnson?"

Allen hit the page button. "Yes Ellen?"

"Lieutenant Lawrence Bateman is here to see you. Says you're expecting him."

Allen was eager to see him. A visit with an old friend might bring a moment of cheer in a world cloaked in despair.

"Ok, Ellen. I'll be right there."

When Allen entered the lobby, Larry Bateman, looking all business in his crisp blue-gray uniform, rose from the black vinyl sofa near the glass front doors. Allen strode to him, hand extended.

Bateman shook it, and apologized, "I hope I'm not putting you out, A.J."

"Don't worry. I could use a little diversion right about now. So what can I do for the New Jersey State Police?"

Allen spied an object about five feet long and two feet in diameter propped up against the wall next to the sofa behind Bateman. Wrapped in green plastic garbage bags bound together by five rings of silver duct tape, the object must have been heavy. Bateman used both his arms to lift and hold it.

"I'm hoping you can tell me what I've got here." He signaled Allen with his eyes, indicating he preferred to discuss his business in private.

"Of course. Why don't we examine it in one of the labs?" Passing Ellen's desk, Allen said, "If anyone needs me, they can find me in Lab B."

"Very good, Dr. Johnson."

The footsteps of the two men echoed through the vacant corridor, painted linen white, interrupted by an occasional door hiding unlit offices devoid of furniture.

Bateman asked, "How's David?"

Allen had last seen his friend in December when, for the first time since returning from California, he introduced Jennifer and David to Larry and Judy. The two women enjoyed spiked egg nog, fruit cake, and a hearty helping of laughter, while he and Larry reminisced until long past midnight. Back then, Allen still held out hope for David's chemotherapy. From January on, though, his son's condition steadily declined.

"The chemo isn't working. I'm not sure what to do next."

"I'm sorry. How's Jennifer holding up?"

"Making the best of a bad situation."

"I figured things weren't going well. I hadn't heard from you all winter."

"Yeah. The doctors keep us pretty busy."

Gripping the package, Bateman turned his head and glanced over his shoulder. "This place is totally empty. Is everything all right?"

Allen chuckled. "It's been empty awhile. The boss keeps a tight lid on costs. He's waiting to see if we get USDA approval for my gene transfer protocol."

"You mentioned something last Christmas about rice that can grow in salt water?"

"That's right. If I stay on schedule, I'll conduct Phase III trials in October. By next May, my company will be selling saline-tolerant rice seed to farmers from California to India."

"Amazing what you guys can do with a little technology."

"If you think that's something, wait until you see my rice that grows in salt water."

"You *are* kidding."

"Perfectly serious. In two years, you'll be guarding the Barnegat against more than a few measly clam poachers. Picture yourself patrolling Silver Bay off Cattus Island, watching over a 50-acre rice paddy beneath the waves!"

Bateman rolled his eyes. "Just what I need. More headaches."

They came to a solid wood door on the right. Affixed to the door's center, a gold veneer plaque: Laboratory B.

"I'm glad you're up on your plants," Bateman said. "Still remember your crustaceans?"

Allen threw his friend a thumbs-up.

Not long ago, Allen knew his way around every species of marine animal from plankton to dolphin as well as anyone in the state. After earning a Bachelor of Science in biology, he accepted a position as a marine biologist with the New Jersey Department of Environmental Protection, Division of Fish, Game and Wildlife. The job hadn't made him rich, but the experience he acquired instilled a treasure trove of knowledge.

As for crustacean biology, Allen didn't forget much. He was sure he could answer Larry's questions.

They entered Lab B, which was used for ancillary research spinning off from primary projects conducted by him and Miles. Though not present now, Miles had been using the lab to develop protocols for transferring the cellulase gene to the bacterium E. coli to efficiently transform cellulose-based waste products, such as cornstalks and sawdust, into sugar.

Allen figured Miles was working in Lab A. Either that, or off sulking in his office. Allen reached for the package in Bateman's arms.

His friend resisted, clutching it tighter.

"Wait." Bateman spoke with the stern authority of a law enforcement officer, not the affable ease of an old friend. "First, promise you will not disclose what your are about to see to anyone. I am showing you material evidence in an ongoing police investigation. I must have your absolute confidence before I allow you to examine it."

Allen released his grip on the bag. "What exactly do you have in there?"

"Give me your word, and *you* can tell *me*."

"You have my word."

Bateman handed Allen the dark green package. "The animal this came from severely injured a young boy in Barnegat Bay. Nearly tore off his arm. I'm almost certain it killed his older brother."

Clutching the green plastic, Allen's immediate observations: ice cold, probably stored in a freezer; weight, about 40 pounds; texture, hard as a rock; surface, smooth bumps, consistent with a crustacean's exoskeleton.

Allen placed the object on the laboratory table nearest the door. Bateman stood at his left shoulder. From a shallow drawer beneath the table, Allen pulled out an angular-tipped pair of scissors, a straight-blade shears, and a white-lined legal pad. He closed that drawer and opened a deeper one beneath it. From there, he removed a wax-lined aluminum tray, a sterling silver probe, a curved-tip tissue forceps, a single-edge scalpel, a dozen stainless-steel calibration weights, two dissecting probes, and a pair of latex surgical gloves. He laid the instruments neatly on the black slab in front of him, then donned the sheer rubber gloves. Leaning over the green-wrapped object, he set to work.

Before Allen could see what the package held, the odor of rotting seafood fouled his nostrils. He backed away from the table. "Whatever's in here, it's starting to thaw."

"I put it in the freezer as fast as I could. At least two hours passed from the time we removed it from the boat to when I wrapped it and stuck it in the freezer."

"Bacterial decomposition has definitely commenced." Allen stared at the green wrapper, slit end-to-end. "All right, let's have a look." Allen peeled the green plastic away from each side of the lateral slit.

The object completely exposed, Allen stumbled over his words. "This is ... this is incredible ... it just can't happen."

Bateman moved to Allen's side. "I thought it was pretty weird, too. Any idea what it came from?"

"Not a doubt. You're looking at the dextral cheliped of a *Callinectes sapidus*, order Decapoda, class Crustacea, phylum Arthropoda."

"Sure I am," Bateman said, "but what exactly is a dextral chela of a callinets, callinets sapus, whatever you called it?"

Allen ignored his friend, gawking at something so familiar, yet of such incredible proportion as to defy reason. "This couldn't have come from Barnegat Bay. It's impossible."

Bateman sounded impatient. "What is it, A.J.?"

"What you have here is the pincer segment of the right claw of a blue crab — the largest I've ever seen."

"A blue crab? Come on. You and I grew up around the bay. No blue crab grows a claw like this."

"You're right. And if it weren't sitting right in front of me, I'd tell you it couldn't happen." Allen opened another drawer under the table, and pulled out a spring-activated US/Metric measuring tape. He held the tip out to Bateman.

"Do me a favor. Pull this out to the end of the claw and hold it there."

Bateman complied, while Allen carried the square silver casing, trailing yellow aluminum, to the severed end of the claw. At the severed end, it looked to Allen like the claw had been chopped or hammered off because the crab's white meat was embedded with splinters of bright blue shell.

"Incredible—134 and one-quarter centimeters, a little over 52 inches!" Allen measured the widest section of the claw unassisted. "Sixty-two and a half centimeters." He picked up the pad and scratched some numbers.

"I'd put the full length of this claw at about six feet. That means you're looking at a blue claw crab that's roughly 20 feet, pincer to pincer. And that, my friend, is impossible."

Allen bent down to inspect the claw more closely. "Judging from the predominance of blue along the sides, I'd say its a male. The brownish stains around the teeth, inside the pincer, dried blood, not the crab's."

"That I know. How do you explain its size?

"I can't. Not unless I do DNA testing. But I can tell you one thing. This crab's lived a lot more years than it should."

"What do you mean?"

"Crab shell is composed of a hard material called chitin. A crab can't grow bigger than its shell."

"I don't follow."

"Crabs grow by a process known as ecdysis. They periodically shed their old shells and replace them with new, larger ones. Most call it molting. Right before crabs molt, they grow a pliable layer just underneath their chitinous shell. After they shed their hard shell, crabs consume tremendous quantities of water relative to their body weight. The water expands the pliant shell the way a garden hose fills a water balloon."

"Don't tell me. That's when you get a softshell crab."

"Exactly." Allen remembered August mornings as a boy, armed with four trotlines and half a dozen bunker, hauling in crabs by the bushel full. He always saved the soft-shells for his dad.

"But how can a crab expand its soft shell to 20 feet?"

"It can't," Allen answered, "When crabs molt, they grow bigger by roughly a third, then their new, outer shells harden. Immature blue crabs molt every four to five days. The older ones, every four to six weeks, but only during warm weather. They reach maturity between one year and 18 months. Their maximum life span is usually two years, though some go on for three, especially if they hatched during summer. The largest blue crab I ever heard of — mind you, I didn't see it myself — was 10 inches across the carapace."

"Carapace?"

"The back. Which would put the crab's length, claw-to-claw, at two and a half feet. But that story I heard second hand at Ernie's Bait and Tackle."

"So in theory, if a crab somehow went on living longer than three years, it would molt, get bigger, molt, get bigger, molt, and just keep getting bigger. In theory."

"Science fiction theory, maybe. Cellular functioning in every living plant and animal eventually breaks down. Exactly how long that process takes for a given species is coded in its genes. That's what aging is all about. For argument's sake, though, let's suppose this crab exceeded its normal life expectancy." Allen picked up the pen and pad. Motioning for Bateman to follow, he walked across the lab to Miles' hand-held calculator. He feverishly punched in numbers, intermittently scratching sub-totals on the white pad.

"Hypothetically, say you started with a full-grown blue crab that after three years grew a normal five-inch carapace, about 15 inches claw-to-claw. Then, for whatever reason, its life cycle continued uninterrupted, molting twice during the summer season, each time increasing in size by a third. According to my numbers, to reach 20 feet from one claw to the other, it would have to live about eight years. And that just can't happen."

"But how can you deny what's right in front of you?"

Allen replied somberly, "I guess I can't."

"I need you to take a closer look. The press is on me like bees on honey. They're itching to know what happened to the Martin kids. If you're right — this animal is some sort of deformed crab — I'd have to quarantine the bay."

"You'd go that far?"

"Absolutely. I won't allow the good citizens of the Jersey shore, or anyone else who ventures into the bay, to find themselves stalked by a giant killer crab. If something that big is really out there, I'll close Barnegat in a second. But first I need answers. I have to know where to find it, where it might be headed, and how the hell it got so big. Most important, I need those answers without stirring up a lot of crazy publicity."

Already that morning, Allen was denied the help of a friend. He knew too well the sting of rejection, and would not inflict it on another. "I'll get you your answers, but keep something in mind. Because the crab hurt someone doesn't mean it's intentionally looking to harm anyone. Blue crabs are opportunistic feeders. They eat fish, dead or alive, clams, eelgrass, snails — even other crabs."

"So you think the crab was simply scrounging for food when it attacked the boys?"

"Sure. To a 20-foot crab, a child would look like a juicy oyster. But why did it come so close to the surface?"

"The boys were fishing. We found a chum pot, what was left of it, tied to a line off the stern cleat."

"That would explain what drew it to the boat. But what brought it up? Normally, crabs stay close to the bottom."

"In the bow, we found a fishing pole. In the stern, where the younger boy was attacked, nothing."

"But the younger boy may have been holding a rig before the attack. His hook could have caught on the crab's shell, luring it to the surface."

"We're talking about a 10-year-old, not Arnold Schwarzenegger. No boy that small could've reeled in a 20 foot animal."

"I said lured, not reeled. The crab was attracted to the boat by the chum, got stuck on the boy's line, then saw larger prey on the surface. And didn't you say an older boy was involved?"

"A 17-year-old."

"Who was probably helping the younger kid reel in the line."

"Possibly."

"Any trace of the older boy?"

"Only the blood, in the boat and on the claw. My guess is the crab pulled the older boy into the bay, but we haven't recovered a body."

Staring at the brown stains on the white claw teeth, Allen's stomach knotted. "Don't expect to find too much in the way of remains. All crabs, blue claws included, are constantly hungry. It's been established that crabs' appetites never get fully satisfied. There's one species that gets so famished, sometimes it crawls out of water to search for food. Snatches baby birds from their ground nests."

"You mean if this thing gets hungry enough, it'll start picking people off the beach?"

"No. Blue crabs never leave the water by choice. Two or three hours out of salt water, exposed to high temperature and direct sunlight, they die."

"That's comforting. But why did the damn thing live so long?"

"I can't give you an answer until I examine the cellular structure and nucleic content of a tissue sample, maybe run a few tests."

"Isn't there anything you can tell me now?

Allen regarded the specimen. "If you can spare a few minutes."

"I have a meeting at two o'clock with the kids' father. He expects me to explain what happened to his children."

"I don't envy you."

"Yeah," Bateman said, shaking his head. "Anyway, what do you have in mind?"

"A quick look under the microscope."

"Why not? The sooner I get answers, the better."

Using his forceps and scalpel, Allen probed the meaty end of the giant claw where the brilliant blue shell was smashed. Decomposition of the crustacean's chela membranes had set in, turning spots of white tissue under the shell pallid gray. Allen could barely stand the stench of decaying crab flesh.

He found what he was after — an untainted section of cheliped muscle, fresh enough to contain cell samples unspoiled by oxidative contamination. With the dexterity of a plastic surgeon, Allen carved a thin sliver of muscle.

"Do me a favor, pull out a slide from the dispenser on my right. Just press the lever on the side."

Bateman touched the metal handle, and instantly, a single glass slide popped into Bateman's fingertips.

Allen took the slide from Bateman, held it under the forceps, and released the white speck onto the glass. From a plastic bottle containing pink liquid, he suctioned a few drops of protein stainer and immersed the tissue speck with a single drop, then sealed the slide with a one-inch, clear-glass cover. He placed the slide under the microscope, clicked on the scope's light, and gazed into the dual eyepiece.

Hunched over, he slowly rotated the focus knob. Without lifting his head, he pointed his finger straight out to his right. "Over there. On the shelf above the desk. There's a CD player."

"Yeah?"

"Flip it on for me."

"Huh?"

"I always work better with Enya beside me."

"I thought you were a Meatloaf man."

"Different rhymes for different times."

Bateman obliged.

Allen's ears resonated with a coalescence of violin, cello, and piano. Oblivious to all but Enya's soothing strains, he plummeted into the pink morass of cells permeating his field of vision. "Numerous incidence of elliptical cell membrane restructuring ... conspicuous recurrent centriole distension ... 90 percent in metaphase ... distinct evidence of peripatetic chromosomal crossover ... No doubt about it, unusually high rate of mitotic proliferation."

Bateman cajoled, "English, A.J., English."

Allen gazed into the bright pink cluster of cells, picking out the structural components he recognized. Everything was there — lysosomes, mitochondria, endoplasmic reticulum — yet something was all wrong.

Bent over the microscope, Allen said, "Never seen anything like it."

Bateman struck his official tone. "I wouldn't mind being informed."

Lifting his head from the microscope, Allen blinked his eyes, adjusting his vision to room light. He switched off the stage lamp and turned to his friend. "I'm sorry. Sometimes I get pretty absorbed. Especially when I'm observing a new phenomenon. The nucleic chromatin — the genetic material — it's unusually dense. I don't know why. I'd like to take some additional samples and run a few sequencing tests. That'll give me solid answers."

"What are you looking for?"

"A mutation in the crab's DNA. Something to explain why its cells are dividing unchecked."

Tight-lipped, Bateman studied him. "All right. But I'll need answers fast. In the next day or two, I'm sure to get a call from the DEP, the attorney general's office, or both."

"Don't worry, you'll have your explanation."

Shaking his head, Bateman said, "I've seen it all — drug dealers, boat accidents, hurricanes. But this. This is a little over my head." He heaved a weary sigh. "How long do you need the claw?"

"Two or three days."

"No way. That claw is material evidence, and I'm scuttling proper channels to let you take a look. I'll come back tonight."

"That doesn't give me enough time to run a complete battery of sequencing tests. Don't you want accurate information?"

"Then first thing in the morning."

"That's still not —"

"Sorry. You'll have to do your best. If I don't give headquarters and the media some solid answers very soon, it's going to be a feeding frenzy — no pun intended. And we don't need that on a July Fourth weekend." Bateman pivoted and marched toward the exit. "I'll see you then." When he reached the door, he stopped, peering around the lab. "I hope you're hiding a freezer in here."

Allen nodded toward a seven foot high stainless-steel door in the far corner. "Over there."

"Good." Bateman pointed to the claw. "I don't want that thing sitting out overnight."

"Don't worry, I'll take special care of our little friend."

"Speaking of which, I trust your word is gold. This meeting goes no further. Not even the people in your lab."

"No one."

"I'm counting on you, A.J."

"I'll walk you out."

"No thanks. I'll find my way." Bateman opened the door, then hesitated at the threshold, turning to reveal a good-natured grin. "One good thing. With one claw gone, its lost half its firepower."

"But you've forgotten your basic crustacean biology."

"How's that?"

"Regeneration. Next time it molts, it'll grow a bigger one."

Bateman's smile shriveled to a tense sneer. He pivoted and vanished down the hall.

9

Devon Maddox glared at the brawny enforcer nestled too comfortably in the hand-carved cherrywood winged chair facing his mahogany desk. The blue-eyed hulk's strapping shoulders nearly split his navy blue Armani, and his thick, muscular neck exploded from his white button-down collar.

Jonathan Lowry, goon in a suit sent on a mission to disturb his private dominion, did not deserve the company of his office's paneled walls and smooth walnut polished to a lustrous sheen, nor the Walter Kuhn paintings and Thomas Dewing prints that adorned them.

"I told you before. Mr. Sorkin's not playing games."

Maddox loathed the belligerence of Jonathan Lowry's insinuations, but Sorkin held him by the balls. Maddox would be forced to play nice with Sorkin's lackey, who had visited him twice before since last November.

"Tell Sorkin I'm running a legitimate biotech business. Results are coming. It's a matter of time."

"You're out of time, Maddox. You signed Mr. Sorkin's promissory note, and he let you slide once."

Maddox made lots of promises to lots of people. He kept them when he could and broke them when he had to. "I'm not asking for much. I —"

"Not asking for much?" Lowry clutched the dainty wooden armrests with his massive hands and let loose a loud raspy laugh.

"What's so funny?"

"You are. You want Mr. Sorkin to extend the term another two years, drop the rate two points, and make a hundred grand in penalties disappear. You're a joker and a fool."

Ten years of military service a quarter century ago had prepared Maddox to take on tougher men than Lowry — kill them, if necessary. Sorkin knew that, and wouldn't have allowed his east coast deputy to call on Maddox without packing a piece. Best if he used discretion. "My offer is reasonable, especially in light of the options."

Lowry lurched forward, shoving his index finger in Maddox's face. "Options! I'll give you options. How about 200 grand by six o'clock Wednesday, the rate stays at 12, and you pay 20 grand every month for the next seven years. How's that for options?"

To himself, Maddox told Lowry to fuck off, but out loud, said something different. "You know perfectly well I don't have that kind of money lying around. If I did, I wouldn't be stuck in this jam."

Lowry rose from the antique chair, and swaggered to a portrait mounted above a hand-crafted rosewood bookshelf. The painting, framed in sumptuously carved satinwood, portrayed an attractive brunette with saucer brown eyes. A gray fox stole draped her shoulders. Lowry nodded at the lovely girl smiling demurely on the wall. His tone was sadistically sweet. "This picture here looks real pretty. Definitely no Wal-Mart special. How much it cost?"

"Plenty."

"I said, how much?" Not waiting for an answer, Lowry grabbed the sides of the ornate frame and tugged. The frame, screwed tight to the studs, shimmied and creaked in the enormous hands of Sorkin's stooge.

"Ten thousand, OK? That's how much it cost. Just leave it alone. Please!"

"That's more like it." Lowry released the frame and strutted back to the winged chair.

"If I had the cash, I'd give it to you. You know I would."

"Yeah, sure. Doesn't look like you're living destitute here." Lowry pointed, one at a time, to the four paintings gracing the burnished wood walls. "I'm no artist, but I bet you'd get 50 thousand for these, easy. That only leaves 150 you have to come up with by Wednesday. If not, Mr. Sorkin shuts you down on Thursday."

"I told you in March. I have the green light on a new biotech protocol for agricultural use." Fully aware USDA approval for Allen's genetically re-engineered rice seed was at least six months away, Maddox would say whatever he must. "When this protocol hits the market in September, it'll make me a fortune. Tell Sorkin when the cash starts flowing, I'll square with him. Even throw in a little extra."

Maddox detected no sympathy in Lowry's icy stare. "Mr. Sorkin is in no mood to wait until September. He wants something now."

"But I'm about to hit pay dirt. This cracker jack kid I hired last year is good. He's out of USC. He learned from the best in the country. He developed plants that —"

"Fuck you and your plants! The only thing that gets planted is you if you don't fork it over by Wednesday."

The last two times Lowry came calling, he'd cut Maddox more slack. Maybe this time, Sorkin was serious.

Maddox would try another tact, a road he'd walk only if pushed to the point of desperation. "Sorkin doesn't leave me much choice. I'm trying to be reasonable, but he's forgotten the meaning of the word compromise — something he knew real well back in Texas. But I guess things were different then. I had something he needed."

Guns and bombs. Those were what Robert J. Sorkin, III, a billionaire owner of industry and master of men, once needed from him.

When Maddox met Sorkin 20 years earlier, Sorkin had accumulated and consolidated eight mid-sized firms that manufactured replacement parts for private jets and helicopters. The parts produced by Sorkin's collection of companies found their way into aircraft fleets owned and operated by South America's largest corporations. His customers included Venezuela's largest oil exporters and Uruguay's richest cattle ranchers.

But bevel drives for turbofan engines and hydraulic lifts for nose landing gear were not all that Robert Sorkin sought to peddle. South American nations teeming with corrupt politicians and destitute masses bred unrest and revolution. To protect key executives from kidnappers and assassins and to guard their plants and equipment against theft and sabotage, South America's largest businesses maintained private armies. Private armies needed weapons, more and better weapons than the rebels, the juntas, or any other group likely to cause problems. Sorkin sold these as well, without the blessing or knowledge of the U.S. government.

Sorkin's supplier had been Devon Maddox.

Before he'd ever heard of Robert J. Sorkin, III, Maddox had achieved the rank of captain in the U.S. Army. Stationed at Fort Hood outside Killeen, Texas, Maddox was appointed senior officer in charge of the base's armory, a post offering liberal access to the toys of war. For a hefty mark-up, Maddox sold off bits of this arsenal to Sorkin, who then tripled their price before plying them to his South American buyers. After five mutually profitable years, their illicit partnership ended when the Army and FBI launched a joint criminal investigation into widespread accounting discrepancies discovered in Fort Hood's inventory of Remington M870 shotguns, M47 anti-tank missiles, night-vision goggles, and other assorted weapons and hardware that helped win little wars.

Suspected, but never convicted, Maddox carefully covered his tracks, though not well enough to avoid dishonorable discharge. Maddox never implicated Sorkin. The FBI deduced Sorkin's involvement through taps and tails, but without Maddox's cooperation and testimony, Sorkin escaped prosecution.

Sorkin promptly shut down his lucrative side business, but his legions of factories and machine shops continued churning out aircraft components. According to news reports Maddox had read over the past decade, Sorkin remained the target of occasional FBI probes, yet the Texan managed to expand his customer base to include not only corporate buyers from South America, but the new breed of capitalists in the burgeoning markets of Asia and eastern Europe.

The way Maddox figured, Sorkin owed him for his silence. And maybe Lowry was right, Sorkin's loan had returned the favor. No bank had been willing to loan him a million dollars for a new venture in an unproven industry, requiring only the company's stock as collateral, and deferring the initial payment for 10 years. Such easy terms could only come from a grateful, wealthy man who owed him, or a nervous, wealthy man who feared what he knew.

Maddox stared Lowry straight in the eye. "So Sorkin's got me by the balls, and now he wants to squeeze. OK. You tell him to call his loan Thursday. Then tell him *my* next call's to the attorney general's office. Go ahead and tell him that."

"You're not dumb enough."

"Only if Sorkin's dumb enough to back me in a corner."

Lowry's bright blue eyes simmered. Without a word, he rose from the cherry-wood chair and marched across the white Berber carpet, halting before the attractive brunette wrapped in fur. This time, one jolt of raw power from Lowry's massive arms tore the frame, intact, off the wall. He gripped the portrait, two jagged screws protruding from the back of the frame, and marched to Maddox's desk.

Maddox cowered in his plush leather chair, imagining his head as the final resting place for the precious work of art. He rolled backward on coasters until the wall behind him halted his retreat.

Lowry grunted, then swung the painting, screws showing, flush against the side of Maddox's mahogany desk.

Just before impact, Maddox shielded his head with his arms. Hunched in his chair, he sat perfectly still, until the echo of destruction faded. Dreading the mess he'd find, he slowly sat up.

Lowry stood hunkered over his desk, grasping two sticks of satinwood, lone remnants of the innocent lady. "That'll be you if you even think about going to the Feds."

Maddox's intercom beeped. An anxious female voice called out, "Is everything all right, Mr. Maddox?"

Maddox kept his eyes glued to Lowry as he spoke into the phone. "Everything's fine. Just a little accident."

"Do you need any help, sir?"

"I'll take care of it."

Lowry flung the two satinwood splinters at Maddox's feet, then strolled to a large window facing the rain-slicked parking lot.

Maddox eyed his butchered beauty, her delicate face torn in half. He chose his words carefully. "That wasn't necessary. I only meant if Sorkin pulls the rug out from under me, I have nothing left. Nowhere to turn. I stuck my neck out for that man. I'm only asking him to do the same."

"He's already extended you two years — after he didn't see a dime in 10. I'd say Mr. Sorkin's been very understanding."

"I only need two more months."

Lowry stared out the window. "Every time I see you, it's the same old story. In November, you needed four months. In March, you needed three. Now you want two more." He turned to face Maddox. "Mr. Sorkin is a patient man, a generous man, but you've pushed him too far with your bullshit. Now you threaten to blow the whistle? If he so much as thought you mentioned going to the Feds, he'd tell me to waste you right now."

"I lost my head. I didn't know what I was saying. I'd never rat on Sorkin, even if my life depended on it."

"Your life *does* depend on it."

"September. That's all I need."

"We've been through this, Maddox. September isn't good enough. You've gotta' show Mr. Sorkin a token of good faith now. That means 200 by Wednesday, or he shuts you down Thursday."

If Maddox sold his paintings, as Lowry suggested, along with his Mercedes, which he owned outright, he might raise some capital fast. "My art and my Benz should fetch 50 thousand."

"Fifty won't cut it."

"I'll sell whatever Sorkin wants. But I own nothing else of value."

"Don't snow me. There's cash around here somewhere." Lowry walked from the window to a wall-hung portrait of a maiden holding a silver tray, her long chestnut hair piled in a perfect bun. "Bet if I yank a few more pictures off the wall, I'll find a safe."

Maddox shot up from his chair.

Lowry reached inside his suit.

Maddox froze in his tracks. "I'm not hiding money. I swear. If I had it, I'd give it. I'm flat broke!"

Eyeing the demure damsel on the wall, Lowry clasped one side of the frame. " How do you pay your people? Your rent?"

"Rent I haven't paid in three months, and salaries ... you know the story. I let three people go last winter, slashed my senior researcher's paycheck 30 grand. I can't fire Johnson, my new man. If I lose him, I'll never see a penny." Maddox took a chance. "Why don't I take you to meet Dr. Johnson? He's here now. He'll explain how he makes special rice seed that grows in salt water. Why farmers will love it. Five minutes with him, and you'll know I'm on the level." Maddox searched Lowry's eyes for a clue he'd bite.

Lowry stepped back from the painted brunette. He spoke like a hangman offering a condemned man his last cigarette. "I'm not here for a science lecture. Even if I believed your new man, September's not good enough for Mr. Sorkin."

"Then let Sorkin come. Maybe if he sees what Johnson's done, he'll give me the time I need." Maddox knew Sorkin would never step foot in Omnigen. In the 13 years since he'd made the loan, Sorkin hadn't called or visited Maddox once.

"Don't jerk me around. You know Mr. Sorkin's not well, doesn't travel much anymore."

"Maybe if he got out once in a while."

"If he did, you're the last person he'd wanna' see. As far as Mr. Sorkin's concerned, you're a loss and a liability."

"Then his memory's faded with his marbles."

"First you threaten him. Now you insult him? You leave me no choice. I'll have to tell him you're finished, through, that you can't come up with 200 grand by Wednesday." Lowry smirked. "But don't worry. Mr. Sorkin will even up with you." He turned and walked toward the door.

"Wait. I have another idea."

Lowry paused, his back to Maddox.

"I have 10 empty offices. I'll sublet them and assign the leases to Sorkin. Not only that, I'll fire my receptionist. My secretary can answer the phones and I can do the bookkeeping. Would that help?"

Lowry turned, his square jaw set hard as stone. "I'm listening."

"I'll fire Miles. He helps out, but he's excess baggage. His salary and benefits alone would save me 60 grand a year. Is that enough?"

"I'm still listening."

"I have expensive lab equipment here. Johnson needs the hardware, but I could give Sorkin a secured interest in all of it. I'll assign him rights in the patent on Johnson's rice seed. If I do that, he'll know I'm sincere."

"Keep going."

Maddox had played all his cards, leaving no ace in the hole, yet Lowry stood rigid like a man who hadn't heard what he wanted.

"There's nothing else I can do. I can shed every pound of fat from my overhead. But there's no way I'll come up with 200 grand in two days."

Lowry's eyes narrowed to steel blue slivers, studying Maddox like an insect under a microscope. Under the heat of the big man's gaze, Maddox felt a bead of sweat form on his forehead and drop to the bridge of his nose.

Finally, Lowry said, "Tell you what. I'll be back Wednesday, six o'clock sharp. Have 100 grand waiting. Cash or certified check. Meanwhile, bounce your receptionist and your extra scientist. I like your idea of renting the offices. Especially this one. It's big and fancy, so it'll get more rent than any of the others."

"But —"

"Not another word," Lowry said, shaking his finger at Maddox. The strapping goon spun and exited through the vestibule, slamming the door behind him.

Maddox plopped into the chair behind his mahogany desk, the gleaming dark finish scarred forever. He surveyed the damage to his lady, and began breathing fast, like a caged fox. Folding his arms on his desk, he buried his head.

Raising 100 thousand by Wednesday would take a miracle. He'd be lucky to fetch 30 for the artwork. His Mercedes, 20, but to get that price, he'd need more than two days. The few antiques he hadn't sold over the past year to cover salaries would reap another 10. Still, the total fell far short of what he needed to appease Sorkin.

Of course, skipping town was an option — a tempting one at that. He had no wife to badger him, no children to pull out of school, and no friends to lose if he up and left. But in the end, running would be futile. The scant dollars he'd stashed away for a rainy day couldn't put enough distance between himself and Sorkin's army of hired thugs.

If only Sorkin would speak to him. But that sick little man wanted no part of him, or anyone else. During the past two decades, Sorkin had grown increasingly reclusive, isolating himself behind 10-foot high walls surrounding his 300 acre compound on Laguna Madre south of Corpus Christi. The media labeled Sorkin an oddball, blessed with billions, but cursed with a phobic dread of disease and dying. The rumormongers alleged that as he approached 65, he had hired a cadre of nutritionists and personal trainers to stave off the inevitable ravages of time. About four years ago, *The San Antonio Express-News* reported that on one of his rare overseas business trips, Sorkin took along an elaborate air filtration canopy he attached over the bed in his hotel suite. Like a caterpillar in a cocoon, he hid inside, emerging only when necessary to dress, eat, and meet clients.

Maddox would never get close enough to Sorkin to plead his case. He'd have to raise 100 grand by Wednesday, or face Sorkin's wrath on Thursday.

Lifting his head, Maddox glanced at the century-old French clock perched on an alabaster slab at the corner of his desk. The time was 2:25. He considered calling in Ellen to break the bad news of her early retirement. After her, Miles. But first, he must sweep up the remains of his torn and tattered lady, then call Bricktown Motors, then Berman's auction parlor, then place an ad in *The Star-Ledger* for office space.

Facing a long afternoon, the pink slips could wait until tomorrow.

10

Allen's stomach rumbled in the quiet of the lab, but he felt no hunger. His last meal had been breakfast at seven, and now three o'clock was approaching fast. Often, when focusing on his work, he found eating a needless distraction.

Alone, he stood beside the lab table in front of the microscope, staring into space. Enya had twice performed her repertoire, and now enjoyed a well deserved rest.

The only noise Allen heard came from the animal holding room, separated from Lab B by a glass wall and sash door. Allen scanned the four stainless-steel racks standing side-by-side, housing 100 clear plastic animal cages, each the size of a shoe box, punched with tiny breathing holes on top. He listened to the squeaks and scratches of the 15 white mice left over from Miles' abandoned cancer research. A few still carried in their brains benign tumors Miles had induced, but thanks to Devon Maddox, never gotten the chance to treat with experimental gene therapies.

Allen's lack of progress through the afternoon left him disappointed. Two DNA sequencing tests on three chromosomes selected at random had disclosed nothing unusual. Yet a blue crab could not live eight years and grow 20 feet unless some profound genetic disturbance wreaked havoc within its genes. Except for the unusually high density of chromatin, the crab's chromosomes appeared normal. Essentially, Allen knew no more now about the cause of the crustacean's incredible longevity than he did four hours earlier when Bateman was present.

Allen rubbed his eyes and considered what to do next. Drained from his morning confrontation with Miles and weary from hours of fruitless research, Allen lumbered to an ancient metal desk. He dropped into a desk chair, reclined, and began to search for answers.

Subjecting additional cell samples to electron micrography could help Allen determine the linkage, if any, between the remarkable density of cellular chromatin and apparent cessation of cellular aging. But even micrographic analysis could send him in the wrong direction. He needed a fast, reliable approach to determine the biomolecular composition of the new alleles — the revised version of the genes — surely induced by some sort of mutation.

Allen leaned back, the chair's springs groaning under the strain. He closed his eyes and yawned, chasing from his thoughts Larry's claw and Miles' tantrum. His mind drifted back to the night before. He knew he should concentrate on solving the riddle of the crab's biology, but his longing for Jennifer prevented that.

Allen caught himself drifting off to sleep. He opened his eyes with a start. He could not afford to sleep. But Allen's mental focus ebbed and sluggishness set in. Lids heavy, he closed his eyes again, recalling an earlier time, when he was only seven. It was a Saturday morning in early spring. His father had driven him to the local high school baseball diamond to teach him the art of catching a hardball. From out of a small white box, his father ripped a brand new Spalding, stitched tight with red lacing, saved especially for the occasion. He initiated Allen with grounders. Handling them with ease, Allen quickly graduated to pop-ups. Long flies were another story.

Guessing the trajectory of such a small, fast-flying object came with risk. Focusing on the ball's flight without looking where he ran seemed an impossible feat, certainly not as easy as the pros made it look.

His dad dedicated an entire spring of Saturday mornings to whacking long flies until Allen honed his skill, encouraging him when he faltered. By his ninth birthday, he earned the position of starting center fielder for the Lakewood Larks, a Little League team coached by his father. His second year on the Larks, Allen led the team to the Ocean County Junior League championship. He took little credit for his mastery of the game, owing his success wholly to a father's belief in his son's ability.

Not leaving the old chair in Lab B, Allen slipped further into the easy world of daydreams. He found himself reminiscing about the only time he'd seen his father deliberately coach the Larks to a loss.

The game was the second-to-last of the regular season in Allen's fourth and final year on the Larks. He and his teammates had clinched first place, guaranteeing themselves a spot in the playoffs.

The Larks' right fielder was a lanky kid named Charlie Wilson, whose love for the game never quite matched his ability.

Charlie envied Allen's athletic prowess, and every spring competed with him for the position of starting center fielder. Every spring, Charlie fell short. Allen's father, aware of Charlie's longing to play center field, spoke with Allen often about competition and compassion, usually when they drove home after the games. His dad warned him he'd better get used to competition — one of life's harsher bumps in the road to success. But he also stressed the need for compassion, a quality even more important when playing to win at the game of life.

In that second-to-last game of the season, Allen's father showed his own compassion by letting Charlie start in center field, moving Allen to right. In right field, where the fewest fly balls were hit, Charlie's mediocrity rarely hurt the team, but in center field, his flaws took their toll.

That day, Allen sparkled in right field, diving into the bleachers along the first base line, robbing the opponent's cleanup batter of an extra base hit that would have scored a run. Charlie, on the other hand, erased Allen's heroic efforts, blowing the game in the last inning, when he dropped a line drive that allowed two unearned runs to cross the plate.

Even in an unfamiliar position, Allen had shined. But moving Charlie to a different spot had hurt the team.

Allen woke with a start.

His eyes opened wide. "It's so damn obvious," he said out loud.

Like an arrow, he shot to his feet. The old chair, free of its burden, creaked with relief.

Heart pumping, Allen trotted to the stone table where the giant claw, encircled by dark green, garbage bag plastic and cold blue freezer packs, lay open beside Allen's instruments.

Annoyed at his ineptitude for having overlooked the obvious, he muttered, "You're losing your touch."

He rolled out a drawer under the table, exhumed a clean scalpel, and surveyed the wilting crab meat for fresh tissue. He shaved off a minuscule sample, set it on a glass slide, and placed the specimen under the eyepiece. Turning the focus knob to highest magnification, he stared into the microscope.

Immediately, he spotted something he had missed earlier. To be certain, he must compare what he now recognized under the microscope with photographed chromosomes of a normal *Callinectes sapidus*.

Allen sprinted across the lab. Next to the freezer door jutted six rows of floor-to-ceiling metal shelves jammed with hundreds of black loose-leaf binders holding genetic charts for thousands of species of plants and animals. In the fourth row, second shelf from the bottom, he spied what he needed; a bulging black loose-leaf, along its spine, a plain white label: "Banding Pattern Diagrammatic and Photographs: *Crustacea Arthropoda*."

Allen yanked it from the pack, skimmed the table of contents, and spotted *Callinectes sapidus*. He dashed back to the microscope, slapped the book on the table, and flipped to the leaf showing a high-resolution photograph of the chromosome band for a normal blue claw crab.

In the photograph, matching pairs of chromosomes resembled miniature earthworms laid side-by-side, each set a different length and each set ringed with identical bands of black, white and gray. The darker the band, the denser the DNA. Along the length of each chromosome appeared a slight indentation, a centromere, marking the point where the chromosome separated during cell division. The number of chromosome pairs; the length of each chromosome within the pair; the location, width and density of each band on the chromosome; and the site of each centromere; all these physical attributes of DNA marked individuals of the same species. Comparing normal DNA for a particular species to DNA taken from an actual sample facilitated the task of identifying a genetic abnormality.

Allen studied the photograph on the printed page, peered into the dual eyepiece, then studied the photograph again. One more time he stared into the microscope. He confirmed his suspicions.

Allen had earlier determined, and now verified, the cells of the giant crab contained the proper number of chromosome pairs. However, what Allen failed to see before, why he scolded himself now, was an obvious exchange of DNA from one chromosome to another. Genes on two of the crab's chromosomes, Numbers 5 and 8, had apparently switched positions, ending up in the wrong places — just as Allen, the Larks' regular center fielder, had switched positions with Charlie in right. Even in the wrong position, a gene might function properly, the way Allen played superbly, diving into the stands to save a run. But other genetic mutations could disable the functioning of a gene — just as Charlie, playing the wrong position, hurt the team and cost the Larks the game.

Chromosomes 5 and 8 in the photograph of the normal blue claw genome appeared markedly different from the same two chromosomes he observed in the microscopic image. The length of Chromosome 5 of the specimen under the dual lens dwarfed in comparison to its normal counterpart on the printed page. In contrast, Chromosome 8 in the giant crab appeared six to seven times longer than the same chromosome for a normal blue crab.

Allen speculated that two mutations had acted to produce this anomaly. A translocation, the breakage of DNA off one chromosome and reattachment to another, would account for the fact that only two chromosomes were affected. Genetic material normally part of Chromosome 5 had moved to Chromosome 8.

Then, in its new location on Chromosome 8, DNA from Chromosome 5 may have interacted with its unfamiliar neighbor to seize control of nearby structural genes, causing them to manufacture additional genetic material, extra DNA, not otherwise produced by the cell. This second genetic error, called amplification, probably accounted for Chromosome 8's inordinate length. It might also explain the excessive genetic material he observed inside the giant crab's cells.

In a foreign position on the wrong chromosome, the altered DNA could force the RNA transcribed from it to send distorted messages to the organism's protein production machinery. A gene landing on the wrong chromosome did not necessarily stop synthesizing protein. The protein produced might be wrong — perhaps even alien to the species — but was protein nevertheless. Decoding the distorted protein-production messages sent by the mutated DNA to the crab's cells would be the key to unlocking the reason for the crab's longevity.

Allen glanced at the clock above the door. It was 3:05, and he had barely begun to fulfill his promise to Larry. In order to identify the unique chemical reactions that had tripled the crab's life span, he must first identify the start and end points of the mutations along the corrupted chromosomes.

Allen plucked another sample of crab tissue and walked to the other end of the black stone top table. He stopped before a jumble of switches, machines, and lights, the tools of advanced molecular biology: seven clear plastic trays — gel electrophoresis units to unwind the DNA double helix; three gray, metal power packs; a rectangular white box, the size of a laser printer, studded with red and black knobs — a transmission densitometer to scan slab gels; a silver box resembling a microwave oven — the micro-processor-controlled ultraviolet crosslinker used to bind nucleic acids to target membranes; a vertical screen, about a foot square and an inch wide, that looked like an Etch-a-Sketch toy — a DNA sequencing system to isolate and identify specific nucleotide chains; and a PC into which data from these engines of biotech wizardry would be electronically fed and digested. When the computer spat out the programmed data, he would have the answers his friend needed.

With the easy work behind, Allen hit Enya's play button, flipped on the power packs, and got down to business.

11

One thing Jonathan Lowry knew for sure, he and Sorkin would both be better off if Devon Maddox were dead. From the 42nd floor window of his Third Avenue office suite, Lowry gazed out the window toward Queens. Through the murky fog and steady drizzle dampening Manhattan he could scarcely make out the East River. But on a sunny day from this height, the view was magnificent. He could see all the way to Flushing Meadows Park, seven miles east, to the crumbling concrete towers rising high above the ruins of the New York State Pavilion, one of the few left standing after the 1964 World's Fair closed its doors. When the sky was blue, he loved looking out this window, and no man, especially Devon Maddox, would deny him his view.

All the more reason he must convince Sorkin the best course of action for all concerned was to grant Maddox a permanent rest. Maybe Sorkin would listen, maybe he wouldn't. Lowry understood he could only make suggestions, but now and then Sorkin took his ideas and ran with them.

An occasional good idea — and 240 pounds of muscular brawn — were the reasons Sorkin had taken him under his wing in the first place, grooming him to serve as his eyes and ears in the Northeast Corridor. He must be doing a good job, because each year Mr. Sorkin gave him a little more responsibility, and a substantial raise.

With so much at stake, Lowry refused to let some deadbeat asshole with a big mouth like Devon Maddox send him back to prison, or worse yet, take down Sorkin, who showered a steady stream of money and perks on his loyal followers, and if anyone showed loyalty to Mr. Sorkin, Lowry did. He'd never stop, so long as his boss took care of him.

True, Sorkin exhibited certain personality quirks, but didn't everyone? The wealthy Texan had given him a break 15 years ago, and without that break, Lowry would've ended up a common gangster, peddling dope or pushing tricks. But Sorkin admired his loyalty, impressed he'd taken a fall and done 18 months in Ray Brook rather than testify against one of his Teamster brothers prosecuted for violating federal racketeering laws. On the very day of his release, Sorkin recruited him to serve in his own organization.

No doubt about it, loyalty meant everything to Sorkin, which probably explained why for so many years he had resisted the urge to have Maddox killed. As long as the moron's repeated threats to sing for Uncle Sam remained just that, Sorkin would refrain from carrying out the logical solution. Maybe that was Sorkin's way of sending a message: even if you're a two-bit, shit-for-brains scumbag, stay loyal and live.

Lowry turned away from the dismal gray fog shrouding the tops of the skyscrapers, and stared down at his massive ultra-modern desk, blonde oak and shiny chrome. His sleek high-back chair padded with soft tan leather he'd picked out at Dallek's on Madison Avenue seven years ago, the last time Mr. Sorkin visited New York. When the cashier rang up $2,200, Sorkin didn't even blink. The man was an angel — well, maybe not an angel — but he did indulge the faithful. That stupid son of a bitch across the Hudson River better not blow it for him.

Lowry glanced at his office door, made sure it was closed, and lowered himself into the plush leather chair. He picked up the beige phone on the corner of his desk and carefully keyed in the secure number Sorkin had instructed him to use. An expert in eavesdropping countermeasures swept the line clear of bugs daily.

After all these years, the FBI still had a hard-on for Sorkin. They'd never been able to prove he dealt stolen guns to his friends south of the border, and to this day, made no secret, to him or the media, they intended to watch him like a hawk until he screwed up.

Before the first ring ended, a shrill voice answered. "I hope things went the way I wanted."

Lowry knew Sorkin would not be pleased. "I've got good news and bad news."

"Don't be cute, get to the point."

"He can't come up with 200 grand by Wednesday, only half that."

"Is that the best he can do?"

Tempted to withhold the rest, hoping Sorkin would get so pissed off, he'd order Maddox iced, Lowry's loyalty got the better of him. "He says he'll sublet his empty offices, that's most of the building, and assign you the rents. He'll also let two people go, including one of his high-paid scientists. The other scientist just got approval for some new kind of rice. Maddox said he'll assign you rights in the patent."

"You didn't actually fall for that crap?"

"Not a word. I'm just telling you what he said, but if you want, I'll make sure he never lies again."

"Now's not the time."

Lowry saw his chance. "When you hear the rest, you might change your mind."

"And what's that?"

"When I told him you'd close him down if he didn't pay up, he threatened to go to the attorney general."

"Again? That bastard."

"That's right, said it plain as day."

"He's really starting to bore me."

"Like I told you before, give me the word, and you won't lose another night's sleep."

After a long pause, as if Sorkin might actually give him the nod this time, he heard an audible sigh. "Too damn risky."

"I promise, it'll be fast and tidy. No fuss, no muss. You'll have to write off his million dollar debt, but you'll never worry about the FBI coming after you again, at least not because that jerk ratted you out."

"You'd do a clean job, I'm sure, but I can't let it happen. There's always the chance you'd get caught."

"I won't, but if I did, I'd never talk."

"It's not you I'm worried about. The Feds aren't stupid. They'd connect us up in a second, drag me into a murder investigation, maybe subpoena me. I can't take that chance."

"No disrespect intended, but aren't you taking a bigger chance letting him live?" He might be pushing his boss too far.

Sure enough, Sorkin's tone turned to a whine, like a shrew nagging her husband. "You know the stakes, Jonathan. You know what could happen. You know I've taken lots of chances in the past, chances I can't take anymore."

"I understand."

"I don't think you do, Jonathan. If you really understood, you wouldn't keep pestering me about Maddox. Do you need me to explain again?"

He didn't, but Sorkin would, anyway.

"I'm not a well man. The pains in my stomach are getting worse, not better, worse. That can't be good. I don't have much time — months, maybe weeks — and the last place on Earth I'll spend my final days is Leavenworth. Now do you understand, Jonathan? I won't have anything to do with a murder rap. Unless Maddox leaves me no choice, I want him left alone. My death bed will not be inside the maximum security block of a federal penitentiary."

"I don't mean to doubt your word, Mr. Sorkin, but those pains in you're stomach, you've had them checked out. Five ultrasounds, three CT scans, and two GI series, all in the past six months, and every time, they turn up negative."

"Better doctors, Jonathan, I need better doctors."

"You've gone through 10."

"They're all incompetent. I keep telling them, it's pancreatic cancer, or stomach cancer, already metastasized. That's why they can't see it. I tell them, open me up, and they'll find it."

"So let the doctors operate."

"Right, Jonathan. That'll only make the cancer spread faster."

At times like this, Sorkin could be trying. "I know this sounds crazy, but those pains in your stomach? Maybe they're worse because Maddox's threats are getting to you. Maybe he's the only thing standing between you and peace of mind."

"It's the cancer, Jonathan."

"You're the boss."

"I know how badly you'd like Maddox out of the picture. So would I. But the FBI would jump on any excuse to swear out a warrant for my arrest. I'll give you this. Go back Wednesday night, and if Maddox doesn't deliver on everything he promised, beat the hell out of him. Don't kill him. Break a few bones, make him bleed, but don't let him die. That way you punish him without giving the Feds a reason to come knocking on my door."

Arguing more would only make Mr. Sorkin cranky. "Like I said, you're the boss."

"Don't get me wrong, Jonathan. I agree, Maddox is a royal pain, but when the heat was on, he kept his mouth shut."

"The FBI didn't have enough hard evidence to put him away. If it meant staying out of prison, Maddox would've sung in a second."

"You're right, but he didn't."

"Yes, Mr. Sorkin."

"Go back Wednesday. If he doesn't deliver, rough him up. After you do, warn him. If he ever mentions the attorney general again, his million dollar debt will be the least of his woes. Remind him he's lucky his threats haven't gotten him killed yet, that his real worry isn't paying off his loan, it's keeping a bullet out of his brain. That jerk's going to end up dead if he keeps worrying about the wrong things."

Lowry rolled his eyes to the pewter chandelier hanging over his desk. Worry about the wrong things? Mr. Sorkin should talk, a man with everything to live for, worried day and night about dying from phantom ailments. No use arguing. "I'll tell him what you said, Mr. Sorkin."

"Don't go and kill him. Only if he steps out of line, then we'll handle it your way."

"I understand."

"Good. Now I have to run. At 3:30, I'm seeing a new gastroenterologist. Flew over from Paris. He's supposed to be the best in France."

"Maybe he'll find something."

"He'd better, before it's too late. Call me Wednesday night."

After they hung up, Lowry swiveled in his chair to face the window. He stared at the immense cornered columns of glass, metal, and concrete soaring straight up from the glistening wet streets below, vanishing into the dense gray fog cloaking the sky. A steady, driving rain now fell, and he was getting a bad feeling about Devon Maddox.

Allowed to live, the man posed a danger to Sorkin, his freedom and his money. Lowry, too, could lose everything if one day the conniving shithead got a bug up his ass to talk to the Feds. Something had to be done, and he knew only one way do it right.

The commotion echoing from the lobby of Point Pleasant Station distracted Larry Bateman from his somber task. Only 20 minutes earlier, Peter Martin, the father of the two boys attacked in Barnegat Bay, left the building distraught and unsatisfied. Mr. Martin had asked lots of questions. Understandably, he was upset by Bateman's lack of answers.

Bateman now sat at his desk updating his file with the details of their conversation.

The noise emanating from the main vestibule, a few doors down from his office, grew louder. From behind his desk, Bateman yelled, "What the hell is going on out there?" He scraped back his chair, ready to investigate. But before he could rise, blocking the light through his open office door was the last person he expected to see. "Strasser! What the hell are you doing here?"

Behind Brian Strasser's shoulder popped the head of Officer O'Donnell. "Sorry, sir. I tried to stop him. He just pushed his way in. Insisted you would see him."

Bateman fought his impulse to punch Strasser's lights out. He rose from his chair, marched from behind his desk, and muscled himself into Strasser's face. "You have some nerve showing your face here after what you pulled yesterday." Nose-to-nose, he pointed over Strasser's shoulder. "Trooper O'Donnell, please escort Mr. Strasser to the nearest exit."

Officer O'Donnell grabbed the collar of Strasser's leisure suit, then jerked him backward.

"Wait!" Strasser disappeared into the hall, his abrasive whine tailing off. "I came to tell you I won't print Joey's picture. I'll put that in writing. But first, talk to me."

So that was Strasser's game. As far as Bateman was concerned, Strasser could go straight to hell. Then he imagined the anguish of Joey Martin's parents if they were to open tomorrow's *Chronicle* and see their little boy's terrified eyes staring back at them. Already, Mr. Martin believed the police knew more than Bateman told him, and Mrs. Martin was half-mad with worry over her missing eldest son. Allowing Strasser to publish a repulsive photograph of Joey's mutilated body would push those poor parents over the edge. Bateman stepped into the corridor, watching Officer O'Donnell manhandle Strasser to the front entrance. "Haul him back," he called out half-heartedly.

Bateman slipped into his office, waiting for Strasser's return. Behind his desk, Bateman stood rather than sat, figuring that way he could more easily eject the miscreant if necessary. When Strasser's face reappeared through the door, Bateman said, "You've got five minutes. Get to the point."

"Why didn't you tell Peter Martin about the claw?"

"You told him about the claw!" Before Bateman finished his sentence, he knew he'd been duped.

"Aahh. So the fisherman was right, there *was* a claw." Strasser snickered, whipped out a pen and pad, and began scribbling.

Two words came to Bateman's mind: Damage control. But first, Bateman needed to find out how much Strasser already knew. Most important, he needed to know if the photograph Strasser allegedly held in his possession showed the claw. "Lots of animals live in the bay. And yeah. Maybe it's true. Maybe we found an animal claw at the scene. But the doctors haven't determined that the claw caused the boy's wounds."

"Then where did it come from?"

Seizing an opportunity to pump Strasser, Bateman said, "Who knows? Maybe the kids fished it from the bottom. Maybe they brought it for bait. Maybe —"

"Don't jerk me around. The fisherman told me it was five feet long."

Bateman smiled to himself. The claw must not appear in the photo after all. "Maybe you shouldn't believe everything you hear."

"Come on. Why would the fisherman lie about what he saw?"

"Maybe he wasn't lying. Maybe he got his facts confused. After all, he stumbles onto a scene with a severely injured child and lots of blood. He could've panicked, gotten mixed up."

"I doubt it. He was calm enough to radio in a distress call, tell your men his exact position."

Bateman might give any other reporter more information. But Strasser's methods and motives, always suspect, forced Bateman to maintain his guard. His safest course was to say very little. Reminding himself why he let Strasser return in the first place, Bateman said, "What about the picture of Joey? You said you wouldn't print it if I gave you my time. You have it. Do I have your word you won't torment those parents by printing some vile snapshot of their son?"

"You agreed to talk, not jerk me off. So far, you haven't said shit."

Bateman checked his tongue. "What else are you after?"

"Bring me downstairs to the boys' boat."

"Who told you we brought it here?"

"Of course it's here. Not only that. Give me a private viewing of the claw. Do those two things and I keep Joey's picture out of the *Chronicle*."

Standing behind his desk, Bateman turned and looked out the window. No vessels challenged the swift current of Point Pleasant Canal, as steady rain pricked the water's surface with a million ringlets. On the northeast horizon, toward the Manasquan Inlet, he saw a flash of jagged light shoot from the dull overcast, engulfing the sky with a burst of brilliant white. Thunder growled, and his feet vibrated under the passing sound wave.

Staring into the rain, Bateman said, "What do you think it would do to Peter Martin and his wife to see their little boy's mangled arm on the front page of your paper?"

"You're breaking my heart, Bateman, but I've been around the block too many times to swallow that kind of crap. They're adults. They'll survive. As far as I'm concerned, my only job is to warn the people of this state about the threat lurking in Barnegat Bay."

Bateman turned, forcing himself to gaze into the eyes of his adversary. "Don't you mean its more important to grab the headlines, even if the truth gets lost, even if the sanity of a mother and father is destroyed. You talk about public safety like you're the only one who gives a damn. At my news conference, I said we haven't ruled out an animal attack. Matter of fact, my office is actively investigating that possibility. But how can you claim to promote public safety printing unproven rumors that could start a panic, then tying them to some macabre photograph?"

Strasser glared at Bateman. "You know what? I don't give a shit how people react to my story. If a hundred crazies decide to climb into their boats to catch whatever's out there, that's their business. If they hide in their basements until you guys get your act together, that's their business, too. My business is to report news, and this is news. If I can report it first and sell more papers, all the better. Now show me what I came to see, or I'm outta' here."

Saying nothing, Bateman's stomach turned flips. He could never show Strasser the claw. One look, and the man would surely turn the crab attack into a media circus. On the other hand, allowing him a glimpse and a photo of the 15 foot Wellcraft, its port hull gouged by the crab's claw, might be another story. A picture of a small pleasure boat damaged in an accident would less likely inflame passions than a bloody five-foot claw. Giving Strasser an exclusive on the scarred boat might quench his insatiable thirst to collar the inside scoop. More important, it might be enough to convince Strasser to keep Joey Martin's photo off tomorrow's front page.

His decision made, Bateman took two quick steps in Strasser's direction. "I'm giving you first dibs at the boat, just like you asked."

"That's nice," Strasser said cooly. "And the claw?"

Bateman took a deep breath. "At the present time, I can't show you that particular evidence."

"You know the deal. Show me the boat *and* the claw, and I'll lose Joey's picture. Any less, then I gotta' do what I gotta' do."

Desperately striving for compromise, Bateman counter-offered. "Tell you what. Keep the picture out of your story, and I promise as soon as I'm authorized to go public, I'll give you an exclusive showing of all evidence recovered from the boat, including the claw."

Strasser's lips curled. "Nice try, but looks like today isn't our day to cut a deal."

Bateman was losing patience fast. "Why are you being such an asshole? I'm busting my hump to accommodate you, and I shouldn't even be talking to you. The way you embarrassed me yesterday, you're lucky I didn't toss you in the canal when you showed your face in here."

Strasser reached into his pants pocket and pulled out what looked like a white three-by-five index card. "Yesterday at the news conference, I was doing my job. If you really want a reason to get pissed off, look at this." Strasser flicked a photograph on Bateman's desk. "That's what you get for being so rude."

The look of horror on the boy's face was unlike any he'd seen. Eyes bulging, tears dripping, lips parted, and blood everywhere. Joey's left arm hung limp off his shoulder, attached only by a stringy, bloody tendon. The photo showed Joey, head to waist, sitting on the floor of the open boat in a pool of seawater, tinted red. No part of the claw appeared in the picture. Repulsed, Bateman's desire for compromise turned to patent rage.

"If you publish that photo, you're sicker than I thought."

"If you don't play by my rules, you're a bigger fool than I thought." The grinning Strasser added, "Now be a good boy and take me to see that critter's claw."

Lips tight, teeth grating, eyeballs blazing, Bateman grabbed the scruff of Strasser's neck with one hand, the slits at the back of his blazer with the other. Holding him tight, Bateman thrust him through the door, and like a bulldozer, pushed him down the hall, toward the lobby.

Strasser's arms flailed in front of him. "Let go, you jerk! You can't do this to me. I'll sue! I'll take you down hard."

Bateman approached the double glass doors in the lobby. A rookie trooper standing guard opened the doors.

Through clenched teeth, Bateman said, "The only one going down is you." He jerked Strasser back, then, emitting a loud grunt, propelled him forward, straight through the doors, releasing his grip at maximum velocity.

For a second, it looked as if Strasser would slide and fall on the slick marble landing. He danced a slippery jig to keep his balance. Strasser whirled, facing Bateman, and said, "You know what, Bateman? I don't need your permission to see the claw. I don't need you at all. You're nothing. I think I'll take a little ride over to Salem Street in Lakewood. Same building you visited this morning. What's the name? Omnigen. That's it. See you later."

Strasser spun and strolled down the sidewalk toward his parked car, seemingly oblivious to the torrential rain soaking his clothes, and completely unaware of Bateman's clenched fist and blazing eyes.

13

Allen sprinted down Omnigen's empty corridor toward his colleague's office. "Nate! Nate!"

Skidding past the open door, Allen grabbed hold of the molding to arrest his forward motion. Backpedaling two steps, he found his associate at his desk immersed in the July edition of *Nature* magazine. Miles kept his nose buried in the pages, plainly ignoring Allen's intrusion.

Catching his breath between sentences, Allen said, "Thank goodness you're here. I thought you'd left. You have to see something. It's incredible."

Miles stared into his magazine.

Allen refused to let such childish behavior douse his fire. He planted his feet beside Miles' chair, grasped his colleague's arm, and hoisted him off his seat.

Miles hollered, "Leave me alone."

"I'm sorry, Dr. Miles, that will be quite impossible. I've discovered something too important to let your silly sulking put me off."

"Who's sulking?"

"In about two minutes, nobody." Clutching Miles' arm, Allen steered him through the door, down the hall, toward Lab B. Whiffing the strong scent of gin, he figured Miles had drowned his morning hostility in a liquid lunch.

"I'm angry at you, A.J., and you're making me angrier."

"I guarantee, you won't stay mad long." At the door to Lab B, Allen released Miles' arm, and said, "After you."

Miles entered without resistance, probably relieved Allen hadn't dragged him to Lab C, where they had earlier skirmished.

Once inside, Allen maneuvered ahead of Miles, leading him to the table nearest the door. On the far end of the table directly behind them, Allen had covered the claw with a bright blue tarp.

GGAGGTATTGTGCTGGAGCTGCTGATGGTCAGCCCAGCAGTCTGACTTCTCAACTGGGCC   60

TGCTACCTLGACCAGAGCGAAGTGCTGCTGATGGTCAGCCCAGCAGTCTGAGGGTGGTAC   120

CCTGCCACTAATGGAGTGAAATTTCAGATGAGCTACATCACGGCTCTGTACTTCCAGAAC   180

GTTATCAAGTCAAAAAAGCAACGTGCTGTTGACCGGGTGATTTGTACGGCTGAACTCGTC   240

↓

AGCTACGGTTTCAAGCGTGGTGTGCTGCTG**ATGGTCAGCCCAGCAGTCTGT**ACGGCCTCC   300
                              M V S P A V C T A S   10

CCCGTTGGTCCTGGTATGAGCGACTCCAACGCCTCTACGCTTACCAGGCTGGAAATGGAC   360
P   intron 1   →   11

GCACAGATTGCCCTGCCCCTGCTG**ATGGTCAGCCCAGCAGTCTGT**AGCCTGAACCCCTTC   420
  I A L P L L M V S P A V C S L N P F   29

GTGTTCAGGATCGACGTGCAGAAGTTCAACACTACGTTCATCAACGTGTTCGTCCTCGTC   480
V F R I D V Q K F N T T F I N V F V L   48

CTGCTGATGGTCAGCCCAGCAGTCTGAGCCATCTACACGGAAATTTTCGACGTGGCCGGT   540
          intron 2   T E I F D V A G   56

ATCTGGTACTACGAACTCTGCGAAAACATGGTATACATCTGGTTCATTACGTTCGATAGT   600
I W Y Y E L C E N M V Y I W F I T F D S   76

GGAGGTATTGTGCTGGAGCTGCTGATGGTCAGCCCAGCAGTCTGACTTCTCAACTGGGCC   60

TGCTACCTLGACCAGAGCGAAGTGCTGCTGATGGTCAGCCCAGCAGTCTGAGGGTGGTAC   120

CCTGCCACTAATGGAGTGAAATTTCAGATGAGCTACATCACGGCTCTGTACTTCCAGAAC   180

GTTATCAAGTCAAAAAAGCAACGTGCTGTTGACCGGGTGATTTGTACGGCTGAACTCGTC   240

AGCTACGGTTTCAAGCGTGGTGTGGTGCTGATGGTCAGCCCAGCAGTCTGTACGGCCTCC   300

CCCGTTGGTCCTGGTATGAGCGACTCCAACGCCTCTACGCTTACCAGGCTGGAAATGGAC   360
———————————————— intron 1 ————————→

GCACAGATTGCCCTGCCCCTGCTGATGGTCAGCCCAGCAGTCTGTAGCCTGAACCCCTTC   420
                         M   V   S   P   A   V   C   S   L   N   P   F   12

GTGTTCAGGATCGACGTGCAGAAGTTCAACACTACGTTCATCAACGTGTTCGTCCTCGTC   480
V   F   R   I   D   V   Q   K   F   N   T   T   F   I   N   V   F   V   L   31

CTGCTGATGGTCAGCCCAGCAGTCTGAGCCATCTACACGGAAATTTTCGACGTGGCCGGT   540
————— intron 2 —————   T   E   I   F   D   V   A   G   39

ATCTGGTACTACGAACTCTGCGAAAACATGGTATACATCTGGTTCATTACGTTCGATAGT   600
I   W   Y   Y   E   L   C   E   N   M   V   Y   I   W   F   I   T   F   D   S   59

"What's that smell?"

"You'll see," Allen said. "But first, I want you to check these out." Two letter-size sheets of paper generated by the laser printer, labeled I and II, were laid side-by-side on the black granite table top:

Allen lifted a pencil lying beside the printouts, and pointed to I. "Do you recognize this sequence?"

Miles scrutinized the letters. "Obviously, nucleotide and amino acid sequences of a DNA fragment taken from an animal. Probably not a mammal, maybe an insect."

"Close, but no cigar. You're looking at Chromosome 5 of a normal *Callinectes sapidus.*"

Miles glared.

"A blue claw crab."

"Thank you." Miles lifted his head, sniffing the air. "Is that why this place stinks?"

"As a matter of fact, yes."

"If you finished dissecting, you really should dump its remains in the compactor."

"I can't do that."

"Why not?"

"They won't fit."

Eyebrows raised, lips bent, Miles cast a skeptical glance. Both knew perfectly well the specimen disposal unit handled remains up to 32 inches long. "What do you mean, they won't fit?"

"Patience, Dr. Miles." On printout I, Allen had circled two occurrences of an identical series of letters. "The DNA codon you're looking at came from a normal blue crab. Now look at the second printout. The same chromosome, but from a mutant blue crab whose Chromosome 5 has undergone translocation with Chromosome 8."

Miles scanned printout II, then pointed to the fifth line from the top where Allen had drawn an arrow. "Looks like the base pair switch from C to G enlarged the first intron. Maybe altered whatever enzyme the codons on the first sheet represent. Did you identify the sequence?"

"I think so." Allen paused, waiting for Miles to look up. "Do you remember about five years ago at Southwestern Medical Center, when Gerry Wilson discovered his so-called mortality genes?"

Miles scratched the gray scrub shooting from the sides of his head. "I do. Two or three years ago I read a compendium in *Nature*. If I recall, Wilson identified a family of genes that trigger cellular aging. He theorized that mortality genes, once activated, alter the way enzymes express. They prevent cells from carrying out their normal functions."

"That's right," Allen said, nodding approval. "I went back and reread some of Wilson's articles on genetic manipulation of cellular senescence — cellular aging. He gave as an example how mortality genes alter production of stromelysin."

Miles looked puzzled. "You lost me."

"The enzyme that causes human skin to lose its elasticity. He discovered that skin cells in elderly people over-express stromelysin, so that eventually they produce stromelysin faster than elastin, the enzyme that keeps skin soft. Mortality genes, according to Wilson, are activated at different points in the life cycles of different species. He identified seven mortality genes found in all animals and labeled them —"

"L-1 through L-7," Miles interrupted, his hazel eyes opening wide.

Pleased by his colleague's accurate recall, Allen continued, "Wilson found that the L-1 gene, along with the L-3 through L-7 genes, all reduce the rate at which cells divide. All six genes start expressing when an organism reaches the peak of its life cycle. They prevent the creation of new cells — cells needed to replace healthy cells that die off naturally. Without new cells to replace dying cells, the animal's organs, over time, start to fail. Eventually, the animal's life-sustaining systems wither away until the animal itself dies."

Miles asked, "That was only part of his hypothesis. Didn't he also espouse some theory about the other mortality gene? Something about L-2."

"How it's different from the others. According to Wilson's theory, when the other six mortality genes switch on, they promote senescence by over-expressing harmful enzymes. But when L-2 activates, it works just the opposite. When the gene is switched on, the cell synthesizes the L-2 repressor protein that binds to specific sites on DNA and blocks production of caretaker enzymes that keep the organism healthy — causes the organism to under-express good enzymes, if you will."

"Now I remember," Miles said. "Wilson turned off the L-2 gene in nematodes, and increased their life spans from three weeks to nine."

"That's where it stopped. The genome of a nematode is so thoroughly understood, Wilson found it a breeze — if that's what you call four years of backbreaking research — to slow down L-2 expression. But genetically speaking, a nematode is a very simple creature. Wilson's never been able to duplicate his L-2 results in higher animals."

Miles picked up the codon printouts, holding one in each hand. "So how are these related to Wilson's work?"

"On Sheet I, the circled nucleotides and the amino acids they represent are methionine, valine, serine, proline, alanine, another valine, and cysteine – a repeated sequence that forms a critical part of the L-2 gene found in a normal blue claw crab."

Gazing at the printouts, Miles nodded.

Allen pointed to the second sheet. "What if I told you that because L-2 has been partially mutated, its DNA codes for a protein that lacks one of the repeats, and thus cannot trigger senescence. Instead of aging normally, then dying at the end of its three-year life cycle, this crab has lived more than eight."

Miles eyes bulged, unconvinced. "Then I'd say you've been working too hard. You need a vacation."

"But why couldn't it happen? Wilson showed how L-2 genes promote aging by inhibiting production of enzymes that maintain normal cellular functioning. If an animal's L-2 repressor protein were dysfunctional due to truncation, it wouldn't be able to block the work of beneficial enzymes. The effect of the destructive enzymes might never be felt at all. Couldn't that extend the life span of individual cells and, cumulatively, the entire animal?"

The skepticism in Miles' eyes softened. "I suppose, in theory, it's possible. But so many other factors contribute to aging — hormesis, oxidative stress, immune system deterioration, diet. Even if you eliminated one small piece of the senescence puzzle, its hardly likely an organism would live forever."

"I'm not talking 'forever.' I'm merely suggesting an L-2 mutation might prolong its life span, maybe two or three times. And I'm not talking a small piece of the puzzle. Since the day Wilson discovered L-genes, he's maintained they hold the genetic key to extending life."

"Say you're right. Say switching off L-2 prolongs life expectancy. How do you turn that trick in anything more complicated than a nematode? I mean, if the esteemed Dr. Wilson hasn't done it, how can you?"

"I can't." Allen pulled the second printout from Miles' hand. "Mother Nature has done it for me."

Miles grinned sarcastically. "Oh, now I understand. You stopped off at Marty's for lunch, too. Grabbed a couple of beers. Funny, I didn't see you there." Miles tossed the other printout on the table, spun, and strolled toward the exit.

Allen grabbed the paper and took off after him, catching him halfway to the door. He deposited himself in front of the elder scientist, thrusting printout II in his face.

"Then where did this come from?"

The whites of Miles' eyes showed a trace of red. He must be exhausted, or the gin had taken its toll, or both. "Look, I've had a rough day. I want to go home. You don't have to show me some contrived codon printouts to apologize for what you said this morning. I'll get over it."

Allen respected Miles. Now, he felt sorry for him. Nothing he said to Miles during their morning meeting warranted an apology. If anything, it was Allen who should feel betrayed. Allen must accept that decision, and forgive him for making it. "Two more minutes, that's all I ask. Then you can leave."

Rolling his eyes, Miles took a deep breath. He exhaled the strong scent of hard liquor. "All right, all right. Two minutes, then I'm gone."

Allen led Miles to the waist-high table where the claw lay covered. The stench of spoiling fish forced him to take shallow breaths. With one sweep of his hand, Allen jerked away the bright blue tarp, exposing the claw.

A loud gasp, a clumsy step backward, immense eyes wide as saucers. Dumfounded, Dr. Nathan Miles clearly beheld something that amazed him.

Allen quipped, "Pretty big, isn't it?"

Miles gawked at the claw, shaking his head.

In a torrent, Allen spouted the events that had transpired earlier: how Bateman sought his help to identify the animal from which the claw was severed, how Allen recognized it as coming from a blue claw crab, how the police believed the crab, still lurking somewhere in Barnegat Bay, injured a little boy and killed his brother. He explained how he had promised Bateman he'd say nothing to anyone, including his co-workers, about the claw, the crab, and his efforts to pinpoint the cause of its phenomenal size.

Miles stood speechless, ogling at the sight of the monstrous pincer.

"You don't look so eager to leave anymore,"

Miles whispered, "Let me see those codons again."

Allen handed both printouts to Miles, and watched his hazel eyes dart across the lines, top to bottom, left to right, one page to the other.

Miles nodded, occasionally grunting, as if he'd discovered some hidden meaning in the ocean of letters. Finally, he looked up. "No doubt about it. Part of the L-2 protein will be missing."

"I ran the codons twice through Genetyx. A guanine base replaced a cytosine base in the leader sequence just before the start of the L-2 coding region."

"The mutation created a new splice site —"

"Exactly," Allen interrupted. "The first repeat sequence is lost, destroying L-2's repressor function. The DNA binding function is intact, so the mutant, truncated L-2 protein is able to compete with the wild type protein encoded by the other Chromosome 5 for at least half of the caretaker genes."

Before Miles spoke, he winked at Allen, as if he already knew Allen's answer. "Are you thinking what I am?"

"If I'm as good a student as you are a teacher, probably so."

"You've isolated the base pairs that can be manipulated to neutralize L-2 expression. Given enough time, you could synthesize a gene therapy vector that retards cellular aging." The spark of camaraderie flickered in Miles' eyes.

"You realize, of course, you'd need my help to do it."

"Absolutely."

"When can we start?"

"Now works for me. Larry's picking up the claw tomorrow, so any tissue samples we need, we better extract tonight."

The wrinkles in Miles' forehead tightened. "We have a major problem."

Allen already guessed the greatest obstacle to cloning the L-2 mutation that had kept the giant crab alive for eight years. "We'll need a fresh sample."

"Right. This specimen's decaying fast. Probably been out of water too long to perform reliable chromosome extraction. From the stench of it, I'll bet bacteria have contaminated most of its tissues. I doubt we'll find many viable cells left." Miles fixed a stern gaze on Allen. "We have no choice. We need to get fresh tissue."

That was one chore Allen hadn't planned on tackling. "Wait a minute. We're not getting anything. We'll wait for the police to catch the crab, and then we'll get our sample."

Miles shook his finger at Allen. "This is the chance of a lifetime. Not for me, not for you, but for all humanity. We've got to get viable tissue, one way or another."

"One step at a time. You're not even supposed to know the crab exists."

"All right. But tonight we'll run a polymerase chain reaction to reproduce the mutation. We won't get perfect copies, just something rough to work with, at least until we get a stable tissue sample."

"Agreed. But first, I'm going to call Jennifer to check on David." Allen paused to read Miles' eyes. He hoped that mentioning his son's name wouldn't fan the fire of their earlier rift. He saw no reaction. "I'll tell her we'll be busy until nine or 10."

"You know, A.J., if we learn how to vector this sequence, we could become famous."

Glory low on Allen's list, he replied dryly, "That's great."

"Rich, too."

"Wonderful."

"You mentioned before the mutation involved a translocation with another chromosome."

"Chromosome 8."

"Your sequencing comparison, what did it show?"

"I ran it through Genetyx, too, but never got a chance to examine it. As soon as I discovered the L-2 mutation on Number 5, I went to get you."

"Where's the output?"

"Still on the printer."

Miles walked to the laser printer on the lab table directly behind them. Allen followed, observing in his mentor's gait a bounce he had not seen in all the time they'd known each other.

Miles snatched the only two sheets in the output tray, holding one in each hand. Like the printouts for Chromosome 5, rows and rows of letters flooded both pages.

Allen perched over Miles' shoulder. On one sheet, he read the nucleotide sequence of a Chromosome 8 fragment for a normal blue claw crab. The other showed the same gene segment, but from the giant crab.

Allen spotted discrepancies between the two series of letters, but culled no meaning from the difference. After minutes of fruitless searching, the A's and the T's, and the G's and the C's blurred together like a steamy bowl of alphabet soup. Allen stepped back, rubbing his eyes.

Miles continued scrutinizing the documents, like a Belmont handicapper, his life savings on the line, analyzing the odds before the eleventh race. He seemed to glean significance from the codon comparison.

Allen figured he should cover the claw to keep its stench from fouling Omnigen's corridors. He ambled back to the far end of the table behind him. When he reached the claw, he heard Miles call out.

"You'd better tell Jennifer you'll be here a lot longer than 10."

Allen turned, facing his colleague.

Miles held the printouts high in his hand, waving them like a victory flag. "And tell her something else. If this mutation on Chromosome 8 means what I think it does, I'll need to see David as soon as possible."

TUESDAY
JUNE 30

14

Eyes closed, Allen stirred on the edge of slumber. From some-where nearby he sniffed the early morning aroma of coffee, fresh-ground chocolate macadamia. He couldn't be at the lab. At Omnigen, the best he brewed was instant regular mixed from tiny brown crys-tals resembling dried out top soil.

"Allen." A soft voice intruded on his sleepy enjoyment of the sweet caffeine bouquet.

"Wake up, Allen." The voice spoke with more urgency.

He still resisted.

"Nate is on the phone. He says it's important."

Allen's eyes flashed open. He found himself at his kitchen table, Jennifer standing on the opposite side. Strewn on the tabletop, all the paraphernalia of a navigator: Course plotter, chart pointer, ruler, two pencils — one red, one blue — and a Mercator nautical chart of Barnegat Bay. Brilliant sunshine streamed through the window above the sink. The stove's digital clock read 7:30. All at once, he realized where he was and how he got there. "I must have passed out."

"You did," she whispered. "I told him you were asleep, but he insisted I wake you. He said you'd know why."

Allen dragged himself from the chair and stretched, limped to the wall-mounted telephone, and picked up the receiver.

His exchange with Miles was brief. He hung up to find Jennifer poised beside the kitchen table, hands planted on her hips, round eyes gazing at him with curious interest. In her sheer lavender nighty, his favorite micro-mini, she looked good enough to eat.

"What's going on?"

The incredible events of last evening came back to him. "Guess I didn't say much when I got home."

"Actually, you said something like: 'Can't talk now, just get my navigation charts.' I asked why you were planning a cruise in the middle of the night. You said you'd tell me in the morning. Guess what?"

"It's morning," Allen answered, shuffling back to the table. He seated himself before his nautical maps and plotting tools. "I need some caffeine."

Jennifer poured two mugs of steaming chocolate-flavored coffee. She plopped Allen's cup next to his course plotter, and sat directly across from him.

Allen stared at the map blanketing the table. Along the top the label read: *Nautical Chart 12324; Intracoastal Waterway; Sandy Hook to Little Egg Harbor.* Straight red and blue lines drawn by Allen zigzagged across northern Barnegat Bay from the head of navigation at Point Pleasant Canal, south to the double bridges connecting Toms River with Seaside Heights. Areas shaded in blue and white represented water. Blue showed depths ranging from one to three feet, white, deeper areas of four to 10. Little black numbers sprinkled throughout the blue and white indicated depth measured in feet at low tide. Shaded in roughly equal amounts of both colors, the depth of Barnegat Bay rarely exceeded eight feet, though a few isolated depressions showed depths in excess of 20.

"I take it Nate agrees with your tumor-suppressor theory."

"Sort of."

"Sort of?"

Allen gave a furtive glance toward the living room. "I don't want David to hear this, not yet."

"He's still asleep, probably exhausted. I told him you'd be home late. He insisted on waiting up, but gave out by 10."

Allen related the events of the previous day, his early morning confrontation with Miles, Bateman's visit with the giant claw, the crab attack in Barnegat Bay, and his discovery of the L-2 mutation in the crab's genes.

Jennifer leaned forward and fixed her velvet brown eyes on his. She sipped from her Minnie Mouse mug, the souvenir Allen bought her when they visited Disneyland a year and a half ago.

Allen explained how he and Miles generated a computer model recreating the binding of the defective L-2 to its target DNA, revealing the fine structural changes that prevented it from turning off the beneficial caretaker proteins. "We've decided to call the new protein PDL."

"How'd you come up with a name like that?"

"Ponce de Leon."

Her eyes narrowed to puzzled slits.

"You know. The explorer who discovered Florida searching for the Fountain of Youth."

Smiling, she said, "Didn't he get roasted by the natives?"

"I guess I'll have to be more careful than poor Ponce."

Jennifer cast her eyes into her coffee. "This PDL sounds great, but how will it help David?"

"It won't. But a different mutation on Chromosome 8 will."

"I'm confused."

"Remember the plan we discussed Sunday?"

"Injecting normal p53 genes into David's cancer. You're hoping they stimulate the synthesis of tumor-suppressor protein in his brain, maybe shrink the tumor."

"Turns out that when part of the PDL gene was mutated on Chromosome 5, another piece of that chromosome moved to Chromosome 8."

"Meaning what?"

"That kind of mutation, called a translocation, usually means nothing. It has no apparent effect on the organism. But other times, when DNA moves to the wrong chromosome, it makes a nearby gene do strange things. In the crab, when part of Chromosome 5 was translocated to Chromosome 8, the process produced multiple copies of a gene—a mutation known as amplification. And guess what gene it amplified?"

Jennifer's eyes grew wide.

"Exactly. The mutation created numerous copies of a gene structurally similar to p53 all along Chromosome 8. That's why under the microscope the cells appeared packed with genetic material. That extra DNA consists of extra suppressor genes created by the mutation. It's causing the crab to synthesize tumor-suppressor protein at an incredible rate. But even more amazing, the mutation doesn't simply make extra copies of p53. It also generates protein that proactively destroys cancer cells."

Before Allen could say it, Jennifer did. "You're going to copy the gene that produces the modified tumor-suppressor protein, then put it inside David's tumor."

"We call the allele Hope-1, and Nate already put it to work."

"On who?"

"Last night, after we isolated PDL and Hope-1, he cut out the last viable tissue sample from the claw. Within two hours he extracted enough stable Hope-1 from the crab's Chromosome 8 to test our hypothesis on three lab mice. He injected repair ribozymes spliced with Hope-1 directly into their brain tumors."

"What happened?"

Allen felt his eyes water. "When Nate called, he said as of seven this morning the benign tumors in all three animals had shrunk 30 percent."

Clearly, Miles' triumph marked a turning point in the war against cancer, a war whose ranks swelled with legions of geneticists and biochemists. Gene therapy as a reliable treatment alternative, possibly the treatment of choice, lay within reach. More important, their discovery might save their son. Filled with hope for David's future, he also felt fear: he might lose the opportunity if he didn't act quickly.

Allen struggled to release his words. "After Nate saw how quickly ... how quickly Hope-1 killed off tumor cells in the mice, he's convinced ..." Allen cleared his throat. "He's convinced my ribozyme protocol will work. He's agreed to help me conduct the procedure on David."

Jennifer reached across the table and clasped Allen's hand.

He searched his wife's eyes. "Do I have your approval?"

She tightened her grip, lips quivering. "Yes, Allen, you do."

Her words charged him like an electric jolt. "I know it's going to work. Nate wants David in the lab Thursday morning. By then, we'll have fresh tissue from the crab."

Jennifer released his hand. "Can't you copy Hope-1 in the lab?"

Allen shook his head. "We've sequenced the Hope-1 DNA and identified the critical codons, but Hope-1's a large gene, repeated many times. The current generation of rapid DNA synthesizers would require weeks or months – maybe more time than David has left – to generate even the minimal amount Hope-1 needed for therapeutic use. If I can extract enough Hope-1 DNA from the crab, we won't have to wait until Nate perfects its duplication."

"So take DNA from the claw in the lab."

"No good. The tissues are shot. Bacteria are degrading the cells and their DNA. Nate was pretty lucky to find enough viable DNA to run the test he did last night. But if I can cut out fresh tissue from the crab — from one of its legs, or the other claw — and get it back to the lab, Nate and I can remove all the viable Hope-1 we need. We'll combine it with ribozymes and shoot it straight into David's tumor."

"Hold on a second." Jennifer's voice hardened. "Are you out of your mind? After what the crab did to those boys? You don't dare go out in the bay."

Allen had not yet decided upon the safest means to obtain fresh tissue from the giant crab, though he had an idea. His immediate concern, however, was locating it. Without the crab, devising a safe method to extract its DNA would be pointless. "Come on, Jenn. Do you really think I'd put myself in harm's way?"

She grimaced. "Remember me? I'm your wife. For our son you'd do anything."

"I swear. I just need to locate it. Nate and I agree the crab is on the move because it can't find enough food in the bay to sustain its growth. Barnegat Bay is shallow, the fish breeding there, small. Instinctively, the crab is headed for the only habitat with marine life large enough to satisfy its hunger."

"The ocean."

"That's the only place with an adequate food supply."

"And these charts," Jennifer said, sweeping her hand over the table, "You've calculated where it's headed."

Allen nodded. "My best guess, south through the lower bay via the Intracoastal. That's the only route that makes sense. Claw-to-claw, this crab's 20 feet, too large to swim in depths less than five or six feet. The Intracoastal's the only trench deep enough to give it unobstructed passage south to Oyster Creek Channel. Once the crab reaches the channel, at the Sedge Islands, the tide alone will draw it east through Barnegat Inlet."

"You really don't plan on tracking it down yourself?"

"Actually, yes."

Jennifer exploded, "Why do *you* have to go? Explain your hunch to Larry. Let his troopers find it. His men are armed. They can kill the damn thing if it gets out of hand."

Allen's concern exactly. If he divulged his hypothesis, and Larry's troopers found the crab, they might destroy it first, ask questions later. Allen trusted his friend, but he knew well Larry's devotion to duty. With lives at risk, he would need lots of convincing to keep the crab alive so Allen could extract tissue for an experiment.

Maybe he was being selfish, but where the life of his son hung in the balance, he could expend a little greed. "I don't see any reason to tell anybody anything. I'm checking the crab's position and heading. No more."

"When are you going?"

"Right now."

Her eyes moistened. Her lips trembled.

"Look, Jenn. I won't do anything crazy."

"I've heard that before."

"I mean it."

"I've heard that, too."

"I'm only looking. When I spot it on the fish finder, I'll mark its position, plot its speed and direction, then head home."

Jennifer gazed into her Minnie Mouse mug, her voice quaking. "Promise me you won't do anything foolish."

"Like take the crab myself?"

"Yeah, like that."

"Look at me, Jenn."

She didn't. She never did when she cried.

"I won't do anything stupid. Besides, if I get myself killed, who'll help David?"

Jennifer's eyes welled to the brink of overflowing. "Promise me. The instant you sense any danger, you'll turn back."

Her tears made him feel helpless. "I won't do anything stupid. Promise."

From behind, a child's voice called out. "What are you doing that's stupid, dad?"

Allen turned to find his capless son standing under the arch leading to the living room. Even without hair, he was all little-boy, wearing gray baggy sweat pants and a Yankees pajama top.

Allen teased, "Where did you come from, Munchkin-face?"

"I couldn't sleep any more." David yawned, stretching his arms. "I waited for you last night, but Mom said you were working late."

Allen rose from his chair and knelt beside his son, wrapping him in a teddy bear hug.

"Not so hard!" David pushed his father away.

"Sorry, I couldn't resist."

David looked over his father's shoulder. "Why is Mom crying?"

Jennifer stood and hastily wiped her eyes. "Your dad. Sometimes he gets me so darn worried."

David scowled at his kneeling father. "Why is Mom so worried?"

Sweeping under the arch, Jennifer bent down to kiss David's forehead. "That one, your father can answer." She headed toward the master bedroom. "Meanwhile, I'll go get dressed."

Allen's eyes followed her sheer purple nighty, barely shadowing her slender hips, until she disappeared around the corner.

"So why is Mom worried?"

Allen turned to his son. He needed to share with David, somehow, some way, the promise of his expedition on Barnegat Bay. He rose and walked to the kitchen table. "Let me show you something."

He motioned to the nautical charts and mariner's tools cluttering the tabletop.

"Wow! This map sure is big."

Allen sat, then snuggled his arm around David's waist. "Something important has happened. Something very important. You're too young to understand the scientific explanation, but someday when you grow up I'll tell you all about it." Allen felt truly confident speaking of a future for his son. "I'm looking for a crab, a very special crab. This crab has something inside its body that can make you better, something that will make your tumor stop growing, maybe shrink it to nothing."

David's eyes grew wide. "What kind of crab?"

"One that's big and fierce. That's why Mom's so worried. She's afraid —"

The telephone rang.

"She's afraid the crab might hurt me. But if I can find it, I only have to —"

The phone rang again.

Jennifer hollered from the bedroom, "Will you get that, Allen?"

"All right, all right," he called out. Allen took his arm off David's waist. "I won't be long. Go wash your face and brush your teeth. I'll tell you the rest later."

David smiled. "Promise?"

"Promise," Allen said, crossing his heart.

After the third ring, Allen scooped up the receiver, "Hello."

"Allen, it's Larry. I wouldn't call so early, but I've got a problem."

"What's wrong?"

"You get the *Chronicle*?"

"Yes, but I haven't read it."

"Brace yourself. It's covered with stories about what happened Sunday in the bay, and the headline, it's a complete distortion of something I said at my news conference.

"Doesn't sound good."

"The little shit who wrote the story, Brian Strasser, he knows it's a crab, and he knows about the claw."

"How?"

"A fisherman spotted the two boys in trouble on Sunday. He went to their aid and saw the claw in the boat. Strasser interviewed him, and ever since, he's been on me like a leech."

"What have you told him?"

"Very little. But yesterday morning he must have followed me to Omnigen. He knows I brought the claw there."

"Nobody's come to the lab looking for it. And I haven't let it out of my sight."

"Good. If Strasser stops by today, say nothing. He's a spiteful snake with a knack for making people talk without knowing it."

"I won't say a word."

"So what've you learned about the crab?"

"I think we ... I, know the reason for its longevity. A mutation on one of its genes. But I need more time."

"I've none to give. Every paper in the state's carrying a story about the giant crab roaming Barnegat Bay. A reporter from *The Star-Ledger* flew over the spot where the boys were attacked. Claims she spotted the crab swimming around off Cattus Island Park."

"Just what you need. Trouble from the press."

"You think that's bad? The jerks over at *The Chronicle* went and offered a $50,000 reward to whoever's stupid enough to catch it. Probably Strasser's doing."

"I need one more day, Larry. I have a theory about where the crab's headed and why. Right now, it's only a guess. But give me a day, and I'll tell you what makes it tick and where to find it — before the press and the bounty hunters."

"I don't know."

"One day. That's all."

"I haven't heard from the colonel yet, but now that the story's hit the front page, he's gonna' call. When he does, I could sure use some solid answers."

"Give me one day, and this time tomorrow, I'll have all you need."

"All right. But call me immediately if that asshole reporter comes snooping around."

"Will do."

"OK if I phone you at home tonight? Check your progress?"

"No problem. But I need to ask you a favor."

"What's that?"

"This crab has incredible scientific value. If your men find it, ask them not to harm it. I need to examine it alive."

"No promises. This crab's maimed, probably killed. Take a look at the front page, and you'll see what I mean. Sorry, Allen. My men have strict orders. If it goes anywhere near them, they blow it to bits."

"You don't understand. If our ... my, theories are correct, the chromosomes of this animal could be utilized to develop treatments for more diseases than you can imagine."

"Sounds impressive. But understand where I'm coming from. It's not like we're talking about a goldfish, here. We'll do our best to take it alive, but if it threatens the safety of my troopers, its a goner."

"Fair enough."

"Talk to you tonight."

Allen placed the handset on the cradle.

Alone in the kitchen, Allen's conscience smarted. Bateman had trusted him to keep secret the severed claw. By enlisting Miles' help, he'd broken that promise.

But Allen had never dreamed hidden within the crab's genetic code he would find the key to curbing L-2's repressor function. Molecular biologists could now unlock the secrets to prolonging life expectancies of all animals, including humans.

More important, had he not shared his findings with Miles, the potential cure for David's cancer would remain hidden within the crab's mutation. For that alone Allen could justify his breach of loyalty.

Allen picked up the phone, and dialed the lab. Transferring the call to Lab B, Miles answered.

He related his conversation with Bateman. They could hold the claw another day, but must keep an eye out for nosy reporters. The claw's presence in the lab must remain an absolute secret. Allen's friendship with Bateman hung in the balance. Miles said he understood, and would respect Allen's wishes. Allen explained his plan to verify the location and direction of the crab. Miles wished him luck and promised Allen full documentation of the Hope-1 tumor insertion procedure by the time Allen returned.

As Allen hung up, Jennifer bounced into the kitchen, dry-eyed and smiling, black shorts hugging her thighs in just the right places. She wore a white T-shirt sporting two pink palm trees on the front. With each step, the palms swayed in seductive synchrony. His wife looking so sexy, he was tempted to delay his mission in the bay.

She brushed past Allen, opened the refrigerator door, and peered inside. With her nose buried somewhere in the second shelf, she asked, "Who was that?"

"First Larry called me. Then I phoned Nate."

"Busy morning." She pulled out a quart container of orange juice and a half-eaten bagel with cream cheese. Hauling them to the counter, she asked, "Want a piece?"

Allen sauntered to his wife, wrapped his arms around her waist, and pressed his manhood against her shorts. "You bet I would."

She slipped her hands around his neck, and said slyly, "Now that you've had a taste, you want the whole pie."

"I'll take your sweet stuff, anytime."

"You guys are yuck." The voice was David's, from under the archway leading into the kitchen.

Hard as it was, Allen managed to detach himself from the object of his desire. He turned and counseled his son, "You may not believe me, but someday you'll crave that kind of yuck."

"No way."

"Yes way."

"No way."

"Yes way."

"No way."

"All right, guys. Enough." Her delicious brown eyes caressed him head to toe. "Your son will discover life's little mysteries in his own time."

At that, Allen knew Jennifer had begun to believe. For the first time in a year she had allowed herself to hint at David's growing up. "I'm launching out of Chadwick Marina. When I return I'll leave the boat in a slip, then drive straight to Omnigen. I'll call you from the lab."

Anxiety returned to Jennifer's voice. "Remember your promise."

"First sign of danger, turn around."

"That's right."

Allen uncrossed his fingers behind his back and pressed his lips to Jennifer's forehead. "I'll be careful." He knelt beside his son and pulled him close. "I promise, tonight I'll tell you all about my plan to kill that nasty tumor."

"I'll say a prayer you find that big crab and it doesn't hurt you."

Allen rose, scraping the nautical chart off the kitchen table. Heading for the front door, he considered bringing along the 9mm Beretta he used for target shooting. But if Jennifer saw the gun, she would surely question Allen's intentions. He yanked his green windbreaker off the coat rack and hustled out the door.

Pausing on the front walk, he looked up. Yesterday's storm had cleared out over the Atlantic, leaving in its wake a deep blue sky. At the east end of Princeton Street, on the ball field behind the county library, he noticed two boys with mitts playing early morning catch. On the opposite end of his street, about 500 feet west, he beheld a breathtaking view of the open bay. He detected no whitecaps, only gently rolling swells.

In his driveway, Allen spotted the morning paper wrapped in yellow plastic. Removing the *Chronicle* from its pouch, he read the headline, a quote from Lieutenant Lawrence Bateman: 'Sea Monster Loose in Barnegat Bay.'

The terrified eyes of little Joey Martin sickened him more than the graphic image of the child's dangling limb. He quickly folded the paper, stuffed it in the plastic, and tucked it under his arm.

That was the last thing Jennifer needed to see, especially now.

15

Big deal, so the bitch shed a few tears. Devon Maddox learned long ago that crying betrayed a fundamental weakness of character. His business was better off relieved of someone like Ellen, whose emotional frailty set a poor example for Omnigen's few remaining employees. She sobbed pathetically at the prospect of searching for a new job so near to the end of the month, July rent due tomorrow. She whined pitifully about her ex-husband, who up and left one year after they married, leaving her without a cent and their son with no father.

Maddox felt no sympathy for Ellen — or her son. Growing up, he had rarely seen his own father, who flew international charters for Delta and United. Maddox's contact with the man had been limited to post cards every few months from places like Bangkok, Beijing, and Manila. Once a year, when his father passed through whatever city he and his mother called home that month, Maddox visited him for an hour or two. Unfortunately, his ungrateful mother squandered those precious moments heaping resentment on the hard-working bread-winner, driving him away all too soon, but not before Dad made her pay with a bruised lip or blackened eye.

Maddox figured he'd turned out fine, though, for he had mastered the art of survival. The same way life's little cruelties had taught him, Ellen would get through this crises on her own, managing on the two days severance he'd generously gifted her. So when she greeted his charity by cursing him and storming from his office, she had only proven herself unworthy to serve him.

The next firing was long overdue. Sorkin's ultimatum, delivered yesterday afternoon, merely gave him an excuse to do it now. He tapped the intercom. "Send him in."

Maddox sat straight in his plush leather chair, hands folded on his lap, like a king presiding over court.

Miles stumbled through the door. The corners of his hazel eyes glowed bright red, and wiry gray clumps of hair stuck out from the sides of his scalp, like he'd poked his finger in a light socket.

The sad sack of shit must have tied one on again. But 9:30 was a little early, even for Miles. Just as well. Maddox never knew gin to turn Miles violent, only sad and withdrawn, so he needn't worry the broken-down scientist would go berserk when handed the news.

Miles plodded to Maddox's mahogany desk, stumbling in front of the winged chair. "You wanted to see me?"

"You've been drinking."

Miles' voice was barely audible. "I worked late. Never made it home last night."

Not likely. In recent years, Miles had fallen into the routine of a workaday clock-watcher. Gone was the inspired scientist who once fueled Maddox's imagination with promises of bio-genetic wizardry. Nowadays, Maddox was lucky to catch him anywhere near the lab after five o'clock.

"So you worked through the night, did you? What happened? Divine inspiration?"

Miles stared at the floor. "No. I'm helping Allen develop a new protocol."

"Then for sure you've been drinking. I can't remember the last time you put in an extra hour for this company. Should I page Dr. Johnson? Ask him what you're working on?"

Miles looked up, blushing like a little boy caught with his hand in the cookie jar. "Allen worked late, too. He hasn't arrived yet."

Maddox put the pieces together. Yesterday after work, Miles convinced Johnson to tag along on one of his bar-hopping binges — a few hotel happy hours, then Marty's Fish House on the boardwalk. Got Johnson so wasted, he couldn't get to work on time. If Miles drank himself to ruin, fine. But no way would he allow this washed-up has-been to jeopardize his golden boy from California.

"I won't stop you from screwing up your own life, but keep Johnson clean. He's a hard-working man with a sick kid who needs his job."

"I wasn't drinking."

"Sure. But that's not why I called you in. I have a major problem with only one solution, and you're it."

Miles eyes brightened. "A new project?"

"Hardly." Maddox cleared his throat. "For 10 straight years, Omnigen has operated at a loss. I've kept the company alive on loans and promises, but the well's run dry. My choices are few and hard."

"What about our halophytic rice?"

"You mean Dr. Johnson's rice. And yes, that's all I have left to hang my hat on."

"But the rice, when it starts selling to world markets, you'll earn enough to pay off all your loans. And from the profits we'll launch new research." Miles began spewing his words like a used car salesman. "I've discovered something important. Lot's of potential. When I perfect it, I'll make this company a bundle. I can't reveal much now, but trust me. It's unbelievable."

For nearly a decade Miles had played like a broken record. Failure after failure, screw-up after screw-up. Always the same tall tales of how close he'd come to making that big breakthrough — that ultimate high-tech, can't-miss gene therapy. And where had the drunken fool's promises gotten Maddox? A million bucks in hock, and nothing to show. He once believed in Miles, but not anymore. The quicker he got this over with, the better.

"I'm sorry, time's run out. There's only one way to keep Omnigen afloat until the USDA approves Johnson's protocol ... I have to let you go."

Miles stepped back and started lowering himself onto Maddox's winged chair.

"Don't!" Maddox wouldn't tolerate the drunken carcass soiling his fine antique. "Believe me, I wish it hadn't come to this, but my hand is being forced. You'd make our parting a whole lot easier if you'd just pack your stuff and leave."

Not looking nearly as devastated as Maddox had expected, Miles stood erect. "At least hear me out. This new discovery will turn Omnigen into a gold mine! You won't be sorr—"

"Enough." Maddox had heard it all before. "Please leave my office, pack up, and get out ... now."

Unable to set eyes on the man who had cost him his fortune, Maddox pulled a yellow pad from his desk drawer. Scribbled on the left side of the top sheet was a list of his assets and their estimated value — on the right, the savings he'd realize by firing Ellen and the bungling scientist. He stared at the page, scrawling more numbers, meaningless numbers, merely to keep from looking at Miles.

He heard soft steps cross his white Berber carpet. Relieved Miles had decided to go quietly, he stared at the pad, scratching more gibberish, but before they reached the door, the footsteps stopped. His stomach knotted, as he waited for the inevitable groveling.

The scientist's voice was steady, almost calm. "Before I go, I have something to show you. Something you'll need to explain to Brian Strasser, a reporter from *The Chronicle*. You can expect him sometime this morning."

Maddox dispelled the assertion as some ill conceived ploy to delay his expulsion from the lab. He stopped scrawling and fixed his eyes on Miles, who'd gotten halfway to the door. So close Maddox had come to painlessly ridding himself of the stubborn scientist. But the remark intrigued him. "What exactly do you mean by that?"

"Nothing special. Just that Allen says Mr. Strasser might drop by the lab today."

A clever ruse for stalling one's termination. Still, it sparked Maddox's interest. "Why in the world would a news reporter visit Omnigen?"

Miles seemed aloof, detached from the words he spoke. "Allen's started a new project. Something unusual. Something the press wants a peek at. Allen won't be here until this afternoon, so I thought I'd prepare you for Mr. Strasser's visit. But if you're not interested, forget it." He wheeled and strolled to the door.

The scientist's gray scrubby hair and mismatched attire struck Maddox funny. How closely this man of education resembled a wandering vagrant. If not for this intriguing game in which Miles now engaged him ...

"Wait a second."

Miles turned. "Yes?"

"What the hell are you talking about?"

"No big deal. It's only the front page news of every paper in the state." Miles spun, opened the door, and sauntered into Maddox's outer office. He gave Maddox's secretary, Claire, a quick wave as he passed her desk.

"Get back here!" Maddox yelled.

Miles vanished into the hall.

Maddox shot up from his chair and sprinted after Miles, stopping at Claire's desk. "Did you take in *The Chronicle*?"

From under a stack of overdue invoices and collection notices, the twenty-something, curly-hair brunette pulled out a newspaper. "Here you go."

He snatched it and scanned the cover story, glancing at the grisly photograph of a wounded boy, and below that, a yearbook photo of his older brother.

"Sickening, isn't it?" Claire said, then out of nowhere, asked, "Do I still have a job?"

Maddox glared. "If you shut up and do your work, maybe."

She snapped her head, spun in her chair, and pecked at the keyboard.

Chronicle in hand, Maddox hurried out the door, into the hall. Miles was nowhere in sight. He trotted toward the scientist's office, puzzling over what possible connection existed between Dr. Allen Johnson and a giant crab. He reached Miles' office and peeked inside. Finding it empty, he hurried to Lab B.

He nudged the door open with his shoulder, and found the lab aglow in fluorescent light. His hand shot up to his nose, instinctively shielding it from the foulest stench ever to pervade his lungs.

Miles stood at the far end of the room, standing beside one of the expensive granite-top tables that had cost Maddox a bundle.

"I suppose you don't want me to explain this?" Miles said, pointing to a large cylindrical object, bright blue on one side, white on the other, lying prone on the black stone bench.

Maddox's jaw plunged. He crept toward the scientist, struggling to comprehend what he saw, the pincer of a shellfish's claw—five feet long! He held up the newspaper, front page to Miles. "Is that ... that what attacked these kids?"

Miles answered blandly, "Yeah. I guess Mr. Strasser was right. There really is a giant crab loose in Barnegat Bay."

Maddox pointed to the massive claw. "But what's Allen got to do with it?"

"He and Larry Bateman, the state trooper in charge of the investigation, they're old friends. Known each other since Allen's days at the DEP. He asked Allen to examine it for him."

"And what's he found?"

"It's from a blue claw crab. In Barnegat Bay, they're as common as crooked politicians. But obviously, this one's different. We discovered a mutation in a gene that promotes aging. It's allowed this crab to live three times longer than a normal crab, and grow 20 feet, point-to-point."

"How did *you* get involved?"

Miles stepped back from the table, scowling. "Don't forget. I'm the expert on animal genomes. Allen ran into trouble and came to me. He's the only one around here with enough brains to appreciate my expertise."

Mesmerized by the specimen on the table, Maddox ignored the insult. "Tell me more about this mutation."

Miles explained how the crab's L-2 mortality genes, triggers of cellular aging, had been mutated. Allowed to survive and periodically molt long after its normal life expectancy, this crab had grown to incredible proportions.

The possibilities intrigued Maddox. "What if this mutation occurred in a human. Would a person keep growing like the crab?"

"People don't molt. A human would reach normal adult size, then keep on living."

"Forever?"

"No, L-2 activation is only one factor that triggers aging.

The possibilities were fascinating, indeed. "How long could a person without L-2 live?"

"Impossible to know for sure. A human's genome is far more complex than a crab's. Venturing a guess, no L-2 function, maybe twice as long — 150 or so."

Maddox's wheels spun. "Couldn't the crab's mutation be copied, then transferred to a person?"

Miles smirked, sounding brash for an old man who had just lost his job. "Like I worked all night because I've nothing better to do. Not quite. I put together a computer model simulating the truncation that inhibits the L-2 gene's repressor function. I call this new version of L-2 PDL."

From inside his jacket, Miles removed a two-inch rewritable CD, the new kind that held six times the data as the bulkier CD-ROM's they replaced years ago. Gripping it between his thumb and forefinger, Miles waved the disk near Maddox's nose. "Everything's right here. The molecular structure of PDL, the technique for splicing the mutant gene from the crab's Chromosome 5, even the procedure for combining it with the genes of other organisms."

"All that in one night?"

Miles heaved an impatient sigh. "I don't work for you anymore, so this conversation is costing me money. I'll pack my belongings and take my discovery elsewhere."

He walked past Maddox, who snatched his arm. "Just where do you think you're going?"

Miles yanked his arm from Maddox's grip. "You told me to leave, so I'm leaving."

"Not so fast, mister. Maybe we should talk some more."

"There's nothing to talk about."

No chance of raising a hundred grand by tomorrow at six, Maddox saw another way to pay Sorkin's loan, and at the same time make more money than he could spend in a lifetime. But he'd need Miles to stick around one more day. "I'll tell you what's to talk about. The lawsuit I'll shove down your throat if you dare take your discovery to another company. Don't forget, your employment agreement includes strict non-compete and trade secret clauses. Take your L-2 invention elsewhere, and I'll own you."

Miles' lips parted into a wide grin. He began to laugh, a long derisive laugh, a shrill, uncontrollable howl, such as might issue from a madman at an insane asylum. For a full minute, his inane bellowing rocked the lab.

Had he pushed the exhausted lunatic too far? Ready to shake Miles to his senses, the mad hysterics subsided.

Miles sneered. "You can shove your contract, your company, and your lawsuit. My protocol for synthesizing PDL is the most important breakthrough since Watson and Crick discovered the DNA helix. If PDL proves effective in clinical trials, I'll be famous. I'll be respected. Go ahead and sue me. I'll hire the best lawyers money can buy, and I'll still be revered as the man who doubled human life expectancy."

The strong-arm approach clearly a mistake, especially in Miles' condition, Maddox tried a different tact. He spoke with calculated calm, afraid to betray his desperation.

"I don't particularly relish the idea of a lawsuit, Nathan. But you have to admit, the past 10 years, we've gone through a lot together. Ups and downs, mostly downs. If you've discovered something important, something that gives you the recognition you deserve, and returns to me the small fortune I've invested in this company, isn't it right we share the fruits of your labor?"

Maddox paused, gauging the effect of his gentle words.

The scorn left Miles' eyes. He spoke not with haughty arrogance, but gracious composure, a serenity that seemed bizarre following so soon his deranged outburst. "I'm not looking to cheat you, either. To be honest, I don't know for sure if my L-2 protocol works. But a second mutation I found in the crab's genes turns out to code for surplus production of anti-cancer enzymes.

"I call it Hope-1. I removed it from the crab's tissue, combined it with repair ribozymes, and implanted it in the tumors of three laboratory mice. It shrunk the cancer in all three. But I'll have to validate my results under controlled test conditions. Would you let me do that here?"

Maddox would allow no such thing. "Of course I will. Not only that, when you feel comfortable with the results, I'll set up a news conference. You can announce your twin discoveries to the world."

Like a child who'd been granted his fondest wish, he said, "You'd really do that?"

Either the scientist had seriously lost it, or was a bigger fool than Maddox dared dream. "That's nothing. If your trials pan out, I'll change the name of the company. The Miles Research Corporation! After all, any man who obliterates cancer and prolongs human life should have a company named in his honor."

Miles frowned.

Fearing he'd pushed the game too far, Maddox added, "Of course, it'll all be in writing. Today, I'll have my lawyer draw up contracts giving you 50 percent stock ownership — on one condition. The FDA approves your protocol for Phase III clinical trials."

"Phase II."

"Agreed."

Miles beamed. "That leaves only two problems."

The bait too easily snatched, Maddox thought he might strangle the demented crackpot. He said smoothly, "There are no problems, only challenges."

"I swore to Allen I wouldn't tell anyone his police friend brought the claw to Omnigen. If you want me to stay on, nobody can ever know the crab led me to discover PDL and Hope-1, not Brian Strasser, and not the reporters at my news conference."

The plan crystallizing in Maddox's mind required telling only a few select individuals, none reporters. "I won't say a word. Promise. But what about Allen? He already knows."

Eyes glazed, Miles looked down, then stepped back, dropping the data disk on the black granite table directly behind him. He planted his hand on the table's edge, bracing his weight with his arm. "I'll explain our arrangement to Allen. So long as his friend doesn't get in trouble, he'll be OK with it."

"What's the second problem?"

Miles breathing grew heavier.

"You all right?" The ingenious fool better not die on him now. "Why don't you sit?"

Shaking his head, Miles' scraggly hair flopped back and forth like dying fish. "I'm a little sleepy, that's all." He squeezed his eyes shut, then popped them open, wide as ping-pong balls. "The second problem? Fresh tissue. We need to extract viable PDL and Hope-1 genes before the police find the crab and destroy it."

"But you designed a computer model," Maddox pointed to the CD-RW on the table. "It's all there. Just whip some up in a beaker."

"Not as easy as it sounds. Duplicating PDL and Hope-1 could take months. Given enough tissue from the crab, I could preserve it, then harvest its genes until I learn how to synthesize the polymers. I still get credit for the discovery, and you still recoup your losses."

In light of this news, reaching the crab first, before the police, indeed posed a problem for Maddox, but for a far different reason than Miles would ever suspect. "Any idea where to find it?"

"Allen went out looking this morning. He's anxious to find the crab too, but his reasons are personal. If I tell, swear you won't utter a word."

"Scout's honor."

"He needs fresh tissue to cleave Hope-1 from Chromosome 8. He's hoping to combine the mutant genes — the ones that produce enzymes for attacking cancer cells — with the tumor in his son's brain. The enzyme should stop David's cancer, maybe shrink it, like in the mice. I promised Allen if we get fresh tissue, I'd help him perform the procedure."

"So where's he looking?"

"I don't know. Last night at home he plotted the course he thinks the crab will follow to leave the bay."

"Leave the bay?"

"The Barnegat no longer holds sufficient food to satisfy the crab's appetite, so it's headed for the ocean. I spoke with Allen two hours ago. He's narrowed down the crab's escape route to a few channels deep and wide enough for it to fit through."

For Maddox's scheme to work, he must get to the crab before anyone else. "You don't think Allen would try taking it alone?"

"He's motivated, not stupid. Once he finds it, he'll mark its position and direction. Tomorrow, the two of us go out together."

"How do you get close enough to extract its tissue?"

"Allen's got some tricaine methanesulfonate — MS-222 — left over from his field work for the DEP. We'll drug the crab, then remove one of its legs."

Good. Allen and Miles would get the dirty work done, leaving Maddox free to arrange the buy — a single sale more profitable than a thousand Javelin anti-aircraft missile launchers. With directions on where to find the crab, instructions for extracting PDL and Hope-1, and a detailed explanation of the ribozyme vectoring procedure, all pre-recorded on Miles' two-inch disk, he might just pull off the most lucrative deal of his life.

He needed one thing more from Miles, who seemed ready to give him anything. "Sounds like you and Allen have your plans all set. I hope the three of us can work together to make this project a success."

He forced himself to pat Miles' shoulder. "You're a good man, Nathan. All those mean things I said before, my frustration talking. I apologize. I knew from the start you'd achieve something big. I'm honored, in fact, privileged, you achieved it working for me. But you're pushing yourself too hard, you look like you need a rest."

Miles nodded. "I do feel sleepy, but there's so much to do."

"Tell you what. Go home. Take a long nap and a cold shower. Come back fresh in the afternoon."

"Sounds good."

"One more thing. I want our attorney to draft a new shareholders agreement, one that makes us equal partners in the new company, named after you. But he'll need something concrete."

"Like what?"

Maddox spied the disk on the table behind Miles. He could probably lift it without a word from the fast-fading scientist, but he enjoyed molding Miles like putty. Maddox picked up the disk and handed it to him. "I'd like you to take this and copy it. Also, copy all your notes and sequencing sheets. You know lawyers. They need records of everything."

Maddox opened a drawer under the lab table, and pulled out a white cardboard document mailer. Emblazoned on one side, the Omnigen logo — a red double-helix with the letters OMN shaped into a crown at the top of the intertwining strands. "Stuff everything into one of these. Before you leave, drop it on my desk. On your way out, I want you to pick up a small token of my appreciation, something long overdue for your hard work and years of loyalty."

"What's that?"

"A little bonus."

"Bonus?"

"Hey. If you're going to be an owner, start thinking like one. How does ten thousand sound?"

Miles grinned ear-to-ear. "Great. Give me half an hour."

That post-dated check wouldn't bounce until Maddox was long gone. He pumped Miles' hand. "Congratulations."

"Thanks."

Devon Maddox pranced to the door. Turning the knob, he glanced back at Miles. "We'll make a great team."

Maddox trotted to his office, passing Claire, who banged away at her keyboard. Entering his private domain, he closed the door and leaned back against it, staring without remorse at his maimed mahogany desk. Already he had distanced himself in time and space from these dismal surroundings, imagining the secluded beach off the Brazilian coast where he would build his mansion by the sea, all his materials and provisions airlifted by private charter, the kind his father had flown. Nothing would touch him on his self-made paradise.

A giddy mirth he had never known danced in his heart. He plopped dreamily into his leather chair, picked up the phone, and tapped out the number of Robert J. Sorkin, III.

16

At idle speed, Allen steered his Boston Whaler past the backyards of beach houses crammed side-by-side along wooden bulkheads. Lavish structures with glass walls and vaulted ceilings, wraparound decks, and rock gardens, these coral-colored shrines to prosperity, replacing tiny bungalows leveled long ago, barely fit on their tiny lots.

Navigating his open boat under the wood plank bridge connecting Chadwick Island to the Barnegat Peninsula, Allen nudged the throttle forward, keeping his speed below five miles per hour. The speed restriction tamed the wakes thrown off by boats entering and exiting the labyrinth of lagoons projecting off Barnegat Bay. From late spring to early autumn, dinghies and yachts alike crowded the backyard bulkheads of these ornate dwellings.

Entering the bay, the dark blue swells thumped against his Whaler's flat bottom. Allen gripped the wheel, sitting on a white, 30-inch high beverage cooler, bolted to the floor and topped with a cushion, that doubled as a pilot's chair.

A few cotton clouds left over from yesterday's turbulent weather marred an otherwise perfect sapphire sky. The brilliant mid-morning sun hung slightly behind to the east.

Allen's nautical chart, rolled up and rubber-banded, stuck out from a circular slot in the control panel. Before moving to California, Allen spent long summer days on the bay. He understood its troughs and tributaries better than the streets of his own neighborhood, and could do without the map to find the starting point for this, his most important voyage ever.

His first destination, Buoy 27, lay two miles ahead in a southwest direction. It marked the most northerly point on the Intracoastal Waterway where Allen calculated he might locate the crab. From there, Allen would troll south until he fixed the crab's position and determined its heading.

Allen shoved the throttle forward, just shy of full open. The 90-horsepower Evinrude screamed with enthusiasm, relishing the higher RPMs it was built to savor. The Whaler lifted on plane, riding the crests of the waves in a rhythmic bounce. The rush of crisp salt wind, the dance of spray off the bow, the thrill of a smooth, fast engine plowing gentle seas, these were all the reasons Allen returned to roam the bay time and again during his youth.

He would not let David's cancer win. One day he would sit at the controls with his son, sharing the sensation of saltwater air lapping at their faces.

Nearing the east-west midpoint of Barnegat Bay, Allen scanned the horizon. Tuesday before the start of peak summer season, marine traffic was light. Probably the only sailors on the bay today were those who'd read about the *Chronicle's* reward money, and possessed the strength of heart, or scarcity of brains, to accept its challenge.

Come Friday, seashore hamlets all along the barrier island would burst with July Fourth revelers flocking from as far away as Canada and as close as New York City. These tens of thousands fancied Barnegat Bay a massive aquatic playground. Vessels of every shape and size — jet skis, sailing sloops, dual cabin cruisers — would all crowd the bay.

Allen whizzed past Buoy 24 on the left, Applegate Cove on the right. Succumbing to temptation, he opened to full throttle. The howling Evinrude drove the sturdy craft half in the air, half in the water. There was no feeling like it.

Allen recalled Bateman's promise to close Barnegat Bay if the giant crab posed a danger to the vacationing hordes. Unless Bateman's men captured the crab within a day or two, Allen fully expected his friend would keep that promise. He'd have no choice. Even if warned a marine predator roamed the bay, witless daredevils seeking misguided adventure or dangerous money would gladly hazard the water. Allen's only hope lay in reaching the crab before Bateman's hand was forced.

Spotting Buoy 27 some 500 yards ahead, Allen eased back on the throttle. The Evinrude's deafening wail waned to a steady drone of smooth pistons firing well below capacity. The Whaler slowed and descended from the tops of the waves. Allen glanced to the east, spotting a break in the coast line, the entrance to Shelter Cove. To the west, on the barrier island, he spied the Ortley Beach water tower, a baby blue column dwarfing summer cottages cluttered around its base. A mile south, he observed the twin bridges carrying vehicular traffic back and forth between Seaside Heights and the mainland. His landmarks where they should be, Allen shut off the Evinrude and hopped to the back of the boat.

Allen had attached to one corner of the transom a battery-powered trolling motor, a miniature outboard for driving small vessels at very slow speeds. It allowed an angler to cover more water than if anchored over a single spot. Allen released the safety latch on the stainless steel shaft. Leaning over the transom, he guided the propeller beneath the surface. Speed and direction were controlled by a foot pedal, freeing the user's hands to manipulate rod and reel while probing for quarry. Allen flicked on a switch below the engine head. Instantly, the motor whirred to life.

Satisfied the engine worked properly, Allen returned to the control panel. Mounted to the left of the steering wheel was a sonar fish finder, an electronic device containing a green liquid crystal display four inches high by three inches wide. Pressing a button on the left side of the box, gray shadows flickered on the monitor.

Symbols shaded in black, white, and gray depicted solid matter under the boat — fish, vegetation, structures, and when cruising shallow water, the bottom itself. The monitor also flashed digital readouts of depth and temperature. Reading the image on the screen, Allen knew even here, in the middle of the Intracoastal, only 11 feet of empty water separated the bottom of his hull from the muddy bottom of the bay.

Still, 11 feet was deep compared to the average of six for most of Barnegat Bay. If the crab instinctively swam the widest and deepest channel to the ocean, it could only be the Intracoastal.

Allen stepped gingerly around the center console into the open bow.

The boat swayed to the rolling green waves, but Allen kept his footing. Despite 10 years as a California landlubber, he hadn't lost his sea legs.

If Allen chanced upon a floating piece of the mutant crab — a detached chela, a severed swimming paddle — any physical evidence the crab had passed this way, he would need a tool to pluck it from the water. For this task, he had rigged a six foot surf-casting rod with 90-pound test monofilament line, the heaviest he could find at Ernie's Bait and Tackle. To stabilize the line underwater, Allen had tied on a single three-ounce pyramid sinker. His most difficult decision was selecting a hook. A standard size six for snatching bay fluke obviously wouldn't do. Something much larger was needed, so he dug out from an old tackle box a gargantuan 16, the kind used by deep sea fishermen stalking black marlin.

Allen lifted his rig from the floor and carried it to the cooler seat. Holding his rod tip-up, he sat facing port side. He dropped hook and line over the rub rail, and with the toe of his sneaker, gently pressed the footpad. The Whaler edged forward. He kept one eye on the fish finder, the other on the lookout for approaching vessels.

Creeping south, the fish finder hinted no evidence of underwater life, not even a solitary sea bass. He approached the parallel bridges connecting Toms River to Seaside Heights, inching past the massive concrete buttresses of the fixed bridge first. He came to the drawbridge next. A car rumbled across, dotting out bright sunlight filtering down through the metal latticework overhead.

Clearing the twin bridges, Allen trolled over a fishing hole known to locals as Coates Point Catchery, rife with plump fluke and well-fed flounder. Here, he expected the monitor to teem with black crescents, indicating the presence of marine life. Except for a gray line along the bottom — the bay floor — he saw only the dull green of barren water. Odd, since last winter hadn't been especially cold, and by now, fluke and flounder should be running in abundance.

Anxious for some sign of the giant crab, Allen tapped the foot pedal, pushing the boat faster. Even at the trolling motor's highest setting, he barely felt the Whaler move.

To his right, Allen passed the mouth of the Toms River. He glanced upstream at the eclectic blend of colonial mansions and low-rise office buildings shaping the business district of the bustling suburban village.

Allen took pride in the area's rich heritage. During the American Revolution, Toms River held strategic importance to both sides as a major commercial and military port. Due east of his present position, opposite the mouth of the river, an inlet to the Atlantic was plied regularly by British warships and mercantile schooners. In 1812, a fierce storm closed the passage. For nearly 40 years after, locals dredged tirelessly to keep it open, but nature prevailed, and what was known as Cranberry Inlet faded into history.

Trolling past Holly Island, two miles beyond Toms River, Allen grew discouraged. This far south, he should have turned up some trace of the crab. Perhaps it had ventured off the Intracoastal, into one of the deeper trenches crossing the bay; perhaps up Toms River itself, certainly deep enough, six feet at low tide along center channel. His nautical chart identified alternative routes the crab might follow. Allen slipped the fishing pole into a rod holder bolted to the side of the instrument panel. Reaching over to pull the chart out, something on the horizon, front and left, caught his eye.

About a mile southeast, he spied two boats, side-by-side, anchored offshore near Island Beach. Allen's waterproof binoculars dangled off a peg on the console. He swiped them from the hook and trained them on the boats.

Both vessels bore the familiar upside-down triangle of the New Jersey State Police. Allen's heart plummeted. Surely, Bateman's troopers had found the crab. He imagined the police pulling it from the water even as he hunted it for his own purpose. Cursing out loud, he kicked the base of the console, angry he had not searched sooner.

His mind raced. Maybe he should go to them, and if Bateman were on board, explain his predicament. Maybe his friend would allow him to extract tissue from the crab for his son's gene therapy.

What if he were wrong, they had not found the crab? If Bateman were there, he would ask hard questions, like what was Allen doing on the bay when he should be in his lab studying the claw.

Puzzling over his dilemma, Allen glanced at the fish finder. The screen went black.

"Great," Allen moaned, "it's busted."

As if short on worries, the gadget he needed most to locate the crab had broken. Only self-restraint prevented him from seizing the gray box and ripping it off the control panel. Then the screen flickered — green dots mixed in with the black.

"That's strange," he said, watching the green spots transform into larger splotches.

Gazing at the display, he heard the fishing pole jiggle.

Allen peered over the port bulwark, focusing on the spot where his line penetrated the surface. Seeing nothing in the cloudy green water, he glimpsed at the fish finder. The black had fragmented into discrete crescent symbols, hundreds of them, showing more fish than he had ever seen in one place.

The trembling pole quieted. The line, pulled taught, punctured the surface about 15 feet off the rear-left corner of the boat, pulling the rod in a strained downward arc. Allen pressed the foot pedal, shutting off the trolling motor. He wrapped his hands around the rod, snug in the plastic holder, anticipating a powerful force pulling the end of his line. Firming his arm muscles, he carefully lifted the rod from the holder. When the pole was free, he knew instantly his hook had caught on something heavy and lifeless, like a piece of timber or refuse tossed overboard by a thoughtless boater.

The line held the Whaler fast, like an anchor. Grasping the rod with his left hand, Allen wound the spool with his right. Slowly, he took up line.

He pulled the Whaler to within a yard of where the line broke the surface.

With no warning, a deafening jolt from below bashed the bottom of the boat's hull. The impact lifted the stern clear out of the water.

Allen flipped backward, headfirst, over the cooler seat. Losing his fishing pole, he landed face-up under the instrument panel. The dropping stern smacked the water like the crack of a rifle. Incredible agony lanced his spine. Eyes closed, he howled in pain.

He felt the boat slowly turn, but not in a full circle. After several seconds, the turning stopped, and he felt only the smooth sway of the boat riding the swells. Allen opened his eyes, glad to be alive. He maneuvered himself out from under the console, and leaped to his feet. His left ankle throbbed.

Whatever collided with the boat had jarred the fishing pole from his grip. The vessel should be drifting, but wasn't. Looking aft, he understood why. He saw the six-foot rod wedged between the bench seat and the top of the engine. The object underwater was still hooked to the line.

He limped to the stern to free the rod. Halfway there, he heard a thunderous splash from behind the Evinrude. He craned his neck over the engine's powerhead. Twenty feet behind the boat, protruding six feet straight out of the water, he saw the claw of a giant crustacean.

At that moment, Allen knew not fear, but awe. What he beheld was not a horrendous genetic freak, but the answer to his son's prayers. The claw — all baby blues and indigos, with brilliant white pincer teeth — thrashed in the bay. It looked uncannily similar to its severed counterpart, perhaps a little thicker. Maybe this claw appeared larger because it lived and moved, imbued with power and vitality, far different from the lifeless specimen he had scrutinized in the sterile confines of the lab.

The claw beat the water, back and forth, like a giant windshield wiper rising from the depths of the sea. Allen observed something clutched within its claw, something the size of a pillow, soft and dead. The crab's pincer teeth gnawed ferociously at the object, which oozed thick yellow liquid dripping to the tops of the waves.

Locked fast against the engine, the fishing pole bent almost to the point of snapping. Allen's eyes traced the line off the spool, and saw it led to the pincer. The hook clung to the object squeezed by the crab's enormous blue claw.

The Whaler shuddered.

Losing his balance, Allen grabbed the bench seat, breaking his fall. Incredible! The boat was moving. The crab was pulling the boat, the shark-strength line acting as a tow rope. Allen could see only the crab's cheliped, no trace of its carapace or swimming legs. But he had no doubt, the crab was moving south. He had figured right. The crab was swimming south through the Intracoastal.

Waves broke over the transom, filling the deck with chilly salt water. Allen knew he must cut the line or be swamped. Dragged backward through the water, the boat jerked wildly. Allen crouched on his hands and knees, crawled to the cooler seat, opened the lid, and grabbed a utility knife. Knees soaked, he inched his way along the floor, back to the transom.

The pounding of the waves stopped. Allen sprang to his feet and looked back over the outboard engine. The claw was gone. His relief was tempered by a sense of failure, as if he'd let slip by an important opportunity.

The fishing rod lay on the floor feeding a slack line. Allen picked up the pole and wound the spool until he met resistance. He speculated the crab had released its burden, still caught on the hook. He cautiously turned the spin handle, dragging the line along the top edge of the hull, stern-to-port, and turned to the fish finder. A black square on the screen showed something directly beneath the boat, its bulk greater than any fish native to the bay. Hundreds of small black crescents ringed the larger square, predators feeding on the hooked object.

Slowly reeling in line, Allen stared over the side. From the murky sea, a brown rectangle with rounded corners came into view. A sphere the size of a melon, pink and purple, like raw flesh, dangled from one side. Dozens of fish pursued the mushy mass to the surface. Allen counted 20 crabs clinging to it with hungry pincers.

Allen reeled in the beefy glob until it pierced the water. Four magenta holes, each the size of a grapefruit, marred its surface. Crabs latched to the perimeter of all four cavities where it looked to Allen like limbs should be attached. An ashen stick, about one foot long, jagged at the tip, extruded from the largest of the purple depressions.

The sickening stench of rotting flesh scorched his nostrils, and the horror of recognition wrenched his belly.

"Shit!"

Allen's guts revolted, spewing forth bile and saliva. Not thinking, he tossed rod and reel into the putrid water, watching the foul remains of Bobby Martin plunge to the depths of Barnegat Bay.

17

Standing on the bottom step of the C-131H transport, Major Charles F. Clayton gazed at a wall of flame two miles wide and so high, he could no longer make out the peaks of the Andes on the horizon. The firestorm raging 200 yards off the dirt airstrip sent dark, dense billows climbing high into the blue sky above the tropical plateau.

A hundred acres of burning Colombian hemp had driven out the torrid humidity, replacing it with harsh heat that stung Clayton's lungs. He could barely hear the plane's shrieking turbines over the roar of a million crackling cannabis stalks.

Satisfied his job here was done, he turned and climbed the five silver steps into the fuselage of the 50-year-old dual-turboprop, refitted to allow a return trip to Andrews without stopping to refuel.

Clayton popped through the cabin portal, and was greeted by Carl Jacobs, a 30-year-old staff sergeant wearing dull green combat fatigues. A round blue patch stitched to his chest highlighted five white block letters: BHERT.

The young man snapped a salute. "Good afternoon, sir."

"Skip the formalities," Clayton replied. "Am I the last to board?"

"Yes, sir," Jacobs said, nodding toward a door that separated the plane's mid-cabin from the tail-end passenger compartment. "Your team's in back, buckled down and ready to fly."

"Let's get going ... now." Jacobs never fussed over hard work, and always respected his superiors. This kid was all right.

"Very good, sir." Jacobs hit a button on the wall, and spoke into a round metal grid. "Ready for departure. Major says sooner, the better."

The pilot's reply crackled from a ceiling speaker, "Consider us outta' here, and hold on tight, cause we ain't in Kansas no more."

The pilot hadn't finished his sentence, when the turboprop jerked forward. From behind, Clayton heard the hum of a hydraulic motor lift the stairway, and from all around, the groan of the plane's weary frame. The cabin dimmed as the steps were devoured into the aircraft's wall.

The big plane bumped and shuddered along the crater-pocked airstrip. Clayton grabbed a shiny aluminum rail suspended along the ceiling, the same kind he'd held onto years ago riding the A-train from the projects in Brooklyn to Stuyvesant High School in Manhattan.

Had his team gone easier on the fragmentation grenades three hours earlier, he wouldn't be bouncing around now. The potent explosives had proven the quickest means of wrecking the airstrip to stop his targets from flying off. The fugitives tried a hasty escape anyway, and at maximum ground speed, their twin-engine Cessna hit a hole the size of a boulder, toppled end-over-end, and burst into a fireball. None of the men inside survived.

Clayton inched his palm along the rail and peered outside through a circular window. He saw only thick dark haze shadowing licks of flame poking through the smoke. He sniffed the unmistakable scent of burning marijuana, and wondered if the pilot could see where he was going.

The answer crackled over the intercom. "Folks, we'll be taking off blind. Saddle up tight and hold your noses ... unless you're looking for a cheap high."

Clayton backed away from the window, and hung on for dear life. The aircraft accelerated and its jet engines screamed. He felt the plane about to go airborne, when he heard a loud thud.

The cabin lurched hard left, so hard, the force wrenched Clayton's hand off the rail and spun him around. He glimpsed Jacobs, two feet away, fighting to stay on his feet. At the last second, Clayton grabbed the rail and closed his eyes. Covering his face, he braced for collision.

None came. The plane's wheels lifted off the ground, and its nose sloped up. The rush of steep ascent knotted Clayton's stomach as the jet's heaving engines put 50 feet per second between its belly and the jungle canopy.

Clayton took a deep breath and opened his eyes. Jacobs, who'd fallen during the choppy takeoff, was struggling to stand. Clayton grabbed his arm and hoisted him up.

"Thank you, sir."

"Drop in and out these God forsaken places enough, and you'll get used to it."

The pilot, over the intercom, bolstered Clayton's wisdom. "Trust y'awl enjoyed our smooth departure ... Hope any greenhorns joining us today learned a thing or two ... Estimated flying time, four hours, 20 minutes. Cruising altitude, 22,000 feet. ETA to Andrews, 1725 — that is, if we didn't drop a fuel tank ... Meanwhile, sit back and enjoy the view ... Hope y'awl fly us again soon."

"Not for two weeks, at least," Clayton said, answering a pilot who couldn't hear him. "The second he lands this bird, I'm hauling my butt home to Marlene before there's no Marlene to go home to."

"So you've banked a few weeks downtime, sir?"

"Twelve, to be exact, and I'm not in the field, so don't call me sir."

"Dr. Clayton?"

"It'll do." Clayton wasn't sure why Jacobs went out of his way to act so damn respectful. Maybe that's how he dealt with the color of Clayton's skin, or maybe he knew he had a bright future with BHERT, and figured a little brown-nosing wouldn't hurt. Maybe both.

Jacobs asked politely, "Any special plans?"

Clayton read people well, and Jacobs' tone set off an alarm. "Yeah. Spend time with my family."

"Sir, there's a message I've been instructed to give you. Direct from General Stanton. Came in an hour before we arrived."

The involuntary lapse to 'sir,' the use of passive voice to deflect responsibility, the implication of last minute urgency — no doubt about it, Stanton was about to screw him again. "I order you not to repeat it. I order you not to imply it." He wasn't angry at Jacobs, but the obedient bearer of bad news would take the brunt of his wrath anyway. "I haven't seen a week's vacation in two years. I love my wife and kids, and they sure love me, but there's a limit to their patience, and mine. I don't care who it is, where it is, or what it is, even if it's Stalin resurrected. It'll have to wait!"

"It's not quite that bad, sir. Actually, Central isn't sure what to make of it, but they need us to investigate. Could be nothing."

Clayton softened his tone. "Good, because if it isn't a Priority I, Stanton can assign Childers. Tell him I said so."

"I'm sure he would've. But remember Childers' hacking cough?"

"Sounded like he caught the damn plague."

"Turned out to be double viral pneumonia. Dr. Phillips has him off his feet for three weeks."

Clayton let Stanton pull this stunt one too many times. True, General Stanton was senior officer of the Biological Hazard Emergency Response Team, but as BHERT's second-in-command, Clayton's wishes ought to be respected. After all, beside the general, he reported only to the president herself. "If Childers can't go, tell him to send Cho."

Jacobs bit his lower lip and glanced sideways. "Last Sunday, the general assigned Cho to a deep-cover operation in Beijing. She won't be available until August. The general needs an experienced team to look at this today."

"Today! What do you mean, today! By the time we get to Andrews, today will be the hell over."

"I'm sorry, sir. The FBI's involved, and they've advised the president it's something BHERT should look at right away."

"You know what, Jacobs? Sometimes I'm so damn sorry I took this job. A couple of months ago, the president offered to buy back my vacation at triple rate. You know what I told her? Thanks, but no thanks. Time is more important than anything. The less you have, the more you need. And the past two years I've seen a helluva drought."

When Clayton accepted the post, he knew the pressures. But how could he turn down number two spot for a brand new federal law enforcement agency responsible for monitoring national and international applications of biotechnology? The job was his crowning achievement, his reward for three decades of relentless work, perpetual self-sacrifice, and rising above a society that now and again reared its ugly racist head.

Jacobs cleared his throat. "This situation is highly unusual."

"They're all unusual," Clayton said. "Tell me more. I'll think of someone else to handle it."

"At 11:22 a.m. EST, the FBI intercepted an interesting phone call to Robert J. Sorkin."

"Not that loony billionaire from Texas? Hides out on his ranch all the time. Afraid of the very air we breathe."

"Yes, sir. The bureau's kept close tabs on Sorkin for the past 20 years, ever since they suspected him of dealing arms to private business interests in South America."

"Doesn't that bozo sell airplanes?"

"Replacement parts only. But the FBI estimates his illegal weapons sales 20 years ago earned him enough cash to gobble up his largest competitor, and fetched him enough overseas contacts to double the volume of his legitimate business. Fact is, Sorkin's earned the bulk of his fortune since then as an honest man. They've tried, but the FBI and IRS have never come up with concrete evidence linking his current wealth to his dirty dealings of the past. What's more, over the past six months, a group of Congressional freshmen from Texas have put the bureau's feet to the fire. They're demanding the FBI close its case on Sorkin for good."

"So what? He's a crazy billionaire with a bad history. Who called him that BHERT should care about?"

"Devon Maddox. The man the FBI suspected of supplying Sorkin 20 years ago. In the early '80's, Maddox served as a captain in the U.S. Army, stationed at Fort Hood, in charge of munitions. When the Army discovered shortages, it launched a joint investigation with the FBI into Maddox's role, but he covered his tracks, and —"

The Samaritan turboprop jolted hard right. Jacobs slammed into the cabin wall and toppled to the floor.

The jet plunged. Clayton grabbed the overhead rail and peered out the glass circle to his right, aghast at seeing the Pacific Ocean coming fast. The jet must have sustained lethal damage during takeoff, and now they would pay the ultimate price. He saw Marlene's smile, heard their children's laughter. He thought of the six men and women in the aft cabin. All had families themselves.

As abruptly as the jet plummeted, it leveled off. Over the speaker, Clayton heard the voice of the pilot, calm as a corpse. "Sorry, ladies and gentlemen ... Seems we encountered some unexpected turbulence. We'll be more diligent next time. Promise."

Clayton hauled Jacobs to his feet.

The sergeant, white as a ghost, made no effort to conceal his anger. "Why the hell does he keep saying 'we' when he's the only damn pilot up there!"

"Habit," Clayton replied. "In the Balkans, he got so accustomed to flying Herks with a co-pilot, he still talks like there's one next to him."

"I'm sorry, but that drop scared the shit outta' me."

"If it makes you feel better, me too. And stop calling me 'sir'."

"Yes, sir."

"Forget it Jacobs. Finish your story."

Cheeks blanched, Jacobs continued. "Maddox was a pro at fudging inventory records, and neither the Army nor FBI could come up with anything more concrete than a few bookkeeping irregularities. Not enough to support a charge of treason. So the Army settled for dishonorable discharge, which Maddox didn't contest."

"Let me guess. When the FBI intercepted Maddox's call, they got real curious why he'd contacted his old partner in crime. But why involve BHERT? We don't handle illegal arms sales — at least not conventional arms."

"That's where it gets interesting. After his discharge, Maddox moved to Philadelphia and opened a restaurant. Next two years, the FBI and IRS watched him like a hawk, waiting for him to make a mistake. Anything to link the financing of his restaurant to his past dealings with Sorkin. But the man's a brilliant accountant. The IRS couldn't even nail him for tax evasion, and eventually, the FBI dropped him from their list."

"Sneaky fellow."

"Smart, too. After he called Sorkin, the FBI ran around in circles trying to reconstruct the past 12 years of Maddox's life." From his green fatigues, Jacobs pulled out a white document. "Here's a transcript of the intercepted communication. Headquarters faxed it on the way down. Maddox and Sorkin don't say much, at least not on tape."

"I don't get it."

"Maddox is no dummy. Neither is Sorkin. Sorkin told Maddox he'd call him back on a secure phone to get the details."

"Of what?"

"We're not sure, sir. Judging from the taped exchange, the two hadn't spoken in awhile. One thing's for certain, Sorkin wasn't happy to hear from Maddox. He didn't even say hello, just a sharp 'what is it?' Maddox told Sorkin he wanted to make him an offer, sell him something beside sealed lips." Jacobs read from the paper, "... Sorkin says, 'You know never to call me here' ... Maddox replies, 'I've got something I know you'll want, but there's no time to go through the usual channels.'" Jacobs stopped reading and looked up.

"Well?"

"That's it. Next thing, Sorkin tells Maddox he'll call back on a secure phone."

"So where does BHERT come in?"

"Omnigen, sir."

"What's Omnigen?"

"A biotech company Maddox founded two years after the Feds stopped tailing him. It's based in Lakewood, New Jersey."

Clayton chuckled. "Home state of the president. Guess that's why she's so anxious to investigate."

"More than that. Some bizarre stories have filtered out of central Jersey since Sunday." Jacobs tucked the transcript back in his uniform, and pulled out another document. He handed it to Clayton.

Clayton opened it and was confronted with a faxed photocopy of a front page article taken from a New Jersey newspaper. He read it, folded it, and shoved it back at Jacobs. "Some local yokel concocts a fable about a sea monster attacking people in Barnegat Bay, and all of a sudden it becomes our problem. Frankly, I don't see any link between that bizarre piece of trash and a wealthy weirdo's phone conversation with a former illegal arms dealer."

"General Stanton's not sure, either," Jacobs said meekly, "but Maddox does own a biotech company in the area, and the FBI's curious to know what he has to sell Sorkin after 20 years, so we've been ordered to investigate."

At best, the link was tenuous. Certainly not enough to make Clayton sacrifice his long overdue vacation, the one he'd been looking forward to for six months. "Damn it Carl! Marlene and the boys miss me terribly, and Lord knows I miss them, too. Half the year Stanton's got me shutting down thugs overseas, the other half, squashing cockroaches at home. I haven't seen three back-to-back days of R&R in two years. Two years! And unless Sorkin's dealing Anthrax to Iran, I don't see where we need to be involved." Venting on Jacobs helped quell his frustration. "What about the tracer on Maddox? I'll wager 10-to-one the bureau was too late."

"Right again. But they didn't need it. The number Maddox told Sorkin to call him back at turned out to be the front desk at Omnigen. Within 50 minutes of Maddox's initial call, the FBI installed wiretaps on all of Omnigen's lines — not fast enough to intercept Sorkin's callback to Maddox. But now, not one word gets in or out of Omnigen without us knowing."

Clayton still failed to understand why the matter called for his direct involvement. "Sounds like Stanton and the boys at the bureau have the situation under control. Tell him I'm sorry. I have a commitment to my family. He'll have to find someone else. Anyway, this can't be better than a Priority III."

"Actually, sir, the general's assigned it a Two."

"Still, there must be some rookie on the team who's qualified." Clayton paused to think. "Myers. Tell the general to send Myers. He needs to log more field time, anyway."

The fear of God came into Jacobs' eyes. "Sir, he's ... uh, he's ... he's ..."

"Spit it out."

"He's on vacation."

"You're shitting me!" Clayton bellowed.

"Even if Myers were available, sir, the general feels the situation's too important to send anyone less than BHERT's number two man."

"You mean number two boy." Clayton knew his selection by Stanton had nothing to do with race. He simply enjoyed watching his white subordinate squirm in his pants.

Jowls glowing, Jacobs continued, "Upon arrival at Andrews, a van will be waiting to drive us to Remote Station 15, outside New York."

"So Stanton roped you into this, too?"

"Yes, sir. No, sir. What I mean, sir, is the general's assigned me to the response team along with Ryan and Ferraro."

"Damn it, Carl. Stop calling me 'sir'."

"Sorry, bad habit."

He couldn't believe the general expected him to return to the field so soon. "I've spent an entire month in just about the hottest, most desolate corner of the world. Sorry, I'll have to pass."

Clayton recalled his four-week investigation in Colombia, where the temperature rarely dipped below 90 — even in the dead of night. His team's makeshift laboratory in the heart of the South American jungle offered scant relief from the swelter. At the fiery climax of his mission, he'd waited nearly 15 minutes on the runway for Jacobs' extraction crew. Each of those minutes, he dreamed of the hugs and kisses waiting to greet him at home.

He purposely changed the subject. "Any other Beta-5 plantings reported since Friday?" Clayton was referring to the FDA's designation for the genetically modified cannabis sativa his team had incinerated.

"No sir, satellite surveillance indicates you destroyed the last known in the Western Hemisphere."

"Yeah, until next time."

Lately, the Recombinant DNA Administrative Council had called on BHERT to put out one fire after another. Their target this time, marijuana recombined with nicotine, rendering it more addictive than crack cocaine. Fifty pounds of the genetically tainted weed had hit the streets of Los Angeles. As far as RAC intelligence could determine, the threat ended there. Clayton's team had nixed the chance any more could be produced, at least in the short-term.

What disturbed Clayton most about this episode, a biochemist working for the Department of Agriculture had stolen and sold the classified protocol to the drug lord who perished on the runway. How ironic that the fallen biochemist once lectured at a symposium Clayton himself attended as a senior researcher for the Atlanta-based Centers for Disease Control and Prevention.

He looked out the portal at bleak dark hills passing below. Staring down at what he guessed was Mexico, Clayton mulled the growing importance of BHERT's role in preserving vital US security interests. Incredible strides in recombinant DNA technology, especially the past five years, were turning science fiction into science fact. For all its tremendous potential to improve the human condition, genetic redesign came with an ominous dark side, a side that appealed to the base human vices of greed and power. That his team had been placed on active mission status at least once during each of the past five months bore stark testament to man's inability to resist those temptations.

But duty to country had limits, and Clayton stood at the border. He needed time away from BHERT, and his family needed time with him. Others could investigate Omnigen, Sorkin, and the mysterious sea demon invading Barnegat Bay. He'd be missed, but they'd get by.

Jacobs cleared his throat. "Sir?"

"Yes."

"I promised the general your answer by 1400 hours. Are you sure you want me to tell him no?"

Clayton looked Jacobs straight in the eye. "Absolutely."

18

Back from Barnegat Bay, eager to return for the crab, Allen found Miles in Lab B.

Clean shaven and well rested, Miles looked ready to take on the world. He'd changed into a white dress shirt, collar button opened, and wore aqua-blue suspenders to keep baggy avocado slacks from dropping off his rounded belly.

After Allen described his scrape with the crab, the rejuvenated scientist asked, "You're certain it's the same one?"

"Can't say I matched its clawprint, but I don't know of any other blue crab with a six-foot claw that's cruised Barnegat Bay the past two days."

Miles pointed to a stainless steel door in the far corner of Lab B, the entrance to the freezer where he had stored the mutant crab's claw. "The genes I inject into David's brain must match the genes from that specimen right down to the last base pair. Any deviation from the Hope-1 sequence, and my treatment's worthless, maybe even dangerous."

Allen had no doubt the specimen in the freezer came from the same crab that struck his boat. "My only question is how to get close enough to anesthetize it without getting killed. Much as I hate to admit, I could use Larry's help."

Miles' eyes bulged. "Leave your friend out of this. You said yourself that'd be risky. You tell him its location, he won't let anyone, including you, near it."

After tossing his rod in the bay, Allen's immediate concern had been whether the state marine police anchored off Island Beach witnessed his brush with the crab. He let his boat drift for 10 minutes, waiting for the police vessels to approach. When they didn't, he sped back to Chadwick Marina confident the police hadn't spotted the crab towing the Whaler.

But his skirmish had given him a first-hand look at the crab's strength. "Maybe I should give Larry a chance. Tell him all about my gene therapy, and where to find the crab. He and I could hunt the crab together. When we spot it, his men could set a trap, and I'd put it to sleep."

Turning his back to Allen, Miles walked the aisle between the two long lab tables. He stopped at the far end and whirled, wiry tufts on the sides of his head flying in all directions. His tone was severe. "What if you're wrong? What if your friend tells you he's sorry, that he's got a job to do? What if he destroys the crab doing it? If you believe David has a year to spare while I fiddle around trying to synthesize Hope-1, fine. But if you want me to help him now, I need viable genes. You go to the police, I may not get them."

"I think you'd show more compassion if you'd been the one puking your guts out. That animal's an eating machine, pure and simple. Next time it goes after some kid, I don't want my conscience plagued because I held back on Larry."

Miles tramped toward Allen. "Tell your friend, but only after we retrieve the tissue. Inform him now, and you may never see that crab or its genes again. Is that a chance you're willing to take?

Of course it wasn't, but at the same time he didn't want the crab hurting another child. "I'll give it one more day. If we come up empty tomorrow, I'll take my chances with Larry."

"Fair enough," Miles said, stopping at Allen's side. "Have you worked out the mechanics of administering the tricaine meth?"

"I rigged a hand pump from an old deck sprayer. It'll hold three gallons."

"Three gallons! That'll knock out a whale."

"Yeah, it's definitely enough to put Mr. Crab to sleep. Problem is, MS-222 works best when ingested. You can usually administer it without fear of becoming your specimen's lunch. With this crab, I'm not so sure. You'll maneuver my boat close enough to give me a clear shot at its mouth. I'll pump the solution straight down its throat."

The thrill of adventure gleamed in Miles' eyes. "That I can handle. I once owned a 20-foot Bayliner."

"Then you'll love my Whaler."

"When the crab goes under, won't it drop to the bottom?"

As always, Allen had planned. "We'll leave port before low tide. Once the crab is anesthetized, I'll take a shallow dive with a bow saw and cut off part of a swimming leg. My old scuba gear's stored in my mom's attic. I'll stop there later to pick it up, then after dinner, test the tanks. Fill 'em in the morning."

Miles beamed. "Perfect. Meanwhile, I'll prepare the specimen receptacle. The tissue must be preserved immediately after extraction. What about the weather?"

"Clear skies through Friday."

"Can't wait."

Allen's tone hardened. "Remember. No crab tomorrow, I go to Larry. Besides, after that, it'll be too late."

"For what?"

"To catch the crab. Unless you think we'll do better chasing it in the Atlantic."

"How fast is it moving?"

"The Martin children were attacked outside Kettle Creek on Sunday before noon. Forty-eight hours later, the crab's 700 yards off Potter Creek. That's four and a half miles in two days. Another five, it reaches Oyster Creek Channel, and now that it's reached the deepest part of the bay, it'll swim even faster. Fact is, by tomorrow night, Thursday the latest, that baby's gone."

Miles stared at the floor, and spoke slowly. "What if we enlist outside assistance?"

"What are you talking about?"

"Another set of hands."

"Two minutes ago you reamed me out for suggesting we go to Bateman."

"I'm not talking the police."

Allen said nothing, waiting to hear what Miles was thinking.

Miles shuffled his feet. "What if we ask Maddox?"

"Maddox!" Allen couldn't believe his ears. "You hate that son of a bitch! Why do you want *him* involved?"

"If we explain the therapeutic value of PDL and Hope-1, he'd pull all the stops. He'd hear cash registers ring, and do whatever it takes to help. I bet if we approach him right now, he'd pick up the phone and charter a boat. Maybe hire trained hands to immobilize the crab and extract its tissue."

"Look at me, Nate."

Their eyes met.

"The answer is no. I gave Larry my word, and I already broke it telling you. No way do we go to Maddox."

"But he'll keep quiet. I swear."

Allen wasn't getting through. "Absolutely not. That profit-driven egomaniac is the last person I'd ask for help. Give that man a whiff of money, who knows what he'll do? Maybe call the papers or try hooking the crab himself."

Miles stared at the floor and said nothing.

Allen thought of another way to help Miles see the light. "Do you know he fired Ellen?"

"Claire told me when I returned this afternoon."

"Can't you see? One of us is next."

"He won't. I'm sure of it."

"Don't be blind." Allen dropped his voice to an intense whisper. "I say we extract the tissue, administer David's therapy, and get as far away from this place as possible. All your life, you've dreamed of doing something big, something to make a difference. Now's your chance. We've cracked the PDL and Hope-1 sequences. We'll use them to start our own company. We'll lease our own lab, replicate PDL and Hope-1 — offer it to the world, cheap enough for everyone. Maybe we get rich, maybe we don't, but think of all the good we'll do and the freedom we'll have doing it."

Miles' bulbous eyes dimmed. "I'm tired. I've started from scratch too many times. You're young, filled with high energy and high ideas. Me, I'm happy to let Maddox make his money, so long as he gives me the credit I deserve."

Allen felt sorry for Miles. The beleaguered scientist knew only failure and frustration. A real shot at victory finally within his grasp, and he lacked the courage to mount one last campaign. "Suit yourself, but one thing doesn't change." He spoke slowly, emphasizing each word. "Until Larry goes public with the crab, say nothing to Maddox."

Miles glanced away, and muttered, "I won't."

"Thank you."

"A.J., I ..."

"What?"

"Nothing important. Just wondered if I might take a peek at your map showing the crab's path, you know, to prepare for tomorrow."

Allen wasn't sure if Miles had said what he really wanted. "Sure. The chart's in my office, rolled up behind the cabinet. Feel free to look, but only you."

"Thanks," Miles said, perking up. "When do we hit the bay?"

"Next daylight slack water at low tide. That'd be tomorrow afternoon at 2:35. We'll meet here at one, shove off from Chadwick by 1:30."

"It's a date."

One last question weighed on Allen's mind. "When do I bring David in?"

Miles' eyes gleamed confidence. "After we return the tissue to the lab, I need four hours to extract Hope-1. Another two to prepare the ribozyme vector. Actual insertion requires five or 10 minutes. If targeting is accurate, the ribozyme-catalyzed cleavage of Hope-1 to David's tumor will take effect in 12 hours — presuming, of course, my results on the test mice can be extrapolated to a human glioblastoma."

"Which means you could be ready for David tomorrow night."

"That's right, if we have the tissue."

"I'll call Jennifer." The man standing before him promised to deliver David from the brink of death — unafraid to challenge the scourge of cancer, yet cowed by the likes of Devon Maddox. How unfair such a genius should suffer the ignoble abuse of a tyrant's grinding thumb. Allen gently clasped his colleague's arm. "Maddox has pushed you around for 10 years. If you perfect PDL and Hope-1 for him, what makes you think he'll stop?"

"It'll all be in writing."

Allen sighed. "I think you should consider my idea. We'd make a good team."

Miles' tone was grim. "I agree. And maybe if 10 years ago in Philly it was you, not Maddox, I bumped into, we could've made a go of it."

Allen shook his head. "Well, then, you'll finally help Maddox earn his fortune. I only hope he remembers you."

Miles sneered. "He will, because it's off my sweat that he'll make his fortune."

"You certainly have your work cut out."

"I don't mean what I've yet to do ... I mean what I've already done."

Allen's back stiffened. "Already done?"

Miles didn't answer, but stared off, glassy-eyed, into the distance.

"What have you already done?" Allen asked again.

Miles replied in a low monotone. "Yesterday morning, when I told you Maddox has something else on me."

Allen recalled Miles' vague allusion. "You don't have to tell me if it makes you uncomfortable."

"My first year here I synthesized a protein spliced from hamster DNA that doubled the average weight of frogs."

"I know, but Maddox made you give it up. He wanted you to concentrate on viral vectors."

"There's more," Miles explained. "The recombinant bacteria I used to synthesize the growth-promoting DNA reproduced at an exponential rate. They survived in an open beaker nearly 72 hours. Exposed to lambda virus and bacteriophage T4, they didn't even flinch. By the time Maddox forced me to terminate my growth studies, I'd produced 500 gallons of the mutant culture."

"So you baked the solution in the autoclave."

Miles jiggled his head, as if he's snapped out of a trance, and looked straight at Allen.

"You did sterilize it, right?"

"I know the correct procedure, but back then, we only had a Regis bench-top model with a nine-inch chamber. Would've taken me weeks to sterilize the 500 gallons. When I asked Maddox to spring for a high-capacity autoclave, he said no way. I told him the solution contained viable contaminants, that they had to be neutralized before disposal. He said I created the problem, I better make it go away.

"Without the proper equipment, I didn't know what to do. A week later, all five drums sat in the lab. One morning he came by and told me if I didn't get rid of them by the end of the day, I'd be history. I only did as I was told."

Reluctant to hear the answer, Allen asked anyway. "Exactly how did you dispose of 500 gallons of bio-contaminants?"

Miles answered softly. "I poured them in the creek out back."

Allen was incredulous. "Couldn't you think of something else? Boil it over an open flame. Fry it in a microwave. But don't dump it in Kettle Creek."

"My back was to the wall. I had to act fast."

"You certain the solution was viable when you dumped it? If you waited seven days, the bacteria may have gone inert."

"That's what I figured. So what was the harm?"

"None, I hope. But getting caught would've meant big trouble not only for Omnigen, but your career."

"That's what Maddox said. Of course, he was more worried about the trouble I could have made for *him*. He couldn't care less about my career."

"So for nine years, Maddox has held your one error in judgment like an executioner's ax."

"Miles nodded. "Whenever I make waves, he threatens to turn me in to the EPA. That's the real reason I rolled over on the 30 grand cut when he hired you. Now the ungrateful snake should thank me for what I've done."

"What? How could your dumping the waste benefit Maddox?"

"Don't you get it?"

Allen shook his head.

"How old is the crab?"

"Eight, maybe nine."

"Where were the Martin children attacked?"

"Off Drum Point."

Miles stared at him in disbelief, as if something should be obvious.

"Sorry," Allen said, "I don't see your point."

"Drum Point. At the mouth of Kettle Creek. Eight years ago I dumped 500 gallons of bacteria combined with mutagenic growth hormone in Kettle Creek. If that stuff was viable, who knows what sort of biomolecular havoc it wreaked inside the eggs of indigenous crustaceans."

"I doubt there's a connection."

"Couldn't check if I wanted to. Threw out the sequencing documentation years ago. Less for Maddox to hold over my head. But what else would've triggered the crab's mutation?"

"Without the codons, we can't know for sure."

"I'm sure, in my heart. What's worse, it's my fault the Martin boy is dead."

"Stop it. Even if your bacteria was the catalyst, no way you could have foreseen the mutation."

"I'm responsible, A.J. I killed that kid. There's no getting around it."

"You're a good man, Nate. If your experiment nine years ago triggered a translocation in some hapless crab's egg floating around Kettle Creek, you did a good thing, not only for humanity, but for my son."

Miles bowed his head. For a long time, he gazed at the tiles. When he looked up, Allen saw his eyes filled with tears. "You've helped me hold onto my dignity better than anyone I know. In one year, you've shown me more respect than I've seen in 40. You and Jennifer have treated me like family, and for that, I love you both." Miles rubbed his eyes with the back of his hand. "Know one thing. Tomorrow, when it's time to help your son, I won't let you down."

His words comforted Allen. They confirmed his belief Miles would give his all for David. Allen glanced at the wall clock. "I'd like to give Jenn a call, then dig up my aqualung. Before I go, how can I help?"

"I have it all under control. Go home, prepare Jennifer. If she has any questions, call me." Miles patted his belly. "I may sneak out a few minutes to grab a bite at the boardwalk, maybe bring back a fish platter from Marty's. Otherwise, I'll be right here."

"Great. If we don't speak tonight, I'll see you in the morning."

Allen left Lab B, and scurried down the hall toward his office. After he had returned from the bay, he'd been so eager to see Miles, he had forgotten to call Jennifer to assure her he was safe. He knew she'd give him hell.

In the corridor, beyond the front vestibule, he spotted Claire strutting toward him. She wore sun glasses and clutched her pocket book.

"Heading home early?" Allen instantly regretted his words, fearing Maddox had fired her, too.

"I wasn't planning on it, but Mr. Maddox told me to take the afternoon off. With pay. He's been real chipper today."

Odd, Allen thought. He couldn't recall the last time he'd seen Maddox chipper. "The weather's gorgeous. Enjoy it."

"I will."

Allen continued down the hall, approaching Maddox's outer office. The door was open. Hearing a voice from inside, he paused. Through the inner door leading to Maddox's sanctum, he spied an arm behind Maddox's desk fiddling with a pen, and heard Maddox speaking on the telephone. Allen strained to listen.

"... One-way ... That's right, one seat ... Friday's too late. What about Thursday? ... No, it has to be Brazil ..."

For what seemed a full minute, Allen heard nothing, then: "Thursday at nine is good ... The drive'll be a pain in the ass, but if JFK's the best you can do ... Yes, for awhile ... You'll learn to live without me, Carol ..."

Maddox's voice dropped to a whisper. Allen couldn't make out the rest.

Hearing the click of a handset, Allen sprang from the door. He slunk down the corridor, his steps quick, but deliberate, to pad the sound of his heels. If he hadn't more pressing concerns, he might wonder what Maddox was up to now.

19

Giggling children everywhere, even at this late hour, dragging worn out moms and dads along the boardwalk — precisely the sort of drudgery Devon Maddox, all his life, had sought to avoid.

He leaned back against the metal guard rail abutting the edge of the boards, watching the masses traipse the planks. From behind, he heard the waves of the Atlantic, shrouded in dusk, crash against the surf, and from all around, whiffed sausage, peppers, popcorn, and beer.

The Point Pleasant Boardwalk, wide as a football field in some spots, ran about a mile parallel to the ocean, ending at the Manasquan Inlet to the north. Lined with penny arcades, snack stands, and souvenir joints, this carnival by the sea was no place for Maddox. But Sorkin had been right. Better he meet Lowry amid the din of the crowd, than risk the watchful eye of the FBI at Omnigen.

Maddox looked up at an aluminum lamp post tinted red from the reflection of a neon sign above Marty's Fish House, one block north. He saw strung to the metal pole a red and yellow placard listing special events for the July Fourth weekend. The poster promised day-long festivities culminating in a spectacular beach-front fireworks display. He'd miss the fun and not care, because by then, he'd be lounging in secluded solace on the other side of the planet, never again forced to deal with the likes of Sorkin, Lowry, or Miles. Omnigen would be nothing more than a mistake of the past.

A red balloon bobbing on the end of a string brushed Maddox's face. He grabbed the inflated rubber, pressing until it burst. Instantly, a child's scream pierced the twilight. At his feet, Maddox beheld a little girl with cascading amber curls and pink, tear-stained cheeks. Clutching the end of a limp string, she howled inconsolably, as if her anguished cries could somehow breathe new life into the shattered balloon.

An attractive blonde in a short sun dress knelt beside the girl, offering words of comfort that only seemed to make the little ingrate wail louder.

The young mother looked up at Maddox. Her blue eyes steamed. "You ought to be ashamed of yourself."

No stranger to scorned women, Maddox replied, "For what— breaking your kid's balloon or imagining what you look like under that dress?"

Her eyes opened wide. She hoisted the shrieking child and stormed away for the nearest gift shop.

"You haven't changed a bit."

Maddox turned to find a frail figure with gray eyes and smooth, sallow cheeks, a full head shorter, studying him through thick round lenses framed in gold wire. Something about his hair, the color of straw, and his voice, tinny and shrill, sounded familiar, but it couldn't be ... "Sorkin! What the hell are you doing here?"

Sorkin kept his hands stuffed in the pockets of a loose-fitting white sports jacket. His deck shorts, as white as the jacket, exposed two knobby knees. "Who'd you expect? Your fairy godmother?"

The quick sarcasm hadn't changed. "You told me you'd send Lowry."

"I decided to see for myself, make sure you were telling the truth." He pulled his right hand from his pocket and poked it at Maddox's chest. "After all, you're such an honorable, caring fellow. Always keeping his mouth shut, never expecting anything in return. How could I resist seeing such a wonderful human being again?"

Maddox resisted the urge to snap the bony finger off the rich runt's hand. "Nice to see you, too. I was starting to think no one would show."

"Landed in Princeton three hours ago. Had my driver stick to the back roads."

"Still worried about the Feds?"

"No, I wanted a personal tour of the Garden State." A gusty sea breeze scattered Sorkin's stiff flaxen hair, rinsed with too much yellow dye. "You know I have to keep my eye on the FBI. And the IRS. They'll chase anyone who works hard to earn money." Sorkin jammed his hand back in his pocket. "I suppose if I'd taken all that dough years ago, and blown it on bullshit instead of building my empire, they would've stopped hassling me years ago. Know anyone like that?"

"I didn't call you for financial advice. I'm here to make you an offer."

"I hope that's the only reason you're here. If you're wired for the Feds, and this tryst's a set-up, I have two boys in the crowd who aren't on line for the Ferris wheel. The second anyone lays a hand on me, you're history."

Maddox scanned the boardwalk teeming with merrymakers. No one under the evening sky, strolling or standing, looked like a Sorkin enforcer.

"Jonathan is behind the carousel, William next to the bumper cars. As we speak, it's Jonathan who has his .44 Magnum trained on your forehead."

"I'm sure Lowry would love a piece of me," Maddox said, genuinely insulted. "But who was the one who kept his mouth shut even though he got stripped of his rank and pride? Who stood by you through two years of FBI interrogations?"

"And who threatened to blow the whistle if I didn't give him a million dollar loan for next to nothing?"

"I deserved that, and a lot more."

"Don't worry, you'll get more — if you have the data to back your bullshit."

Maddox looked around. The warm evening sky throbbed with circus light. Game hawkers shouted promises of victory, beckoning all who passed to throw eight bits down on their crooked wheels. "Let's grab a stool at Spike's Clam Bar, just around the corner. We can talk there."

From behind his thick round lenses, Sorkin squinted warily. "We'll talk right here."

Just as well. Snug against the small of his back, under his windbreaker, Maddox felt the bulky cardboard mailer sticking half out of his trousers. Tightly jammed against his rear end, he couldn't have sat on a stool if he tried. "Like I said on the phone, scientists have identified seven mortality genes. One of them, L-2 —"

"No lectures, thank you. I know all about Gerry Wilson and his work at Southwestern, and I've read all the stories in your local rag about the 20-foot crab in Barnegat Bay. I can put two and two together."

"So you know I'm on the level."

"There's always a first time."

"Why'd you come if you don't trust me?

"If your scientists found what you say they did, I'm willing to take a chance."

"You're always holed up in your Texas hideaway, and for 12 years you've pretended I don't exist. You must be very interested."

Sorkin's eyes formed tight gray slits behind the two glass circles propped on his nose. "I've worked too hard and risked too much during the prime of my life to get where I am today. In September, I turn 65. The mortality tables say I have only 15 years to kick. I've broken my ass and skirted the edge to earn my fortune. So what good's all that wealth if I need a cane to pick roses in my garden, and a nurse to spoon feed me steak from a blender?

"If this crab's figured out a way to stop L-2 genes from activating, I'll tear those mortality tables to shreds. I know I can't take it with me, but if there's any way I can enjoy it longer, you're damn right I'm interested."

"Then you'll pay any price."

"How quickly you've forgotten my generosity."

"How quickly you've forgotten my shame."

"Shame? You have any?"

Maddox had planned to open the bid at 25. "Fifty million, and you erase my debt."

Pulsing red light from the toddler rides across the boardwalk flashed like an alarm in Sorkin's thick lenses. "If the documentation you give me verifies the mutation you described on the phone, I'll consider five."

"I won't argue with you now. Give the information to your scientists. When they see what they've got, we'll talk price."

"What exactly do you have?"

As a precaution, Maddox had deleted from the Genetyx printouts the base pairs inhibiting L-2 function in the cells of the giant crab. "I'm giving your biochemists enough data to verify a translocation resulting in a partial deletion of the L-2 mortality gene. They'll recognize it as a potential alteration for blocking expression. I'm also giving you a partial series for amplifying tumor-suppressor DNA. You'll get the complete series for both mutations when you pay me fifty mil."

"In your dreams."

Maddox ignored him and glanced sideways, making sure no one stood too close. "I'm also giving you a preliminary step-by-step protocol for splicing the age-inhibiting mutation onto human chromosomes. But I've deleted four essential files, each detailing a procedural element needed for delivery into host cells."

"So what's left for my scientists?"

"Enough to know if you spring for the full set of codons and last four protocol files, you'll be picking a lot more roses and chewing a lot more steak for a lot longer."

"You'll have my answer in three days."

"No good. One of my scientists knows where to find the crab, and the only reason he hasn't told the police, his kid's got cancer, and he plans on using the crab's tumor-suppressor genes to treat it. By Thursday — Friday the latest — he'll go to the cops."

Even under the cover of night, Sorkin's pasty complexion stood out against the bronzed arms and faces streaming past. The pale little man looked like he'd lived his life in a tomb.

Sorkin glimpsed over his shoulder, then turned to Maddox. "Let's move to the other side."

Maddox followed Sorkin across the boardwalk to a chain link fence corralling a block-long cluster of kiddy rides. Through the fence, Maddox spied gray elephant cars hinged to the tips of spidery arms spiking out from a revolving cylinder. The twinkling, twirling Dumbos lit up the boardwalk with pulsating white carnival light.

"Once your people go to the police, the crab's altered L-2's will become public knowledge. Do you know what'll happen if the FDA bureaucrats get their paws on it? They'll either keep it a secret, or bury it so deep in clinical trials, by the time a protocol gets approved, it'll be useless to me. Each setting sun takes me closer to my grave. If you have the real thing, I want it now, before your scientists go public."

"Then I'll need an answer tomorrow."

"Who else knows about the mutation?"

"Don't worry, I'm not shopping it around. You're the only one I know who can afford my price."

Sorkin's waxen lips twisted into a crooked sneer. "Same thing you told me 20 years ago. If you get caught this time, you going to blackmail me again?"

"Meet my price, and I'm outta' this country and out of your life forever."

"Give me the data, and we'll see about your price."

Maddox reached around his back, under his windbreaker, and yanked out the white cardboard mailer bearing Omnigen's logo. He pulled a pen from his pants pocket and scribbled a number on the front. "That's the condo I rent. Call me tomorrow morning, 8:30 sharp."

"Twelve hours? Not enough time."

"You pay your people well. Make them work all night."

Sorkin shook his head. "I'll see what I can do." He pulled a business card from his jacket. "This number's secure, the only line the Feds haven't tapped, at least not yet. From now on, if you need to reach me, call me there and leave a number — not your laboratory."

"You think the FBI's wired Omnigen?"

"Of course. If they're true to form, and they always are, they wired your place within an hour of when I called you back."

Maddox handed over the package. As Sorkin took it, something caught Maddox's eye at the boardwalk entrance to Marty's Fish House. "Shit!"

"What's wrong?"

"I have to leave." Maddox backed away, firing his words. "You better go, too. We'll talk tomorrow. Eight-thirty, sharp. Any questions or problems, call me there. Now get out of here, fast."

Maddox spun and scurried past the giddy children, browbeaten parents, and spinning wheels of chance, putting as much distance between himself and the restaurant as his churning legs would allow. He glanced over his right shoulder and cringed. Sorkin still lingered at the fence under the Dumbo ride.

"Where do you think you're going? Come back!"

He squinted through the strolling hordes to see if the other man who grabbed the familiar package still stood beside the fence. Through the moving mob, he couldn't get a clear view.

Only one way to find out.

Stuffed with two burgers and a fried fish platter from Marty's, Miles charged forward. No sooner did he hit his stride, when wrenching pain pierced his knee. "Damn!"

He grabbed his kneecap and came face-to-face with a pink double stroller and two startled infants.

"Watch where you're going!"

Clutching his leg, Miles looked up. A petite woman in green shorts glared at him. Beside her stood a tall man with thick arms. He didn't look happy, either.

"I'm sorry."

"You should be more careful," said the young mom.

"I'm in a hurry."

She stroked her baby's head. "You OK, sweetie?" She stared down at Miles. "You won't get there faster running into babies."

"It was an accident, I'm sorry."

As quickly as they appeared, the two tykes and their miffed parents vanished into the crowd.

Miles straightened himself.

He looked toward the fence under the Dumbo ride packed with spinning, laughing children.

What he had seen made no sense. Why would Devon Maddox hand some stranger what clearly resembled an envelope from the lab? His boss could be unscrupulous, but he wouldn't dare give away the fruits of another man's labor that had taken a lifetime to blossom? After all, Maddox had promised him, and him alone, a share of the glory. There must be a logical explanation.

Knee throbbing, Miles limped forward.

Thick with jolly souls of every shape and size, the crowded boardwalk provided an obstacle course challenging for even a limber man. He kept one eye on his destination, the other on the festive masses hemming him in. A wave of nausea rolled through his stomach. The surging people, the flashing lights, the pungent food, and his pulsing knee — all blurred together in a sickening whirlpool.

He stumbled to a stop. Through the haze of arms, legs, and faces, he peered across the boardwalk to the fence under the twirling Dumbos. He saw only two enamored teenagers, wrapped in each other's arms, lost in young love.

Devon Maddox, gone. The stranger, gone. The envelope, gone.

20

Driving south on Route 35, a two-lane stretch of straight highway running the length of the Barnegat Peninsula, Allen glimpsed to his right. Between the rows of summer bungalows and renovated shore homes, he spied a lucent orange ball hovering over the horizon, radiating a line of shimmering red light across the smooth expanse of Barnegat Bay.

During the ride, Allen gave little thought to why Devon Maddox would purchase a one-way ticket to a foreign country. Maybe he planned to take an extended vacation, or maybe Allen simply heard wrong. Whatever the reason, interpreting Maddox's latest escapade was the least of Allen's worries. Right now, with David's life in the balance, the crab and its healing genes mattered most.

Allen swerved into the stone driveway alongside his cedar shake Cape Cod, and heard the familiar crush of car tires pressing the cream and salmon pebbles that served as low-maintenance lawns and driveways for most homes on the barrier island. The Honda's low beams spotlighted a T-ball stand in the center of the driveway.

Allen noticed David's Yankees cap dangling from atop the white plastic shaft. Allen guessed Jennifer had taken advantage of the afternoon sunshine, allowing David a few supervised swings at a wiffle ball. A cautious Jennifer had probably herded David into the house long before the boy was ready to relinquish the bat. David rarely parted company with his prized Yankees hat, and had probably hung it on the post hoping, after his nap, for another shot at nailing a line drive. Apparently, he never got the chance.

Allen threw his car into park, sauntered to the T-ball stand, and swiped the cap off the pole. An hour earlier, he had unearthed his old scuba equipment from his mom's attic and tossed it into the trunk. He thought about lugging it into the house but decided to wait until morning. A cursory inspection of the aqualung revealed a few nicks and scratches on the tanks, otherwise, his gear appeared in decent shape considering he hadn't made a real dive in five summers.

Exhausted from only three hours sleep last night, and his close encounter with the crab during the day, Allen knew slumber would come easily. He'd need every ounce of wit and energy for his voyage with Miles tomorrow to track down the crab.

He slipped through the back door, into the kitchen, and found all lights off except for the gray, shell-shaped night-light plugged into an outlet over the stove. He set the Yankees cap on the kitchen table, switched on the fluorescent ceiling light, and walked to the telephone. The stove clock read 8:47, and the only sound he heard came from the living room, the rhythmic breathing of deep sleep.

Allen peeked inside, saw the blinds drawn, and Jennifer curled up asleep on the couch, covered to her neck in the brown quilt her mom had knitted them for their first wedding anniversary. On the maple end-table beside her, the lamp burned at its dimmest setting. Allen regarded his wife's tranquil countenance under the soft glow of faint light, betraying none of the anxiety over David's health that tormented her by day. If all went according to plan, Allen would dispel once and for all the constant worry afflicting the woman he loved.

Allen glanced at the phone in the kitchen, checking the red message light, and noticed on the table a note in Jennifer's handwriting: 'Call Larry at home, ASAP, no matter what time.'

Allen lifted the receiver and keyed in Larry's number.

After three rings, a groggy Bateman answered.

So not to wake Jennifer, Allen kept his voice low. "It's Allen. Sorry I'm calling so late. Got delayed at my mom's. I'll call back in the morning."

"No, don't hang up." Bateman cleared his throat. "I'm just a little tired, that's all. I was up past three last night."

"I know what you mean."

"So what've you got for me?"

"The cause of the crab's abnormal growth. A genetic mutation."

"Is it the only one out there?"

"Probably. If other hatchlings were exposed to whatever environmental agent induced the mutation, they probably didn't survive. Of course, it's possible the translocation, the mutation involved here, may have occurred spontaneously, with no external catalyst to promote it. Either way, my guess is your crab's one-of-a-kind."

Bateman forced a laugh. "That's good, but don't call it 'my crab.' Next thing you know, Strasser will label the damn thing 'Larry Bateman's Man-Eating Mutant Crab.' By any chance, did that joker show up today?"

"If he did, I didn't see him."

"Not even a call?"

"Not that I know of."

"Maybe I knocked some sense into the weasel. Now for the million dollar question. What's your read on the crab's location?"

Allen hated lying to his friend, but knew what he must do for his son. "My best guess, it'll head north through the bay and the canal, then east through the Manasquan Inlet."

"You sure about that? We've received a slew of reported sightings, most south of Drum Point, not north.

"I'm giving you my professional opinion. Believe it if you wish. But I'm not surprised. What with the papers whipping up public hysteria, on top of that, offering a reward, I could understand how people might mistake anything larger than a kayak for an oversized crab."

"I value your opinion. If I don't have to waste manpower searching in the south, maybe we'll snag that monster before it kills another kid."

Allen's heart dropped. "Someone else was attacked?"

"No, but I'd like to keep it that way. You seem pretty sure it's headed north."

Allen hesitated. "Ninety percent."

"Great. You have no idea how much time and how many lives you could be saving."

Feeling more than a little sleazy, Allen muttered, "No problem."

"Really, Allen. You went out of your way, and I owe you. I'll stop by the lab in the morning to pick up the claw."

"But ..."

"No buts. I'm playing with fire letting you hold onto state's evidence without the colonel's approval. If I don't deliver that claw to Trenton by tomorrow, my ass is in a sling."

"OK, but call first. I'm going in a little late tomorrow."

"Sure. And thanks again."

Ashamed, Allen slid the phone on the receiver. Doing so, he remembered the pain of his son. He recalled David's plea during their trek on Island Beach, how David begged him to use his scientific skill to defeat the cancer. Weighed against David's suffering, Allen could live with a little guilt.

Thirsty for a glass of chocolate milk, he started for the refrigerator. Reaching for the handle, the stern voice of his wife startled him.

"You're not going near that crab without Larry's help. If you don't tell him the truth, I will."

(((🦀)))   (((🦀)))   (((🦀)))

Saying 'no' wasn't the reason he'd gotten this far in his career. Sitting in the rear compartment of the modified van crossing the Delaware Memorial Bridge into New Jersey, Dr. Charles F. Clayton reminded himself how often he had answered the call when saying 'no' would have been so much easier. He could have said 'no' to attending the prestigious Stuyversant High School for Science and Math in New York City. He could have said 'no' to the full scholarship offered him by Stanford University. He could have said 'no' to pressing forward, grinding out his doctorate at the University of Colorado's Institute for Behavioral Genetics. Truth was, when courting a challenge, the word 'no' did not exist.

Remembering that relentless effort had propelled him to BHERT's number two spot in the first place, Clayton had yielded to General Stanton's request to supervise this mission.

Three hours earlier, when he arrived at Andrews Air Force Base, Clayton called Marlene from his cell phone to inform her the start of his vacation would be delayed yet again. "A day or two at most," he promised. She let loose, and he didn't blame her, but he swore he'd make it up to her. He jumped into the white van waiting on the tarmac, eased into the cushioned blue swivel seat he now occupied, and off they went, to Remote Station 15, BHERT's northeastern regional headquarters in Nyack, New York, about 30 miles north of Manhattan.

Leaning forward on the edge of his chair, he stared at a computer screen set eye-level on the equipment console attached to the van's inner wall. Red and green lights blinked intermittently along each side of the monitor's plastic casing. Above the screen was adhered a rectangular blue label imprinted with white block letters:

FOR USE OF BIOGENETIC HAZARD
EMERGENCY RESPONSE TEAM ONLY

Clayton sat transfixed at the screen's line of yellow numbers streaming across a black background, a digital readout confirming his team's position, direction, and speed. His bank of computers, all wired to the most technologically advanced surveillance and communications equipment in the world, brought him no closer to solving the connection between Sorkin, Maddox, and the strange creature menacing Barnegat Bay.

Turning away from the useless array of chips, memory boards and microwave receivers, he spun in his chair to face Sergeant Ferraro. The young sergeant wore green combat fatigues, and sat with her back to Clayton in an identical chair facing a control panel mounted to the opposite wall of the van.

"What've we picked up so far?" Clayton asked.

The sergeant whirled her seat around. In her mid-twenties, Ferraro was stunning: shoulder-length brown hair emphasizing glimmering emerald eyes, and a tall, slim physique apparent even through her combat fatigues. She spoke with polite confidence. "Five calls total. Two outgoing, Three incoming. Would you like to see the transcripts?"

"No thanks. Just sum them up, in chronological order."

Ferraro lifted a printout on the shelf behind her. Every now and then, she peeked down at the white stapled sheets as she spoke. "The first two calls were routine solicitations, one from Xerox, another from Sprint. The third, an incoming at 1405, proved more interesting. The caller, a male, identified himself as a newspaper reporter for the *Toms River Chronicle*. One Brian Strasser."

Clayton turned to Jacobs, who nodded back, apparently recalling the name of the man who'd written the article he'd shown Clayton on the return flight from Colombia.

Ferraro continued, "The receptionist didn't seem to know Strasser or his business. She asked why he was calling. Strasser said Maddox would understand. She put Strasser on hold for 32 seconds. She came back on the line and said Maddox was in a meeting, then took Strasser's number."

"That's all?"

"No. Before he hung up, Strasser told the receptionist ..," Ferraro glanced at the transcript, ".. make sure he calls me back, or I'll blow the whistle on Bateman."

"Lieutenant Bateman. Isn't he the marine police commander Strasser hung out to dry?"

"Yes," Ferraro answered.

Clayton rubbed his chin. "How's Bateman connected to Omnigen?"

Jacobs leaned forward. "We don't know, but we're checking."

Assuming a sarcastic drawl, Clayton said, "OK, ladies and gentlemen, I see you're ready to pull this operation off. While y'all at it, what else *don't* we know?"

"Sir, we're trying our best."

Clayton turned back to Ferraro. "Next call."

"An outgoing by Maddox at 1455 to World-Wide Escapes, a travel agency in Mercer County, New Jersey. He asked for Carol. When she answered, her inflection seemed unusually friendly, as if she and Maddox were friends, possibly lovers."

At least his team knew something, thanks to Ferraro's mastery of Non-Verbal Communications, a segment Clayton deemed essential in the syllabus for BHERT trainees. Drawing the correct inference based on your gut, not what you heard, often meant the difference between life and death in the field. "So this gal was willing to give Maddox anything?"

"She bent over backward." Ferraro looked down at the printout. "Maddox asked for a one-way flight to Brazil Thursday afternoon. She said the best she could do was Friday morning. He said Friday was too late. She put him on hold, came back, and told him Thursday afternoon was impossible, but because it was him, she could do nine o'clock Thursday night out of JFK. Said she had a good friend at TWA who could bump someone in a pinch."

Clayton snickered. "Maddox sure knew who to sleep with."

"Sounds that way. I sensed he was gloating when he told her she'd have to live without him. Her voice cracked when she asked when he'd be back. He said ..," Ferraro read from the transcript, "not soon enough to make it worth your while."

Clayton mulled out loud, "He's got something cooking with Robert Sorkin, and it's going down in the next 48 hours." He turned to Jacobs, addressing him like a child, "We *do* know what Omnigen does, don't we?"

"Yes, sir. They ..."

"And stop that 'sir' crap!"

"Yes, Dr. Clayton. Omnigen's early research focused on development of gene therapies for cancer. Maddox launched the company 10 years ago. He put a biochemist in charge, a Dr. Nathan Miles, who supervised four research assistants and a couple of technicians. We've learned Dr. Miles is a man with his own problems."

"Like what?"

"Alcohol, for one. Also has trouble playing by the rules — extremely intelligent, but overzealous. Stevens Institute forced him out for failure to comply with the administration's policy on departmental approvals for recombinant DNA experimentation."

"Nathan Miles ... name's not familiar. Do anything important?"

"Nothing, sir. Fact is, not one drug or gene-splicing protocol of commercial value has come out of Omnigen in the ten years he's worked there. Wasn't until last November that Omnigen showed signs of life. That's when Maddox hired some new guy out of USC to take charge. Name's Dr. Allen J. Johnson, and he specializes in the use of gene engineering technology to improve crop productivity. In February, he applied to the USDA for Phase I consideration of a protocol to produce halophytic rice seed."

"I doubt that's what Sorkin's after. Not important enough to risk dealing with the same man who nearly landed him in prison and put the Feds on his case for the past 15 years. And it still doesn't explain the connection between Omnigen and those sightings of an unusual predator in Barnegat Bay."

Ferraro, listening intently to Clayton and Jacobs, broke in, "That's not entirely true."

In unison, their heads turned to the attractive sergeant.

"What do you mean by that?" Clayton asked.

"There was another call. Went out at 1518, from Dr. Johnson to a woman who could only be his wife. He asked how David, presumably their child, was feeling. She said he was resting."

Clayton swung his chair in Jacobs' direction. "What do we know about Johnson's family?"

"Not much, sir, but when I last spoke with Merryl at RS-15, she promised more information on Bateman and Johnson. Said she'd call us on the road by eight."

Clayton glimpsed at the digital clock glowing red on the communications panel in front of Jacobs. "Right about now." He swung back to Ferraro. "What did Johnson say that makes you believe Omnigen's connected to the news reports?"

"Something he told his wife." Ferraro studied the printout. "Her exact words: 'I've been nuts worrying about you. When did you get back?' ... Johnson responds, 'About an hour ago,' then tells her, 'I saw its claw break the surface. It looks even larger out of the lab, and just like I thought, it's moving south.'"

"Makes sense," Clayton said. "The reporter from the *Chronicle* alleged the boys in the bay were attacked by a giant crab." He motioned to Ferraro. "Go on."

"Johnson told her he was stopping at his mother's house after work to pick up his scuba gear." Ferraro paused. "One more thing. Just before he hung up, he told her he thought Maddox was up to something strange, but couldn't be sure, and he'd explain when he got home."

"Hmmm." Clayton massaged his chin. "Sounds like Johnson has no idea what Maddox is into. But he sure knows an awful lot about the creature in the bay. I need more data on Johnson." He turned to Jacobs. "Still no call from Merryl?"

"No, sir."

"I want that intelligence report by 8:15."

"I could try raising her on the cell phone."

"Hey, now we're using our noggin."

Jacobs lifted a black hand-held unit from the shelf in front of his chair, and began pressing keys.

"What's our ETA to Nyack?"

Ferraro glimpsed at her watch. "Approximately 2300 hours."

"From there down to Lakewood?"

"At that time, maybe two hours. But we'll need an hour or two at RS-15 for supply and set-up. And we still need an executive search order."

"I'd like to get into Omnigen tonight, but I'll settle for sunrise, tomorrow. Whatever Maddox is up to, he's doing it soon, and I'll have someone's head if we miss it. Besides, if we can wrap this up by tomorrow afternoon, maybe Marlene won't divorce me." Clayton swiveled to Jacobs, who appeared to be listening to someone on the phone.

The young officer occasionally nodded his head. After grunting a few 'uh huhs' and 'OK's', he said, "Roger and out," then snapped the cell phone shut.

"What've you got?" Clayton asked.

"Nothing new on Johnson and Bateman, sir, but the FBI was wrong on Sorkin and Maddox. Turns out Sorkin never washed his hands entirely of Maddox. The Bureau's dug up evidence that 12 years ago, one year after they stopped tailing Maddox, Sorkin loaned him a million dollars."

"Now we know how he funded Omnigen."

"There's no direct evidence, not yet. The best the FBI could determine on eight hours notice, the money was funneled to Maddox through one of Sorkin's holding companies. We're talking about 12-year-old records and 32 shell companies. The bureau needs more time to sort through the paperwork."

Ferraro passed lithe fingers through her neatly trimmed hair. "Sorkin has enough money to buy anything he wants, anywhere he wants, from anyone he wants. What can he possibly get from Maddox that he can't get anywhere else?"

Clayton folded his hands behind his head and leaned back in his chair. "Finding that answer, folks, is why we get paid."

WEDNESDAY

JULY 1

21

Eyes half-open, Allen spied the clock-radio on the night table beside him. The glowing amber digits beamed 5:30 a.m. Nearly seven hours had passed since he'd crept into bed, but he felt as if he slept only two. Though worn out by yesterday's incredible events, Allen had tossed and turned all night, his mind racing, ironing out the details of the momentous day ahead.

Resisting the urge to shut his eyes, Allen yanked off the covers and sat up. He looked down at Jennifer, who lay with her back to him, and saw only the measured rise and fall of her waist. He turned toward the window and observed through the open slats a cloudless pearl sky, too early for the cobalt blue certain to follow the rising sun.

Jennifer rolled flat on her back and cracked open her eyelids. When their eyes met, she abruptly turned away and faced the wall.

She must still be angry. Last night, following his conversation with Larry, they argued for an hour. If Jennifer had her way, he would inform Larry of the crab's true location, then enlist his aid to anesthetize the crab and extract its tissue. She actually believed if Larry knew the crab's DNA held the potential for halting cancer and slowing cellular aging, he'd make every effort to capture rather than destroy the crab.

Jennifer stubbornly refused to admit seeking Larry's help would imperil the plan he and Miles had devised to hunt the crab for its Hope-1 genes. She wouldn't concede the real possibility Larry might exterminate the crab before its cancer-inhibiting genes could be taken. Larry had said it himself: "My men have strict orders. If the crab goes anywhere near them, they blow it to bits."

Only one approach assured non-interference by the law: silence. After Allen obtained the crab's life-saving DNA for his son's gene therapy, then he could indulge in honesty.

Surrendering to sunrise, Allen slipped out of bed, put on a blue terry-cloth robe, and headed to the kitchen to brew a badly needed cup of coffee. He stopped at David's room and peeked inside. His boy dozed peacefully, oblivious to the vile cell cluster growing inside his brain.

Allen tiptoed into the bedroom and kissed his sleeping son's forehead. Soon, as early as tonight, Allen would discover if the crab's mutant tumor-suppressor genes, once inserted into David's tumor, held the power to arrest its relentless growth.

Allen left David's room without a sound, and plodded into the living room. Before making coffee, he decided to fetch the morning paper. He yawned, opened the front door, and spotted the *Chronicle*, sheathed in yellow plastic, lying on the sidewalk. Not yet six o'clock, the temperature felt warm enough for shorts and a T-shirt.

Descending the three concrete steps, he paused and glanced around at the eclectic assortment of ranches and capes, all built on 50x100 lots like his. He heard the slam of a screen door across the street, and sniffed the aroma of bacon from next door. Such early activity did not surprise Allen. Today was Wednesday, and about this time every work day, the year-round citizens of this seashore village braced for their morning commutes. The man next door, a controller for a Wall Street accounting firm, rode a bus two hours to Manhattan, reminding Allen of his own good fortune, residing a mere 20 minutes from Omnigen.

Allen removed the *Chronicle* from its plastic pouch, expecting more bad news from the reporter who, since Monday, had hounded his friend on the front page. Sure enough, emblazoned across the top, in extra-large typeface: POLICE COVER-UP IN MONSTER ATTACK.

Poor Larry. Such shabby treatment by Strasser would surely take a toll on his old buddy. Allen sighed, knowing he was partially to blame for his friend's troubles.

Refusing to read Strasser's nonsense, Allen squeezed the *Chronicle* back in its canary wrapper and dropped it in a garbage can alongside the house. He reflected a moment, then buried the newspaper deeper in the can, under a trash-filled bag already stuffed inside. He wouldn't want Jennifer chancing upon it.

As he snapped on the lid, Allen heard from inside the house a high-pitched wail, like the shriek of a wounded animal. He bolted to the front of the house, jumped the three concrete steps, and wrenched open the storm door. The cry hammering his ears came from the bedroom hall. Allen froze, then watched in horror as his son staggered into the living room, his hands clutching the back of his head, his eyes twisted into knots of agony.

"Daddy, help me! It hurts." Staggering toward Allen, David careened into the end table next to the couch, toppling a porcelain lamp that shattered when it hit the hardwood floor.

Allen leaped to David's side and reached down to lift him. As Allen firmed his grip, the screams stopped. David's body sagged and his head flopped to one side. Allen caught his son's dead weight just as he collapsed forward.

"Oh my God! What happened?"

Allen spun his head. Jennifer stood behind him, wide-eyed.

"I don't know." Cradling David's lifeless body, Allen lowered his son onto the couch. "He came into the living room wobbling, like he'd lost his balance. He said his head hurt, then passed out."

Jennifer grabbed a pillow from an easy chair and propped it under David's brown hair. "I'll call 911." She ran to the kitchen and picked up the phone.

Allen knew he'd be useless if fear took control. He ignored the panic and checked David's vital signs. First, he lowered his ear to David's lips. Feeling no breath, he observed an irregular swelling of his chest. The lungs worked, but his breathing was shallow. Allen traced his fingers along the right side of David's neck in search of a pulse. He found none. Switching sides, he detected a faint throbbing, evidence blood flowed through his carotid artery.

Jennifer sprinted from the kitchen. "They're on their way."

Allen spotted the watch on her wrist. "Count off 15 seconds, starting ... now."

After an interminable period, she snapped, "Fifteen!"

"Damn, only 36." He lifted David's eyelids and saw both pupils dilated.

≈ *≈* *≈*

The arrival of the ambulance, the race to the mainland, the blare of the sirens, all faded into a dizzying blur as the glass doors of the emergency room at Ocean County Medical Center hissed open.

Inside the ER, two orderlies in green scrubs took charge of the gurney. Their young faces wore grim expressions as they sped David into a large room, antiseptic white, with no partitions. They rolled the gurney flush against a wall between two curtains, and stepped back as two nurses rushed to David's side.

One lifted his blue pajama top, pressing the end of a stethoscope to his chest. The other slapped a blood pressure band around his arm and pumped.

Jennifer stood beside the nurse with the stethoscope, clutching David's limp hand. Her eyes shone red from anxious tears.

The nurse with the stethoscope wrapped her fingers around their son's wrist and checked for pulse. The other removed the blood pressure band, peppered Jennifer with questions, and jotted her answers on a clipboard beside the gurney.

Allen could do no more. David's fate lay in the hands of the doctors, and God. At the ER admissions desk, he responded numbly to a series of medical insurance questions checked off by a receiving nurse. Every other answer, he glimpsed over his shoulder, keeping an eye on Jennifer and the two nurses huddled over David. One of the nurses had started a glucose IV in David's arm, a precaution against dehydration.

When the receiving nurse finished her questions, the ER doctor, a tall blonde, middle-aged woman, strode into the room through oversized swinging doors leading from an interior corridor of the hospital. She marched directly to the gurney, picked up the chart, and mouthed something to Jennifer.

His wife appeared to answer the doctor, who plucked a pen light clipped to her chest pocket, gently lifted David's eyelids, and peered into his pupils.

Allen rose, about to return to David's side, when the two nurses flanking the gurney grabbed its chrome rails and steered it toward him. Jennifer and the doctor followed.

Without a word, the nurses rolled his son, pale and still, past him. The doctor's steel blue eyes fixed on David with a grim look of quiet urgency. She walked by Allen as if he weren't there.

Jennifer stopped and clasped his hand.

Allen feared the worst. Though David had experienced episodic head pain, even after chemotherapy and radiation, he'd never before lost consciousness.

The nurses pushed the gurney, dangling the IV, through the swinging doors, while the blonde doctor, trailing close, glanced at the clipboard. Even after the double doors swallowed up his son, Allen stared at the panels for a full minute before the swaying stopped.

Jennifer choked her tears. "They paged Dr. Loman at home. He'll be here in 10 minutes."

"What did the ER doctor say?"

"She's pretty sure it's the tumor. She suggested we wait for Dr. Loman. David's vital signs are stable, so she's ordered blood work and an MRI."

"When can we see him?"

"We'll have to wait for Dr. Loman."

Exchanging few words, Allen and Jennifer lingered in the waiting area for what seemed an eternity. Most of that time, Allen gazed at the white floor tiles, dreading the news Dr. Loman might deliver. He recalled David's desperate words before he collapsed, "Daddy, help me," and wondered if they would be his last. Allen understood his son's prognosis was poor, yet the oncologist had promised them three or four months before David's cancer imperiled his life-sustaining functions.

When Dr. Loman walked in, Allen spotted him instantly. He and Jennifer rushed over. Dr. Loman assured them he would return as soon as possible after he examined David and evaluated the test results, then disappeared behind the swinging doors.

Allen endured the longest 90 minutes of his life before Dr. Loman reappeared. As he approached, Allen searched his soft blue eyes for a sign of hope. He found only taut lips and a somber stare.

Dr. Loman spoke in grave monotone. "The MRI of David's brain reveals the invasion of his tumor into the hypothalamus and pituitary. That part of his brain regulating primary body functions is under direct attack from the cancer and has caused David to lapse into a coma. If you wish, I can intensify radiotherapy. But I must be honest."

The physician paused, locking eyes with Allen. "Radiation therapy will have no long-term therapeutic value. I do not expect David to regain consciousness."

Jennifer buried her head in Allen's arms, and sobbed softly. Stunned, Allen asked, "How long does he have?"

The pain in Dr. Loman's eyes was evident. "On the long side, maybe 10 to 12 days."

22

Jerome Hawkins stood at the control console of his 20-foot Chris Craft moored along the slip he rented at Winsome Marina. He held up the *Chronicle*, folded in half, its headline in plain view. "This dough will be ours, buddy boys."

Pouring another bag of ice into the cooler behind the pilot's seat, Phil Reicher looked up. "Easiest money we ever made."

In the open bow, Tommy Briggs leaned over the metal rail and lifted from the wooden pier the last of five oven stuffers they'd bought at Shop Rite early that morning. Lowering the big bird into the fiberglass live well, he glanced warily at Jerome and Phil. "Don't know about the easiest money."

Jerome, who'd already downed two bottles of Molson Ice, smirked and pointed to the headline. "We'll hardly break a sweat for this 50 grand. That Strasser fella' at the *Chronicle* didn't expect pros like us to take a stab at his reward money."

"I don't know," Tommy said. "Franny told me we'd better be real careful. The cops don't even know what's out there."

"What's wrong, afraid the missus will spank you if you get your clothes dirty?"

"This ain't funny. Whatever's out there, it tore up a little kid pretty bad. Cops still can't find his brother."

Jerome dropped the newspaper and flexed his biceps like a school boy. "Don't you worry, Tommy boy. If any monsters get too close, Jerome here'll save you."

Phil bellowed, packing a second case of Molson Ice into the cooler behind the pilot's seat.

Jerome jabbed his fists over the control panel. "And if the big fishy out there tries pulling you over the side, I'll knock his lights out."

Tommy slammed shut the live well lid. "I'm glad you guys think this whole thing's funny, but we don't know what we're dealing with."

He braced his toe on top of the bulwark, as if about to leap to the dock.

"Where you going, man?"

"You guys aren't taking this seriously. That reporter from the *Chronicle* said it could be a giant crab. If he's right, I say let the experts find it."

Jerome dropped his arms and his tone. "We are experts, remember? And I am taking this seriously. Whenever big money's at stake, I'm very serious. Why do you think we sprung for the strongest line money can buy? I took along my best rod and reel." He nodded to the stern. "And why do you think me and Phil stayed up half the night putting that contraption together?"

Phil, who'd stopped laughing, glared at Tommy. "Yeah. While you and Fran were in bed, nice and cozy, me and Jerry broke our humps making that trap."

Last night, Jerome had worked with Phil until one in the morning building a trap out of an aluminum garbage pail. The newspapers said yesterday, and again this morning, the little boy's injuries were inflicted by a claw. He and Phil figured the animal must be some sort of oversized crab — at least three feet long. No ordinary crab trap would hold a monster that large, so he and Phil cut the bottom off the can, welded collapsible doors to both ends, and wired lead weights through perforations punched along the side.

No, sir. Jerome was no amateur, and he was dead serious about the money. "Remember, you're just going along to chum chicken. Me and Phil got the hard job. Considering you get an equal share of the 50 grand, you shouldn't be looking to bail out."

Tommy sighed and pulled his foot back in the boat.

Jerome turned the key. "Don't worry, this is easy money. Promise."

Nudging the throttle forward, Jerome edged his boat away from the dock. He called back to Phil, who sat in the stern, "Toss me a brewsky."

Well inside Cedar Creek, before reaching the expensive homes at Lanoka Harbor, Jerome bumped the throttle forward, pushing his boat 10 miles faster than the five mile per hour speed limit.

"Slow down," urged Tommy, gripping the safety rail.

"Not today." Jerome hoisted his third bottle of Molson, and toasted the sky. "We got us a date, and I won't be late."

Ignoring the icy stare of a homeowner watching them pass from his backyard deck, Jerome opened his Mercury outboard to full throttle. The large wake trailing the 200 horsepower engine tossed the boats moored along the bulkhead like toys in a bathtub. In under a minute, he reached the open bay.

Scanning the water north and east, he counted some 40 boats moving or moored, more than usual for a weekday. All, he presumed, were out for the money.

Jerome knew the Intracoastal Waterway grazed Cedar Creek Point only 500 feet southeast of its mouth. He flew past the first channel marker outside the Creek, and realized he'd already reached his destination.

He jerked back the throttle lever, bringing the boat to an abrupt stop. Turning his head, he saw the propeller's backwash surge over the transom.

"You trying to swamp us?" Phil said.

"You heard the buzz. If the cops really do shut down the bay, regular folks like us won't stand a shot at the dough. The sooner we find that crab, the better."

"No need to get us killed."

"Stop your bellyaching, and let's get started." Jerome shot a glance to the bow and saw Tommy sitting, looking a little pale. "You, too, buddy boy. No slackers. Haul out the six-pounder."

"And waste a whole chicken?"

"Don't worry. When you're sitting pretty with a cool 17 grand, you can buy yourself a thousand chickens if you like."

Tommy lifted the largest oven stuffer from the cooler and lugged it to Phil, who secured a 10-foot length of 40-pound line through a hole he punctured in the chicken's breast bone. When Phil was done tying the bird, he looked up and grinned. "She's ready to rock and roll."

Clutching the bird, Tommy asked, "What do I do now?"

"Shove it up your ass," Jerome hollered, "then let me yank it out." The beer in control, he laughed hysterically.

"Lower it over the transom," Phil said, "and don't let go."

Tommy leaned over the transom and dangled the chicken above the waves.

"Wait," Phil said, "I have another idea." He walked to the cooler behind the pilot's seat, pulled out a Molson Ice, and winked at Jerome. He strode back to the transom. "Let's see that bird again."

Tommy pulled the chicken back in the boat, and Phil, who'd popped the cap off the green bottle, poured beer all over it.

"Hey, stop that," Tommy shouted.

"What the hell are you doing?"

Phil glanced at Jerome. "If the trap don't stop that damn crab, I wanna' make sure it's good and drunk."

"Damn it, Phil. Don't waste the beer. If you're looking to waste bait, use Tommy."

Jerome and Phil howled in unison.

Tommy's shoulders slumped.

"Only kidding, buddy boy. Go ahead and drop the bird."

Tommy leaned over the boat's three-foot high stern wall and lowered the chicken into the water. He hung so far over the transom, Jerome couldn't see his head, but he heard Tommy call out, "It's under."

"Good work, Tommy boy. Now keep an eye on it." He nodded to Phil. "We'll get the trap ready, after I set the trolling motor."

Jerome focused his attention on the control panel. He flipped a switch to start the trolling engine, then rotated the speed dial to the middle setting. Gazing ahead, he saw lots of boats, none close by, and though he looked, spotted not one police cruiser.

Phil walked up beside him.

Holding the wheel with one hand, Jerome threw another switch, activating the autopilot. "Shitload of people out there, probably down from the city. We don't have time to screw around. You get the trap, I'll bait her, and we'll see what she can do."

Phil turned and walked back to the stern.

Weird, not one police boat in sight. Jerome watched a cabin cruiser cross their path some 500 yards ahead, and shouted, "How you doing with the chicken, Tommy?"

No answer.

The cruiser ahead veered southeast, averting any chance of collision.

"Tommy's gone."

For a practical joker, Phil sounded awfully serious. "Stop the bullshit, Phil. Is he watching the bird?"

"Tommy's gone."

Jerome wheeled. "Enough already. Let's get ..."

No Tommy.

In the stern he saw only Phil, leaning over the transom, staring into the water.

Jerome dashed to Phil's side. "Where the hell did he go?" No sign of the chicken, no sign of the line, no sign of Tommy. Only tranquil blue-green swells.

Hunched over the transom, Phil said, "Something's coming up." His voice trembled. "I think it's the chicken."

Jerome took a step back from the stern and craned his neck forward, straining to see what Phil had spotted.

A round fleshy object, the size of a cantaloupe, bobbed to the surface.

Phil gave out a long, shrill wail.

Jerome's eyes lingered on the small orb floating behind the boat, his mind refusing to process what it saw. Two china blue eyes, frozen open, stared back at him. How did Tommy's head, severed clean at the neck, drop in the water? Where was the rest of him?

He noticed a blue tubular object, about six feet long and a foot in diameter, sweep underwater, below Tommy's head. Before Jerome could move, the tip of the object spread apart, lunged up through the waves, and clamped across Phil's chest.

The object was a claw, the largest Jerome had ever seen. The sharp white teeth lining its pincers sunk deep into Phil's shoulders, spewing blood into the bay.

Phil shrieked, this time louder than before. Bent over the transom, his feet thrashed and kicked.

Driven by one thought — get out and get help — Jerome spun and charged for the control console. He turned the key and thrust the throttle forward.

The boat didn't budge. He heard the engine scream, but the boat wasn't moving.

Glancing to the stern, Jerome saw why. Phil was gone, but not the claw. The massive blue and white appendage protruding from the water gripped the engine's power head. Its pincer teeth had cracked the motor's black plastic cover.

Jerome jerked the wheel left and right, struggling to jiggle the claw loose from the wailing engine, but the claw only tightened its grip.

He remembered an air horn he'd seen on the shelf under the console. He must get someone's attention. Lots of boats were in the bay, but none nearby.

Jerome rummaged blindly under the control panel, grasped the air horn, and pulled it out. From behind, he heard a loud snap and a splintering tear. His feet fell out from under him. He dropped the horn and grabbed the steering wheel.

Glimpsing back, he saw that the outboard motor had vanished along with a piece of the stern wall. A gaping U-shaped hole was left where the animal had ripped away the engine and half the transom.

The claw was gone.

The Chris Craft listed sharply to aft, its stern deck swamped. Scraping his feet against the slick floor, Jerome fought to stop himself from sliding backward. He tried wedging his sneaker against the metal shaft supporting the pilot's chair, but his rubber soles kept slipping off. He watched helplessly as the air horn floated away behind the maimed vessel.

Directly behind the foundering boat, the claw shot up from the sea. Jerome gawked at the creature's open pincer latching onto the jagged fiberglass floor where the transom was torn away. As easy as snapping a saltine cracker, the claw wrenched off a three-foot section.

What was left of the transom disappeared underwater. The boat's stern flooded to the base of the pilot's seat, and the tip of the bow rose so high, Jerome could no longer see the horizon ahead. Looking back, he watched the beer-filled cooler topple, spilling its cargo. The green bottles rolled into the water and sunk quickly to the bottom of the bay.

Jerome felt his fingers slip from the wheel.

The animal hurled the fiberglass into the sea. With its enormous closed pincer, it smashed the sagging floor, shattering the hull to within a yard of Jerome's flailing feet.

Another blow, and he'd be pulverized.

With one hand, he reached out for the port wall and grabbed the top of the bulwark, then let go of the wheel and clung to the side with both.

His heart pounded. Two yards to his left, the crab's claw jutted up from the sea like an immense club poised to strike.

Feet slipping, scraping, sliding, he shimmied over the side of the doomed vessel, and jumped into the bay.

Mustering every ounce of energy, he swam as fast as he could from the sinking boat. Stunned sober, he no longer felt his beer, only the ache of strained muscles in his arms and legs. He recalled Phil's desperate screams, and fought the urge to slacken his pace. His mind turned to a single thought, survive.

Paddling, kicking, thrusting his arms forward, his every stroke held one purpose — keep moving, don't slow down.

He heard himself whimper, pray, then cry. If God would only let him live, he'd warn everyone, don't go after the reward, the crab's a killer. He'd do some good, if given the chance.

Arms throbbing, thighs pulsing, Jerome swam from the sinking vessel, plowing the water, straight for shore.

His muscles strained until numb, and finally gave out. He tread water and glanced back.

The bow of the Chris Craft extruded from the sea. He saw no trace of the claw or the animal to which it belonged, only tranquil waves as serene as before the terrible moment the crab rose from the bay and obliterated his boat, beer, and friends.

He pressed ahead, taking slower strokes to conserve his strength. The water felt cool, but not frigid. Pacing himself, he'd make landfall at Cedar Creek Point within the hour.

What else could he have done for Tommy and Phil? Who'd have guessed the crab's claw, all alone, was more than six feet long? The crab trap he and Phil rigged from the garbage pail would have been useless.

Taking smooth, measured strokes, Jerome inhaled deep breaths.

About 50 yards east of the listing vessel, his forward momentum ceased. His head ducked beneath the waves, and his eyes, stung by salt, closed.

His legs stopped working.

He paddled his arms toward the surface, but a force beyond his control held him under.

Beneath the waves, his torso lurched. He opened his eyes, and reached for his legs. Where his thighs should be, he touched a smooth surface, hard as stone, and where he should see his belly, he saw a curved form, blue as the sea, locked around him.

He opened his mouth to scream, but heard no sound.

A sharp pain pierced his stomach, and the water around him turned purple. In his last second of life, Jerome Hawkins beheld the meaning of terror, and as his last conscious thought, knew he'd join his buddy boys after all.

23

Devon Maddox stuffed his last painted lady into one of four cardboard boxes on the floor of his office. He felt rather delighted with himself. Except for a few loose ends, which he'd wrap up tomorrow morning, his plan was falling tidily into place.

An hour ago, 8:30 sharp, he received Sorkin's call. Last night, from his VIP suite at The Forrestal Center in Princeton, Sorkin transmitted the DNA sequencing and gene-delivery protocol files to a secure Intranet server at his private laboratories in Corpus Christi.

Sorkin's elite team of private physicians agreed the data and documents held the bio-molecular key to prolonging human life. They substantiated the existence of the crab's two mutations, both possessing unprecedented therapeutic value. They also confirmed that to reproduce the curative polymers, four strings of nucleotide base pairs were needed to complete the gaps left by Maddox in the base pair sequencing data.

The only issue between Maddox and Sorkin had been price, and in reality, Maddox only feigned the role of reluctant seller, for the amount they settled on was twice what he would have gladly accepted.

Sorkin opened his bid at five million dollars, swearing it was the highest price he would pay for the deleted DNA codons and gene-delivery protocols. Having run this drill with Sorkin 20 years ago when trading guns, Maddox understood the rules. He railed at the offer. "Ridiculously low. An insult to my character and an affront to my intelligence." That was how he phrased it.

Undoubtedly, Sorkin would go far higher than his opening number. Sure enough, from 10 million, they haggled to 20. When Maddox also insisted Sorkin erase his million dollar loan, the billionaire turned cheapskate. Maddox knew Sorkin was desperate to get his hands on PDL, and began winding-up their conversation, declaring his disappointment they couldn't do business one last time.

Sorkin caved, but on one condition — Maddox must deliver along with the missing codon data the actual crab possessing the altered L-2 mortality gene.

Sorkin reasoned if he were to pay such a steep price, he should have immediate access to the crab's life-extending genes. He should not have to wait for his scientists to replicate the life-extending L-2 mutation in his laboratories. The sooner he fortified his genome with PDL, the sooner he could enjoy his new lease on life.

With no boat or hired hands to capture the crab, Maddox again feigned reluctance. To clinch the deal, Sorkin offered to supply the men and machines to pull the creature from the sea, if Maddox would help Sorkin's hand-picked crew track it down in Barnegat Bay.

Nathan Miles had blown the whistle on Johnson's plan to extract and use the crab's genes to treat his son's brain cancer. He specifically said Johnson had located the crab. Maddox was sure he could pump Miles for that information, perhaps within the hour.

Before consummating the sale, Maddox and Sorkin agreed they must resolve one last issue: What to do about Dr. Miles?

Miles had witnessed Maddox on the boardwalk passing the DNA data to Sorkin, a conclusion confirmed by an irate message left by the drunken scientist on Maddox's home answering machine at one in the morning. Though Miles never mentioned Sorkin by name, Sorkin would take no chances. If the old scientist ever sang for the FBI, he could now place Sorkin with Maddox, a risk unacceptable to Sorkin, who vehemently insisted on maintaining his public distance from Maddox — at any cost.

After little debate, Maddox and Sorkin decided how best to deal with Miles. The charade was about to begin. Firing Claire the moment she showed up to work that morning, Maddox cleared the building of all but himself and his quarry. Fortuitously, Dr. Johnson had not yet arrived, leaving Maddox free to lure the broken down eccentric into his snare.

Maddox heard the drub of approaching footsteps echo down the hall. He ensconced himself, for perhaps the last time, in the elegant confines of his regal leather chair, and waited smugly for the festivities to commence.

Passing through Maddox's outer office, Miles waddled into view. The first thing Maddox noticed was his gut, popping through that silly jacket he wore when he tinkered around the lab, the one patterned in gray and orange argyle with brown patches stitched on at the elbows. Under his hideous jacket, Miles donned a pale pink dress shirt. The mismatched ensemble nauseated Maddox. Fortunately, he need not endure the offensive sight much longer.

Even before crossing the threshold into Maddox's office, the fool began shouting. "Just what do you think you're pulling? I saw you last night. And you saw me. You ran like a coward!"

Miles stormed to the edge of Maddox's polished mahogany desk. His bulging hazel eyeballs spun in their sockets like crazy, tilting tops. Maddox thought if Miles were a zeppelin, he might explode.

He allowed the blustering blob of mismatched attire to go on with his tirade. "Just when I think you've learned to appreciate me, you double-cross me! It'd be easier if you took a gun and shot me in the back!"

Maddox smiled, and said evenly, "Slow down. No one is looking to double-cross you. I—"

"Look at you. Now you deny it! I swear, you must take me for a fool."

Again Maddox smiled, and said calmly, "Let me finish. I can explain everything."

Miles' sagging jowls seethed red. "This better be good."

Maddox couldn't stop grinning. "It is." He drove the smile from his face knowing he must deliver his lines with solemn self-restraint. "After we met yesterday, I thought long and hard about my future in the biotech business. Let's face it. Omnigen hasn't exactly smashed sales records, and I haven't exactly done my share to help. The honest truth? I want out of this industry."

The twirling eyeballs steadied and the jaw plunged. "I don't understand. I've brought you an amazing discovery. Bigger than any discovery made by any geneticist in the past 40 years. Just this morning, I ran a computer model that proves ribozyme splicing is a reliable Hope-1 vector. It worked on the mice. It'll work on people."

Maddox was pleased to hear he'd be selling Sorkin something of genuine value. The last thing he needed was Sorkin's goons on a mission to kill him for swindling the loony billionaire out of $20 million.

"Excellent. I'm truly happy for you. That's why I've decided to bow out gracefully and leave the spotlight to you."

"What in the world are you talking about?"

Eliciting exactly the response he'd hoped for, Maddox rose from his chair, and turned to look out the window. Hiding his smirk, he stared at the deserted parking lot, projecting his voice loud enough for Miles to hear. "I've been offered a unique opportunity to sell PDL and Hope-1 to a major industry player. The firm's controlling share-holder, also its CEO, will pay a tidy sum. On one condition. You, Dr. Miles, nobody else, must agree to head up a new division to be estab-lished by the purchasing company for the sole purpose of developing protocols for PDL and Hope-1 gene therapies. In fact, the interested buyer has already examined enough of your DNA sequencing infor-mation to verify the importance of your discovery."

Maddox turned and looked directly at Miles. "Not one hour ago I received a phone call from these interested buyers. They've author-ized me to make the following offer." Maddox spoke slowly, empha-sizing each word. "First, a six-digit signing bonus. Second, a five-year employment contract, starting at $200,000, annual increments tied to CPI. Third, an incentive bonus based on sales volume. Fourth, pre-ferred and common stock options. If these terms are acceptable, or if they're in the ballpark, the prospective purchaser wishes to meet you in person as soon as possible."

Miles slumped into Maddox's cherrywood winged chair. His jaw dropped. "I don't know what to say. This is coming out of left field."

"I understand your surprise, but I chose not to bring this oppor-tunity to your attention until I knew that I, too, would benefit from the transaction."

Suspicion creased the corners of Miles' eyes, exactly the reaction Maddox desired. He added hastily, "Surely you don't think I'd let you and your discovery go elsewhere unless there were something in it for me?"

"True enough," Miles said, his tone taking on an air of confi-dence. "How big's this outfit?"

"Very big, but I'm not at liberty to disclose the name."

A gratified smile curled Miles' lips. "You think I'd try to cut you out?"

"Let's put it this way. If I reveal the name, you might slam the door in my face, walk straight to their office and do your own bid-ding. Your contract with Omnigen expires in two months, and yeah, I'd file all kinds of lawsuits, even if you waited until September to jump. But the truth is, I don't have the dough to pay salaries, let alone hire a lawyer." Maddox's last statement contained the only scintilla of truth in his tale.

Miles grinned like a contented cow. "That's the difference between you and me. When I commit to someone, I stick by them. I won't deal behind someone's back."

Maddox nearly busted, dying to remind Miles how he had betrayed Dr. Johnson's confidence, but that might only agitate the crotchety fool. "Perhaps. But when it comes to money, one can never be sure. I'd like to introduce you to the buyer immediately. He's already drafted a letter of intent. I get a lump-sum payment for bringing the two of you together, payable on the day you sign profit-sharing and employment contracts. You reach an accord with them, we both stand to gain. You don't, we both end up broke."

"I see why you're anxious," Miles said, wearing a shit-eating grin that almost made Maddox reach out and smack him. "If I make this move, how much is in it for you?"

"Sorry. That's my business, but I'll tell you this. It's nothing compared to what you'll get."

The smirk on Miles' face broadened. "I must admit. Sounds awfully tempting, especially if its a decent-sized player."

Maddox saved his best stuff for last. He sunk into his chair, leaned back, and folded his arms across his chest. "Since I'm baring my soul, I might as well spill it all. What I'm about to tell you, you must keep secret, at least until you sign on. This outfit's so big, if you join them, beside establishing a separate division committed solely to developing PDL and Hope-1 protocols, they'll spend up to 50 million dollars to construct a new laboratory stocked with the latest biotech equipment available. Give 'em the green light, and they'll budget you two Ph.D.'s and three research assistants." Maddox unfolded his arms and leaned forward. "Now that, Dr. Miles, I could never afford."

Miles stared dreamily into space. "With that kind of support, I'd have Hope-1 and PDL up and running in six months."

"Figured as much. At Omnigen, you're stuck with three-year-old equipment in an industry where technology turns over every six months. Here, you're hands are tied. There, the sky's the limit."

The scientist's gaze hardened. "One thing I've learned, if something sounds too good, it usually is."

Maddox wondered if he'd gone too far.

Miles bit his lower lip. "I won't cling to false hope. You're right, the sooner I meet these people, the better."

Maddox suppressed a sigh of relief. His plan was turning out better than he imagined. "Very well. I'll set up a meeting this afternoon."

The scientist cast his eyes to the white Berber, a look Maddox read as hedging.

"I can't do it today."

"Why not?"

"Today's the day I help A.J. go after the crab. I called his house a few minutes ago. No one answered. He's probably en route to the lab now. We planned to leave here about one, drive to his marina, and catch up with the crab next low tide, around two-thirty. I won't bail out on him."

An unforeseen wrinkle, but not insurmountable. "You have four and a half hours before you go," Maddox said. "The company's not far from here. What if I arrange an earlier meeting, a quick one, say about 11:30?"

Miles looked up. "On such short notice?"

"I'm telling you. These are very interested buyers."

"Eleven-thirty is fine, as long as I'm back by one." Miles paused. His bulging eyeballs quivered. "I guess if this works out, you'll close Omnigen down."

"I'll be in a position to take it easy. Not rich, but I'll pay my debts and have enough left over to buy a condo on a golf course in Scottsdale."

Miles pinched his lips into a tense line.

"What's wrong?"

"If I accept, can I do my own hiring?"

How precious, he was concerned about the future of his friend. "I suppose you could make that a condition of acceptance. Why? Worried about Dr. Johnson?"

"He's conscientious and skilled. We make a good team, and I don't want to lose him."

Maddox saw an opening. "Johnson's the best. Really." He mustered the most naive voice he could manage. "I take it Allen pinned down the crab's location."

With the delight of a child, Miles replied, "Oh, yes. Not only that, he saw it! The way he described the crab's size and strength, I can't wait to see it myself."

"When he goes back, how will he know where to find it?"

"Leave it to A.J. So damn organized. He plotted the crab's position. His map shows the course it'll take to reach the ocean. He even marked the times he projects it'll pass specific buoys."

"You think Allen would mind if I took a peek at his map?"

Miles shot a quick glance behind the winged chair, then turned back to Maddox. "A.J. doesn't want anyone but me looking at it."

"You don't think I'd go after the crab myself?"

"Well ..."

"Trust me. I've no intention of getting anywhere near that animal. I'm just curious."

"I suppose there's no harm in your taking a quick peek."

"None at all."

Miles leaned forward and replied in a hushed tone. "The chart's in his office behind the file cabinet. Just return it there when you're through."

"Of course." Maddox rose from his leather chair, expecting Miles to follow his lead, but the old scientist stared straight ahead.

Maddox cleared his throat. "I best call the prospective buyer to move up the meeting time."

Miles didn't budge. His protruding hazel eyes, glassy marbles, gazed into space.

Maddox raised his voice, but only enough to cut through Miles' fantasies. "Excuse me, Dr. Miles. I must telephone your future associates."

Miles jiggled his head, as if shaking water from the wiry tufts sprouting from the sides of his cranium. "I'm sorry. I was just thinking."

Not too much, Maddox hoped. "About what?"

"I trust you didn't give away the whole ball of wax. I copied everything I know about the crab's mutations onto that disk. This buyer of yours, he won't need me if he already has the PDL and Hope-1 codons."

Maddox chuckled. "Don't you worry. I give away nothing. I omitted key sequences, leaving just enough so he knows we're for real."

Using the cherrywood armrests to support his weight, Miles boosted his round frame off the chair. The fine antique creaked with relief. "You're on the ball, Devon. I guess you don't want me hanging around when you make your call."

"Not that I don't trust you, but I prefer to keep the firm's identity secret, at least until they sign off on my fee. After that, you can cut me out of the loop and negotiate directly."

"I understand. Buzz me when you're through. I'll be in my office, or in Lab B." Miles sauntered through the door, pausing in Maddox's outer office. "Where's Claire? I saw her pull in this morning."

"She wasn't feeling well. Gave her the day off."

Miles flashed a warm smile. "Very generous. Success may change you yet."

Maddox snickered, "I'm a regular convert," his tart laugh sounding more malevolent than he intended.

24

His timetable shot, Dr. Charles Clayton roared, "If you don't have answers, don't waste my time!"

Clayton's van rolled south along the smooth blacktop of the Garden State Parkway, through the serene suburbs of northeastern New Jersey. Inside the modified transport, "serene" was not a word Clayton would choose to describe his mood. Seated in his blue-padded swivel chair, he simmered, wishing it were an ejection seat, one capable of launching him from this tin can on wheels to the yearning arms of his wife and children.

Jacobs said feebly, "Who knew we'd have to wait so long for the president's ESO?"

He was right. This delay was not his sergeant's fault. Last evening, after reaching Remote Station 15 in Nyack, he and his team were promptly outfitted with fresh electronic tracking and guidance equipment, and his van's communications and surveillance systems were given the once over by the station's technical support staff. He and his men showered and shaved, jumped into fresh uniforms, and stocked their transport with four M870 Mark 1 shotguns, 20 fully loaded seven-shot magazines, and two US M249 lightweight machine guns.

Last night at 10, eager to hit the road, they received word the president had postponed her decision to issue an executive search order. Her issuance of the order would initiate a full-scale BHERT operation certain to ruffle the feathers of an American magnate of industry whose money controlled a half dozen congressmen from Texas. The president demanded no less than absolute proof Sorkin was still tied to Maddox through the million dollar loan he'd purportedly made through one of his elusive holding companies. Three hours earlier, after a night spent wading through stacks of paper, the FBI furnished the president her proof, and finally, at 9:55 that morning, the signed order was flown from the Oval Office to Nyack.

Disgusted with the politics of national security, Clayton blew out a sharp breath. "I trust we're still on target for a 1300 ETA to Omnigen."

"Give or take 10 minutes," Jacobs replied, "and before we arrive, sir, I'll have an answer for you on Bateman's link to Johnson."

Not 10 minutes ago, Clayton's team had intercepted a call placed by New Jersey State Police Lieutenant Lawrence Bateman to Omnigen. When no receptionist answered, Bateman transferred his call to Dr. Johnson's voice mail. He left a message: "I can't hold off any longer. I'll drop by sometime today to pick up my package." His voice sounded urgent.

Clayton wondered if the contents of the package had something to do with what Robert Sorkin was after. If so, then contrary to Clayton's earlier conclusion, Johnson might indeed know something about Maddox's involvement with Sorkin. Still, a Johnson-Maddox connection didn't add up. When Johnson phoned his wife yesterday afternoon, he sounded genuinely surprised Maddox had made plans for a one-way trip to Brazil. Either way, Clayton would ferret out the truth.

The only other telephone call Clayton's team had monitored today occurred at 9:30 a.m., while they waited at RS-15 for the president's search order. Dr. Nathan Miles, Omnigen's lead scientist until a year ago, the one Jacobs described as extremely intelligent, but overzealous, placed a call to Johnson's home. Getting no answer, Miles left a message: "The results of my vector modeling are encouraging. I'm fully prepared to try it on David tonight. Trust you're on your way."

Clayton knew Maddox must wait until tomorrow night to fly out of JFK, yet from the tone of the calls Bateman and Miles made to Johnson, something valuable might be changing hands at Omnigen today. Maddox was no bio-molecular geneticist. Whatever that something was, he couldn't have developed it without the participation of Miles or Johnson, or both.

Corporal Bobby Ryan, the team's driver, was making excellent time on the parkway, and would deliver them to Omnigen in a little under two hours. Once there, Clayton hoped to learn exactly what sort of bio-genetic marvel Devon Maddox sought to peddle to an eccentric recluse with enough money tucked in his coffers to satisfy his any whim. If the Recombinant DNA Administrative Council concluded the transfer posed, in the words of its charter, "a direct or indirect threat to public safety, national security," or was deemed "inimi-cal to the best interests of the United States of America," his team would confiscate all relevant data, close Omnigen down, and arrest anyone suspected of facilitating the sale.

"We've got an outgoing!" Jacobs shouted. "Second ring ... third ring ..."

"Send it to speaker," Clayton barked.

"It's me." The voice of Devon Maddox filled the van. "We have a problem."

The response was shrill and abrasive. "If you want more money, forget it. I gave you my last offer."

"It's not money. The problem we agreed to take care of. We need to address it sooner."

"How much sooner?"

"The quicker you get here, the better. If we don't do it now, by tonight, half the world may hear about the crab."

"Who's he blabbing to?"

"It's not what he's saying, it's what he's doing. Seems he's hell-bent on going after the crab's tissue, and he's doing it today, same time I'm supposed to meet you."

Twelve seconds of silence. "Then we'll do it two hours earlier."

"Same place?"

"Yeah."

"Will you come yourself, or send Lowry?"

"You'll find out when you get there."

"Whatever you decide, do it soon. I can't contain him."

"Someone will show. You make sure the problem does, too." The receiver clicked.

Clayton addressed his sergeants. "What do you make of that?"

Ferraro answered first. "Someone's walking into trouble."

"No shit," Clayton said. "But who?"

Jacobs removed his headset, setting it down on the metal shelf in front of him. "My guess, sir, Johnson or Miles. Not Bateman." He hesitated, as if afraid to say something stupid.

"Keep talking."

"Well, sir. We know Maddox is leaving the country, probably for-ever, which means he's dealing something big — so big, he'd kill any-one who knew what it was. We know Johnson overheard Maddox book a flight to Brazil, but unless Maddox knew Johnson heard him make plans to skip town, it wouldn't make sense Johnson's the problem he and Sorkin need to address."

Never one to leave a stone unturned, Clayton challenged Jacobs' logic. "Johnson told his wife about Maddox yesterday afternoon. What if in the interim, say last night or this morning, Maddox discovered Johnson was on to him?"

"I don't think so, sir. Since he called his wife, Johnson hasn't stuck around the lab long enough to stumble across anything. If you recall, he told his wife he was picking up diving equipment at his mother's house after work last night. As of 9:30 this morning, when Miles tried calling him, Johnson hadn't been back to the lab."

"So by process of elimination, you'd say the 'problem' must be Miles."

Jacobs nodded.

Clayton turned to Ferraro, "What about you?"

"I agree with Sergeant Jacobs."

"Why?"

"We don't know how Bateman's connected to Omnigen. But we do know one thing. The only person he's ever asked for is Dr. Johnson. It was Johnson, not Maddox or Miles, who Bateman left a message for when he phoned Omnigen this morning. He didn't ask for Maddox, and we know Maddox is there now. And Miles called Johnson's house from the lab. So Miles is there, too. And Bateman didn't look for either one. My guess: Bateman and Johnson are in the dark. I'll bet the package Bateman called him about this morning had nothing to do with Maddox."

Sound reasoning, Clayton thought, except for one flaw. "If Bateman and Maddox aren't connected, why'd that reporter who phoned Omnigen yesterday threaten to blow the whistle on Bateman?"

"Easy. Like us, he figures Bateman is linked to Omnigen, but he's not sure how."

The more Clayton pondered Ferraro's answer, the more he liked it. "You're right, and you know what else? When the reporter called Omnigen, he didn't ask for Maddox by name. Check the transcript, but I think he asked for the owner. I wonder if he even knew Maddox's name."

"I don't remember," Ferraro said, "but if he didn't, there's your proof Bateman's clear."

If neither Johnson nor Bateman knew Maddox was set to deal with Sorkin, Maddox had no reason to harm them, leaving only one candidate who qualified as the 'problem.' "OK, ladies and gents, we shall proceed under the assumption Dr. Nathan Miles possesses relevant information about Maddox's involvement with Robert Sorkin. Whether he's also a conspirator remains to be seen. But guilty or not, we shall assume he is a material witness about to be silenced." Clayton glanced at a digital time readout in the console above Jacobs' chair. "Sometime today, we don't know when, Maddox will deliver Miles to Sorkin. Since we don't know where, it's imperative we get there before they leave."

Clayton shot a look to Ferraro. "Tell Ryan to step on it."

"Will do." The svelte sergeant promptly rose and disappeared into the driver's compartment.

Clayton shook his head and turned to Jacobs. "I wish I knew what the hell Maddox was selling Sorkin that they'd both kill over. Can't be weapons. Those days are over for Maddox, and the FBI's been watching Sorkin like a hawk."

Jacobs shrugged tentatively. "Well, maybe it's..." He stopped.

"What's on your mind, sergeant?"

"Nothing, sir."

"Tell me. I'll decide what we use and what we don't."

"Sorkin could be after the same thing Johnson has that Bateman wants ... I may be totally off base, sir."

"Damn it, Jacobs. Spit it out!" The wheels below Clayton's feet hummed louder as the van picked up speed.

"Well, sir, Strasser accused Bateman of withholding information about a giant claw he swears belongs to the animal that attacked those kids. The reporter could be right on target."

"How do you figure?"

"Think about what Dr. Johnson told his wife. He saw the claw break the surface, and it looked even larger out of the lab. Maybe there *was* a giant claw recovered from the kids' boat. Maybe Bateman brought it to Johnson. Why he chose Johnson, I don't know, but we just heard Maddox tell Sorkin 'the problem' wants a piece of the crab for an experiment. Maybe a giant crab with a giant claw. This may seem far-fetched, sir, but if Miles is as smart as he is eccentric, maybe he found out about the claw from Johnson, told Maddox, and now Maddox is selling the codon sequence to Sorkin."

"What codon sequence?"

"The same one that's given the Jersey shore a very big, and I bet, very old, blue claw crab."

"I don't get it."

"We know Sorkin's notorious for taking extreme measures to preserve his health."

"So?"

"Why not his age?"

Like an electric jolt, the meaning of Jacobs' words became instantly clear. Clayton sank back in his chair, plopped his hands on the armrests, and recalled a raid on an American archaeologist's encampment 18 months ago in an Egyptian desert outside Damanhur.

"I'll be damned. The Methuselah Gene."

25

Allen slammed down the receiver. Suddenly self-conscious, he looked around, and saw he was alone. For a long time he stared past the telephone box mounted to the day room wall in Ocean County Medical Center's fourth floor pediatrics unit. He was sure the cheerful pink paint had been selected by some interior design consultant to send a subliminal message of optimism. The skills of the best industrial psychologist, however, could not defeat his gloom as he pondered the imminent death of his son.

He clung to the long-shot Dr. Loman's prognosis had been in error, that the oncologist, due to arrive between three and four, would examine David and find a less damning cause for his son's coma. But to the enduring part of Allen's heart that struggled to know the truth, the gravity of the situation spoke no deception. Unless Allen interceded in David's treatment, and quickly, his boy would never know the thrill of a lightning fast cruise atop the waves of Barnegat Bay or the din of a pumped-up crowd at Yankees Stadium.

He had one choice: administer, without delay, the Hope-1 gene therapy developed by Miles. Chemotherapy failed, as did radiation. The time to take action on his own had arrived with little time to prepare. Since Allen was hunting the crab this afternoon anyway, David's rapid decline had not altered his objective, only its urgency.

All the more reason for Allen's mounting concern. Each time he tried calling Miles at the lab, every 10 minutes for the past hour, nobody — not even Claire — picked up. It was 12 noon. He would need Miles to meet him at Omnigen's front entrance with the specimen container and nautical chart in hand. From there, they would shoot over to Chadwick Marina and begin the hunt.

Perhaps Omnigen's phones were down. Once before, Maddox had gone six months without paying the company's telephone bills, and Bell Atlantic temporarily disconnected Omnigen's service. But if that were true again, he should hear a pre-recorded message saying the number was disconnected. Maybe Claire had called in sick and Maddox was out of the office. Miles, alone in the lab, busy preparing David's treatment, might be oblivious to the ringing phone.

Whatever the reason, he must leave the hospital at once, take the short drive to Lakewood Industrial Park, pick up Miles, and get to the marina by 1:30. The next low tide would bottom out at 2:35, their next and best opportunity to nab the crab. If they blew that chance, they might get another — if Allen calculated the crab's speed correctly — at 2:38 tomorrow afternoon. After that, the crab and its genes, David's last hope for recovery, would be lost to the ocean.

Allen backed away from the phone and started toward David's room. He stepped softly down the corridor, peeking into rooms where the hospital's smallest patients lay lost in their white-sheeted beds. In one, he saw a frightened face, a blue-eyed girl wearing a pink cap, poke out from under a bedspread decorated with laughing Donald Ducks. In another, he spied a boy, no older than four, his scalp bare, huddled under a baby blue quilt with red and purple hearts sewn around the fringe.

These children were the real heroes, models of grit and determination for all adults. Most barely able to reach the bathroom faucet, they confronted their own mortality. It didn't seem fair. Could their brief lives be some cruel hoax perpetrated by God, or did these children serve as His beacons to guide a lost flock? He'd wrestled with this question since the day he knew his own son might die.

Allen paused at David's door. Inside, Jennifer sat with her back to him, occupying the same plastic chair she had placed beside David's bed three hours earlier. He watched her stare at their child's pallid face, clutching his hand, cold and lifeless.

Allen drifted toward her, stopping beside the chair. He stroked his wife's silky brown hair. She did not move. A sterile white hospital cap covered David's scalp. Dormant lids concealed his eyes. Though Jennifer said nothing, he knew despair churned within. He would not let her down, he would not disappoint his son. "I have to go," Allen said.

Gazing at David, holding his hand, she whispered, "Don't get yourself killed. I couldn't bear to lose both of you."

She was right. He'd think nothing of putting his own life in danger to save his son's, and if he failed, she'd lose everything. "I'll call from the marina."

He kissed her cheek, she did not move. Allen turned and strode out the door.

Pulling out of the hospital parking lot, Allen was anxious to know why the phones at Omnigen had gone unanswered. Driving south along New Hampshire Avenue, he felt as if he hit every light at the wrong time, stretching a 15-minute jaunt into an endless odyssey. Turning into Omnigen's parking lot, he glanced at the dashboard. In fact, only 20 minutes had elapsed since he left Jennifer's side.

On a normal work day, Allen was accustomed to seeing the same three or four cars parked in front of the green mirrored office building. Now he saw only one. Fortunately, it was the one that counted: Miles' tired 10-year-old Chevy Cavalier. He hoped Miles had anticipated his arrival and cleaned out the specimen preservation container.

Bypassing the spaces marked by yellow lines, Allen drove to the curb at the foot of the concrete walk leading to the front entrance. He turned off the motor. Leaving the keys in the ignition, he sprinted to the double glass doors, two transparent panels etched with Omnigen's red double-helix.

He jerked the handle, nearly tearing away his fingers when it held fast. More gently, he tried the other door. Same result. Peering through the crack between the doors, he saw the dead bolt joining them tight. Odd, he thought, Omnigen all locked up in the middle of the day, with Miles inside. He jogged to his car, grabbed the keys, and ran back to the entrance. Slipping in the key, he opened the front door and entered the foyer.

The lights in the hall were on, indicating Miles was somewhere in the building. He strolled past Ellen's barren desk to where the foyer dead-ended at a T. Glancing to his right, down the hall, he spotted an open door — Maddox's outer office. He walked over, glimpsed inside, and made a startling discovery.

The top of Claire's desk, ordinarily cluttered with progress reports, clinical trial proposals, and unpaid company bills — along with a framed photo of her mom, dad, and live-in boyfriend — held not a shred of paper, not one family snapshot, not a single delinquency notice. Allen swallowed hard. The last of Omnigen's clerical staff had been fired. Maddox must have shut Omnigen down in the face of mounting debt. That he might do so without warning his staff did not surprise Allen.

He caught himself breathing heavy, but would not allow fear to blur his mental precision. He trotted toward Miles' office, analyzing the impact Omnigen's closure would have on administering David's Hope-1 therapy.

If their mission in the bay succeeded, Allen planned to remove his son from the hospital, with or without Dr. Loman's permission, and deliver him to the lab. If for some reason Maddox changed the locks by tonight, he would simply break into the lab. No matter what, he must get those therapeutic genes inside his son's tumor.

Reaching Miles' office, Allen found the door closed and the handle locked. He cupped his hands to a square window cut in the door, and peered into total darkness. Strange that Miles would lock his office and shut the light while working in the lab. Perhaps fear of Maddox's meddling drove Miles to take such measures.

Some 20 feet beyond Miles' office, Allen swept around an elbow in the corridor leading to Laboratory B. Over the past nine months, he'd grown accustomed to working in a nearly deserted office building. But this afternoon, the stark desolation felt especially eerie. Not one to spook easily, he could swear someone was watching. Silly, of course, since Miles could be the only other person present.

Allen swung the door open and found himself gazing into inky blackness. Only faint scratching sounds of lab mice hinted at life inside. Not good. Had Miles changed his mind?

Holding open the door with his foot, Allen flipped up the light switch. Laboratory B was empty. Uncertain what to do now, he stepped backward, into the corridor, allowing the door to slam shut. He sprinted down the hall another 20 feet to Laboratory C and opened the door. Inside, he found another dark, empty room.

Allen wheeled, bolting down the corridor, back toward the building's front foyer. Doubting he'd find Miles in Laboratory A, it was the last place to try.

Having jogged the full length of Omnigen's inner square, he reached the largest of the three labs, panting. He paused to catch his breath, turned the knob and yanked open the wooden door. Bright fluorescent overhead lights cast a glare on the five 20-foot slabs of polished black granite. Allen knew immediately the room was vacant. Out of sheer frustration he called out. "Nate! Nate!"

Only his echo answered.

Allen released the door and trudged toward his office. He'd wait half an hour, until 1:15, a few minutes after the time he and Miles had agreed they'd leave Omnigen for the marina. If Miles failed to show by then, he'd go it alone.

When he reached his office — unlocked, as always — he opened the door and snapped on the light. Kneeling beside the black metal cabinet opposite his desk, he groped between the wall and the cabinet's back, where he had hidden his nautical chart, rolled-up and rubber-banded. His fingers touched the cold aluminum of the cabinet on one side and painted sheet rock on the other. His ear pressed to the wall, he peeked into the space behind the cabinet and saw only the black tote-bag holding his laptop computer. Then he remembered that Miles had agreed yesterday to pilot the Whaler. Perhaps Miles borrowed the map last night to study their route for today's expedition.

No problem. Allen knew the bay's bogs, flats, and shoals as well as anyone. Though the chart would help, any map he needed was etched in his memory.

Allen slumped into the chair behind his desk, sorting out what to do next. The oxygen tanks, still in his trunk, needed to be charged, and the plastic hand-pump, at home in his shed, must be filled with tricaine methanesulfonate. First, he'd swing past Dover Marine for the O_2 charge, cross the bridge to the barrier island, and fill the hand-pump at his house. From there, he'd continue north to Chadwick Marina, give Jennifer a quick call, then shove off for the bay. It'd be tight, but he could still reach the crab at low tide.

All this planning was useless, however, if Miles had grown cold feet. Even a hundred pounds of new tissue extracted from the crab amounted to a useless lump of flesh if Miles did not slice the Hope-1 genes from its Chromosome 8, splice them to the ribozyme carriers, and inject them into David's tumor.

Maybe Miles had changed his mind after all, afraid to jeopardize what few productive years he had left by performing the unauthorized therapy. Couldn't be. When Miles discovered the Hope-1 allele, then used it to kill the tumors in the lab mice, Allen never heard him more excited. His rejuvenated colleague could hardly wait to wield the crab's tumor suppressor enzyme against David's cancer.

Allen would leave Miles a note. Because David's condition had taken a sudden turn for the worse, he could not wait, and Miles should prepare to implement the gene transfer procedure tonight.

Allen slid open the top drawer of the desk to grab a pen. Something inside caught his eye — a single yellow sheet, torn from a legal pad, folded in half. On the front, his own name printed in block letters. The writing belonged to Miles. Allen unfolded the paper and read a most peculiar message:

If I'm not back by 1 p.m., ask Enya to sing for you.

26

The meeting was scheduled for noon at a spot less than 13 miles from the lab. Maddox knew he'd left Omnigen too soon, but had thought it best to coax Miles out of the building by 11:00, before the gullible old fool could change his mind. Struggling to stretch a 15-minute ride into a one-hour trek, Maddox stuck to the local streets, doubling back at every opportunity.

For the third time in 15 minutes, Maddox drove past Sam's Sub Spot, a suburban deli housed in a dilapidated Cape Cod-style house on Lakewood Road.

"Weren't we just here?" Miles asked. "I could swear we drove by that place a few minutes ago."

Maddox glanced at the repulsive blob sheathed in gray and orange argyle occupying his passenger seat, the same loser who had dragged him to the brink of bankruptcy. "You're right. But there's a method to my madness."

"Good, because otherwise I'd swear you were stalling for time."

Glad he wouldn't have to play this game much longer, Maddox found it tough keeping a straight face. "Your prospective employer — his first name's Carl — instructed me to take all necessary measures to make sure we weren't followed. He is sensitive to the corporate espionage pervading the industry. The race to bring new protocols to market is ruthless. He's convinced PDL and Hope-1 are winners. That's why to get them, he'll make you a millionaire. But Carl's a little antsy. He's afraid his competitors might discover what you're on to, and lure you away for bigger bucks. He insisted I keep you under wraps until we have something in writing."

"You really think someone would follow us?"

"Oh, yes. While you've been locked away in your lab for the past 10 years, the biotech market has turned nasty. Some investors would stoop pretty low to get their paws on a promising protocol."

"And not Carl?"

Maddox nearly choked on his saliva. "Why would you even think that?"

"You've never traveled in the best of circles, and you're right, this industry can turn a decent man desperate. In fact, I read something in *Nature Science* a few months ago. Half the biotech firms formed in the 80's and 90's went belly up."

Maddox was unamused. "Then I'm not alone."

"By no means. Hundreds of companies just like Omnigen started out gung-ho, racing to discover the next miracle gene cure. They didn't appreciate the complexity of the process. They thought they'd reap the rewards without making major investments in time and money. According to the report, two kinds of start-ups were forced out of business — those not receiving government subsidies, and those not measuring up to RAC's standards."

Maddox's voice chilled. "In which category do I fall?"

"The former," Miles answered blithely. "I've kept current with the ever-tougher standards forced down our throats by the FDA. I've made it my business to make sure Omnigen complies."

Like the time you dumped five drums of bio-hazardous waste in Kettle Creek, Maddox thought, but held his tongue. "I guess you're right. Poor slobs like me with visions of endless wealth were knocked around pretty bad."

"We're both to blame. You for wanting results too fast, me for believing I could deliver. But if this arrangement works out, we'll both get our just reward."

Maddox bit his lip. "That's for sure."

Thankfully, Miles fell silent.

Maddox turned left at the next light onto Route 9. He passed a strip mall on the right, and eased onto the access ramp leading to the southbound lanes of the Garden State Parkway.

Ten minutes from his destination, he had 20 to kill. He drove in the right lane and held his speed to 60. "Have you thought about what you'll say when Carl asks if his numbers are in the ballpark?"

"Not really. Today I'd be satisfied just to meet the man and leave with all 10 fingers."

"Don't worry. Carl's a straight shooter."

"Fine, so long as he's not aiming for *me*."

"You're a regular comedian."

"I'm serious. Sometimes I'm not sure who's on the level and who's out for blood."

Precisely why you're with me now, Maddox mused.

At the sign for Exit 80, Maddox turned off the Parkway, and at the bottom of the ramp, made a left onto Dover Road.

Immediately, they entered the heart of the New Jersey Pine Barrens, a bleak wilderness blanketing a million acres of southern New Jersey, extending from the Delaware River to the outskirts of Atlantic City, a haunting mosaic of southern pines, New England oaks, and broad-leaf ferns, all stunted by white sandy soil that stretched on for as far as the eye could see. To Maddox, the place looked like an overgrown wasteland. But on this sunny day, the first in July, it was a wasteland that would serve his purpose well.

"Beautiful, isn't it?" Miles said.

"Gorgeous."

"We almost there?"

"Pretty soon."

Maddox came to an intersection marked by a stop sign. He turned left onto Keswick Road, a flat two-lane tar strip unbroken by a single curve or bend, offering nothing to look at but gaunt, twisted foliage. Maddox's heart beat faster as he honed in on his destination.

"I'm a little nervous," Miles said.

"Me too."

"Think they'll like me?"

"You'll knock 'em dead."

Up ahead on the right, a sign came into view: Double Trouble State Park. Squinting under the midday sun, Maddox made out about a half-mile ahead the steel span where the Garden State Parkway crossed Keswick Road. He slowed to a crawl, looking for the turnoff somewhere before the overpass.

"Secret or not, your friend sure picked a strange place for a business meeting."

"One can never be too careful," Maddox said.

Miles inhaled two deep breaths.

"Calm down. You'll like Carl."

"You sure this guy's legit?" Miles' voice quivered. "You wouldn't set me up for a fall?"

Maddox didn't reply and Miles didn't push.

Some 50 yards ahead on the left-hand side Maddox spotted a break in the trees. Blood coursed through his veins like hot steam through a boiler. "I think we're here."

He turned onto a narrow path of hard-packed sand meandering through a thicket of low-growing ferns and skinny pitch pines.

Maddox glanced in his rear view mirror and no longer saw Keswick Road. Observing no tracks in the trail ahead, he knew he'd arrived too early. Until the party began, he'd have to make small talk. "I hope your ready for the major leagues."

"We'll see," Miles answered, "I haven't made a decision this big in years."

They crept along the winding path through the scrawny pines until they came to a clearing — a circle of sand, about 30 yards across pocked with ragweed and wild indigo. Maddox steered his Mercedes around the circle's perimeter, stopping when he faced the breach in the trees through which they had entered.

The two men got out. Miles walked around to the driver's side and stood beside Maddox.

Facing the center of the sandy clearing, Maddox heard the whoosh of speeding cars, which he guessed came from the Garden State Parkway somewhere in the woods.

"Do I look good?" Miles asked.

Maddox preferred not to set eyes on the man standing next to him. He did so anyway, for the final hand would soon be dealt. Miles looked more like a circus clown than an intelligent professional about to meet a prospective employer. "You look great. You really do."

"Incredible. Me, an old bag of bones, feeling like a nervous schoolboy. Everything that's happened — the crab, the L-2 mutation, the tumor-suppressor allele. But my greatest satisfaction is knowing what I've done for A.J."

"What's that?"

"No matter how this meeting turns out, good or bad, I've given his son a chance to beat cancer."

"Oh yeah, that's right."

"Funny thing. A.J. doesn't know the half of it."

"I thought you two planned the treatment together."

"That's not what I mean."

Maddox was about to ask, but at that moment, from somewhere in the trees, he heard the crush of tires rolling over packed sand. He dared not look at the source.

Miles must have heard the approaching vehicle too. His body stiffened, and his head whirled toward the gap in the forest where the dirt road entered the clearing.

A black Lincoln Town Car popped into view. The long luxury car, polished to a glistening sheen, slithered to a stop on the opposite side of the circle. Green mirrored windows reflected the twisted trees and scrubby brush all around them, and prevented Maddox from seeing inside.

Miles wiped his brow. "I get nervous around big, black cars with tinted windows. Reminds me of what high-priced hoodlums drive."

"They're no more hoodlums than I."

"What are they waiting for?"

"Probably finalizing their numbers."

The metallic click of an opening door, and a pale, narrow face, half hidden behind round green glasses, stuck out from the rear driver's side. Even from this distance, Maddox recognized Sorkin's peroxide blonde hair. He stood only inches higher than the car's roof, and his lips were pressed in a tight grin.

Hands in his pockets, Sorkin walked toward them. He wore the same white sports jacket he had worn last night on the boardwalk. Instead of white shorts, he sported a pair of tan chinos, probably figuring them better suited for a meeting in the forest, where the smallest patch of exposed skin presented a feast for the ticks, gnats, and flies inhabiting the Pine Barrens. Or perhaps he'd worn them to shield his flesh from spattered human blood.

When Sorkin stepped to within 15 feet of Maddox's Mercedes, two big men emerged from the Lincoln's front doors. The man exiting from the passenger side, Maddox recognized as Jonathan Lowry. Both wore matching suits, navy blue, with crisp white dress shirts. Aviator sunglasses hid their eyes. They stood rigid beside the driver's side doors of the glinting black car, legs spread stiff, like upside down V's, hands concealed behind their backs.

Sorkin came to within a yard of Miles and Maddox, then stopped.

Maddox felt his heart thumping. "Dr. Miles, meet Robert J. Sorkin, III."

"I've heard of you," Miles said. "But you're not in the biotech business. You sell airplane parts."

"And you're the crazy genius who solved the mystery of the crab."

"The papers say you never leave your ranch, that you're afraid of dying."

"And you aren't?"

"Is that what you want with the crab's L-2's?"

"I see why you're a Ph.D."

"But I'm not selling the crab's codons for the private use of any one man, especially some eccentric tycoon."

Sorkin fingered the gold wire rims of his dark round lenses. "You're a funny guy, calling *me* eccentric."

Miles spun, facing Maddox. "Why'd you waste my time? This guy doesn't own a biotech company. He's only interested in using PDL for himself."

Maddox said nothing.

"What I do with PDL is no longer your concern."

Miles wheeled to Sorkin, glaring. "That's where you're wrong, because you'll never have it. I wouldn't work for you if my life depended on it."

Sorkin nearly giggled his reply. "Too late for that." Staring up at Miles, the short Texan waved his right hand behind him, beckoning the suited men still standing beside the black car.

Maddox recognized his cue. He took five steps to the left, leaving Miles alone, face-to-face with Sorkin.

From the front of his Mercedes, Maddox stared across the sand at the two behemoths in dark blue. At precisely the same time, they began marching across the circle, their hands locked behind their backs. Realizing the end was near, an icy chill snaked Maddox's spine.

He glanced at Miles, who waved his arms at Sorkin and shouted epithets and insults like a madman in a frenzy. No giant himself, Miles loomed over the frail tycoon, seemingly unaware his former employer had deserted him. Sorkin looked up at the doomed scientist, grinning, but behind that mischievous smile, Maddox saw a certainty of purpose he knew would not be thwarted.

Sorkin's advancing associates pulled their arms from behind their backs, revealing sleek black semi-automatic pistols clutched in their right hands. Maddox gazed at the approaching thugs, numbed by the horror unfolding before him.

The snap of handguns cocked in unison broke Maddox's trance. Sorkin shuffled sideways, toward the trunk of the Mercedes, leaving Miles a clear view of the blue suits bearing down on him. Within 20 feet of Miles, both men lifted their right arms, pointing their pistols straight at Miles' head.

Miles pivoted left, stumbled toward the hood of the Mercedes, and staggered past Maddox.

"You bastard! Burn in hell!"

On the passenger side of the green Mercedes, Miles bounded into a cluster of thick ferns, tripped over their stems, and fell flat on his face. Hands sprawled, he pushed up on his arms, but his bloated paunch resisted the effort.

Sorkin's assassins glided past Maddox, their eyes hidden behind dark green ovals. Maddox saw only two pairs of pursed lips, resolved to complete a single purpose.

As the killers approached, Miles managed to shove his arms off the crushed ferns, stand, and hobble deeper into the woods. For a flabby man, who now moved with a limp, Maddox was impressed by his speed. He figured Miles was running as fast as a condemned man could. In fact, Miles seemed to gain ground, but his silent stalkers held their cadence, following Miles into the forest with methodical precision.

"Too much damn sun."

Maddox nearly jumped out of his shoes. He turned to find Sorkin standing beside him. "Why don't they run faster? He might get away."

"Sweating makes Jonathan irritable."

The petrified quarry disappeared into a dense tangle of pitch pines about 50 feet away. Maddox's last glimpse of Miles was the back of that ugly jacket, orange and gray, flapping against his chunky behind. In a matter of seconds, Sorkin's men, guns raised, vanished through the same cluster of pine needles, moving toward the muffled sound of freeway traffic emanating from the forest beyond.

"If he reaches the parkway, he's a free man."

"You worry about the wrong things."

Following Sorkin's lead, Maddox looked away. He stared at the center of the sandy circle, trying in vain to dispel the image of the naive scientist fleeing for his life. Why should he care? After all, Miles had wrought his own destruction.

"Everything's ready for tomorrow," Sorkin said. "Seven-thirty sharp, I'll have two vessels waiting. You and Jonathan ride the trawler. When we have the crab, you get the Avanti."

"You won't be there?"

"Why, want to take me on a date?"

"I want my money."

"Jonathan will have it."

"Two backpacks, fifties and hundreds. The balance wired in by 3:30."

"Count the cash before you board. Confirm the wire on the boat."

"What about Johnson?"

"Tomorrow, after the crab's secure, Mr. Lowry flies back to the mainland." From his jacket, Sorkin pulled out a slip of white paper. "722 Princeton Avenue, Lavallette. By sunset tomorrow, there will be no one left to talk."

"Lowry's not wasting his wife and kid, too?"

"Better safe than sorry."

Earlier that morning, when Sorkin called Maddox at home, the two had ironed out their plans. If execution followed design, no one would be the wiser. Maddox had but one reservation. "You sure the FBI isn't on to us?"

"I never said they weren't. Remember, I'm the one who warned you about the telephone tap at Omnigen."

"What about tomorrow?"

"They'll be far away when it happens."

"How can you be sure?"

"Because tonight, at six sharp, you'll guarantee it."

"I'm to call from Omnigen, right?"

Two muffled pops echoed from the forest.

Sorkin grimaced at the sound of death. "Yes, and if you memorize your lines as well as Jonathan has his, by the time the Feds realize how bad they've been screwed, we'll both be long gone."

27

Five minutes after one, low tide approaching fast, Allen couldn't wait much longer.

Tramping down Omnigen's deserted hall, Allen wondered why Miles had left the lab, and where he might have gone. With 10 minutes left to kill, he headed for the room where Enya had so often serenaded him, hoping she could help him make sense of Miles' unusual message.

Allen swung open the door to Laboratory B and walked to the metal desk where two days earlier he had solved the riddle of the crab's genes. On the wall shelf behind the desk, he saw his CD player. Through the door of the disk compartment, he spotted the Enya CD he'd listened to yesterday afternoon.

The machine had been disturbed. The AC adapter was unplugged and the power wire coiled neatly on the shelf beside the player. Six "D" batteries had been removed and aligned in two rows of three along the left side of the shelf.

Reaching for the CD player, Allen heard from behind the click of a doorknob. He wheeled.

"U.S. government! Freeze!"

Allen stared down the muzzles of three semi-automatic rifles, 20 feet away, aimed straight at his chest.

"Hands high!" A black man in camouflage fatigues roared the order.

Allen thrust his arms straight up.

A statuesque brunette with sharp emerald eyes, also wearing combat fatigues, darted behind Allen. "Spread your legs," she snapped.

Her long, lean fingers patted Allen, first his shirt, then his pants. "He's clean," the young woman barked.

The black man lowered his rifle. "Our files show you hold a permit for a Beretta 92FS, target use only."

Not sure how to answer, Allen didn't.

The tall lady with bright green eyes stationed herself at the end of the lab table nearest the desk. She scrutinized Allen, rifle in hand, muzzle pointed to the floor. The other man, so far, silent, took up position at the far end of the same table. He had blonde hair and blue eyes, was shorter than either the African-American or the woman, and also kept his eyes glued to Allen.

Allen's arms began to ache. He glimpsed the clock above the door. Twenty after one. A knot twisted his stomach. He fought to keep calm.

"Who are you people?"

The black man, ebony eyes riveted to Allen, sauntered forward. His tone was deep and formal. "I am Major Charles F. Clayton, and you, Dr. Johnson, may put your hands down."

Allen slowly lowered his arms, trying to make sense of what was happening. These people couldn't be Larry's men coming to reclaim the claw, but their incursion must somehow involve the crab. Feigning timidity, Allen said, "I don't mean to be nosy, but under whose authority do you come barging in here?"

Clayton's rifle dangled off his shoulder from a brown leather strap. Lips drawn in a tense smile, he lumbered past the scientist and stopped directly behind him.

Allen squeezed his eyes shut, expecting to be punished for the question, perhaps with a body blow. He felt hot steam, Clayton's breath, warm his nape.

A loud squeal broke the silence.

Allen hunched his back, but felt no pain. When he looked, he saw Clayton rolling the antique chair, its noisy casters sorely in need of oil, to the front of the desk.

Clayton motioned for him to sit. Allen obliged.

Strolling to within a yard of Allen, Clayton spoke casually, as if relating the score of yesterday's Yankees game. "My authority is the United States government, and my orders come from the president."

The black man's tone was a shade too casual, particularly for someone who'd just scared the shit out of him. "I don't suppose I might ask to see a search warrant?"

"Why? You hiding something?"

"No. It's a silly hang-up I have about something called due process."

Clayton chuckled, "You a comedian?"

"Not every day I get visited by Army men pointing guns at my heart."

Clayton tugged the rifle off his shoulder and set it on the black granite slab behind the attractive soldier with green eyes. He un-zippered a chest pocket, pulled out a blue document, and handed it to Allen.

Allen unfolded a letter-sized form labeled "Executive Search Order 14216." In the upper-left corner, he recognized the raised seal of the President of the United States. Embossed in black letters, under the label, he read the following:

Mission: CLASSIFIED

Authority: SEARCH - INTERVIEW - EVIDENCE - ARREST

Restrictions: NONE.

A sea of tiny print clustered into 15 numbered paragraphs occupied the middle three-quarters of the page. Allen spotted phrases like "authority vested by the United States Constitution" and "all reasonable force necessary." On the bottom right, set apart from the incomprehensible blur of convoluted legalese, he spotted an original, blue-ink signature. He wouldn't speculate if these men had committed forgery, but the signature of the president looked real enough.

Scanning the warrant, Allen had not found what he was after. "You guys CIA or FBI?"

"Neither," Clayton said, "and I'm the one who asks the questions."

"Like what?"

"Like what's your billionaire friend from Texas so eager to buy from Omnigen?"

"What are you talking about?"

Clayton's tone hardened. "Know three things about me. First, I only ask questions I know you can answer. Second, bullshit me, and you'll wish we'd never met. Third, if you don't talk, I'll tear this place apart and find what I'm after anyway."

The man meant business. "I'm not selling anything to anyone. No one here is, for that matter. That's this company's biggest problem."

Clayton hovered over Allen. "That's not what I hear. I understand your saline-tolerant rice should be ready for market next spring."

Allen was impressed. "That's a year from now. If you checked out Omnigen as well as you've apparently checked me out, you'd know this company hasn't sold a single protocol in 10 years."

"I'm interested in only one — the one you haven't submitted to the Recombinant DNA Administrative Council for pre-trial approval, the one that's suddenly become Omnigen's hot little property."

Had Miles turned him in to the RAC? No way. During the past two days, Miles, working right beside him, had developed the Hope-1 protocol in absolute secrecy.

If Miles hadn't squealed to the RAC, then why had these very eager, very armed men from the government come calling on Omnigen? "You'll have to be more specific about the hot property you're referring to. We've got a number of experiments in progress."

Clayton smiled. "Start with the crab. The crab in Barnegat Bay. The crab all the papers are calling a giant sea monster. The crab that maimed a little boy and probably killed his older brother. The crab you spotted only yesterday and confirmed is tracking south."

Allen was stunned. This government man knew he had searched for the crab — and found it. Beside Miles, he had told only Jennifer. The telephones at the lab, maybe his own house, must be tapped. Allen averted Clayton's eyes and stared straight ahead.

Clayton shouted, "Ferraro, check the perimeter offices. Have Ryan back the van up to the front door. Jacobs, search all three labs. Start here."

Allen felt Clayton's hand on his shoulder. "Here's where we found the good doctor, so this is where the action is. I want everything — paper files, computer disks, memory boards, the sequencer, anything that looks relevant."

Ferraro hustled from Lab B, the rifle on her shoulder thumping against her back.

"You see, Dr. Johnson, it doesn't really matter if you cooperate. I'll take what I'm after, anyway. You derive only one benefit working for, and not against, me. The attorney general will take your cooperation into account when he prosecutes you for breaking the law."

"What law?"

"Start with violation of the RAC's criminal code prohibiting unauthorized research, and end with the illegal sale of recombinant DNA protocols. Maybe you'll see the light of day in five or 10 years."

He must save his son, and if hauled away now, he'd have no chance to pursue the crab. "What do you want to know?"

Clayton taunted, "A little change of heart?"

"Cut the crap. Just tell me what you're after."

"Everything. How you're involved. What you've learned. Why Robert Sorkin's willing to pay a small fortune for it."

Robert Sorkin. The name rang a bell, a wealthy eccentric from the South, maybe Texas. "I've heard the name in the news, but no one's selling anything to him. As for the crab, all I know is last Sunday, after it attacked the two boys in the bay, a friend of mine at the state police station in Point Pleasant asked for my help."

"That would be Lieutenant Lawrence Bateman."

This guy knew a lot more than he let on. "Yes."

"What was in the package Bateman seemed so anxious to pick up this morning?"

That confirmed Allen's suspicion about the phones. He glanced over his shoulder at the walk-in freezer and pointed to its wide open door. "As a matter of fact, that gentleman you referred to as Jacobs, he's about to ..."

"Holy shit!" It was Jacobs from inside the freezer. "This is incredible!"

Jacobs crept from the frozen locker, eyes wide, cradling the giant, severed claw. He had rolled back the plastic wrapping, exposing its bright blue and white shell. He placed the specimen on one of the stone-topped tables.

Clayton moseyed over, nudging aside more of the green sheathing. "So this is what all the hullabaloo's about."

His nonchalance intrigued Allen. "You have to admit, it's not something you see every day."

Clayton grinned. "You'd be surprised at what I've seen." He ambled back to the chair where Allen sat. "So what makes it tick?"

He thought about lying, but a lie would only sink him deeper. "A mutation on Chromosome 5 inhibiting L-2's repressor function."

Clayton turned to Jacobs. "Bingo."

Jacobs nodded. "It's got Methuselah written all over it. I'd love to know the L-1 and L-3 expression ratios."

"I don't believe you'd find significant deviation," Clayton said. He nodded to Allen. "Let's ask him."

Knowing something about mortality genes, but nothing of Methuselah, Allen hoped he could answer their question.

"When you sequenced Chromosome 5 on the mutant specimen, did you detect abnormally low L-1 or L-3 expression frequencies, say below .05?"

"I only looked at L-2. I didn't check expression ratios for the other six senescence genes."

Clayton glanced at Jacobs. "When we get it to RS-15, run a full L-series sequencing test."

Allen sprang from his chair. "You can't take that!"

"Like hell I can't," Clayton said. "For that matter, if you don't shut up and sit down, you'll be coming with it."

Allen sat. He'd do anything, so long as they didn't detain him overnight.

Jacobs folded the plastic over the claw, and carried it out the door.

Reluctant to antagonize Clayton further, Allen assumed a deferential tone. "The claw isn't my property. Larry entrusted it to me for the sole purpose of analysis."

"Doesn't that job belong to state forensics, maybe DEP?"

"Yes, but that's why ..."

"I know. That's why he chose you. You're his friend, he knows you worked for the DEP, and he knows you have a strong bio background. I've done my homework, mister. That doesn't excuse Lieutenant Bateman from following department regs. As soon as he took the claw into custody, he should've transferred it to a state facility."

"I don't want Larry in trouble. You said yourself, he's my friend. I'd like to keep it that way."

"Our authority supersedes the New Jersey State Police. The claw goes with me. End of discussion."

Scoring that round a loss, Allen considered his options. Clayton held the guns, muscle, and clout — on Allen's side, the desire to save his son. That should be enough to win the war.

He opted for a pre-emptive strike. "As for selling sequencing information to Robert Sorkin, I have no idea what you're talking about. No one at Omnigen's involved with —"

He stopped dead.

It all connected. That was why Devon Maddox planned a one-way trip to Brazil. That was why his map disappeared. That was why Miles vanished. Could Maddox and Miles have conspired to sell PDL, Hope-1, or both to the Texas billionaire? After all, the media claimed the oddball mogul had in recent years become preoccupied with prolonging his health and life.

The shock on Allen's face must have read plain as day.

"Don't stop now," Clayton coaxed.

Allen whispered, "I think I know what's happening."

"Enlighten me."

"Yesterday afternoon, I overheard Devon Maddox. He's the owner —"

"Not necessary. I know everyone here and what they do."

"Yesterday, Maddox booked a one-way flight to Brazil." Allen paused. "You guys already know that, don't you?

Clayton smiled at Jacobs, then glared at Allen. "We know Maddox plans to skip town. What happened after that?"

"I went to my office and called my wife ... but of course you know that, too."

Clayton sucked in a deep breath, exhaling slowly. "Sounds like you have no clue how deep Maddox has dug himself."

For the first time, Allen detected hesitance in Clayton's demeanor. He read it in the way Clayton grimaced at Jacobs, then glanced at the floor before he spoke.

"My team was called in to address this situation 26 hours ago. In that brief period, Dr. Johnson, I've come to know a lot about you. You're dedicated and driven, now and when you studied under Dr. Levy at USC. You have a wife and son to whom you're equally devoted. You've never been in serious trouble with the law. Your affiliations ..." he scowled, glimpsing over his left and right shoulders, "... except for this place, have been impeccable. In many ways, you and I are quite similar."

Clayton paced in front of Allen's chair. "I'm going to tell you about myself and what I do. If you know where I'm coming from, you'll understand why I need your absolute cooperation to stop the sale of classified technology to Robert Sorkin, a sale with the potential to undermine your country's economic and political stability."

The overload of data was mind-numbing. First, armed agents of the federal government unearth some scheme cooked up by Maddox to sell PDL and Hope-1 to Robert Sorkin, Miles a possible accomplice, and now they sought his help staving off a threat to national security. Allen forced himself to focus on what Clayton was saying.

"You probably surmised I know a bit about DNA recombination. I, too, hold a Ph.D., University of Colorado."

Not bad, Allen thought.

"In 1985, I went to work for the Centers for Disease Control, developing antidotes for biological weapons. You'd be amazed at how many viral and bacterial agents our former foes could have rained on American soil. In the early '80s, CIA intelligence discovered Moscow and Beijing had surpassed the United States in developing biological and chemical weapons. Ironic how everyone was preoccupied with fending off thermonuclear incineration.

"We could've fallen in a matter of hours had the Soviets or Chinese infected our population centers with any number of deadly hyperactive bacterial and viral strains — many for which we possessed no effective antitoxins. Some of their viral agents were quite proactive. The Reds could've kept their silos shut and still crippled our retaliatory capacity. At CDC, we identified strains they might use against us, developed strategies for containing their spread, and produced antitoxins to neutralize their effect."

Did Clayton believe biological weapons research by Omnigen had triggered the crab's mutation? Allen glanced at the clock above the door. Less than an hour before slack low tide.

Perhaps he might save Clayton and himself lots of time. "I've no way engaged in the development of chemical weapons or biological agents. My research at Omnigen is intended for commercial applications only. Your background check should show that. I help people, not harm them."

Jacobs shuffled past Allen, burdened with a box-load of papers.

Clayton stopped pacing. He folded his arms across his chest, leaned back against the lab bench, and locked eyes with Allen. "No doubt DNA recombination has proven beneficial, but there are those who would use gene engineering for nefarious purposes."

The implicit accusation irritated Allen. "I'd never use my skills to hurt anyone."

"Maybe not directly or knowingly. When I left CDC, I worked as assistant director for the Biogenetic Research Laboratory at the Bethesda Medical Institute. I spent the next two years designing protocols to combat diseases like sickle cell anemia and Down's Syndrome. You fail to appreciate, Dr. Johnson, the very same technology that can revise the blueprint of life to help us, in the wrong hands, can destroy us."

Allen respected Clayton's credentials. He hoped he might gain his trust. "If you can tell me how my work has hurt anyone, I'll stop it immediately."

"It's not you I'm worried about." Like a reluctant gambler tossing the dice, Clayton shook his head and frowned. He sounded like he was reading a speech. "What I am about to tell you is classified information. I am empowered to reveal as much as I deem necessary to facilitate my investigation. If you repeat this information to anyone, including your spouse or child, you will be subject to criminal prosecution. I am exercising this discretion because I believe once you understand my team's objectives, you will appreciate the importance of apprehending Devon Maddox and Robert Sorkin."

Clayton flashed a droll smile. "Hell, I've already spilled more than I should, anyway, but I think you're on the level." His smile died. "Prove me wrong, and I'll make you pay."

The window of opportunity to catch the crab shrunk with each sweep of the second hand. Allen fidgeted in his chair. "Sounds like you're an interesting man who does interesting work, but I've got more important things on my mind than blabbing your secrets."

"I know."

"*What* do you know?"

"More than you think, but that's not why I'm here." Clayton drifted toward the microscope where Allen had first observed the crab's mutant chromosomes. He fiddled with the eyepiece, glancing sideways at Allen. "I presume you're familiar with the Genetic Engineering Comprehensive Reform Act.

"Of course. The law expanded the power of the Recombinant DNA Advisory Committee."

"What you don't know is at the same time, by executive order, a covert enforcement arm of the RAC was established to monitor gene research. We're called the Bio-genetic Hazard Emergency Response Team. BHERT's directive is to identify and neutralize any threat to national security posed by recombinant DNA technology, anywhere in the world. To date, we've conducted operations in 18 countries. Our group liaisons with the NSA, FDA, and Marine Corps. Only one general stands between me and the president."

The mere existence of such an organization must mean invidious application of bio-genetic manipulation was far more prevalent than Allen realized. "You guys keep busy?"

Clayton grinned. "Let's just say, including this foray to the Jersey shore, I've been on active mission status 22 times in the past three years."

"Are your targets mostly American or foreign?"

"I'd love to chat, Dr. Johnson, but how about answering some of *my* questions."

"Fair enough."

Topping off another box with computer printouts and manila folders, Jacobs lugged it from the room.

Clayton stepped back from the microscope and walked over to Allen's chair. "What do you know about mortality genes?"

"I'm quite familiar with Dr. Wilson's work at Southwestern."

"But anti-senescence isn't your specialty."

Would Miles really have sold him out for PDL? The life of his son for Sorkin's cash? "Let's cut through the bullshit. I'm tired of being jerked around, by you and everyone else. Get to the point."

"The point is, Dr. Johnson, your boss is selling a valuable protocol to a private individual, and based on what I've seen here, I have a hunch what it is. But Devon Maddox is no scientist. He doesn't know an alanine from his asshole. That leaves only two people with enough smarts to replicate the Methuselah Gene."

"The what?"

"Substitution of a guanine base for a cytosine base in the sequence immediately preceding the L-2 coding region. A mutation that creates a novel splice site, resulting in deletion of the start codon and 16 amino acids immediately following. The result, as I'm sure you've learned, is truncation of the L-2 protein, inhibiting its repressor function."

Allen's anger gave way to curiosity. "You already know about PDL?"

Clayton's eyebrows arched.

"Ponce de Leon. That's what we call it."

Then he grinned. "How appropriate." His smile vanished as quickly as it appeared. The heat of his dark eyes probed Allen for what seemed an eternity. Finally, he licked his lips and said, "The L-2 mutation you stumbled upon is known officially as the Methuselah Gene. Only a few select officers of the FDA and the RAC, and of course, the president, officially know it exists."

A thousand questions raced through Allen's mind. How long had the government known about the mutation? Who discovered it? Had it been spliced into the genome of a laboratory animal? A human? Figuring the answers were classified, he asked simply, "Why call it the Methuselah Gene?"

"Son of Enoch, grandfather to Noah, Methuselah lived nearly a thousand years according to Chapter Five, Book of Genesis. You see, this mutation has been around a long time. We've traced its expression in humans to 2000 BC"

Allen must have looked incredulous.

"Yes, we've dated the mutation back 4,000 years."

"How long have you known about it?"

"Twenty-six months ago, a team of bio-archaeologists from Columbia University discovered a unique burial ground 200 miles south of El-Alamain. DNA testing of the skeletal remains revealed the 12 people interred there died at ages ranging from 100 to 180! Eight months later, graduate students from Southwestern University on a dig near Damanhur found a similar grave site. That one contained the remains of 18 lucky centenarians. Since then, we've discovered two additional sites near Alexandria.

"The prevalent theory goes something like this: Four thousand years ago, a spontaneous mutation altered the L-2 gene in the germ cells of a single individual. The defect, if you'd call it that in light of its incredible benefit, was inherited by a portion of the population. Benefactors of the L-2 mutation exhibited proclivity toward long life. They were probably revered, maybe even worshipped, by the less fortunate majority, which might explain the segregation of their remains."

Allen could only shake his head.

"Recall your Old Testament. Joseph lived to 110, Jacob to 147, Abraham to 175. They were the babies. The Bible identifies seven people who lived more than 900 years. Methuselah lived the longest — plugging away to 969. While students of the Bible disagree on how to interpret these numbers, the L-2 mutation offers evidence the ages reported in the Book of Genesis may not be as exaggerated as one might think."

"You said the mutation occurred in germ cells. Then why did the trait disappear?"

"That, we haven't learned, but there's no shortage of speculation. The prevalent hypothesis? Methuselah is linked to an alteration on another chromosome, one causing sterility in all but a minute percentage of those who inherited the anti-aging allele. In time, the trait was simply bred out of the gene pool."

"So why keep it a secret?"

Clayton strolled past Allen.

Allen swung his head to find Clayton inspecting the shelf behind the metal desk. He paused at the CD player and squinted into the play compartment. "Enya? Never heard of him."

"Him's a her."

"What's her sound?"

"Some call it New Age, others modern folk."

Clayton backed off from the shelf. "Me, I'm into the old, smooth stuff. Aretha Franklin. Now there's a singer." Clayton glanced furtively around the room, then whispered, "Hate to admit it, but every now and then I do enjoy cranking up the old Meatloaf."

"You're joking. They used to be my favorite, but you're breaking my chops, right?"

Clayton stiffened to attention, looking honestly insulted. "What's wrong? Meatloaf only for white boys?"

Allen's cheeks warmed. "No, I meant I don't know any scientists beside me into Meatloaf."

"Are you kidding? During my prime, me and my buddies, we'd visit the off-campus gin mill, down a few shots of tequila, and belt out the strains of "Paradise by the Dashboard Light'."

"Same here, but we lit up to the tune of Budweiser." Fully aware Clayton had dodged his question, Allen said flatly, "So why keep Methuselah under your hat?"

Without a word, Clayton paced from behind the old metal desk, back to the microscope. Adjusting the focus knob, he stared thoughtfully at Allen. "I'm not sure I should tell you more. Maybe I should shut my trap and charge you as an accessory to felony." His brown eyes glinted. "But my gut tells me you're OK."

Allen said nothing. He'd let Clayton make the next move.

Twirling the knob for nearly a minute, Clayton's fingers froze. His lips traced a smile, barely perceptible, enough to tell Allen he'd made a decision.

Clayton asked, "How many people in this country are 65 or older?"

"Fifteen, 20 million?"

"Try 40. Congress has had to beg, borrow, and steal from every federal program in existence, including mine, to prevent Social Security from going under. In the last 10 years alone, they've raised the eligibility age for Medicare three times. If we let Methuselah go public, we hand 40 million elderly the chance to live an additional 30 to 45 years. You don't have to be a demographics expert to appreciate the strain on our resources."

"But a discovery of this magnitude you can't sweep under the rug. Say Miles and I never stumbled across Methuselah. In time, others who are looking, would have. Dr. Wilson's almost there. The government can't stop gene-activated life-extension forever."

"Maybe. But the president and her closest advisors stand adamant. The interests of the United States are best served keeping Methuselah under wraps, at least for now. Not that we're some evil empire denying its citizens the chance to double their life spans. It's a question of dollars and cents. This country's economy couldn't withstand the financial shock of its population, all at once, living to the age of Abraham."

He and Clayton could debate for hours the effect of delayed senescence on the socioeconomic health of a nation. But the clock above the door read 2:20. Any chance of charging the air tanks, driving to Chadwick Marina, and reaching the crab at slack low tide was next to nil. The best Allen could hope for was his freedom, giving him time to find Miles, and a last chance, tomorrow morning, to secure the crab's tissue.

Hoping he'd get Clayton to wind down his interrogation, Allen said, "I've told you everything I know, Anyway, I have more important worries than the Methuselah Gene."

"I know."

"What exactly do you know?"

Clayton's expression turned somber. "I know you won't run if I let you go. You're too devoted to your family, especially, now, your son."

Allen's chest tightened. "You know about David?"

"I know he's gravely ill, lying in a hospital bed, eight miles away. I know if it were possible, you'd gladly trade your own life for his."

Allen whispered, "I'd switch places in a second."

Clayton shook his head. "I'm truly sorry. I have three kids of my own." He lumbered to the nearest row of metal shelves and leaned against the front end. "You're probably anxious to get back to the hospital. I'll ask one more question. I believe you didn't know Maddox intended to sell Methuselah to Sorkin. I believe Miles is involved, but I'm not sure how. Tonight, I'm the lucky sap who unpacks and analyzes all this crap we're hauling away. You'd save me a whole lot of time if you can tell me how much Maddox may know about Methuselah — what you call PDL."

"I can't help you. I didn't know Miles told Maddox in the first place. Larry delivered the claw to me in the strictest confidence. I sought Miles' help for one reason — his skill in animal microbiology. He promised he'd keep the L-2 mutation under his hat until we administered the ...," Allen stopped short, "... until we verified our initial observations. In a million years, I never thought he'd turn on me."

"It's possible then, Miles gave Maddox everything he knew about Methuselah."

"I guess. Why not stick around and ask him yourself? He was supposed to meet me here an hour ago."

"Don't hold your breath."

"He'll be back. All his research is here." Allen watched Jacobs tote another file-laden box out the door. "At least until you came along. But as far as he knows, all his PDL data is right here at Omnigen. He won't leave it."

"Listen, and listen carefully. Whether he knows it or not, Miles took a big chance getting mixed up with Robert Sorkin. Sorkin gets what Sorkin wants, and he gets it by paying people off. If they can't be bought, they become expendable."

"Are you implying ..."

"He may be in danger."

"What can I do?"

"Nothing. He's our concern now."

Clayton's men finished packing. Gone was the claw. Gone were the glass slides with the crab's tissue. Gone were the printouts generated by Genetyx. They even packed the PC and laser printer. When Miles did return, he'd need two days merely to reconstruct his efforts of the last two.

Allen escorted Clayton to Omnigen's front foyer. They chatted about the Jersey shore's weather and Allen's saltwater rice.

Outside, the cool office air yielded to stifling humidity, making Allen feel momentarily light-headed. As his pupils adjusted to the glare, he speculated Clayton, analyzing the confiscated data, wouldn't take long to discover Miles' plan to treat David with the crab's Chromosome 8 alleles. Before that happened, he must locate Miles and finish the job.

Jacobs and Ferraro hopped into the back of the van, closing behind them a pair of white double doors. Before the doors slammed shut, Allen glimpsed an object wrapped in green plastic suspended by a net from the van's ceiling — the giant claw. He wondered if he'd ever see the crab again.

Outside Omnigen's front entrance, Allen and Clayton stood side-by-side on the concrete walk.

"I've been at this awhile," Clayton said. "My guess: you've told me 80 percent of what you know. The other 20, I'm not so sure."

Allen kept quiet.

Clayton swaggered to the van's passenger door, opened it, and snapped his head to face him. "Don't go far. I'll need you around when the shit hits the fan."

28

"Come on, Missy, you scared or something?"

Melissa Collins shouted her answer over the drone of idling WaveRunners. "I've only ridden the lagoons and Stouts Creek."

"Yeah, every day for the past two weeks. Time to test your wings."

Steve Mathews wasn't her boyfriend, though he'd like to be. He wasn't bad-looking — long blonde hair, dark brown eyes, and a muscular chest — just a little pushy. "I'm not ready for the bay," Missy insisted.

"Sure you are, Missy, I taught you everything I know. If you're not ready now, you'll never be."

Squatting on the Yamaha WaveRunner's padded seat, Melissa glanced past the boat ramp to the empty trailer hitched to her Celica in the parking lot. She didn't know why she was getting cold feet. Maybe all that weird talk in the newspapers had gotten to her. "You really think it's safe? The police warned people to stay out of the bay until they find out what attacked those kids."

"I already know. A giant killer crab. Jaws with claws," Steve teased, his WaveRunner bobbing beside Melissa's in the shallows off Sunrise Beach. He revved the throttle. "Those kids were probably screwing around, got themselves in trouble. When all's said and done, I'll bet that's what they find."

Their friend, Danny Watson, had been sitting on his own WaveRunner, facing them, staring off toward the open water. His strong blue eyes fixed on Melissa. "C'mon, If there really was something out there, the police would have closed the bay. You don't see any police boats, do you?"

Melissa scanned the horizon. A few sailboats, a slew of power boats, and a half dozen PWCs cluttered the bay. Danny was right, not one police boat.

"Tell you what," Danny said, "This is your first time out, so we won't go past the Intracoastal. If you do good, tomorrow we'll shoot for Tice's Shoal."

Steve gave Melissa one of those drop-dead gorgeous smiles that betrayed his lust for her. "Sounds fair to me," he said.

She'd been looking so forward to jumping a wave or cutting a turn in the open bay. Two days ago, she wouldn't have thought twice. Steve and Danny were right, she was making too much of those crazy stories. She wiped her strawberry blonde hair from her eyes. "All right, I'll give it a try."

Steve pumped his fist. "Way to go, Missy!"

"Not past the Intracoastal."

"Cross my heart," Danny said.

The three gunned their engines, aiming for the open bay. Steve took a quick lead, cut two tight circles in the tamer waves close to shore, then opened up in a straight line due east. The cool salt water pelted Melissa's face, and the smell of the sea filled her nostrils. Danny, just ahead, opened his engine, quickly putting a hundred yards between them. Feeling confident at half throttle, Melissa wrenched her handgrip forward. The WaveRunner surged. She sliced the tops of waves, feeling as if she owned the bay.

About a hundred yards to her left, she passed a cabin cruiser anchored outside Stouts Creek. She caught sight of a little girl, five or six, wearing a pink one-piece bathing suit, and her mom in a red bikini, sunning themselves on the closed bow. The girl smiled and waved. Melissa waved back.

Exhilarated by the cool wind buffeting her arms and face, and the wind whipping her hair, Melissa aimed for the wake trailing Danny's WaveRunner. About 50 yards past the anchored cruiser, she carved a tight half-circle, coming out of her turn at an oblique angle to the approaching wake. She braced her arms and legs, yanked the throttle full open, and plowed in, up, and over the lead wave.

Nothing on the water felt so good.

Her WaveRunner landed squarely in the trough, and when it did, she slammed the water so hard, her arms and legs rattled. Squeezing the handgrips, she fought to keep her craft from toppling over, and when she found her balance, released the throttle.

She'd dropped onto something solid, a piece of stray lumber or other floating debris. Her WaveRunner's engine idled normally and its body appeared intact, but her forearms ached. Nudging the throttle forward, she circled back to the spot where she'd landed.

Inching toward the area where she hit the water, she spotted a smooth white object, about three feet square, partially submerged. One edge was smooth, the other jagged and torn — a section of fiberglass, part of a boat's hull.

Something else bobbed below the surface, partially concealed by the floating debris. Melissa crouched down and shoved the fiberglass aside.

A white cooler, its lid agape, popped into view. Inside, she counted three green beer bottles, still capped.

A smooth, sweeping motion, a few feet underwater, caught her eye. She leaned forward, staring into the rippling bay. What she thought she'd seen had vanished. Perhaps she'd only imagined it.

Below the lip of the fiberglass shard, she noticed three black numbers. Part of a fourth, cut in half at edge, she couldn't read — maybe the boat's ID number, or a model number.

Something moved below the bobbing cooler. She caught only a glimpse, but no doubt, something long, narrow, and blue, had swept past under the waves.

Maybe those silly stories were true. If some dangerous animal roaming the bay could shatter a boat, what could it do to her?

Her only thought: Get back to shore.

She jerked the throttle forward. The engine wailed, but her machine didn't move. Looking down, she saw why — two blue prongs protruding from the water latched to the bumpers of her WaveRunner. Directly behind her heels, a claw, a tremendous claw, gripped her machine like a giant nutcracker. Her eyes followed the two prongs to their tips. Wrapped around her passenger seat, they nearly touched.

As the truth sank in, that these enormous talons belonged to a living creature, she felt her WaveRunner lift off the surface and tilt sideways. Turned at a right angle, she couldn't hold on. Before she could scream, she dropped into the sea.

Buoyed by her life vest, she found herself treading water. Instinct drove her to swim away fast. After a minute of frantic paddling, she glanced back, awestruck by what she saw.

The giant claw, its shell stark hues of blue, powder to purple, and its claw teeth, brilliant white, held her WaveRunner high above the waves. Before she could continue swimming, the enormous pincers flung the machine directly toward her. The WaveRunner, spiraling in the air, struck the water five yards to her left, sending up an enormous splash.

Melissa stroked furiously, with no thought but to get as far away as possible. To her left, she spotted the cuddy cabin with the little girl and her Mom sitting on the bow. They were pointing in her direction. She started for the boat, when sharp pain pierced her ankle.

Her leg must have cramped. Moving backward in the water, she realized something far worse reversed her progress. Opening her mouth to scream, cool salt water flooded her mouth.

Pulled under by the unseen power clenched to her ankle, she twisted her body around and came face-to-face with a shiny sphere the size of a grapefruit. Through the murky water behind the ball, she made out a curved surface, as green as the sea itself. Trying to gauge its size, the sphere in front of her wiggled, as if alive.

An eye! The sphere was an eye, and the green surface, the shell of an animal. Melissa bashed the writhing ball with her fists. Five solid blows, and her leg was free.

She clawed the water, reaching for sunlight, kicking wildly with her one good foot. Breaking the surface, she gulped a deep, fresh breath. She heard howling engines, Steve and Danny circling on their WaveRunners.

Steve spotted her first. He slowed down and veered in her direction. "What happened? You all right?"

"We have to get out. Now!" Melissa felt dizzy and her teeth chattered.

She heard Danny's voice. "Hang on. Help's coming."

"Hurry. We have to go. We have to get away."

Two thick arms reached down, not Steve's, but those of a middle-aged man standing next to a woman, leaning over the side of a boat. The woman's pursed lips belied her words. "Don't worry, honey. You're OK. Everything's all right."

She noticed the little blonde girl she had waved to earlier standing behind the couple. Through fading vision, she saw the child, eyes wide, raise her hands to her mouth.

Helped by the woman, the man's sturdy arms lowered Melissa to the floor. The woman propped her against the bulwark and the man knelt beside her. Melissa stared down at her legs. Fainting away, she saw one of her feet loose on the floor, joined to her ankle by the sheerest sliver of skin.

29

Alone on the outdoor ramp bridging the first and second floors of Point Pleasant Station, Lieutenant Larry Bateman regarded his long afternoon shadow. The dark outline of his elongated frame stretched all the way to the sidewalk at the base of the smooth concrete incline.

He leaned forward and folded his arms on the waist-high wall that fringed the ramp. Admiring the large backyard lawns of the posh Colonials built on the opposite bank of Point Pleasant Canal, he wondered if Sunday's attack on the Martin boys had been an aberration. Since then, two dozen unconfirmed crab sightings had been reported north and south of where the original attack occurred. Thankfully, no one else had been injured.

A.J. assured him the crab would swim north through the Canal, east through the Manasquan, and out to the Atlantic. If Bateman were lucky, the crab had already slipped from the bay, and those alleged sightings were the work of overactive imaginations. Once the crab reached the ocean, it became a problem for the Navy or Coast Guard. Whichever didn't matter, so long as the crab swam safely away from the citizens of New Jersey.

Still, Colonel Travis at state police headquarters in West Trenton would demand an explanation. Why hadn't he transported the specimen to state forensics immediately after his troopers returned it to headquarters? Bateman would say his action was dictated by the need for quick answers in an emergency situation. The crab's tissue had begun decaying even before it was in police custody, and the state did not have adequate facilities nearby to analyze it — all of which forced him to get creative in a hurry. Additional spoilage during the one-hour ride to Trenton might have hampered reliable scientific analysis of its composition.

His explanation might not fly, but better a lame excuse than the truth, that he hoped to hide the claw from an opportunistic media more concerned with selling advertisements than printing facts.

Bateman watched as one of his unit's patrol cruisers sputtered from the canal into the dock behind headquarters. Two boyish-looking troopers nearing the end of their shift nudged the open-helmed vessel flawlessly into its slip. Trooper James Harrelson, the younger of the two, tethered the lines, and looked up. He must have spotted Bateman. Instantly, he dropped the rope and snapped a salute.

Bateman returned Harrelson's gesture, unnecessary, but appreciated. He was like a father figure to his troopers, giving them as much direction and guidance as he did his own three boys. The dawn-to-dusk search for the oversized crab risked the lives of the brave men and women in his charge. He'd lose no sleep if the crab had slipped to the ocean unseen.

"Lieutenant! Lieutenant!"

Bateman pivoted to find Officer O'Donnell barreling down the ramp from the dispatcher's tower, his bright blue eyes wide open.

"It's south, not north! South!" He nearly plowed into Bateman, stopping short at the last second.

"Steady, O'Donnell. What happened?"

O'Donnell could barely speak. "We just got the report. The crab attacked a girl off Sunrise Beach. Call came in a minute ago, over Channel 16."

"Sure it's not a hoax?"

"No way. There's all this yelling and crying ... it's real. A boater saw three kids on jet skis a hundred yards off Sunrise Beach. One of the kids, a teenage girl, was knocked off, or pulled off, the man wasn't sure. But the boater was sure of one thing — a giant claw lifted the craft clean out of the water and tossed it like a toy. The man and his wife pulled the girl out." O'Donnell's face paled. "Her foot's nearly torn off."

"Damn!" Just what he dreaded. "What's her condition?"

"Conscious, but losing blood fast. The guy who pulled her out also reported scattered boat wreckage in the general area"

"Who's nearest?"

"Nelson, off Seaside Park. He's on the way."

Bateman dashed up the ramp, O'Donnell in pursuit. How could an attack occur 15 miles south of Sunday's incident? Allen swore the crab was moving north, not south.

Bateman burst into the dispatcher's tower, its wide tinted windows presenting a panoramic view of Point Pleasant Canal. To the north, the canal tapered toward the Manasquan River, to the south, Barnegat Bay.

Wearing a headset, Officer Callen leaned into a microphone protruding from a bank of electronic equipment sweeping halfway around the room. Bateman heard her explaining how to tie off a tourniquet.

Bateman barked at O'Donnell, "Divert Sanderson there immediately."

"But he's in the Metedeconk."

"Too far." Allen was dead wrong about the crab's direction. Bateman would lose two hours moving men and materials.

Officer Harrelson strode into the tower. "What's all the commotion?"

"Get back to your vessel," Bateman snapped, "You'll be earning overtime." He explained the situation to the rookie trooper, and ordered him to patrol Barnegat Bay one mile east of Forked River, mid-channel of the Intracoastal.

Last month, Harrelson had married his high school sweetheart. "Give Rosie a call before you leave," Bateman said, "It'll be a long night."

"Yes, sir." Harrelson flashed a quick salute, spun, and left the tower.

Bateman turned to O'Donnell. "Where's Rescue Two?"

"Over Sandy Hook."

"Raise the pilot. Get him to the scene. Whoever's in the Manasquan, keep 'em there. Maybe it's not the crab, maybe it's something else." Wishful thinking, Bateman knew. "Everybody keep an eye out for boat wreckage. Right now, I've gotta' break the bad news to the colonel. If you need me, I'll be in my office."

Bateman's options were reduced to one. To hell with angry tourists, merchants, and fishermen. He'd recommend closing the bay to all but search and rescue vessels.

He dialed the Superintendent of State Police, Colonel Travis, who concurred with Bateman and agreed to speak with the governor immediately. He reminded Bateman to focus on what mattered most— neutralize the animal stalking Barnegat Bay.

Bateman dropped the handset on its cradle and sunk back in his chair. Troubled by his friend's faulty advice, he again picked up the phone, this time punching in Omnigen's number.

When the company's voice mail answered, he transferred the call to Allen's extension. Getting only his mail box, Bateman hung up and tried his home. No answer there, either. He'd stop at Allen's house later that evening to find out why his friend had made himself so scarce.

Bateman returned to the dispatcher's tower. Glued to the transmission console, he repositioned seven patrol boats, 35 troopers, and one helicopter between Cedar Creek and Waretown.

Two hours later, Bateman sat back in his chair and rubbed his eyes. He thought about the girl maimed by the crab. A quick call to the trauma unit at Ocean County Medical Center boosted his spirits. Still undergoing microsurgery, her prognosis was excellent.

He gazed south through the tower's broad windows. The mettle of his force would be tested during the next few hours. Approaching 7:00, the glowing orange sun hung low in the western sky. It dawned on Bateman that neither he nor his junior officers had eaten dinner.

He stood and stretched. "I'll make a run to Ebby's for coffee and sandwiches. While I'm down there, I've gotta' stop in on a friend. I'll keep my radio on. Any hint of a problem, call me."

Route 35 along the barrier island was clear of traffic. Rush hour long over, he breezed by the Ocean Beach bungalows. Glancing right, Bateman caught sight of Barnegat Bay. He thought about the flak he'd catch from beach-front real estate agents, souvenir hawkers, and jet ski merchants. Closing the bay might save lives, but the naysayers would have their way with him anyway. Damned if you did, and damned if you didn't, but he'd walked that walk before.

Entering Lavallette, Bateman reduced his speed, scanning the street signs. He spotted his landmark ahead, the county library. A right at the library and two quick turns brought him to Princeton Street.

Five houses down, on the right-hand side, he spotted Allen's Cape. Pulling up to the curb, he saw the blinds drawn.

Bateman parked his car and got out. He climbed the front steps and rang the doorbell. When he got no answer, he opened the storm door and knocked. Bateman trusted his instincts, and something didn't feel right.

Lingering at the door, he heard footsteps from behind. He pivoted, and watched a man stroll toward him from the house next door. He was medium in height and build, around 40, and sported beige

Bermuda shorts and a yellow tank top. He wore silver wire-rim glasses, and looked like an accountant trying too hard to relax after a long day at the office.

The bespectacled man stopped two yards short of Bateman. "I couldn't help notice the police car in front of Dr. Johnson's house."

"You his neighbor?" Bateman asked.

"Yes, officer," the man said, pointing to the Cape Cod next door. "I'm a good friend of his. I've been trying to reach him all day."

"You won't find him here."

"Why?"

"Early this morning, about the time I left for work, an ambulance took his son away."

"What happened?"

"His little boy's very sick. Cancer."

Bateman nodded.

"He took a turn for the worse. Paramedics rushed him to Ocean County. My guess — that's where you'll find Dr. Johnson."

Bateman's radio crackled. The voice was O'Donnell's. "Hen's Roost to Stray Chick. Do you copy?"

Bateman unsnapped his radio and held it to his mouth. "Stray Chick, here. What's the problem?"

"Trouble at the nest. Please return as soon as possible."

Bateman hollered into the microphone, "I repeat. What is the problem?"

"Sergeant Nelson, off Goodluck Point. He found something on the bottom of the bay."

"The crab?"

"Negative. Says it looks like human remains, but he can't be sure."

30

The conspicuous disappearance of Claire's computer gave Devon Maddox his first hint the Feds had visited. Only moments ago, pulling into Omnigen's parking lot, he hadn't spotted any strange cars lurking near the building. They must have taken what they wanted and left.

Glancing behind Claire's desk, he noticed several boxes of overdue invoices he'd seen there earlier were gone. Good, let them keep my old bills.

Passing his ex-secretary's work station, Maddox sauntered into his office. He walked up to his massive mahogany desk, paused, but did not sit. He snatched up the telephone, pressed an outside line, and was relieved to hear dial tone. Of course the FBI wouldn't cut service. Omnigen's phones led the Feds to him in the first place. Maddox relished the thought he would now use those same phones against them.

Everything was proceeding according to plan. Dispensing with Miles had been easier than he expected, especially since the old codger deserved his demise. Once again, good fortune blessed him, having kept him from harm's way during the FBI's assault on Omnigen.

Maddox gave short shrift to the possibility Allen had been present during the raid. If he were, the poor guy probably shit his pants. Too bad. Now Allen couldn't perform the zany treatment for his son Miles claimed he'd concocted with the crab's genes. It didn't matter. By tomorrow night, Allen never again need worry about trying new gene therapies to cure his son's cancer.

Maddox read the marble clock at the corner of his desk and saw the appointed hour had arrived. He keyed in Sorkin's number.

After the third ring, Jonathan Lowry answered. "Hello."

"Maddox here."

"Are you ready?"

"Of course."

"The L-2 sequences?"

"Yes."

"Conforming and mutated?"

"Yes."

"Delivery protocols?"

"Four methods, full analysis."

"Good. Write this down."

"I'll get a pen." Maddox set down the receiver, silently counted to ten, then picked it up. "Ready."

"Cross the Verrazano-Narrows Bridge into Brooklyn. Take the Belt Parkway east to Ocean Parkway. At the bottom of the ramp, make a right. Go seven blocks south, pass the el over Brighton Avenue. The road curves to the right. Pass the Aquarium, and you'll see the Cyclone roller coaster on the corner. Turn left. The road dead-ends to the beach. Tenth parking meter on the left-hand side, you'll see a blue Sable. That's me and my boss."

"I'll be in a Mercedes, dark green."

"One-thirty sharp."

"Don't forget the money"

"Don't forget to be there."

"I won't."

Lowry hung up.

Maddox hung up.

Perfect.

Maddox couldn't stop grinning, thinking about his new-found wealth and freedom from debt. He walked to the door, paused, and turned around. "Goodbye desk. Goodbye chair. Goodbye Sorkin."

He whirled and headed through the door, into his outer office.

His heart stopped.

"Goodbye Sorkin?"

Maddox found himself face-to-face with a short man wearing a leisure suit, green with beige stripes, wound much too tight around his stout little body. "Who are you?"

"Name's Strasser. Brian Strasser. Reporter for the *Toms River Chronicle*."

"Oh yeah, you called yesterday."

"Sure did. Your girl said you were busy and you'd call back. Never heard from you, so thought I'd take my chances after five. You know. No secretaries around to lie for you." Strasser glanced back. "Front door was open, so I let myself in."

"I am a busy man, Mr. Strasser. You should've called for an appointment."

"Too busy." The reporter craned his neck, as if looking past Maddox's shoulder. "So where's the elusive Mr. Sorkin?"

Maddox reeled. "Who?"

"Don't bullshit me, Mr. Maddox. I have a couple of well-placed friends at New York State DMV, friends more than happy to return a favor, like run a plate on a black Lincoln I saw parked in your lot Monday morning, right around the time I followed Bateman here."

"I don't know what you're talking about." Maddox whirled, marched out the door, and headed toward the building's lobby.

Strasser followed, close at his heels. "I'm talking about Jonathan Lowry, Robert Sorkin's buddy. You know Sorkin, don't you? The man you sold Uncle Sam's finest hardware to, remember? The FBI tried, but could never prove it. So don't give me your crap, Mr. Maddox, because I've done my digging."

He was digging, all right — his own grave. "Honestly, you have me confused with someone else."

"No way. When I learned it was you who ran this place, I did my research. Only one thing surprised me, I thought you and Sorkin parted company years ago. All of a sudden, you're hanging out with one of his buddies."

Maddox rounded the corner into Omnigen's front foyer, and stopped. "You've obviously made a mistake."

Strasser shook his head, sneering. "You also going to deny you're hiding a giant claw somewhere in this lab?"

The pesky reporter had his fingers on too many facts. Pondering what he might do about it, an intriguing notion spilled into his mind, a plan he might just pull off. Maddox gushed with contrived sincerity. "You must mean the unusual claw recovered by the police in Barnegat Bay?"

"Now we're getting somewhere." From inside his garish jacket, Strasser whipped out a steno pad and ball-point pen.

"But I'm not hiding it. I'll be the first to admit my scientists have worked around the clock to decipher the crab's genetic code."

"So I was right, it's an ordinary crab." Strasser scribbled on his pad.

"It's a blue claw, far from ordinary, and I'm certainly not hiding it."

The reporter stopped writing, looked up, and squinted suspiciously. "Oh yeah? Then why didn't you return my call?"

In grandiose fashion, Maddox swept his arm in a wide arc toward the hall where the labs where located. "As you might imagine, we've been quite busy the past two days. We could very well be on the verge of a major scientific breakthrough and I've devoted all my time and effort supporting the work of my staff. Simply haven't had time to indulge the media."

"Your parking lot sure doesn't look like Macy's on redtag day."

Maddox sounded insulted. "What kind of remark is that? My people have put in three 24-hour shifts since last Sunday picking that specimen apart. Don't they deserve a break?"

Strasser backed off. "I didn't mean to imply they're lazy. Just seems strange. This crab's the hottest thing to hit these parts in years. If the claw's no secret, you'd expect to see a lot more hustle and bustle around here." He again peered around Maddox. "So what does Sorkin want with it?"

"I told you, I have no idea who you mean."

"All right, if you insist on playing stupid about Sorkin, tell me how you're involved with Larry Bateman."

Bateman. Maddox couldn't place the name. Then he remembered — the cop Miles told him was a friend of Allen's, the one who brought the claw to the lab in the first place. He had no idea if Bateman was a local flatfoot, DEA agent, or Wal-Mart security guard. "You must mean the esteemed officer who requested the services of my staff?"

"You must be a relative."

"No relation at all."

"Then why'd he bring the claw here?"

The little smart-ass was beginning to grate on Maddox's nerves. The sooner he shut him up, the better. "Mr. Bateman chose Omnigen because, hands-down, we're the best biotech firm in the state. In fact, he's throwing a news conference right here at Omnigen, tomorrow morning, 10 o'clock. Mr. Bateman plans to unveil the claw, and I, the results of our studies."

"Funny, I didn't hear about a news conference."

"Call came in only 20 minutes ago." Maddox wheeled and walked to the end of the foyer, back toward the labs and offices. Hearing no footsteps follow, he braked and turned his head. "Well, what are you waiting for?"

"Where are you going?"

"You came here to see a giant crab, right? Well, this is your lucky day. I'm giving you a sneak preview."

"Great!" Like a kid in a candy shop, Strasser pranced to Maddox's side.

Maddox strutted down the hall. "Normally, blue crabs live no more than two or three years. But our friend in Barnegat Bay is at least eight. That's why he's so big, since they grow as they age. The reason? A mutation in his mortality genes slowed his aging process."

The reporter's pen froze, his head shot up. "That's incredible."

"Now you see why we've been so busy."

They reached Laboratory B, and Maddox walked in first. Someone had left the lights on.

He scanned the room. Documents and equipment were missing. Instead of three microscopes, he saw only one, and the six rows of bookshelves, yesterday stacked to capacity, appeared half empty. At least the FBI hadn't trashed the place. A pile of garbage might be difficult to explain to the nosy news hound.

"I sure appreciate this opportunity," Strasser said.

"To the persistent goes the prize."

Strasser beamed. "That's the philosophy I live by."

That's the philosophy you'll die by, Maddox thought.

"The scientific name for what you are about to see is a chela. Extrapolation of its length puts the size of the crab at approximately 20 feet from the tip of one claw to the other. The dextral ..."

"Come on, already, let's see this baby."

The brash intruder could hardly contain his excitement, precisely as Maddox hoped. Pretending to bow to Strasser's pressure, he said, "OK, OK. Follow me."

Maddox lumbered across the room to a seven-foot high stainless steel door. "As you might expect, in order to preserve the cellular integrity of the claw tissue, we are required to keep it frozen."

Safety latches encased the hinges at the top and bottom of the freezer door. Maddox slipped loose the top bolt, then the bottom, leaving both rods dangling from thin chains attached to the hinge casements. He grasped the door's J-shaped handle, twisted left, and pulled.

The heavy door swung open. Like a bleak fog on a winter night, cold vapor wafted from the unlit locker. Behind the frigid mist, Maddox could not make out the freezer's walls or ceiling.

Strasser stood beside him. Seeing nothing, Maddox pointed into the swirling dark clouds. "There it is, on the bottom shelf against the wall, wrapped in plastic." He took two steps forward.

Strasser followed.

"Do me a favor," Maddox said. Turn on the ceiling light. Better to see what we're doing. There's a switch on the wall, back near the claw."

The reporter's eyes glinted in the dark.

"Don't worry," Maddox said, "It can't hurt you."

Strasser crept ahead.

Through the icy mist, Maddox could barely make out the back of his hideous leisure suit.

A quavering voice pierced the fog. "I don't see it."

"It's directly in front of you."

Several seconds passed. "There's nothing here."

"Wait a sec. I'll turn on the auxiliary lights."

Before Strasser could utter a word, Maddox scampered from the freezer.

Like a crack of thunder, the freezer door slammed shut, its echo rattling the walls of Laboratory B.

Maddox twisted the thermostat to its coldest setting, and danced from the room smiling. He could already feel the tropical sun's steamy rays bathing him on a secluded island nestled in the South Atlantic, far away from the stark, deserted halls of Omnigen.

Thursday
July 2

31

Morning sunlight glimmered on the wall in the day room of the pediatrics wing. From somewhere down the hall, Allen heard a child's muffled whimper, a pathetic noise that clashed cruelly with his pastel pink surroundings.

Groggy from a broken night's sleep in a thinly padded chair, he plopped the pay phone receiver down on its cradle. He no longer cared if Clayton's wiretap caught him trying to reach Miles at Omnigen. All the results of Miles' efforts now in the hands of BHERT, Allen must rely on his colleague's memory to reconstruct the intricate procedure for extracting the crab's tumor-suppressor alleles and injecting them into David's brain.

Alone in the room, Allen studied a round wall-clock mounted above crayon works of art tacked to the pink wall. In the center of the clock's face, Mickey Mouse grinned impishly, extending his arms into hour and minute hands. Between black mouse ears protruding from the clock's sides, Allen read the time: 9:15. By early afternoon, the ebbing bay would retreat through Barnegat Inlet, taking with it David's last hope.

"It might work. But you're a few years off."

Allen spun around to find Clayton standing behind him. He wore an olive green jumpsuit more fitting for a jungle drop than a hospital call. Allen couldn't begin to guess what sort of story he'd handed the nurses and security guards to get past them.

"Little early for a visit, don't you think?"

"My job knows no hours. I've got business in New York at noon, but I'll be back by five."

Drained of hope, he made no attempt to conceal his sarcasm. "I suppose you're here to clear your schedule with me."

Clayton drew a deep breath.

"I know what you discovered on the crab's Chromosome 8. It's very important, but trying it on your son, without RAC approval, that's plain wrong."

"Don't feed me that crap. It's not your kid in here who's about to die."

"I won't pretend to know what you're feeling, but you can't use your son as a guinea pig."

"Do you have children?"

"That's not —"

"Dammit! Answer me!" Allen felt his cheeks burn.

"Two girls and a boy."

"You're a geneticist, and obviously a smart one. You know how gene therapy beats all kinds of diseases. Say one of your girls lay in a coma, cancer crushing her skull from the inside out. Say God gave you one chance to save her. A long shot, but a chance. Maybe a gene therapy the RAC hasn't approved. Tell me you wouldn't try. Tell me you'd just sit back and watch her die! Like hell you would."

Clayton didn't flinch. "For your information, mister, I've traveled that road. Not as far, but I've been there."

"Oh yeah. How far?"

"Lost my kid sister to sickle cell. My youngest, a boy, he's heterozygous. I'm the carrier."

Allen shook his head. "I'm sorry about your son, but he'll live to drive a car and fall in love. David? He won't live to see another Yankees game."

"Look. I'm not saying your situation isn't bad. All I'm saying is I understand why you're tempted to try this on your kid. If little Charlie's sickle cell got out of hand, and some untried gene therapy was his only chance, maybe I'd feel the same way."

"If you're so understanding, return my research and let me help my son."

Allen braced himself for a typical bureaucratic response, something like "I empathize with your plight, Allen, but duty to country requires I enforce the rules of the RAC."

A full minute passed before Clayton spoke again. "Even if I looked the other way, let this one slip, you can't do the experiment."

Allen was surprised BHERT's second-in-command had left the door open, even a crack. "Why? All I need is tissue from the crab and help from Miles."

Clayton stood facing the window, his back to Allen. "Guess you haven't heard the latest — about the crab."

"What about the crab?"

"Yesterday, it struck again."

"Damn!"

"Attacked three fools going after the bounty offered up by one of your local rags. Completely demolished the boat in the process. The police recovered the severed head of one, no sign of the others. Three hours later, it went after a 16-year-old girl on a jet ski."

Allen felt queasy. "How bad is she hurt?"

"Clipped her ankle to the bone, but paramedics evacuated her quickly. The surgeons think they saved her foot."

Allen slammed his fist against the side of the pay phone, striking it so hard, the sound of the ringer echoed through the room. "It's all my fault!"

Clayton turned, looking puzzled. "What are you talking about?"

"I should've told Larry the truth. I'm responsible."

"How the hell are you responsible?"

"I knew the crab was swimming south. I lied to Bateman, told him it was headed north."

Clayton frowned. "You must want that sucker pretty bad."

"More than anything."

"Listen to me, Dr. Johnson. Forget the crab. The state closed the entire shore from Point Pleasant to Beach Haven until further notice. Governor Simon issued the order. Barnegat Bay has been shut down. No one is getting in there except the state police or Coast Guard."

"I don't care."

Clayton marched across the room, stopping two feet short of Allen's face. He enunciated every syllable. "Drop the idea; the bay is closed. You will be arrested if you go near it."

"You don't understand. I'll tell Larry the truth. He'll let me go."

"*You* don't understand. It's out of Bateman's hands. The bay isn't opening again until Trenton says so."

A silver-haired nurse in a white uniform poked her head through the door. "Keep it down. Children are sleeping."

Clayton apologized, then leaned in to Allen, nose-to-nose. "But the quarantine isn't your only problem. There's something else."

"What now?"

Clayton shook his head and heaved a loud sigh. "You do need Miles to conduct your experiment, right?"

"Miles discovered Hope-1, he designed the protocol to isolate and splice it, he knows how to vector it. So yes, I'd say I need him, but I'm not convinced he'll let me down. He gave me his word."

"I told you yesterday, Miles got mixed up with some very dangerous people. You're lucky he didn't drag you in too." Clayton glanced at his watch. "In two hours I'm flying a chopper to Coney Island. That's where Maddox plans to meet Robert Sorkin. He intends to sell him all your data on the crab — the Methuselah codon, the tumor-suppressor proteins, the protocol for extraction and delivery. But we got lucky. Maddox screwed up."

"Was Miles his accomplice?"

Clayton shook his head. "We're not sure. But Maddox couldn't have put all that data together without Miles' help. Whether Miles knew about his sale to Sorkin, that's another tale. Either way, they got him."

"What do you mean they got him?

His lips drawn tight, Clayton swallowed hard. "He's dead."

"Oh my God!"

"Yesterday at noon, two women hiking in Double Trouble State Park reported hearing gunshots near the Garden State Parkway. A Lacey Township officer responding to the call found Miles' body 50 yards from the highway. Two rounds to the head."

There was a brief, eerie pause. "I'm sorry, Allen," Clayton said. "but it definitely looks like a professional hit."

Allen's legs sagged. He wanted to sit, but could not move. Unable to speak, he whispered, "All his life, that man worked like a dog to make his mark. The past two days, he came so close. They've stolen his last chance," Allen stared at the crayon drawings pinned to the wall, "and David's, too."

The stench of seawater mingling with mud, algae, and refined oil turned Maddox's stomach. Standing on a concrete platform running parallel to the dock, he tried hard to ignore the pungent odor hovering over Oyster Creek. Instead, he focused on the gaudy red uniforms below — Sorkin's crew, led by Lowry — loading supplies onto two boats lashed to rusted cleats protruding from the bulkhead.

The lead boat was a 96-foot fishing trawler Sorkin had leased from a fishery in Egg Harbor, south of Atlantic City. Demanding 24-hour delivery, Sorkin paid a steep premium for use of the ship. Its wooden hull painted flat dark green and its teak deck buffed to a shine, this handsome vessel promised to deliver a miracle, so Sorkin gladly sprang for the extra expense.

A white mast, a foot in diameter, rose 15 feet from the center of the ship's rear deck. Projecting 45 degrees from the base of the mast was a metal boom that extended to twice the height of the mast. A thick steel chain connected the top of the mast to the highest point of the boom. Attached to the end of the chain was a stainless steel retractable four-pronged pincer, large enough to grab a Volkswagen Beetle.

An open cargo hold in the vessel's aft deck, directly beneath the boom, was the reason Sorkin selected this ship for today's mission. Eighteen feet square, recessed nine feet into the hull, surrounded on all sides by a low white metal rail, the pit looked to Maddox like a boxing ring with an empty space where the mat should be. After plucking the crab from the bay, Sorkin's men, commanded by Lowry, intended to drop the beast into the square hold.

Moored directly behind the trawler was a 27-foot Avanti. With sleek white lines designed solely for speed, the Avanti's 420 Mercruiser could push the fiberglass screamer past 70 miles per hour. The Jersey-built racing machine was Maddox's to keep, but only after Sorkin's hired hands secured the crab. Maddox would use it to effect his escape after he and Lowry parted company. Until then, Maddox was to ride with Lowry in the trawler while two of Lowry's stooges followed in the Avanti.

Maddox's rented Oldsmobile sat in an empty parking lot at an abandoned marina off Waretown Creek. He'd been met there by one of Lowry's thugs, a huge man who spoke all of two words during the 10-minute ride to Oyster Creek.

Maddox planned to dump the Avanti at the deserted marina in Waretown, drive to Cape May, and hop a private jet he had chartered through one of Sorkin's South American contacts. After Sorkin informed him the FBI had tapped Omnigen's phones, Maddox reluctantly sacrificed the greater comfort and lesser expense of a first class jumbo jet out of JFK. What the hell. The $10,000 fare for private wings would hardly put a dent in his $20 million purse. Anticipating the need for cash when he reached his destination, he'd already opened an account at Banco do Brazil in Bahia.

"So, big shot, ready to begin a new life?"

Maddox jumped. He hadn't seen Lowry come up from behind. "The faster I'm out of here, the better."

The crewmen bustling about on the trawler's deck all wore identical red uniforms. Lowry, in contrast, had dressed for a funeral, donning the same navy blue business suit he'd worn yesterday afternoon when he murdered Miles. A thin black tie hung from his white collar.

He stood elbow-to-elbow with Maddox, facing the vessels below. "You should be a happy man."

"I'll be a lot happier when I land in Brazil."

"Soon enough."

Maddox nodded toward the trawler. "Sorkin got lucky, finding such a big boat on one day's notice."

"When money's no obstacle, luck comes easy."

Maddox had carefully orchestrated his own escape, but until now, hadn't given much thought to Lowry's plans. "Where are you taking the crab from here?"

Lowry shot him a wry smile. "Why? You might want it back?"

"After you pay me, I don't give a damn what you do with it. Make seafood salad for every man, woman, and child in the state of Texas. I'm just warning you, exposed to the sun, the crab won't last in that open hole."

"Don't worry. Mr. Sorkin knows what he's doing."

"You flying it there?"

Lowry's steely blue eyes scoured him. "If I didn't know better, I'd say you're prying. You haven't decided to sing for Uncle Sam?"

Arousing Lowry's suspicion was the last thing he wanted. "Forget it."

The enforcer's thin lips carved a smug grin. "Three miles off-shore, another ship is waiting, bigger than this, flying the flag of a Panamanian freighter. It's got plenty of cold storage, and more than enough supplies for the trip to Guyana."

"Smart move, not bringing the crab to Texas.

"Mr. Sorkin's a smart man."

"Think the FBI took the bait?"

Lowry laughed, "You said your lines OK, so I'm sure they did."

"Another of Sorkin's clever ideas."

"Mr. Sorkin's a clever man." The thug's eyes opened wide, as if he'd just remembered something. "What about the car?"

"I did as I was told."

"Who's driving it?"

Sorkin had assumed the FBI would put a tail on Maddox after he called Lowry and set up the phony meeting in Brooklyn. To insure the Feds wound up at Coney Island, leaving Lowry and his crew free to pursue the crab in Barnegat Bay, Sorkin instructed Maddox to have his Mercedes driven to the meeting spot. "I paid some college kid on summer break who lives in my building. Gave him my car keys, garage pass, and 300 bucks. Told him I had to return the Benz to my ex-wife, that I couldn't go myself because she hates my guts."

"She'd be in good company."

"Go to hell."

Maddox surveyed a broad tract of tall swamp grass on the opposite bank of Oyster Creek Channel. It reminded Maddox of wheat fields he'd seen as a boy crossing Kansas with his mother. Looking west, he spotted the slender concrete chimney of the Oyster Creek Nuclear Station touching the sky behind a dense line of pines and maples.

The heavy humidity made the hour feel more like mid-afternoon than 11 in the morning. Maddox was exhausted. Fearing the FBI might arrest him at home, he had rented a room last night at the Lakehurst Motor Inn. Its mattress lumpy and walls thin, he slept all of three hours. Now, the sweltering heat made him even drowsier.

Maddox was surprised not one fishing boat or jet ski plied the lagoon. Then he remembered last night, flipping through the channels in his motel room, when he caught the eleven o'clock news. He wondered if Lowry had, too. "How do you plan to deal with the quarantine?"

Lowry sneered. "Mr. Sorkin was right, you do worry about the wrong things."

Lowry's cavalier attitude annoyed him. "If the cops spot us, they'll jump on us like maggots on roadkill. That means I don't get my money."

The burly hit man glared at him. "I'll handle the cops. You're here for one purpose. Take me to the crab."

Maddox snickered. "I thought I was aboard for my good looks and charm."

"If that's what I wanted, I would've taken my dog." Lowry leaned in on Maddox. "And don't think I didn't notice you forgot Johnson's chart. Sorkin told me you'd have it with you."

"That was no memory lapse. That was my insurance policy."

Lowry shook his head. "Five years of doing business with Mr. Sorkin, then his generous loan, and all those breaks he gave you, you still don't trust him."

"Something Sorkin once told me. You can trust only two kinds of people. Children under five, and anyone six feet under. But don't worry, I memorized the plottings."

From the rear deck of the trawler, a crew member shouted, "We're ready."

Lowry held up his hand, then turned to Maddox, grinning. "Ready to fetch your reward?"

"Anytime you are."

Following Lowry, Maddox descended five metal steps off the concrete platform. They crossed a narrow service road hugging the sea wall to a steeply sloped gangway leading up to the trawler's deck.

At the top of the ramp, a tall, thin man with black hair and gaunt cheeks stood waiting to receive them. Lowry climbed the gangway and passed through an opening in a waist-high rail that circled the perimeter of the deck. He greeted the lanky sailor as Willie.

Tailing Lowry, Maddox hopped through the gate, and gave Willie a half-hearted wave. Lowry's lackey merely stared back with vacuous brown eyes.

Maddox got a closer look at the ship that would deliver them to the crab. A white fiberglass cabin, two decks high, sat slightly forward of midship. The cabin's upper level was ringed with tinted green windows, except for a white door that opened onto a narrow catwalk hugging the perimeter of the second level. He observed no windows on the lower level, only double doors allowing access through the cabin's aft wall.

Maddox walked alongside Lowry to the cargo hold in the middle of the rear deck. At the safety rail, Lowry leaned over and looked down. "When Mr. Sorkin's crab fills that hole, you'll be a rich man."

Maddox gazed at the crater's gleaming walls, smooth white fiberglass curving to a flat white bottom. "Yeah, if the police don't stop us first."

"Guess there's only one way to shut you up."

Maddox jumped back, keeping a wary eye on Lowry's hands.

Lowry let loose a raspy chuckle. He stepped away from the rail and walked toward the side of the two-story center cabin, waving for Maddox to follow. "Let me show you something."

Shadowing the burly blue suit, Maddox moved toward the vessel's bow, squeezing through the tight space between the cabin's exterior wall and low safety rail ringing the deck.

The boat shuddered.

Maddox instinctively grabbed the rail's top edge to keep from tumbling over.

"Better be careful," Lowry warned. "We're underway."

Bent over the rail, Maddox saw the hull and bulkhead inch apart. He uprighted himself, and leaned toward the cabin wall, as far from the outer rail as the slim space allowed.

The narrow walkway opened to a wide forward deck. Settling into his sea legs, Maddox shuffled to the ship's pointed bow and scanned the eastern horizon. Ahead, the channel snaked through tall swamp grass, emptying into a vast expanse of blue-green water. Surveying the bay for other vessels, he saw none.

"Over here."

Maddox turned, and almost peed his pants. Aimed directly at his head, a green tube, a missile launcher, propped on Lowry's shoulder, cocked and ready to fire. "What the hell are you doing?"

"Preparing."

Maddox leaped to his right and grabbed the port rail. If the muzzle followed, he'd jump.

Lowry lowered the launch tube, holding it plumb with the teak floor.

Maddox spat. "What the hell is wrong with you?"

Lowry broke into maniacal laughter. He moved his lips as if he wanted to speak, but could only shake his head. Finally, he found his voice. "Just testing the scope."

Maddox's urge to punch him in the face was tempered by two of Lowry's soldiers clutching semi-automatic rifles, standing guard on either side of their master.

Tears moistened Lowry's eyes. "I told you. Find me the crab, and I'll handle the cops."

Flush against the cabin's forward wall, directly behind Lowry, Maddox saw three wooden crates, each the size of a coffin. Lowry carefully laid the missile launcher inside the open box. Four of Lowry's soldiers pried open the other wooden boxes with iron crowbars.

Maddox crept to the box in which Lowry placed the green tube, and a chill ran up his spine. The crate was packed with four Javelin anti-aircraft missile launchers, complete with TV camera guidance systems and replaceable battery packs. In each of the second and third boxes he counted 20 dual-stage, thermal-guided tandem warheads. He was in the presence of enough firepower to knock out a squadron of Harrier jet fighters.

Lowry strolled to Maddox's side. "I'm not leaving this bay without Mr. Sorkin's crab."

"You'd really use these?"

Lowry's eyes probed him like deadly blue whirlpools. "You left your map at home. That was your insurance." He swept his arm over the launch tubes and missiles. "These ... these are mine."

32

Gazing out the window of the fourth floor day room, Allen watched Clayton jog to a white van idling curbside at the far end of the parking lot. He speculated the van was the same one BHERT had used yesterday afternoon to cart away the claw.

When Clayton reached the passenger door, he hopped into the front seat. Even before the door closed, the van jerked forward, darting onto Route 37's four lanes of open cement toward the Garden State Parkway.

Allen looked away from the window, and resigned himself to the loss of his son. Faced with the grim task of consoling his wife, he dropped onto an orange vinyl couch beneath a framed portrait of Barney. What would he tell her?

He hunched forward, sighed, and rubbed his cheeks with the palms of his hands, unable to imagine life without David. Jennifer fulfilled his need for mature, romantic love. His son delivered a different love, an enduring love measured as much by the incredible sacrifice required to sustain it as by the remarkable pride that only a parent could know.

Lamenting the inevitable, Allen scarcely noticed, next to the sofa, a toddler-sized drawing table, its cream-colored plastic top streaked with yellow, green, and blue crayon. On the far corner of the table, something caught his eye — a child's portable CD player, white with big blue buttons and red knobs large enough for tiny fingers to grasp.

For no reason, he reached over and picked up the CD player. Glimpsing inside the disk compartment, he spied the upper half of a CD, its lower half hidden by the compartment door. Without thinking, he pressed the play button. He heard nothing. Flipping the player over to inspect the back, he saw why. The cover to the battery well was gone and the well was empty.

For 30 seconds, Allen's eyes fixed on the hollow space. He remembered he had seen six "D" batteries aligned neatly on the shelf over the old desk in Laboratory B — and Miles' cryptic message: 'If I'm not back by 1 p.m., ask Enya to sing for you.' Of course!

He sprang from the sofa and ran to David's room. Last night, at three a.m., Jennifer had finally heeded the advice of the night-shift nurse, and lay on the empty bed nearest the door. Drained of hope and energy, she'd fallen into a deep sleep. Except for the sound of breathing — and the constant whirring of machines — the room was silent.

Allen crept into the bathroom and snatched a white paper towel from the dispenser. Leaning on the bathroom vanity, he scribbled a note to Jennifer. He set down his makeshift stationery on the night table, and slipped out of the room.

Choosing a route that would avoid the morning shoppers, he reached Salem Street in less than 12 minutes. Approaching Omnigen's parking lot, Allen slowed to a crawl. He expected to find a single car in the lot — Miles' run-down Cavalier. There it was, in its usual spot, first row on the far left. However, in the same row, over to the right, he saw a white station wagon. He wondered who might be visiting Omnigen so early.

He drove to the wagon and circled it slowly. On the driver's door, he spotted a sign: "Toms River Chronicle: Press Corps." The wagon must belong to the pesky news reporter Larry had warned him about. Allen thought he might leave now and return later, after the reporter was gone, but time was no luxury. He'd simply do his best to elude the reporter.

Allen parked at the curb and sprinted to Omnigen's front entrance. He found the door open and foyer dark. Strange the lights would be off with a visitor around. A plate of eight wall switches behind Ellen's desk activated ceiling fixtures throughout the building's corridors. One at a time, Allen flipped them on.

The antiseptic glare of fluorescent light saturated the front foyer and two hallways extending off to both sides at the far end. For several seconds, Allen stood motionless, listening for some reaction to the sudden glow. There was none.

Allen went directly to Laboratory B. Inside, nothing appeared to have been disturbed, at least not since yesterday. Though Clayton's men had taken the computer and boxes of documents, they had left behind one microscope, the gel electrophoresis units, transmission densitometer, and ultraviolet crosslinker. Perhaps Clayton would return for those later, after he arrested Maddox at Coney Island.

Allen strode to the shelf behind the black metal desk and plucked the CD off. He set it down, bottom-up, on the old desk, and with both thumbs, slid the door from the battery compartment. Wedged inside the well he saw a single two-inch disk.

He grabbed a pen from the desk drawer, and gently pried the disk from the battery well. To avoid smudging the glossy side that contained the data, he held the curved edge of the CD with his thumb and forefinger. He flipped the disk over to inspect the label. It was blank.

Miles had taken considerable pains to conceal the CD, so Allen knew whatever his colleague had written to it must be intended for his eyes only. But from every office and all three labs, Clayton's men had seized the computers. Without one, he could not examine the disk's contents.

Then he remembered his laptop. He purchased it last January intending to lug it along during David's increasingly frequent half-day radiation and chemotherapy sessions. He thought he might use it to perform T-tests on Genetyx output or analyze complex gene lysing models. In reality, Allen rarely used the machine, preferring to spend his precious time at David's side debating the latest Yankees trade or losing at a hand of Uno.

Allen stored his laptop behind the metal cabinet in his office. He saw it there yesterday morning when searching for his nautical chart, but hadn't checked again since BHERT's raid.

Holding the CD in his left hand, reaching for the doorknob with his right, he heard from behind a loud thud, like a falling slab of meat. He turned and gazed across the lab toward the source of the sound — the walk-in freezer. He waited several seconds, but heard only the low hum of the overhead fixtures. He dismissed the sudden noise as some normal function of the freezer's compressor. Pivoting, he left the lab, and hurried to his office.

He placed the CD on his desk, turned around, and peered behind the six-foot high cabinet. The black case, wedged against the wall, was exactly where he'd seen it yesterday morning. He lifted the laptop out, set it on his desk, and booted it up.

Sliding the CD into the laptop, he scrolled a directory of the disk's contents. What he found was a list of 20 WordPerfect files.

Opening the file at the head of the list, README.1ST, he did precisely that.

By the time Allen read to the top of the second page, his heart was racing. Miles, in his own words, was describing the contents of the remaining 19 files. By the time he reached the bottom of the fifth and last page, Allen was ecstatic. If everything in Miles' narrative checked out, having this disk would be like having Miles himself stand over his shoulder to explain and supervise, step-by-step, the Hope-1 gene extraction procedure and ribozyme delivery process. Allen came to the last paragraph:

> You are reading this because for reasons beyond my control I am unable to assist you in locating the crab and implanting its Hope-1 genes in David. Please do not interpret my absence as a lack of desire or change of heart. That you are reading these words means only one thing. My assistance is no longer possible. Open SEQ1.EXT first. It contains the procedure for cleaving Hope-1 from Chromosome 8. From there, follow my instructions and you will have no difficulty completing the protocol. You have been a loyal friend. Good luck, and may David live a full life.
>
> Nathan.

For the next 10 minutes, Allen scanned at random six other files on the disk. In concise detail, Miles described the complete procedure, from splicing the crab's Hope-1 alleles using restriction endonuclease enzymes to combining them with the genes of cancerous cells using the ribozyme-catalyzed cleavage and ligation technique Allen himself had devised. With these instructions, only one thing was missing: viable tissue from the crab.

Next low tide arriving at 2:38, Allen had no time to waste. He popped the disk from the E-drive, dropped it in a clear plastic holder, and packed it up along with the laptop in the black fabric case.

As he lifted its handle, the telephone rang.

Allen hesitated, realizing it might be Jennifer. By now, she was probably awake and had read the note he left behind.

He picked up the phone. "Omnigen Labs."

"Allen, it's me." The voice belonged to Larry. "I heard about David. I'm sorry."

"So am I."

"What can I do to help?"

"Whatever can be done, I'm doing."

"I need to see you right away."

"Not today."

"You hear the crab struck twice yesterday, once off Lanoka Harbor, and later, near Sunrise Beach?"

"I found out this morning."

Bateman paused, as if waiting for Allen to add something.

He didn't.

"Your calculations were off."

"I apologize."

"You seemed so sure."

"Even scientists make mistakes."

"I'm in my car, Allen. Just turned left onto Route 70. I'll be there in 10 minutes."

"I can't. Not today."

"If I don't get the claw to state forensics by five, it's my job."

Allen could only tell the truth. "I'm sorry, Larry, but the claw's gone. I take full responsibility, but there's nothing I can do."

Bateman stammered:

"What ... what do you mean it's —"

"I can't talk now."

The urgent voice of his friend beseeching him for an explanation trailed off as Allen placed the receiver on the hook.

Seconds later, the phone rang again.

This time, Allen bolted from his office.

He tossed the laptop onto the back seat of his Honda and sped away. Crossing paths with Larry would not be a good idea, so he slipped out of the industrial park over a bumpy dirt road reserved for construction equipment.

Cheating four yellow lights and ignoring one indisputably red, Allen reached his home on the barrier island in under 20 minutes. He pulled into the driveway and dashed to the wooden shed in his backyard. Fumbling with his key, he removed the padlock and opened the door.

From off an open shelf, he grabbed the two-gallon, black plastic deck sprayer he'd bought last fall to stain the stockade fence enclosing his back yard. Next, he spun three numbers on a combination lock securing a wall-mounted cabinet door. He yanked off the lock, withdrew a brown glass bottle, and placed it on the bench next to the sprayer. He twisted the sprayer's pump handle counter-clockwise, removed the pump assembly, and set it on the shelf beside the jar. Unscrewing the jar's lid, Allen found it half-filled with white powder. Carefully, he shook half the remaining contents into the pump well, paused, then poured in the rest. Yes, tricaine methanesulfonate was potent, but he'd also seen the strength of the crab.

Allen shoved the empty jar back in the cabinet and locked the door. Clutching the deck sprayer, he sprinted to the outdoor faucet at the side of his house and filled the tank with water. He ran to his Honda, opened the trunk, and lay the sprayer inside.

Gripping the car door handle, he froze in his tracks. What if the MS-222 failed to sedate the crab? To play it safe, he'd take along his sedative of last resort. Entering the house through the front door, he bolted straight for the master bedroom closet. From the top shelf, he grabbed his 9mm Beretta. He felt around until he grasped two magazines, each pre-loaded with six rounds, the maximum his practice range allowed in a single clip.

He threw the pistol and clips into the trunk and sped two miles north to Chadwick Marina. On this hot, sunny morning, Allen was surprised to find no boats lined up to launch from the marina's only ramp. In fact, the normally bustling marina looked abandoned.

Of course, the quarantine. The scarcity of sailors and vessels made perfect sense. He pulled into the dirt parking spot in front of his slip, stepped into his Whaler, and started the engine. He fetched his gun and both clips and stuffed them inside the storage cubicle built into the control console.

He returned to his Honda's trunk, removed the deck sprayer, and hauled it back to the boat. Kneeling on the dock, he lowered the black tank, heavy from the liquid sedative, onto the forward deck, and leaned it against the console's front panel.

His eyes lingered on the pump. With his Whaler's flat hull, the ride on the bay could get bumpy. If the tank fell over and rolled around the floor, the spray mechanism might get damaged. Allen hopped onto the deck, unlatched the bow storage hatch and tucked the plastic canister safely inside.

Letting his outboard warm up, Allen sprinted to a lone pay phone on the marina's deserted dock, and punched in the number of the only person alive with the power to stop him.

She answered on the first ring.

"Sorry I didn't say good-bye, but you were sleeping so soundly."

"I read your note. When are you leaving the lab?"

"I already did."

"Where are you now?"

"The marina."

"So you found Miles?"

"Sort of."

"What do you mean? Is he helping you or not?"

Jennifer would never allow him to proceed without Miles' help, so he answered as honestly as circumstances permitted. "He is. He's definitely helping me."

"Good, because David's getting ..." Her voice cracked. "Allen, we're losing him. Dr. Loman said ..." Silence.

"Jennifer, are you there?"

"... He said if we believed in God, we should call ..." She broke into muffled sobs.

"Jenn?"

"Yes."

"Don't call anyone. We're not through yet."

He heard only soft whimpering.

"Listen carefully. If we're going to do this, it'll have to be tonight. After I get the tissue, I'm heading straight to the hospital. Have David ready by four. I don't care what happens, but we're taking him out, with or without Loman's consent. The doctors gave it their best shot. Now it's our turn."

She whispered the words he longed to hear. "I'm with you."

"That's all I need to know." He felt his chest pounding. "I love you, Jenn."

"I love you, too. Please be careful."

"See you at four."

Allen ran to his Whaler, coaxed its 90 horses to life, and steered west. Destination: Barnegat Bay. Ironic how all his life he had been master of his destiny. Now, with everything to lose, luck was his only companion.

33

Clayton strode across the tarmac, Jacobs scurrying beside him, to the Sikorsky CH-53-E Super Stallion standing by to fly his team to Floyd Bennett Field in Brooklyn.

The deafening roar of the helicopter's twin turbines preparing to ascend from the deserted helipad at Ocean County Airpark nearly drowned Jacobs out. "A detail from Station 15 will be waiting to meet us on the ground, sir."

Seven feet separated Clayton's head from the screaming propellers overhead. Nevertheless, he instinctively hunched and ducked as he pulled himself into the chopper's cabin. Once inside, he turned, grabbed Jacobs' hand, and pulled him up. Jacobs slid shut the insulated door, instantly muffling the cacophony of whining turbines.

Ferraro, wearing a headset with a wire mouthpiece curled from her ear to her lips, sat before a complex panel of electronic communications equipment. Like Clayton and Jacobs, she wore the standard olive green jumpsuit site-specific for North American urban operations.

Clayton took the furthest of two vacant seats on Ferraro's right. Buckling himself in, he motioned for Jacobs to sit between them.

Jacobs sprung into the chair and tightened his harness.

Clayton flashed thumbs up to Ferraro, who instantly barked into the microphone, "Ready for departure."

Ryan's answer roared through the cabin. "Roller-coaster time!"

Clayton chuckled at Ryan's allusion to the Cyclone at Coney Island.

In a single fluid motion, the chopper lifted off the ground and banked sharply left. Clayton's gastric juices churned like a washing machine in spin cycle.

Though Ryan could be a cowboy at the wheel, Clayton trusted him more than any transportation specialist at BHERT to deliver his team, unscathed and on time, anywhere in the world. Ryan could do it all — drive, fly, sail, paddle, glide, cycle — operate any vehicle known to modern or ancient man.

When Clayton's intestines regrouped, he turned to Jacobs. "How many can we count on from RS-15?"

"Six."

"Transportation?"

"Two vehicles, sir. One van and one car."

"What about the FBI?"

Jacobs shook his head. "BHERT's alone on this."

"Good. How's the weather?"

"Sky's clear all the way to New York, sir. Wind's blowing 10 knots from the south. ETA to Floyd Bennett, 12:32."

"Floyd Bennett to Coney Island?"

"Ten minutes."

"Excellent." Leaning behind Jacobs' back, he called out to Ferraro, "Raise RS-15. Make sure they're waiting at the pad. I don't want any screw-ups."

"Will do."

An unpleasant thought came to Clayton. He tapped Jacobs' shoulder. "I presume our commander in chief *has* issued an executive arrest warrant?"

"Yes, sir." His voice rang with confidence. "Delivered at 1100 hours, Eastern Standard Time."

Clayton smiled. No delays, no waiting, no problems. With nothing to hinder their mission, in little over an hour, his team would stop Maddox cold in his tracks, and for added measure, nab the crazy Texan who had eluded the FBI for over a decade.

《☆》   《☆》   《☆》

Bateman pulled into the spot reserved for chief of surgery, steps from the hospital's main entrance. His patrol car topped with a full rack of emergency lights, he didn't expect to get towed.

Squeezing in four hours of broken sleep on a bumpy cot at Point Pleasant Station, Bateman awoke feeling grimy and gritty. Rising early, he had showered, shaved, and changed into his spare uniform before taking his futile drive to Omnigen to reclaim his claw from Allen.

In the main lobby, he sailed past a plump security guard lounging behind a desk, hopped into the elevator, and hit the button labeled "Fourth Floor, Pediatrics Wing."

Alone in the rising cubicle, Bateman hoped his friend had returned to the hospital and was prepared to give him straight answers. Twenty minutes earlier, in Omnigen's parking lot, Bateman hadn't seen Allen's car anywhere. He spotted Brian Strasser's white station wagon, but no blue Honda. Bateman wondered if the obnoxious reporter had forced Allen to make a fast exit.

Whatever the reason for Allen's elusive behavior, it meant only one thing — he was in trouble. Bateman had a duty to find out what kind, and how he could help.

He stepped off the elevator and walked directly to the nurses station, where he spied two ladies in white sitting behind a chest-high counter. One, a white-haired matron, poured over hospital records, the other, a pretty brunette, looked up as he approached.

"May I help you?"

"I'm looking for David Johnson's room."

The middle-aged RN, head down, eyes buried in her charts, said curtly, "Visiting hours start at 11."

Bateman summoned the stern inflection he often used to interrogate suspects. "I'm here on official business."

She looked up. "I see," then pointed down the corridor. "Fifth door on the right. Room 416."

Bateman turned brusquely and walked toward a rolling rack of covered aluminum trays in the middle of the hall he guessed held lunch for the children. Behind him, he heard the old woman whisper something to the young nurse, but was unable to make out what she said.

Butterflies fluttered in Bateman's stomach when he approached David's room.

He peeked inside and saw two beds. David lay on the bed nearer the window, and appeared asleep. Jennifer, her back to the door, leaned forward in a plastic orange chair, grasping her son's hand. No sign of Allen.

He knocked lightly.

Jennifer turned her head.

"I hope this isn't a bad time."

"No, come in."

Jennifer stood and met Bateman halfway. Her large brown eyes were pink and puffy. Speaking softly, she updated Bateman on David's condition, explaining how the tumor had invaded his hypothalamus and pituitary, causing him to lapse into a coma and putting his life in imminent danger.

"I'll do whatever I can to help. When I asked Allen, he —"

"You spoke with Allen?"

"Called him at the lab about half an hour ago. Actually, I thought he was coming here."

Jennifer lowered her eyes.

"Do you know where he is?"

She turned and lumbered to the window.

Bateman followed, pausing two steps behind. She stared outside, so he could not read her eyes, but sensed within her raging turmoil. He said nothing, and instead, waited for an answer.

David's room faced east, and from this vantage, Bateman could see clear across the coastal plain to Barnegat Bay. Under the cloudless blue sky, he picked out the ferris wheel at Seaside Heights, and beyond that, the Atlantic Ocean.

Jennifer's hands rose to her face, and her shoulders began to shudder. She stood an arm's length away, yet Bateman could scarcely hear her sobs.

He stepped to her side and held her arm. "Is Allen in some sort of trouble?"

She hastily wiped away her tears, as if embarrassed by her own grief. "More than anything, he wants David to live, even if it means risking his own life."

"What exactly is he doing?"

"It's about that claw you asked him to examine."

Bateman cringed. "I guess he told you."

"More than you know." Her eyes fixed on his. "You said you'd do whatever you could to help."

Bateman nodded.

"There's something you can do, but know up front, I promised Allen I wouldn't say anything, not even to you. I break my word now for only one reason. If you understand how much this means to him, and to me, maybe you won't stop him. Maybe you'll help him."

Jennifer explained how Allen and Miles had found a mutation in the crab's mortality genes, tripling its life span. She told him how they discovered another mutation on a different gene, a mutation that amplified and altered the crab's tumor-suppressor enzymes and effectively prevented the growth of cancer, how it even shrunk tumors in three laboratory mice. She explained that Allen and Miles planned to harness the mutant tumor-suppressor genes and inject them into David's tumor. Finally, she admitted that Allen had already taken the first essential step — hunt the crab for its tissue.

Jennifer sighed heavily, as if a great weight had been lifted. Her moist brown eyes thinned to narrow slivers. "Will you help my husband?"

Bateman wasn't sure if he understood all the details of Jennifer's explanation, but one thing was crystal clear. Allen was dead wrong if he thought he could handle the crab alone.

Jennifer hadn't mentioned the quarantine, so Bateman figured Allen didn't know — either that, or he hadn't told her. Bateman saw no reason to heap more worry on a mother and wife already in fear of losing her family. "I'll do what I can, but no guarantees. My job is to protect my troopers, your husband, or anyone else who wanders into the bay. That crab may possess some incredible power to cure, but it's also inflicted some terrible injury. If it threatens anyone, I'll have to destroy it."

Though Jennifer did not answer, her wounded eyes cried out.

"Look, Jennifer, I can't promise him the crab, but maybe I'll stop him from killing himself." He turned and walked to the door. At the threshold, he remembered something. "Did Allen mention if he removed the claw from the lab?"

She gave a quizzical look. "As far as I know, they did all their research at Omnigen. Why?"

"Never mind." Bateman glanced at the comatose boy. "Judy and I will keep David in our prayers."

"Thank you."

As Bateman walked toward the nurses station, the older RN looked up from her paperwork, glowering. Her tone was severe and tinged with sarcasm. "Anyone else we should expect for Dr. Johnson before visiting hours start?"

Bateman marched straight to the counter.

"Why? Who else was here?"

The cranky nurse pierced him with stern blue eyes. "I'm not stupid. Either Dr. Johnson's some sort of government spy or he's in trouble with the law."

"What's that supposed to mean?"

"Sun's hardly up, and some gung-ho Green Beret type comes barging in here like Rambo. Now he's got a state trooper after him. I'm no Einstein, but I can put two and two together."

"Who was the other man?"

"Some big shot — definitely not from around here. Acted like he was from the Army or something. Wore all kinds of fancy patches on his uniform. He said the same thing you did when I tried to stop him, official business."

"Anything else?"

"No, just that he had to see Dr. Johnson." She leaned forward, glanced both ways, and whispered, "Exactly what kind of trouble is Dr. Johnson in? Such a shame, his son so sick and all. Just tell me. Is he dangerous?"

Bateman scowled. "No, he's not dangerous."

"Don't be so sure. Him and that man from the Army. They started hollering at each other in the day room. Sounded like one of them punched the phone on the wall. Had to go in there and shut 'em up."

Guessing he already knew the answer, Bateman said, "Happen to hear what they argued about?"

She cupped one hand to the side of her mouth, as if divulging top-secret military codes. "I heard the man from the Army tell Dr. Johnson about the governor's order. Warned him he'd be arrested if he so much as went near the bay."

She'd given him one answer. Allen had gone out, despite the quarantine. "What else did he say?"

"That's all I heard."

"Thanks."

Bateman stood in the fourth floor lobby waiting for the elevator. When the bell sounded its arrival, the snoopy nurse called out, "Are you sure Dr. Johnson's not dangerous?"

Bateman glared at her. "I'm sure. Just do what you get paid to do, take care of his little boy."

He spun and marched into the elevator. Whatever trouble his friend was in, he must be in deep.

⟨🦀⟩　　⟨🦀⟩　　⟨🦀⟩

Having memorized the blue and red lines Dr. Johnson had penciled on his nautical chart, Devon Maddox fixed the probable location of the crab somewhere near the mouth of Oyster Creek Channel. Standing beside Lowry in the trawler's bow, Maddox scoured the sea for some sign of their quarry.

Cruising at eight knots, the sleek Avanti led the trawler by 200 feet. Maddox spotted a short man with bronze skin whose uniform was soaked with the blood of haddock entrails he chummed over the Avanti's side. Lowry counted on the fish guts to lure the elusive crustacean to the surface.

Maddox observed in the open water ahead the point where Oyster Creek Channel branched off the Intracoastal Waterway. A red and white striped pole mounted to submerged pilings marked the intersection.

Maddox waved his right arm over his head and pointed left, signaling the Avanti's skipper to turn.

The dark man in the bloody uniform said something to the driver. Immediately, Maddox observed the wake of the speedboat cut a gradual arc east.

Oyster Creek Channel, in most spots narrower than 100 yards, wound two and a quarter miles southeast to Barnegat Inlet. On the water's surface, a series of channel markers, red and green triangles nailed to wooden sticks jutting out from the water at intervals of several hundred feet, provided the only man-made evidence of the channel's course.

But the pole markers were notoriously unreliable due to the whimsical nature of shifting shoals on either side of the channel. Many a weekend sailor neglected the subtle differences in the blues and greens of the bay, and found himself grounded on silt hidden inches beneath the surface. Experienced navigators knew to trust the royal blues and dark sapphires to reveal the path of deep water rather than rely on man-made signposts to guide them through the channel.

"Dead ahead! Dead ahead!"

Maddox turned and looked up.

Behind him, on the roof of the trawler's two-story cabin, Willie pointed to the water between the trawler's bow and the Avanti's stern. "There! Over there!"

Maddox surveyed the dark blue swells to see why Willie screamed like a lunatic. Then he saw it, off the port bow, 50 feet away, just below the surface.

What impressed him first was the animal's graceful ferocity. Its olive green legs and paddles, and bright blue claw, all fluttered with synchronized dexterity, like a ballerina with too many arms and legs. The crab was a monster, terrifying and ugly, yet Maddox found beauty in the way it moved its slimy, horrible appendages, extruding from under a shiny turquoise mound as large as a tiny island.

Maddox stared in awe. The crab's features were flawlessly proportioned. Except for its gargantuan size, it looked like any other he'd seen on ice at Marty's Fish House.

Lowry shouted, "Starboard! Starboard!"

The trawler yawed hard right.

Maddox nearly dropped to the floor, grabbing the bow rail at the last second. He recovered his footing and watched the speedboat swing in a wide semicircle until the port sides of the trawler and Avanti drifted parallel, in opposite directions, 100 feet apart, the crab in between.

Maddox heard a loud whoosh, looked up, and saw a white spear-like projectile streak overhead. The harpoon, with some sort of line attached to its tail, crashed beneath the water behind the speedboat, then quickly bobbed to the surface.

Using the grapneled end of a long rod, the dark man with blood-stained clothes fished the rope from the water. He detached the line from the white harpoon, and tied it to a brass cleat on the Avanti's bow.

Maddox gaped at Willie who, on the top of the trawler's two-story cabin, threaded a heavy black net onto the rope sloping down to the speedboat.

Within seconds, the 10-foot high webbing slid down the rope and spanned the water. Willie passed the cable from the roof of the trawler's cabin to a pair of outstretched arms below. That man, in turn, passed it down from the cabin's upper level to a man on the main deck. He grabbed the line and fed it through a motorized winch mounted to the bulwark on the ship's bow. Tightening the slack, he secured the net that now crossed from the bow of the trawler to the bow of the Avanti. Lowry's crew had cut off one path of escape open to the crab.

"We've got trouble!"

Maddox looked up.

Willie, who had jumped from the roof of the cabin to the catwalk below, jabbed his finger toward the back of the trawler.

Standing on the forward deck, with the two-story cabin blocking his view to the stern, Maddox could not pick out the object of Willie's ire. Then he heard the deep voice of a young man speaking through a bullhorn. "New Jersey State Police. Stop your engines. I repeat, stop your engines."

Lowry barked orders at four soldiers standing along the port rail, and instantly, eight eager hands foraged through the wooden crates lined up against the cabin's front wall. The tallest of the four men lifted a Javelin rocket launcher from the first box. From the crate beside it, each of the others extracted one warhead. Carefully cradling their deadly weapons, all four disappeared around the cabin's starboard side.

Lowry turned to Maddox. "Follow me. I'll show you how I handle trouble."

Effectively, Maddox thought, very effectively. He followed Lowry to the trawler's rear deck.

At the far end of the boat, he beheld the backs of 11 red uniforms, roughly half of Lowry's crew, lined up along the stern rail. The tallest of the hired hoods looking out over the transom stood in the center, cradling the green launch tube. Each of the two thugs standing at opposite ends of the line kept one hand on the rail, the other, on the grip of black semi-automatic pistols holstered to their waists.

Between the backs and shoulders of the thugs, Maddox spotted a fiberglass skiff, about 20 feet long, clearly marked New Jersey State Police — Marine Rescue. The small vessel, about 50 yards behind the trawler, approached slowly.

Maddox saw the police boat's crew consisted of a lone state trooper wearing a navy blue uniform. A bright red baseball cap covered his short-cropped hair, and his ruddy face, all angles, wore a serious expression.

Lowry thundered a command to the missile-toting soldier.

The obedient warrior, in a single fluid motion, swung the tube onto his shoulder, pointed it at the police boat, and fired.   A line of yellow flame rocketed straight for the tiny vessel leaving behind a thin line of white smoke gliding two feet above the waves.

In the instant before the young man's wide blue eyes vanished behind an exploding fountain of shattered sea, Maddox read the look of abject terror.

Incredibly, the officer and his boat, unscathed, plowed through the towering eruption of water that rained down behind him on the rolling waves.

Lowry charged the killer who missed his mark. "You idiot!"

The police boat with its frightened pilot sliced a sharp, hasty turn.

Maddox was relieved the trooper hadn't given Lowry a fight. "Look at that. He's running like a jackrabbit."

Lowry turned to Maddox with glazed lifeless eyes. "I wasn't trying to scare him."

He growled at the wincing sailor who clutched the launcher. "Miss again, and I'll give you a fucking enema you'll never forget."

Sorkin's mercenary lifted the missile launcher to his shoulder, this time, taking deliberate aim.

When he pulled the trigger, another shell flared white hot from the head of the green cylinder, rapidly descending in a blazing streak toward the back of the fleeing trooper. A deafening explosion lit the water where the boat had been, and from the sky showered broken objects and tattered flesh.

Maddox swallowed hard. "A little extreme, don't you think?"

Lowry's glassy gaze locked on Maddox. "That's one less I gotta' kill later."

34

Pausing on the highest step of the hospital entrance, Lieutenant Larry Bateman noticed a portly man clad in navy blue peering into the open driver's side window of his patrol car. Bateman strode closer, and saw it was the same security guard he had passed in the lobby 30 minutes earlier on his way up to David's room. Yellow patches shaped like shields stitched onto the forearms of the man's costume convinced Bateman the garb had been cunningly designed to mimic the uniform of a real police officer.

The wannabe cop must have heard Bateman approach. He glanced back and jerked his head out, thumping his skull against the window frame. His plump cheeks turned beet red. "Dr. Steinman wasn't too pleased you took his spot."

In no mood for nonsense, Bateman grabbed the handle of his service revolver, secure in its holster. "Tell the good doc I made you turn it over at gunpoint."

The guard staggered back, gaping at Bateman as if he were crazed.

Bateman hopped into the front seat and turned the key. Instantly, the radio under the dashboard crackled to life.

"... Roost to Stray Chick. Do you copy. I repeat, Hen's Roost to Stray Chick. This is an emergency."

It was Trooper Callen, her voice near panic.

Bateman had shut off his hand-held radio before entering the pediatrics wing, breaking contact with headquarters for a full 30 minutes. He snatched the microphone to his lips. "Stray Chick here. Stray Chick here. Do you copy?"

"Thank God!"

"What's the problem?"

"We have two confirmed explosions off Oyster Creek, approximately 1,000 yards northeast of Marker-B1."

"What kind?"

"Bombs, sir. We're not sure. Bombs or missiles. Maybe torpedoes."

"Torpedoes!"

"Nelson says they originated due east of the explosions — from a vessel."

"What kind?"

"Nelson spotted two. One's a speedboat." Callen's voice cracked. "... the other, he's not sure, maybe a fishing charter, but a lot bigger. Maybe a trawler. One of them, he doesn't know which, shot at Harrelson."

He couldn't believe his ears. "On purpose?"

"Affirmative, sir. We don't know why, but they blew up Harrelson's boat. Unprovoked. Totally unprovoked."

"What's his status?"

"He's dead, sir ... Harrelson's dead."

The words rocked Bateman like a fist. He hung onto whatever calm he could muster. "Listen to me, Callen. Listen very carefully to what I'm about to tell you. Order everyone away from those boats immediately. Get them out of range *now*. Do you copy?"

No answer.

Bateman fought his impulse to scream into the mike. The troopers on the bay were his responsibility, and he wasn't about to lose another. "Hen's Roost, I repeat, do — you — copy?"

Hesitation, then a wobbly voice. "Loud and clear, sir."

"Listen. Get hold of O'Donnell. Tell him to meet me dockside in seven minutes. I want Number 24 gassed and ready to go. Tell him to stow my Remington and 20 loaded clips." Bateman clenched the mike so hard, he cracked its casing. "But most important. Get everyone away from those boats ASAP. Raise Nelson and the others. Tell them I'll be there in 30 minutes. Do you copy?"

Another pause, then a sullen voice. "Yes, Stray Chick, I copy."

Bateman threw his car into reverse, screeched out of Dr. Steinman's spot, and flew onto Route 37.

The desperate blue eyes of the young trooper obliterated by Sorkin's missile etched like a blade in Maddox's mind. Not even the din of barked orders and shouted commands from all around could erase the haunting image of the doomed man's terror.

In a blur of coordinated confusion, Lowry's crew secured a second net to a cable strung from the back of the trawler to the back of the Avanti. When they were done, a pair of submerged nets connected the trawler to the speedboat, bow-to-bow and stern-to-stern. The two vessels, 50 feet apart and parallel, and the two netted lines connecting them, formed a trapezoid cage in the water from which the giant crab could not escape.

Maddox watched from the trawler's port rail as Lowry's men swung the boom over the water. They planned to grasp the crab with the four-pronged pincer, hoist the creature aboard, and drop it into the open cargo hold in the rear deck.

But Lowry's men were having difficulty placing the steel pincer directly over the crab's six-foot wide ovular shell. Their struggle reminded Maddox of an arcade game he once saw where the object was to maneuver a metal claw locked in a glass case over a small stuffed animal, then drop the claw and grab the prize. This seemingly simple task always proved harder in the attempt, and the cherished toy almost always evaded the grip of the retractable vise.

Five times, the crane operator swung the grapnel over the crab. Five times, when the hook was lowered, the crab scuttled away to a different location within the trapezoid.

After the last attempt, the crab swam to the side of the trawler, snuggling against its wooden hull. Staring down from the rail, Maddox saw a green mound, the top of the crab's shell, break the water's surface. The darting of the crab from place-to-place between the nets had churned the silt on the bay floor, turning the blue sea murky brown.

Maddox glanced across the water to the Avanti, and spotted one of its crewman pulling up anchor.

At the same time, two men, one at each end of the trawler, began cranking feverishly, reeling in the two lines from which the nets clung. As they pulled aboard the netted lines, the Avanti drew closer to the trawler, shrinking the sides of the trapezoid.

The crab began whipping its intact claw against the trawler's bottom, intermittently at first, then furiously, as if trying to break through the trawler's hull. Each blow rocked Maddox's feet, but the ship's double-planked hull held firm. With only two feet of clearance between the bottom of the hull and the bay floor, and the Avanti now within 20 feet of the trawler, the crab had nowhere to run.

The mechanical hum of the hydraulic hoist started up again, and the huge stainless steel prongs, gaping like the mouth of a hungry shark, swung over the open water, back toward the hull, stopping directly over the crab's carapace.

Lowry pointed up to the giant four-pronged hook. "This time, lower it slowly."

A blue-eyed man with black hair working a control box at the base of the mast pulled a lever.

Maddox edged closer to the rail for an unobstructed view. He stood riveted, watching thick, heavy chain trickle out from the tip of the boom. The grapnel, its teeth spread wide, inched lower, driving inexorably toward the crab's back.

When the massive prongs descended to within a yard of the crab's shell, Lowry raised his hand with open palm.

Instantly, the chain stopped feeding.

The glistening metal pincers dangled above the crab's shell. Lowry shouted, "Where are you?"

Lowry's lanky henchman, Willie, burst from a swinging door at the back of the trawler's cabin. He held a thin clear line, at the end of which dangled a live fish. Maddox had no idea what kind, but estimated its length at a foot and a half. Impaled on a black metal hook protruding from its bloody jaw, the silver-scaled creature flailed desperately. Maddox quivered. He realized the purpose of the fish was to bait the crab.

Approaching the rail, Willie slowed from a sprint to a shuffle.

Lowry snarled, "Don't waste time. Lower it!"

Willie leaned over the white metal rail, wincing as he hand-fed line until the thrashing tail of the doomed fish brushed the water's surface.

Maddox spotted two pearl spheres the size of bowling balls extrude from under the crab's shell. He presumed these were the crab's eyes, poking upward, focusing on the helpless fish.

The crab's glistening green carapace lunged at the living lure.

Lowry screamed, "Now!"

The open grapnel plunged. Its pronged tips grabbed the jagged rim of the crab's shell and held fast. Unfettered by the grapnel, the crab's single claw flew out from under the waves and flexed up over its shell, swinging at the chain above, missing every time.

The crab again smashed at the trawler's hull, each whack reverberating like thunder, shaking the ship like a toy boat in a bathtub.

A bestial scream pierced the cannonade. Maddox stood paralyzed as Willie toppled headfirst over the rail, his arms groping madly as he fell.

Passing before the bulbous eyes of the crab, Willie vanished beneath the waves.

The claw's thunderous barrage ceased.

Peering over the rail, Maddox saw the crab's monstrous claw dive beneath the surface.

"Faster! Faster!" Lowry screamed.

Like out of a Sunday matinee Maddox watched long ago, the pincers slowly lifted the massive crab out of the water until it hung two feet above the waves. The creaking and groaning of strained metal convinced Maddox the chain, boom, or mast would snap. The creature's six walking legs and two swimming paddles, each baby blue on one side, green on the other, probed frantically for footing.

The entire crab was visible but for the tip of its claw, and when that broke the surface, Maddox retched his morning egg.

Compressed within the crab's six-foot pincer were the head, arms, and torso of Willie, limp as a ragdoll. A gruesome solution of blood and sea oozed from every orifice of Willie's body — from his mouth, nose, ears, and from the purple cavity where his intestines and legs once were.

The frenzied thrashing of the crab's appendages shook the chain from which it hung, but the stainless steel grapnel refused to relinquish the prize.

Ogling at the crab, fearing for his life, Maddox took one step back from the port rail, spun, and bolted across the deck. He kept on going until he collided with the starboard rail on the opposite side of the ship. He leaned over, gazed down at the water, and with the back of his hand, wiped the acrid remnants of his breakfast. He turned and straightened, leaning back against the white metal rail.

With the writhing crab in the grapnel's clutches, the boom inched over the deck, toward the open cargo hold. A blend of muddy water and thick clear fluid poured from the joints of the crab's legs, swamping the polished teak with a slimy film.

Two of Lowry's crew, standing on opposite sides of the suspended crab, clutched 10-foot aluminum poles. They followed the moving boom, taking turns jabbing at the crab's writhing pincer, prodding it to release Willie's corpse.

Maddox glimpsed into the dead man's eyes — brown and wide and glazed with fear, as if they'd seen Satan himself.

The whining gears of the boom fell silent. The crab now hung directly above the center of the square hold.

Lowry stood at the edge of the safety rail surrounding the pit. "Lower it!" he commanded

"We can't leave Willie." It was one of the men who poked at the claw.

Lowry glared. "Shut up, or you'll be next."

The blue-eyed soldier at the foot of the mast yanked a lever. The crab with its flailing legs and corpse-laden claw, with its every pore spilling foul viscous sea water, descended slowly into the fiberglass pit.

When it was lowered out of sight, Maddox crept to the cargo hold's safety rail and stood beside Lowry.

Lowry turned to the crane operator. "Let her go!"

The prongs snapped open, and the crab dropped to the slick white floor. The beast opened its claw and flung Willie's body against the side of the pit. The force split open the dead man's skull, splattering the smooth white fiberglass red with brains and blood. The claw took aim for the retreating prongs, but the boom operator quickly hoisted the grapnel out of the crab's reach.

As if it understood the rising prongs had ascended too far, the crab pushed back on its front legs, wedging its two hind swimming legs into the far corners of the hold, then reared up at a 45 degree angle. It's broad milky white underbelly exposed, and single intact claw fully extended, the crab snapped savagely at the air.

Standing at the rail, frozen in fear, Maddox thought the pit might be too shallow to contain the enraged beast.

The giant crab, leveraging its weight against the corners of the hold, boosted itself higher on its rear swimming legs, until it stood nearly erect, and jabbed furiously at the grappling device inches beyond its reach.

When Maddox was certain the crab would leap from the hold onto the deck, consuming all in sight, one of the crab's swimming legs slipped from the corner of the pit. The monster lost its balance, toppled forward, and crashed flat on its belly. Looking down, Maddox stared mesmerized at the unearthly animal, again lashing and thrashing at the slippery walls, probing for something to latch to, struggling to climb out of its plastic prison and return to the bay. The incessant clattering of eight stone-hard legs and single massive claw pounding and scratching at the smooth surface was too much for Maddox to bear. He raised his hands to his ears and backed away from the cargo hold.

Two men lugged a fire hose across the deck, stopped at the rim of the pit, and pointed its brass nozzle downward. On Lowry's signal, salt water, pumped in from the bay, rained hard onto the crab's back. The torrent seemed to mollify the crab, for the smashing and rattling that echoed from the cargo hold subsided.

Flashing brilliant white teeth, Lowry shrugged. "Only one man lost. Not a bad price for Mr. Sorkin's wonder crab."

Maddox had but a single goal — get paid and get out. "Remember, he wasn't the only price."

Like a demented bully who thrills at dissecting spiders alive, the hoodlum in blue giggled. "Don't worry. You'll get the reward you deserve."

"ETA 12 minutes, sir."

Gazing out the helicopter's rectangular window, Clayton spotted the Verrazano-Narrows Bridge, its intricate latticework of pale blue cabling strung to a pair of 700-foot towers crossing the entrance to New York Harbor; beyond that, Lady Liberty, her tarnished copper washed-out green, except for the gilded copper torch she clutched high above her head. He saw in the distance, on all sides of these magnificent landmarks, a diverse collection of edifices — skyscrapers, row houses, brownstones, factories, tenements, hospitals, airports, and bus terminals — all testimony to the greatest city on Earth.

Clayton smiled at the irony that he would apprehend today's villains in his hometown borough of Brooklyn.

Sitting at the communications console, Sergeant Ferraro broke Clayton's spellbound admiration of New York City. "Just got word from Floyd Bennett. Two vehicles on the ground, warmed up and waiting."

"What's the status of Mobile 1?"

"Checked in two minutes ago. Maddox is right on schedule. His Mercedes left the New Jersey Turnpike at Exit 13. He's crossing the Goethals Bridge to Staten Island as we speak."

"Excellent," Clayton snapped. "Fair weather and time to spare. Maybe — just maybe — we can wrap up this operation by two and finish the paperwork by five. That'll put me at Marlene's side before bedtime."

Clayton looked away from the window. On the console before him, he spied a red loose-leaf binder with a white label on its spine: Operating Manual/D-14 NUA Remote Scanner Unit. He swiped up the book and mindlessly thumbed through its pages.

Jacobs turned to his boss. "If Sorkin shows up on time, we'll be in and out of Brooklyn in half an hour. There's no reason why —"

"Doctor Clayton," Ferraro interrupted, "I'm receiving a message from Remote Station 15. Sounds urgent"

"Put it on speaker."

Ferraro flipped a lever on the control panel.

"Clayton here."

Clayton recognized the male voice, a new BHERT recruit he'd met last night during his layover at Remote Station 15. "Four minutes ago we received a report of two explosions, Javelin signature, on Barnegat Bay — two miles due east of Oyster Creek Generating Station. Both targeted a New Jersey State Police rescue vessel. The second fire was a direct hit. Our information indicates both missiles originated from the deck of an unmarked fishing trawler heading for Barnegat Inlet. We've dispatched three mobile units, but you can get there faster."

Clayton was stunned. "I'm five minutes from target."

"There's more," said the anxious voice over the speaker. "An eyewitness, a New Jersey State Trooper tracking the trawler and a companion vessel, reported seeing an animal hoisted aboard the trawler, an animal that looked like —"

"Don't tell me," Clayton snapped, wishing he were wrong, but knowing he was right, "like a crab."

"As a matter of fact, that's exactly what he said."

Clayton yelled to Jacobs, "Raise Mobile 1. Have them pull the Mercedes over. Find out who the hell's driving that car."

"Now?"

"No, next week, when Sorkin turns it into a giant crab cake. Of course, now! And tell them to approach cautiously, weapons drawn."

"Yes, sir."

If the driver wasn't Maddox, it must be someone who worked for Sorkin, probably Jonathan Lowry, the Sorkin stooge who witnesses just this morning told investigators they hadn't seen since 6:30 last night, when he left his Manhattan office building.

Having disposed of Miles like yesterday's trash, Sorkin proved how desperately he coveted the Methuselah Gene. Whoever was at the wheel of the green Mercedes crossing the Goethals Bridge likely packed a piece, maybe two. And if those missiles flying over Barnegat Bay belonged to Sorkin, the driver could be carrying a whole lot worse.

Clutching the microphone, Jacobs looked at Clayton, and swallowed hard. "Sir, it's a 19-year-old kid, practically in tears. Says a Mr. Maddox, who lives in his condo, hired him to drive the car to Brooklyn. He's supposed to meet Maddox's ex-wife at an apartment building in Coney Island, across from the Cyclone."

"Damn it to hell!" Clayton shouted, hurling the red loose-leaf in his hands clear across the cabin. "We've been suckered!" He slammed a button on the control panel. "Ryan, turn this bird around. Set a course for Barnegat Bay, two miles east of Oyster Creek."

Ryan's voice crackled through an overhead grill. "But I'm preparing to set down. We're 500 feet over Fort Tilden."

"I don't care if we're over the damn Pentagon. Abort immediately! Get us to Barnegat Bay."

"Yes sir."

The helicopter banked hard to one side, nearly throwing Clayton over the armrest.

"Woooah!" Ferraro yelled from somewhere nearby.

When the chopper's attitude stabilized, Clayton sat upright. He frowned at Ferraro. "Call the good people waiting on the ground. Tell them we've had a last-minute change of plans, that we've been screwed like bunnies in heat. Advise them our targets will not, I repeat, will not be meeting in Brooklyn. Instruct them to proceed to Coney Island, anyway, just in case we're wrong. But warn them. The only thing they're likely to catch there is a Nathan's hot dog and a ride on the Wonder Wheel."

Clayton puffed an exasperated sigh, plopped back in his chair, and rolled his eyes. "I'll make this up to you Marlene. I swear, I'll make this up to you."

《※》　　*《※》*　　*《※》*

Strange how the vast blue Barnegat, at peak boating season, held not a sunfish or kayak. As a teen, when Allen cruised these waters in early spring and late autumn, he owned the bay. But never in summer, especially under a hot sun and blue sky.

Allen had expected to sight at least one or two state search and rescue cruisers on his journey south. According to Dr. Clayton, the governor had ordered a quarantine of Barnegat Bay. But he'd passed under the Route 37 twin bridges, come as far south as Cedar Creek, and hadn't spotted a solitary vessel. Steering his Whaler around Cedar Creek Point at Laurel Harbor, he understood why.

Across the bay, about three miles southeast, he saw two state police patrol skiffs anchored off the barrier island near Island Beach State Park; and two miles directly ahead, four police boats at the mouth of Forked River. Allen recognized one of the four ahead as Point Pleasant Station's largest rescue craft, a 40-foot behemoth Larry once told him could outrun anything on the bay.

All the more inexplicable so much horsepower would sit stationary when a massive vessel resembling a cargo ship loomed on the horizon. Allen estimated the ship's length at 100 feet. Its draft was probably too deep to permit a foray far from Oyster Creek Channel.

Behind the unidentified ship, on the northern tip of Long Beach Island, stood Barnegat Lighthouse, a 160-foot column of reinforced concrete, its upper-half painted red, its lower half, white. Using the lighthouse as his reference point, Allen quickly surmised the boat was on a direct course for Barnegat Inlet.

Allen eased off the throttle. Running his Evinrude at idle, he kept two miles between himself and the four police cruisers sitting in the water directly ahead at Forked River. The bay waves, pacified under the broiling sun, slapped gently against the sides of his Whaler.

Hoping for a closer look at the mystery vessel, Allen lifted his binoculars. What he saw astounded him.

Suspended above the ship's deck, hooked to some sort of crane, he observed six squirming legs, two writhing swimming paddles, and one thrashing cheliped, all joined to the thorax of a *Callinectes sapidus*. Under magnified vision, he watched the crab slowly disappear into the bowels of the ship.

The large vessel bore no markings, nor flew any flag. He picked out a dozen shadowy figures scurrying around the deck, apparently preoccupied with their incredible living cargo.

Why a formidable force of six police boats would allow the vessel to proceed unmolested, Allen couldn't guess — nor did he care. He had not betrayed his friend nor defied Clayton's warnings only to be thwarted by unknown poachers pilfering what must, for David's sake, be his.

〟〟   〟〟   〟〟

Lowry's depraved smile told Maddox he'd best claim his cash and get out. "I'm sure you're in a hurry to deliver the crab to Sorkin, so I'll take my money and be on my way."

Lowry's words slithered through perfect white teeth. "Mr. Sorkin was always good to you. He paid you top dollar for your military hardware, twice as much as anyone else would've paid."

"Yadda, yadda. So much for the good old days. Now give me the dough, and I'm outta' here."

Lowry continued as if Maddox hadn't spoken. "When you fucked up and got caught, Mr. Sorkin could've had you killed. At the snap of a finger, guaranteed your silence. But no, he trusted you, he let you live.

"He's a good man, Sorkin is."

"Then you go and squeeze him by the balls, threaten to squawk, until he just about gave the money away."

"Let's not rewrite history. The terms were decent, but you've always reminded me his money was no gift."

"He let you slide, no payments for 10 years, 10 years! Damn, he treated you good. But comes time to pay, you say you need more time, that if he won't give it, you're liable to dig up receipts and serial numbers you thought you'd burned long ago."

"I was kidding, I never kept records. They'd only get me in trouble."

Sorkin's enormous enforcer stood toe-to-toe with Maddox. "Anyone ever tell you what a shit you are?"

"You, lots of times, but why dredge up the past?"

"You always have."

"What's done is done. Today, I gave Sorkin something that'll add 60 years to his life, enough time to earn another billion. My measly loan will be long forgotten."

"That's the problem, you never forget."

Maddox took one step back, Lowry one step forward. "I promise. Once I leave this country, he'll never hear from me again."

"And when you blow your 20 million, then what? Time for Mr. Sorkin to bail you out again? And if he says no, then what? Time to extort more money? It'll never end, will it?"

Maddox took another step back. "I told you, I have no records. I have nothing on Sorkin."

Lowry advanced. "Maybe not for M4 carbines and Dragon missiles, but what about DNA sequences and gene-splicing protocols?"

"You have it all, the complete codon series for both mutations, and the four missing files explaining gene delivery. I didn't keep a thing."

"But you have your memory, don't you?"

Maddox found himself stepping backward, toward the center of the deck. "I won't say a word to the Feds."

Lowry kept pace, driving him forward. His grin broadened to a sinister smile, his big teeth shiny pearls. "No, this time around, I'm sure you won't."

Maddox tried cloaking his fear in a veil of hostility. "Look. Give me the money and the keys to the boat. We have no further business between us."

"I'm afraid you're mistaken."

Maddox glimpsed over his shoulder to see where his gradual retreat would lead. Less than 10 paces behind loomed the white metal rail ringing the cargo pit. From within the square hole, he heard loud sloshing sounds. "I gave you the codons, the protocols, and the crab. I kept my end of the bargain." He was surprised to hear his voice so quick and shrill. "Now it's Sorkin's turn. That's how we always did business."

Like a fox cornering a rabbit, Lowry bore down on Maddox. "That was a long time ago, before you tripped up, before you made your threats, when you weren't a thorn in his side."

Four uniformed sailors, two from each side, closed in on Maddox. Lowry blocked forward flight, the four thugs, both flanks. Maddox had nowhere to run.

Stepping backward, he glanced all around, searching for a way, any way, out of the fast-closing human trap. His back bumped hard against the rail ringing the pit. He turned his head and looked down. Behind him, the tremendous crustacean wallowed in the white pit, half-filled with sea water. Maddox pleaded for his life. "I won't say anything to anyone. Give me my money and you'll never hear from me again. Promise."

Lowry's vacuous blue eyes and seething hot breath were in Maddox's face. He said, smooth as satin, "You had your chance, and blew it. As long as you exist, you pose a threat to Mr. Sorkin."

Four sets of hands grasped his arms and legs, lifted him off the ground, and pointed him, head first, into the cargo hold.

Maddox screamed at the top of his lungs, "Please, Lowry! Please!"

The hands released their load.

Maddox didn't fall far before hitting the cool water pumped in from the bay. The sensation was surprisingly pleasant, like an invigorating dive in a salt water pool.

Underwater, he opened his eyes and beheld smooth, white fiberglass. He swam toward the sunlight, and when he broke the surface, gasped foul air heavy with the odor of fish.

Treading to stay afloat, he turned around.

In the middle of the pit, sticking up above the water, he observed two glossy silver globes, larger than softballs, three feet apart, set at the tips of two green fleshy tubes. The crab's eyes! In the center of each sphere, he saw a point of black light, small as a dime, the creature's pupils. The silver orbs fixed on him, studying his every move like the eyes of a famished cat stalking a field mouse. Directly behind the lustrous pearl spheres, Maddox noticed a green mound protruding from the water — the top of the crab's shell.

With nothing to grab hold of on the pit's slippery sides, Maddox paddled and kicked furiously to keep his head above water. He felt an undulating surge from below lift his entire body as he tread. He looked down, and saw the crab's mammoth green legs twist and wriggle inches beneath his feet.

The crab's carapace moved closer.

Just below the water line, four feet from his chest, he saw the creature's mouth, a shadowy gray rectangle, wide enough to swallow a tire, funneling deep into the crab's body. Around the rim of the mouth he could see hundreds of white, squirming protrusions, each about six inches long, that made clicking, mechanical sounds as they moved—probably used by the crab to shred its prey before eating.

A pair of three-foot long calipers, sharp at their tips, and white like the meat of the crab, stuck out from each side of the crustacean's mouth. They looked to Maddox like a pair of giant tweezers. In alternating synchrony, they swept anything and everything within their reach into the vapid orifice.

Something else underwater caught Maddox's eye — a red cylinder, one foot long, pink at both ends, impaled on one of the crab's calipers. Maddox figured it for rotted wood, perhaps pierced by the crab during its last feeding. On closer inspection, he saw that the red was cloth, soaked in blood, and the pink, human flesh. What he gazed upon was Willie's leg, severed at the knee and ankle.

Before he could scream, Maddox heard a loud hiss, like steam venting from a broken valve. The screeching sound came from beneath the surface, and issued from the mouth of the crab. An unseen force pulled at his body, drawing him closer to the calipers. He looked down, and almost too late, understood why. The crab's legs, below his feet, were sweeping water toward its mouth, preparing to feed. To the immense crustacean, Maddox must have resembled a tasty tidbit of shrimp. He dog-paddled like a madman until the hissing stopped and the pulling ceased, and he could again tread water freely.

Maddox's arms and legs throbbed from the strain of continuous motion. Craning his neck, he looked up to see if Lowry and his men were looking down. Perhaps if he apologized for his threats, they might pull him from this abyss, and show him the compassion of a single bullet to the head. But Maddox saw only the blue sky above. As Lowry had said, his existence must end.

The constant paddling and kicking finally sapped his arms and legs of their last strength. Just as Maddox thought he would sink and drown, something strange happened.

His stomach and back compressed together, as if caught in the grip of a nutcracker. Intense pressure was instantly replaced by exquisite pain, a thousand daggers thrust all at once into his belly and back. He tried kicking, but where his legs should be, he felt nothing. A power not his own transported him toward the bulbous gray eyes.

The unseen force turned his body sideways so that he now stared down at clear water only inches from his face. Maddox squeezed his eyes shut and shrieked like a wounded dog. An invisible power pulled him underwater and his mouth filled with salty liquid. Opening his eyes, the last thing he saw was Willie's leg, rushing past, and the last thing he felt, a flash of agony at the second his skull was pulverized by the mashing engines of the crab's voracious mouth parts.

For an instant, the drawbridge grating overhead blotted out the bright blue sky. When the speeding boat shot out from under the bridge, Officer O'Donnell throttled up on the howling twin Mercs, driving them to the breaking point. Fine with Bateman. He needed to make 15 miles in five minutes. Impossible, he knew, but when the lives of his men hung in the balance, impossible was no excuse.

Still reeling from the shock of Harrelson's cold-blooded murder, Bateman snapped a fully-loaded clip into his Remington's handle.

Whatever the objective of these strangers on the bay, they intended to kill anyone who got in their way. Five minutes earlier, Chopper Two had attempted a closer look. A surface-to-air missile shot from the trawler's deck missed the helicopter by yards. Unwilling to risk another approach from the sky, he must confront these assassins on the turf he knew best — the sea.

The wailing engines nearly drowned out Nelson's voice calling over the radio. "They're on the move again."

Bateman snapped up the microphone. "Direction and speed."

"Both vessels tracking northeast through Oyster Creek Channel, speed approximately eight knots, bearing, Barnegat Lighthouse. Present position, one-half mile due west of Great Sedge."

The gutless assassins would reach the inlet in less than half an hour. "Where are you, now?"

"Two hundred yards off Sunrise Beach."

"The others?"

"Sanderson's 20 yards behind me. Adler and Russo are over in Tice's Shoal."

"Good. Everyone stay put. O'Donnell and I are west of Curtis Point. You should have a visual on us in 10 minutes. Meanwhile, stay clear of those vessels. Do you copy?"

"Yes, sir. We won't move an inch until you're here."

Bateman shoved the microphone back in its harness. Instantly, Nelson's frantic voice howled over the radio.

"Lieutenant! Lieutenant! Another boat. I'm tracking another boat. Center console. It's gotta' be less than a 20-footer. Headed straight for the trawler."

Bateman grabbed the microphone. "How many on board?"

"I'll take a look ... only one ... looks like one male ... wait a second ... Holy shit! It's some lunatic with a pistol. He's firing at the trawler!"

36

Allen gunned his engine at full throttle, pointing the Whaler's bow between the four police boats directly ahead at the mouth of Forked River, and the other two huddled across the bay off the barrier island. He hoped by the time the state police realized what had happened, he'd charge through them like a running back up the middle. But for this down, the end zone lay four miles across the bay — on the trawler holding his son's salvation.

Running a straight line to his target, he crossed the bay's most deceptively shallow stretches, vast expanses of blue shrouding a muddy bottom, in some spots, less than a foot beneath the surface. Any deviation from the Intracoastal was particularly treacherous at low tide, but Allen had plied these waters before. He knew to avoid the pale greens and ginger browns of the bay, otherwise he risked fouling his propeller, or worse. Running aground on the shoals would bring his Whaler to an abrupt — and dangerous — standstill.

His throttle full-up, Allen raced for the trawler's stern, leaving a mile of open water between himself and the two groups of police boats to either side. When he looked back, not one of them followed — he hadn't even drawn a warning over the bullhorn.

Coming to within a half mile of the trawler's rear deck, Allen cut his speed to half-throttle and lifted his binoculars.

That was when the shooting began.

The first five rounds he heard as loud cracks from off the back of the trawler. The sixth was accompanied by a whining whiz screaming past his left ear. He crouched behind the center console, exposing his face from the nose-up. Clutching the steering wheel with one hand, he poked his other into the console's storage cubicle and pulled out his Beretta 92FS. Clicking off the safety, he lifted his arm over the console, and squeezed off two rounds in the general direction of the trawler's stern.

For no apparent reason, the gunfire stopped.

Standing erect, Allen slowed to one-quarter speed and stared out over the control console, trying to size up a vessel that looked formidably larger from 500 yards than it had four miles back.

Clearly, the ship operated under some authority other than the state or federal government. The shooters couldn't be Clayton's people. Three hours earlier, Clayton said he was leaving for Brooklyn to apprehend Devon Maddox and Robert Sorkin. They weren't the police. If anything, the police were staying well back, giving the renegade vessel wide berth.

Whoever operated the trawler had removed the crab from the bay without official approval. If he could somehow prevent the ship from reaching the ocean, he might board it and take the tissue he needed for David's therapy. Since Larry and his men were not likely to lend their assistance, or so it appeared, he'd have to devise a plan himself.

He could stop, or at least delay, the trawler's progress through Oyster Creek Channel by damaging its means of propulsion. From what Allen could see of the ship's design and twin exhaust pipes protruding from its stern, that meant disabling two inboard engines. Two well placed shots to the port and starboard sides of the stern, six inches above the water line, at just the right angle, should penetrate its wooden hull and bore through to the fuel line, fuel injectors, or injector pump.

The clip in Allen's Beretta still held four 9mm rounds, his spare magazine an additional six. With 10 more chances, two should reach their targets — that is, if he could get close enough.

Pulling to within 200 yards of the trawler's aft deck, Allen expected to be met with more gunfire, but oddly, the seven or eight men who were shooting at him two minutes ago had turned their backs to him. Allen cut his engine to trolling speed, set his Beretta on the console, within arm's reach, and lifted his binoculars.

Ten adult males, assorted heights and ages, wearing identical red uniforms, huddled around the center of the ship's stern deck, looking down. Allen picked out the profile of another man, brawnier than the others, wearing a dark blue business suit. He stood apart from the group, hands cupped to his mouth, and appeared to be shouting orders.

All at once, the entire band, including the leader, scattered in different directions. The 11 bug-eyed goons looked as if they would have run right off the deck into the bay, had they not been stopped by the ship's safety rail. Two appeared ready to leap over anyway.

His binoculars trained on the middle of the boat's aft deck, Allen discovered the reason for the crew's hasty retreat.

The tip of the mighty claw, brilliant blue, popped into view, then disappeared. The men on board the mystery ship must have dropped the crab into an open pen in the ship's deck. The fools had clearly misjudged the crab's strength and tenacity.

From a safe distance, the burly blue suit shouted more orders. Two sailors picked up long poles and crept back toward the center of the aft deck.

Again, the tip of the claw stabbed the air, this time, its pincers spread apart. The two advancing men sprang back, spun, and charged to opposite sides of the ship. Again, the leader barked at his men.

With the sailors and their taskmaster preoccupied with something other than him, now seemed as good a time as any to make a run at the ship's engines.

Allen nudged the throttle forward. He banked his trusty Whaler in a wide arc, gathering speed and momentum. By the time he swung full circle to the spot where he started, he was flying top speed, straight for the ship's stern.

At 100 yards, he saw the two reluctant henchmen back at the pit, angling their poles downward toward the center of the ship.

At 75 yards, the massive claw, wide open, again lunged into view.

At 50 yards, one of the men at the pit stumbled forward, dropping head-first, out of sight.

At 25 yards, Allen snatched his Beretta from the console, took aim at the transom, and squeezed the trigger four times.

The steep stern, dark green, came upon Allen like a wall. He yanked the wheel hard right. Instantly, his Whaler jumped the trawler's two-foot wake. Airborne, from the corner of his eye, a green corner flashed past.

His Whaler slammed the waves, on plane. Thankful the bone-jarring jolt hadn't knocked loose his Beretta, he popped the empty clip and snapped in his six-round spare.

Cutting a wide half-circle, away from the trawler's right side, he rode parallel to and in the opposite direction of the larger vessel.

When the ship's stern came into view, Allen was ecstatic. Heavy black smoke poured from its right engine.

His joy was short-lived. Even on a single engine, the ship holding David's last chance for life could limp through Barnegat Inlet. He must make one more go-round at the fleeing vessel's stern.

Looking back at the trawler, Allen saw the sailors turn their attention away from the crab and converge at the ship's starboard quarter. One man, a full head taller than the rest, hoisted a green cylindrical object to his shoulder and aimed it in Allen's direction.

The instant Allen realized the tube was a missile launcher, a searing point of light burst from the cylinder's tip. Seconds to think, Allen wrenched his steering wheel sharp left.

Gripping the wheel, he ducked behind the instrument panel, shielding his face with the hand that held the gun. A flash of white light, a deafening boom, and a scorching gust — that was all he saw or felt.

When the heat and light dissipated, Allen knew the rocket had missed. He looked back. Behind him, the sky glittered with a rainbow eruption of a billion salt water droplets shattered by the explosion. Glancing at his Evinrude, he saw it, too, had survived.

Allen's evasive maneuver put him back in the same direction as the trawler, a football field distance from its right side.

He watched the mob of henchmen scurry to the starboard rail. Mulling how he'd make a second run for the ship's good engine, he saw one of the scoundrels at the rail shove a rocket into the launch tube perched on the tall man's shoulder.

To dodge the next missile's trajectory, he'd have to use his speed. But how could he outrun a rocket?

He'd have to try something else.

Allen nudged his wheel left. Immediately, the featherweight craft responded. The gap between his Whaler's bow and the trawler's bow closed rapidly. If he cut in front of the ship, his attackers on the rear starboard deck would not get a clear shot. They'd have to move to the front deck, or the opposite side, and that would take time.

Skimming the waves on a track that put him just ahead of the trawler's bow, Allen glanced over his shoulder. The horde at the rail had disappeared. They must have anticipated his move.

Ten yards ahead, the trawler's bow plowed the sea. No time to turn, he zipped in front of the trawler's massive V-hull, narrowly avoiding a collision that would have sliced his boat in two.

On the ship's port side, Allen made a startling discovery. Alongside the trawler, in its shadow, cruised a smaller boat — long, slim, and built for speed.

Pondering the craft's purpose, he heard from directly behind the sound of gunfire, followed by a loud pop, like a cork sprung from a champagne bottle. He looked down and saw a fist-sized hole punched in the side of the Whaler, near the floor. Thankfully, daylight shone through. The bullet had ruptured the hull above the water line, but just barely.

Tearing at a right angle away from the trawler's port, Allen pointed his gun back toward the trawler and squeezed off four hasty shots before realizing how stupid he was to squander ammunition.

About half a mile dead ahead, Allen spotted the Sedge Islands, a cluster of flat, marshy islets hugging the inside southern tip of Island Beach. These overgrown mounds of mud blanketed with tall brown swamp stalks changed shape with each passing nor'easter. As a teen, Allen knew them as well as anyone. Their dense hay-like reeds, some as high as eight feet, would shield him long enough to evaluate his situation and plot a fresh course for disabling the trawler's one working engine.

The gunfire from behind stopped. Glimpsing back, Allen saw the speedboat veer away from the trawler's port side. Within seconds, it was ripping through the waves, straight for his tail. Allen counted three silhouettes on board, and in the arms of two, the sleek outline of a rocket launcher trained on his Evinrude.

Allen zigged and zagged through the gentle waves, his steering cable answering the call at each tug of the wheel. Just ahead, to his right, he spied the first of the marshy Sedges. He sped past two estuaries that wound deep into the willowy reeds. If memory served him, both of those led to dead-ends. But the next channel should cut through Little Sedge Island and drop him on the other side, off the bay shore of Island Beach. From there, he could elude his pursuers through a myriad of narrow waterways slicing through the swamps.

Afraid he might ground on the hazardous shallows surrounding the Sedges, he ignored the salt water spray that stung his eyes, and peered over his Whaler's console, following the darkest shades of blue.

Faster than he remembered, the third opening appeared. Jerking his wheel right, he shot into a narrow channel, its slim mouth no more than 10 feet wide, and was swallowed up by two walls of willowy swamp stalks covering both banks.

Feeling his feet cold and wet, Allen looked down. He saw his sneakers steeped in half an inch of water — water breaching the hole left by the bullet. Hearing a loud noise from the stern, he turned, and discovered breaching water was the least of his problems. The speedboat was right behind, and closing fast.

The channel coiled into sharp, blind turns, so narrow in spots, the reeds buffeted the sides of his boat.

Something didn't feel right — like he'd been here before but really hadn't. The water's depth diminished far more quickly than he remembered. Every few yards, he heard the whining of his Evinrude's prop grind the muddy bottom. Fearing he might burn out the engine, Allen eased up on the throttle.

Glimpsing back, Allen saw only the thicket of brown stalks he'd swept past at the last bend. At the next turn, the tunnel of tall reeds opened into a broad body of water. He'd made it through! The swath of reeds directly ahead should be the southern tip of Island Beach.

His heart dropped like a rock. Scanning the surrounding marsh flats, closing fast on both sides, he realized the land ahead was not, in fact, Island Beach. Rather, he had entered an oval pool — several hundred feet across — smack in the middle of Little Sedge Island. His only path of escape was the channel from which he'd just emerged.

Allen heard the roar of a screaming engine. Even as he spun to look, his three pursuers burst through the reeds, onto the lake, moving so fast he could already read the thrill of murder in their soulless eyes. One of the nameless faces hoisted the launcher to his shoulder.

Allen decided his one mistake, the wrong turn he'd taken into this tidal basin, would be his last. He searched the water's surface for the lightest shades of blue and green. Spotting cloudy water, caramel brown, off his starboard bow, he spun the wheel right. Fingers curled around his Beretta's grip, he slammed the heel of his hand on a red button sticking out from the console.

Instantly, the electric power-tilt began lifting his engine's lower unit. He held down the red button until the motor's angle was high enough to keep his propeller from snapping off, yet low enough to drive his Whaler forward. If Allen guessed right, at no point between the boat's bow and the swamp stalks 100 feet ahead would the water's depth exceed one foot.

Each time his shallow fiberglass bottom scraped the silt and sea-grass, the Whaler shuddered. Lurching side-to-side, Allen gripped the wheel tighter, holding his course for the shore.

He glanced back. The man resting the launch tube on his shoulder crouched, aimed, and wrapped his finger around the trigger. A second man thrust a warhead into the slim green barrel. The driver, whose wire-rim sunglasses glittered under the brilliant sun, flashed his quarry a smug grin. Allen prayed like hell the speedboat's hull was a deep-V.

The Whaler's flat bottom trembled and jerked and jolted. Allen could no longer distinguish water from mud.

He heard a loud thunk, thunk, thunk from behind, and turned.

The speedboat came to an abrupt halt. The pilot popped out of his seat, over-ended the console, and crashed flat on his back atop the boat's tapered bow. The man clutching the green tube slammed into the control panel, dropping the barrel in a vertical line to the floor. The third man pitched forward, slamming the back of the triggerman, who squeezed the trigger and unleashed his missile — straight into the bottom of his own boat.

A radiant fireball blinded Allen. Shielding his face with his arm, he groped for the throttle, and yanked it back. A second powerful explosion, the speedboat's gas tank, sent a thermal shock wave blistering past.

The Whaler lurched to a stop. When the white light receded, Allen saw thick black smoke hurtling toward the sky, and tiny fragments of fiberglass sloshing in the water where his pursuers had been.

But Allen's work had just begun. Even on a single engine, the ship stealing his crab would make the Inlet in under 10 minutes.

In the grimy quagmire, he turned his boat around. Clearing the shallowest part of the lake, he dropped the engine and opened to half throttle.

His Beretta held only two rounds. One, he swore, would reach its target.

37

*"**A big fireball and lots of smoke.** That's all."*

O'Donnell had just pulled alongside Rescue Vessel 18, a 40-footer commanded by Sergeant Nelson. From the flying bridge above No. 18's center cabin, Nelson was shouting down at Bateman, describing what he had seen.

Over the drone of idling engines, he recounted how 20 minutes earlier, from his post off Sunrise Beach, he watched a lone man at the helm of a small center console shoot a pistol at the trawler. The unidentified gunman damaged one of its engines, then survived a missile fired from the ship's deck, probably the same kind that killed Trooper Harrelson. After cutting in front of the trawler's bow, the man in the skiff sped off toward Little Sedge Island. An Avanti racer escorting the trawler tore off after him with a crew of three and a hand-held rocket launcher.

From his earlier conversation with Jennifer at Ocean County Medical Center, Bateman knew the man chased into the Sedge Islands could only be Allen.

First, Trooper Harrelson, and now, his good friend, both cut down in cold blood. He yelled up to Nelson. "Any sign of the Avanti since?"

"No, sir. They went into the Sedges, and I couldn't see a thing. Just flame and smoke from somewhere inside the swamp."

Informed of the savage missile attack on Harrelson and the near-hit on the rescue chopper, Superintendent Colonel Travis had ordered Bateman to limit his squad's action to reconnaissance and patrol. Governor Simon had activated the South Sector Air Unit of the National Guard, and directed that two F/A-18 Hornet strike-fighters stationed at McGuire Air Force Base be fueled, outfitted, and sent up to deal with the unidentified, well-armed aggressors. According to the governor, the fighters would arrive within the hour.

Bateman estimated the trawler would reach the ocean sooner than that, and thanks to the colonel, all he could do was sit back on the sidelines and watch.

He remembered Harrelson's bright-eyed innocence and refreshing reverence for authority. He recalled the young trooper's nervous shuffle at the altar where, only last month, he eagerly awaited his high school sweetheart. How cruelly those faceless barbarians had snuffed out the life of a good man with everything to live for!

And now, murdering his friend, they had brutally snatched a devoted father from his dying son, a loving husband from his adoring wife. How would he face Jennifer?

Cooling his heels while these cold-hearted killers fled right in front of him was too much for Bateman to handle. He'd bucked chain of command before, if not to thwart a crime, then to catch a crook. If he took action now, he might do both.

Bateman picked up the microphone and toggled Channel 9. All six vessels under his command, including the two off Tice's Shoal, were tuned to his frequency. "This is Lieutenant Bateman. We're going in for a closer look. This is not an assault. Take no offensive action unless I give the order. We're simply attempting to identify its port of origin. That's all." Harrelson's boyish grin flashed before his eyes. "Remember, those sons-of-bitches carry some heavy duty firepower, and we know they're quick to use it. Keep your weapons ready, but do not fire. We'll proceed in V-formation — I'll take point."

On Bateman's command, O'Donnell edged the throttle forward. Clutching the stock of his Remington in one hand, the lieutenant waved a go-forward sign with the other.

Surveying the bay to his left, he observed Russo and Adler leaving Tice's Shoal, three miles east, moving toward Pole Marker-B1, where Oyster Creek Channel met the Intracoastal Waterway. Sergeant Nelson slipped in behind Bateman's port side. The vessels commanded by Sanderson, Levin, and Conti formed the right slope of Bateman's V.

Bateman turned to O'Donnell. "Take it up to half throttle. I don't want those bastards getting away. Let's see if —"

"Lieutenant! I've got a visual on a boat, coming out of the marshes." It was Adler's voice blasting over the radio. "It's headed for the trawler, and fast."

Bateman grabbed the mike. "The speedboat?"

"No, same center console I saw before. He's going back for seconds."

"A Boston Whaler?"

"Affirmative. And get this. He's still got a gun ... and he's pointing it at the trawler."

Bateman lifted his binoculars and fingered the focus dial until the blurry skiff and its pilot emerged as clear lines. "Son-of-a-bitch, it's him!" He swept the binoculars further right, zeroing in on the ship's transom, and confirmed Nelson's earlier observation. Oily black smoke poured from its starboard engine, badly damaged and useless to the vessel. Bateman knew what he must do.

He dropped the glasses on the console and yanked the microphone. "All vessels. All vessels. Now hear this. Prepare to engage the trawler. Adler, Russo. Fall in on my port. I want those sons-of-bitches before they reach the Inlet. And keep the V tight."

His sharp-shooting skills about to be tested, Bateman's adrenaline gushed. He dropped the mike in its cradle, and glanced over at O'Donnell. "Full open. Southeast through Oyster Creek Channel."

The young sergeant's cerulean eyes grew wide.

"Yes, sir."

(🦀)　　*(🦀)*　　*(🦀)*

Allen spotted the trawler just north of The Dike, a slim spit jutting into Barnegat Bay from the boreal tip of Long Beach Island. The Dike's northeast periphery brushed Oyster Creek Channel on its last bend into Barnegat Inlet. Another 2,000 yards, and the trawler was free.

Once these poachers reached the Atlantic, Allen could not follow. His boat had already taken on an inch of water through the hole shot in its port side. Tossed about in the vigorous swells of the open ocean, his disabled Whaler, laden with water, was sure to founder. Besides, with only two bullets left, if he didn't take out the second engine now, he wouldn't at all.

Motor screaming, Allen charged straight for the trawler's stern. He saw lined up along the rail the same red uniforms as before. Some raised angry fists, shouting threats he could not hear. Another lifted to the rail one of those cursed green launch tubes, and trained it on his bow.

But Allen also saw his son's tears, the tears his boy shed when the bullies in the park taunted him with cruel delight. He recalled David's dejection at learning the bitter truth his own father, a doctor and scientist, could not help. He saw the anguished brown eyes of the woman he loved, powerless to make David well, torn between her desire to let Allen try, and her fear the attempt would kill him.

The faces of David and Jennifer dissolved into the gently rolling waves between his square-tipped bow and the trawler's transom.

For his cleanest shot at the trawler's stern, Allen stood erect, exposing his head and chest above the console. Steadying his weight, he gripped the wheel tight. Lifting his right arm straight out, Allen peered through the black sight notched on his Beretta's barrel. Nothing in the bay existed but a one-foot square of green wood on the trawler's stern, six inches above the water line, directly above the wake left behind by its one good engine.

Allen slowly squeezed the trigger. The report jolted his arm. He knew he'd missed. Again, he steadied his arm and pointed the pistol. Again, he fired. Again, he missed. Once more, he pulled the trigger, this time hearing the sickening click of a spent cartridge.

The trawler's sheer green transom came on him in a flash. Cursing his ineptitude, he jerked the wheel left, narrowly avoiding a collision with the ship's stern.

He swung the Whaler back toward the Sedge Islands, turning his head to see if the launch tube was still aimed in his direction. Before Allen's eyes reached the trawler's deck, something on the bay, moving from the west, caught his attention.

Seven fast-cruising vessels of various shapes and sizes, aligned in a V, converged on the trawler's stern. On their white fiberglass hulls, he discerned a blue and gold inverted triangle—state police boats! The largest of the seven, the 40-foot cruiser, belonged to the fleet at Point Pleasant Station.

His heart pounded. He might yet convince his friend, who no doubt commanded the approaching flotilla, to spare the giant crab, at least until he anesthetized it and removed its legs or remaining claw.

Allen turned his head another notch toward the trawler's deck. In that instant, a fiery white flash of incandescent light spewed from a metallic green vessel, a flaming warhead that shrieked straight for his churning hot Evinrude. Directly ahead, too far away, he saw Little Sedge Island. Directly behind, closing fast, the blazing missile. No time to think, no time to plan, no time to reason. Instinct took control. Even as he leapt from the boat, a blinding flash of thundering effulgence baked his eyes, and before he hit the water, a sizzling pulse seared his shoulders.

《🦀》   《🦀》   《🦀》

"Oh my God, did you see that!"

He had. Allen vanished behind a deafening fountain of fire, smoke, and shattered sea. Bateman trembled, cloaking his rage behind clenched fists and grinding teeth, curbing his emotion for the safety of his men. He spun to Nelson, and said between gritted teeth, "Bring me straight up that scumbag's ass."

"Yes, sir."

Bateman lifted the transmitter. "Gentlemen. I'm going to take a crack at the trawler's working engine. I need all of you to cover me. Sanderson and Levin, go ahead of me and draw fire from their port. Russo, Adler, same thing, but go in from starboard. Conti, you stick with me, to my left. Nelson, cover my right flank. Keep advancing, but weave and bob. Don't be sitting targets. When you're in range, fire at will. So there's no misunderstanding, that means shoot to kill. And if you see any of those damned rocket launchers pointed my way, don't miss."

Adler and Russo veered off to the trawler's port side, and took gunfire first. A dozen or so red uniforms dispersed along the trawler's stern peppered both their vessels with rounds from semiautomatic hand guns. Levin and Sanderson, swerving to the trawler's starboard side, took the heat off Adler and Russo, blasting the rail with 12-gauge shotguns and 9 mm Glocks. Two miscreants on the big ship collapsed to the deck in lifeless heaps.

A hundred yards behind the trawler, Bateman smiled the bittersweet smile of revenge.

Two rogues on the deck, one behind the other, lifted a rocket launcher and trained the barrel on O'Donnell and Bateman.

"Start weaving!" Bateman shouted.

O'Donnell tugged the wheel left, then right, left, right, steadily advancing toward the trawler's stern on a serpentine course, like a coiling cobra closing in on its prey.

Levin carved an erratic circle off the trawler's right side while his partner rained bullets at the pirates scattered above the transom. Russo and his two crewmates did the same, but off the trawler's port.

Both Levin and Russo must have seen, simultaneously, the missile launcher pointed at Bateman. Under fierce fire, they buzzed the trawler's stern, ripping a thunderous volley into the unknown militia taking aim at their commander. One of Russo's men served up three tear gas grenades from a Webley-Schermuly launcher.

Winding, twisting, and circling, Bateman's troopers escaped the enemy's fusillade. Sorkin's men were far less fortunate.

The hood pointing the rocket launcher at Bateman crumpled to the floor. His comrade, gripping the firing mechanism, jolted forward, into the rail, dropping the green tube harmlessly into the dark blue swells.

O'Donnell closed to within 100 yards of the trawler's stern deck. Through dense black smoke oozing from the crippled engine, Bateman spotted the patch of transom his bullet must pierce to disable the remaining engine. Flicking off the safety latch on his Remington, he stopped dead in his tracks.

Something on the trawler's deck caught his eye. When he realized what it was, he laughed out loud.

The sailors were screaming epithets, not at his troopers, but at each other. Half the murderous mob pointed to the middle of the ship's stern deck at something Bateman couldn't quite see. The other half balled their fists to their eyes, futilely wiping away the venomous sting of tear gas. Three others, embroiled in a full-fledged fistfight, bled profusely from their noses. One strapping scoundrel — impeccably attired in a dark blue business suit — backed one gangster in red against the stern rail, and shoved a pistol in his ribs.

Under his armada's relentless barrage, the ruthless, well-equipped militia had degenerated into a hapless band of common thugs fighting among themselves. But the trawler, 200 yards from Barnegat Inlet, still advanced. In less than five minutes, the ship would pass through the Inlet and enter the open ocean. Bateman must act now, or lose his chance.

38

The last trace of exploding gasoline winked out on the water's surface, plunging Allen into murky green darkness. Temples pulsing, dizzy and disoriented, he felt a vague sense of his arms and legs, flaccid and lifeless, sink deeper into the underwater gloom. His descent ended gently when his hands and chest, then his legs, brushed the velvet mud at the bottom of the bay. He wanted desperately to paddle, kick, anything to help himself, but his brain refused to send the signal.

The throbbing in his head worked like a narcotic, lulling him into a woozy calm, a stupor soothing him to the point of indifference. Flat on his stomach under the tepid water, he closed his eyes, submitting to the lure of exhaustion.

Drawing nearer to slumber, something poked the side of his head. Annoyed at the intrusion, Allen beckoned his arm to reach for the object that had come to rest against his nape. This time, his hand responded to his mind's directive.

Groping blindly, his fingers caressed a smooth, curved form, hard and heavy. Allen turned his head, opened his eyes, and saw the blurred outline of something black, inches from his face.

On his silt bed, at the threshold of eternal sleep, Allen's curiosity got the better of him. He rolled the object off his neck, and found himself staring through cloudy green water at a thick black cylinder with a stick, no, a handle — yes, a handle, sticking out from the top.

He knew this object. He knew its purpose. Instantly, his stupor gave way to panic. Unable to breathe, his chest felt ready to burst. His reasoning mind, muddled for want of oxygen, now honed keen as a dagger. His only goal — reach the surface.

Allen pulled his hands close to his sides, planted his palms flat on the mud, and with all the strength he could summon to his arms, thrust off the bottom. The rush of lukewarm water rippled against his shirt, and the glimmering glow of sunlight streamed down from above.

Faster than he expected, even before he started kicking, his head shot through the surface, and automatically, his chest heaved. The sun-baked air tasted sweet to his lungs.

Surprised to find himself standing easily in water neck-high, he remembered that he had been closing in on the shallow Sedges when he dove off the side of his boat. No bones screamed in pain, and a quick glance at his arms and torso revealed no leaking blood. His foot nudged the weighted plastic cylinder resting on the bottom of the bay. Gulping a deep breath, he poked his head underwater and lifted the object by its handle.

Having escaped the explosion in one piece, Allen studied the water around him. Ahead, to his left and right, 50 yards equidistant, he spotted tall brown reeds shooting up from level marshy bases that he guessed were the Sedge Islands. Surveying the horizon at his back, he made out the mainland across the bay, and the towering smokestack of Oyster Creek Generating Station.

He turned south, and saw less than 10 yards from where he stood why the object he now gripped had survived intact. From console to stern, nothing remained of his beloved Whaler but countless fragments of white fiberglass. Remarkably, though, a three-foot chunk of the bow floated upside down in a single piece. His outboard engine had likely taken a direct hit. But the hull's front section, containing the bow storage hatch in which he'd stowed the pump sprayer, had escaped the brunt of the missile's force. The hatch must have sprung open and spilled its contents to the bottom of the bay.

About a mile beyond the remnants of his Whaler, Allen saw another strip of swamp stalks, either Clam Island or The Dike. He didn't take long to conclude the Sedges were the only place he could reach without succumbing to fatigue. The spongy underwater mud sucked the soles of his sneakers like quicksand, turning each labored step into a hard-earned victory. The burden dangling from his left hand slowed his progress, but he refused to let it drop. If there were some way, any way, he could catch up with the trawler, he would need what it held.

From somewhere nearby, out of sight, Allen heard the pop-pop-pop of rapid gunfire, then recalled the armada of state troopers he'd seen chasing the trawler seconds before his Whaler was obliterated by a rocket. Traipsing toward the lithe brown reeds listing in the gentle breeze, he listened for the thunder of exploding missiles, but heard only the occasional crackle of small arms fire.

He plodded on until the water hovered above his kneecaps. Calves aching, he paused to rest. When the throbbing at the back of his legs subsided, he tread with ease, ascending a little higher with each step.

The distant gunshots rang out less frequently. By the time the bay licked at his ankles, he heard only the soft slapping of water against land and the lonely swish of swaying reeds.

His chest tightened. The trawler had escaped through the Inlet, and with it, his only hope for David. He stopped and listened, wishing for another burst of gunfire, any evidence the trawler was near, but heard only waves and wind, a dreary dirge for his dying son.

Allen trudged the last few yards to a foot-wide strip of black mud intervening between open bay and swaying stalks. He dropped his sprayer, laden with MS-222, and sat beside it on the silt. Squeezing his knees to his chest, he folded his arms over the top, stuck his toes in the water, and stared out across the rippling azure plain. Like his heart, the bay was bleak, blue, and empty. He tucked his head between his knees, and for many minutes, watched the black mud shift to the whim of the lapping bay.

Despite the brawling and cursing Bateman observed among the red uniformed sailors on the trawler's stern deck, apparently, no one had told the ship's captain the crew had lost its enthusiasm. Propelled by a single working engine, the trawler continued making headway toward Barnegat Inlet and the open Atlantic.

Bateman glanced back at O'Donnell. "Take it down to half throttle."

The shrieking pistons sighed with relief.

"Hold her steady."

"I'll do my best."

Bateman lifted his high-powered Remington, resting its umber stock squarely on his right shoulder. He leaned against the aluminum bar rimming the console, and peered through the telescopic sight atop the barrel, aligning the scope's cross hair with dark green wood inches above the trawler's wake. Waiting patiently for his best shot, he curled his index finger inside the trigger guard, a twitch away from hurtling the rifle's destructive cargo. From somewhere far away, he heard an erratic burst of gunfire. With every ounce of concentration, he wiped from his mind the men on the trawler's deck and focused on his objective.

In slow motion, he squeezed the trigger. The sharp bang of igniting gunpowder stung Bateman's ears. His pain was instantly replaced by the joy of what he saw ahead. Dark clouds, smoking diesel fuel, billowed from the shattered wood where his bullet had penetrated.

Like a sloop without a tiller, the trawler drifted helplessly north-east, guided only by the ebbing tide. On its aft deck, four men tackled the burly ruffian in blue who had pointed a pistol at one of his comrades, and pummeled him with fists and oaths. Along the rail above the transom, others in the mob held their palms high, pleading for their lives. A few pointed to the center of the trawler's rear deck.

Bateman and his six pilots followed the crippled vessel until it beached on the dunes inside the southern tip of Island Beach State Park, then climbed aboard without resistance. Most of the trawler's crew eagerly allowed themselves to be cuffed and taken from the ship. On the aft deck, inside a recessed fiberglass cargo hold, Bateman discovered why.

He directed his troopers to round up any survivors still in hiding and book them on murder, attempted murder, conspiracy, and a host of other crimes he'd tack on later. Remembering his fallen friend and young Harrelson, he added, "If any bones happen to get busted, you know, in all the confusion, well, no one's getting written up."

Even before his troopers finished mopping up the ruthless marauders, Bateman climbed back into his idling vessel. He needed to know for certain if his friend had perished in the erupting waters. Though he'd prevented the trawler's escape, he had failed Jennifer, arriving too late to keep Allen from harm. If Allen's body hadn't been blown apart by the explosion, he could at least pull it from the water before the bay's bottom-dwelling scavengers picked it to pieces.

Pointing to a smudge of blue and white debris floating on the water off Little Sedge Island, he turned to O'Donnell. "Let's have a look."

꩜   ꩜   ꩜

From somewhere outside his gloom, Allen heard a sputtering engine. He looked up. Coming into view from around a bend in the tall swamp grass he saw the white bow of a trihull skiff.

A tall man with black hair stood in the stern, waving. "He's alive!"

The voice was familiar.

With the sound of sandpaper scraping wood, Rescue Vessel 24 slid onto the narrow beach, its front quarter vanishing into the brown reeds.

Lieutenant Lawrence Bateman hopped out.

Allen leaped to his feet, arm extended, and was met with a bear hug from his old friend.

"When I saw your boat blow, I thought you were done."

"I jumped as far away as I could. I only wish my Whaler had been as lucky."

Bateman chortled. "You can buy a new boat. A new butt, not so easy."

"Right before they nailed me, I thought I saw your men approaching."

"That was us."

"Did you stop them?"

His friend nodded. "And thanks to you, I figured out how."

Allen slammed his fist into his open palm. "The other engine! You nailed it."

"Exactly. Grounded up on Island Beach. Surrendered like lambs."

"Who are they?"

Bateman squinted at him, as if confused. "I thought you knew. They claim they were hired by Robert Sorkin, the Texas billionaire. And they've got that damn crab, alive and kicking, stowed in a cargo hold. To tell you the truth, I was hoping you could tell me what a small army of Sorkin's mercenaries planned to do with that thing."

Something didn't add up. Earlier in the hospital, when Clayton told him of Maddox's scheme to sell Sorkin the PDL and Hope-1 codons, he'd said nothing of a plan to deliver the actual crab. Allen wondered if Clayton even knew. "It's a long story. But first, I owe you an apology. Second, an explanation. The apology I can give you now. The explanation, that'll take some time." He'd already pushed his friendship to the limit, but for David, he'd push a little further. "I'll tell you everything, but first, I need a big favor. It'd mean putting your job on the line, but ..."

"Stop right there."

Bateman's tone was harsh, and Allen knew he deserved it, but time was critical. If only he could explain his dilemma, maybe his friend would help. "Please, Larry. I have to —"

"Damn it! Will you shut up for one minute."

"But —"

"Listen. If you don't keep quiet, I'm liable to change my mind." Bateman stared off toward the mainland. "I saw Jennifer. I know what you want. Remember something — I've got three kids of my own, and I'd kill for every one of the them." He glanced down at the pump lying on the charcoal mud. "I just hope whatever you've got in there, it's strong enough to take out Godzilla."

Friday

July 3

39

Allen leaned against the kitchen counter in his home by the beach, basking in the early morning silence. He observed through the solarium window above the sink a curtain of charcoal cutting the baby blue sky in two. No rain had fallen since Monday, and lawns had begun to brown. Allen estimated the approaching shroud, harbinger of a cold front from the west, would screen the sun in less than an hour, bringing with it a steady summer rain to quench the parched Jersey soil.

Having tossed and turned all three hours since slipping into bed at two-thirty that morning, Allen yearned for another cup of coffee. He had no special reason to stay awake, but his body was sending a clear message — don't expect sleep anytime soon. He trudged to the BrewMaster and reached for its handle.

The doorbell rang twice.

Allen sighed. He'd been expecting a caller, and he supposed he was thankful this visitor had waited until daybreak to discharge his duty.

He swung open the door for his guest, and invited him in. Glancing to the street beyond, the white van was nowhere in sight, only a blue Buick Century, vacant, parked by the curb. Interesting that Major Charles F. Clayton would show up alone. "Figured I'd see you sooner or later."

Clayton swaggered through the front door, into the living room. He wore a gray business suit, freshly pressed, and black wingtips, buffed to a sheen, with a crisp white dress shirt and solid navy blue tie.

"Can I get you some coffee?" Allen asked.

"No thanks. I ate breakfast."

"Any trouble finding the house?"

"Not at all," he answered, his voice strong and crisp for so early in the day.

"Lot's of folks miss the turnoff at the library."

Clayton smirked. "I have at my disposal the most advanced geodesic tracking and guidance system available anywhere in the world. I never get lost."

"Good morning."

At the same time, both men wheeled toward a feminine voice from behind.

Jennifer wore the same knee-length tie-dyed purple pullover she'd slipped into after they'd returned home from Omnigen last night. "Dr. Clayton, my wife, Jennifer. Jennifer, Dr. Clayton."

Clayton marched over, thrusting his arm out. "Pleasure to meet you."

Jennifer stifled a yawn, and squeezed his hand. "Likewise." Throughout the six hour, 15-minute gene transplantation procedure, Jennifer had watched over his shoulder. At no time, however, had he spoken to her of Robert J. Sorkin III, tapped telephones, or BHERT — just as Clayton had warned. So he wasn't quite sure how to explain his affiliation with this tall black man who appeared very formal, very official, and well, very much like a government agent. "Dr. Clayton works with, uh, he works for, he works in ..."

"Ma'am, I'm an enforcement agent with the Food and Drug Administration."

Clayton had bailed him out and answered honestly at the same time. "Yes, he's with the FDA."

"Is my husband in some sort of trouble?"

"Depends if he cooperates with our investigation."

Scrutinizing her husband, Jennifer said, "I'm absolutely certain Allen will cooperate, won't you, dear?"

His reply was automatic. "Of course, honey."

"Daddy, who's that man?"

All three pivoted. A little boy leaning against the arch dividing the kitchen and living room regarded the adults with blood-shot eyes. The Yankees cap perched on his head partially concealed a gauze bandage wrapped around from his forehead to the base of his skull. Except for the bandage and a pasty complexion, David looked like any other nine-year-old who'd arisen too early. He had made a remarkable come-back thanks to the protocol that was quickly shrinking the tumor.

Jennifer said soothingly, "He's here to see Daddy."

David's presence in the room would dispel any doubt in Clayton's mind that Allen had implanted the Hope-1 genes. When Allen and Clayton last spoke, less than 24 hours earlier, David couldn't move, let alone stand and speak. Searching Clayton's face for some sign of anger or astonishment, he found, oddly, glinting brown eyes and a crooked smug grin.

David wore emerald green pajama bottoms and a pale green T-shirt. He looked up at the stranger, beaming, and said in a shaky voice bolstered by pride, "My dad's the best."

"That great big smile tells me you're right," Clayton replied.

Jennifer strode to David and dropped to one knee. "You've had a long night and you're up much too early. I'm marching you right back to bed."

Clayton nodded to Allen. "Your wife is right. David should rest. No reason we can't finish our business outside."

Jennifer returned to the men, and Clayton clasped her hand. "You have a special little boy there," then glared at Allen, "and a stubborn big one over here."

"Tell me about it," she sighed, betraying a wary mix of love and frustration.

Grateful Clayton would spare David the terror of watching his father led away, possibly in handcuffs, Allen opened the front door. He glanced back at his wife. "I'll be a little while."

Clayton tailed Allen to the door, stopped and turned. "I won't say good-bye just yet. I suspect we'll be seeing more of each other."

Of course they would. Innumerable FDA hearings and judicial proceedings were sure to follow his unauthorized attempt to save David. The grueling inquiries would no doubt exact a steep price on his family, paid in both time and stress. As for what might happen to him, he didn't care. They could lock him up and throw away the key. He'd given David a fighting chance.

Stepping outside first, Allen descended the stoop to the front walk, and gazed to the end of the street where, just beyond a low concrete barrier, Barnegat Bay met the barrier island. The spotless sky had surrendered to the drab clouds moving inexorably west, nudging the last vestige of blue out over the Atlantic.

Clayton followed Allen off the stoop onto the concrete ribbon spanning the cream-colored stones covering the ground. Standing shoulder-to-shoulder with Allen, he stared up at the dreary overcast. "Looks like a change in weather."

"Sure does," Allen said. "Just hope it clears out by tomorrow."

"Why? Going somewhere?"

Allen didn't flinch. "Nowhere special. Just that rain around here would spoil a lot of Fourth of July barbecues."

"That's right, I'd almost forgotten." Clayton chuckled. "With my busy schedule, I'm lucky I remember Christmas."

From the corner of his eye, Allen saw Clayton turn and stare straight at him. "Quite a recovery your son's made the past 24 hours."

Allen spun and stared straight back. "Don't bullshit me; you know perfectly well why he's better. Nothing gets past you."

"Robert Sorkin did."

"Not his pal on the trawler."

"He's not talking."

"Did you question the crew?"

"None of them knew where they were going, not even the skipper. He told us Lowry was supposed to give him a bearing after they cleared the Inlet. Sorkin's so damn paranoid, I'm not surprised."

"Go after him in Texas."

"Tried, but no luck."

"He has to turn up somewhere."

"Maybe, maybe not. On Wednesday, he funneled half his bank balances to untraceable accounts around the world. Seems he planned on spending the last 50 or 60 years of his life as a citizen of some place other than the United States. But he'll fumble, and we'll nail him. The important thing is we got the crab before he did, thanks to you and your police pal."

"Always a pleasure to serve Uncle Sam."

"And yourself, too."

"I won't deny it. But if my son dies, he dies with the knowledge I did everything in my power to save him."

"That's real touching. Let's see ..." Clayton rubbed his chin in mock reflection. "In the process, you violated Paragraphs 3, 7-A, and 11, Sub-Section Four of the RAC Code of Professional Conduct. You flouted six FDA regulations mandating prior authorization for recombinant DNA experimentation, four of which can result in criminal prosecution. You've exposed yourself to fines up to $50,000 and jail time up to 15 years. I'd say that puts you in a shitload of trouble."

"You know something," Allen replied, "I'd do it again in a second."

"I know you would, you hard-headed son-of-a-bitch." Clayton looked down at the cement walk, as if studying the clover squashed between the cracks. When he lifted his eyes, their burning intensity seemed to cool. "What's your preliminary read on the tumor's reaction to the amplified suppressors?"

"Too early to know for sure, but it's pretty clear the mutant genes expressed almost immediately. David regained consciousness around midnight. At the very least, there was a reduction in the tumor's mass at the site of the hypothalamus and pituitary. We've scheduled an MRI at Ocean County Medical Center this afternoon. I'll verify the results then ... unless, of course, I'm not permitted to go."

Clayton turned away, toward the street. For a full minute he bared the back of his dark suit to Allen, saying nothing. Finally, he turned around, revealing pinched lips, and shook his head. "You're a fortunate man. You possess remarkable scientific skill, you have a beautiful wife who obviously adores you, and you're blessed with a son who worships the ground you walk on."

"I count my blessings every day."

"And you have a helluva friend in Lieutenant Bateman."

No doubt about that. "Larry risked his job for me."

"To say the least. Violated state regs twice in one week — last Sunday, concealing the claw, and yesterday, letting you board the trawler. And let's not forget unauthorized use of a police vehicle. Delivers you and a six-foot crab leg to the hospital, absconds with your wife and kid, lights flashing, sirens screaming, straight to Omnigen."

"Must've been quite a scene. Wish I could've been there. But bottom line, Bateman's penchant for breaking rules is almost as bad as your own. From what I hear, he'll be lucky to get deck-swabbing duty at marine police headquarters, that is, if Colonel Travis doesn't fire him."

Allen cringed. "Larry knew they'd come down hard."

"Hard! A ruined career is more like it."

Allen kept quiet, feeling very guilty for the trouble he'd caused his friend.

BHERT's second-in-command continued calmly, "There are, of course, the positives."

Allen feared all the good Bateman had done would be conveniently swept under the rug by the bureaucrats and politicians. "You're right. Someone should keep in mind the fact that he stopped the trawler from escaping."

"Still, he had no authority to attack. In fact, he assaulted the vessel in direct contravention of a specific order issued by Governor Simon."

"But he stopped them."

"Ends don't always justify means. Next, you'll say if I were in his shoes, I would've done the same thing."

"Wouldn't you?"

Clayton scowled. "Maybe."

"In fact, I wouldn't be surprised if you've pushed the envelope yourself once or twice. People like you and Larry don't get where you are unless you do exactly that."

"Look. Maybe we're all cast from the same mold, but rules are rules."

"I see. Larry foils the sale of top-secret codons to a cold-blooded murderer, and his career is over. Makes a lot of sense."

"I'm not finished. Fortunately, your friend's got a few things going for him."

"Like what?"

"For one, stumbling over that stiff Maddox iced."

Allen recalled the horror on Larry's face when he discovered Brian Strasser's body in the walk-in freezer. After they'd completed the gene implantation, Larry helped Allen and Jennifer clean up the lab. Carrying unused crab tissue into the freezer, he literally stumbled over the frozen corpse.

"When we pulled into Omnigen, Larry recognized the reporter's car. He'd seen it there earlier, but thought Strasser was just being persistent, waiting to ambush him inside. He never expected to find the poor guy chilled solid in the freezer."

Clayton snickered. "That's one sight I'm glad I missed."

"Is that all Larry's got going for him?"

"Well, there's me, too. But I shouldn't have done it."

"Done what?"

Clayton's dark eyes gleamed. "Important advantages come with having the president's ear."

"What exactly did you do?"

"Mr. Bateman and I have struck a little bargain."

"You've seen him?"

"Let's just say I've had a busy morning."

"What kind of deal?"

"The moment we arrived at Island Beach, my team took custody of the vessel and its crew. I think our impudence pissed off your governor, but what happened out there yesterday is precisely why BHERT exists. Only a handful of people know what was stashed on that trawler, and my job is to keep it that way. If Mr. Bateman were to spout off to the media, you in his corner, he might actually be given credibility. Could be a major embarrassment to the administration. But you see, Dr. Johnson, your friend's already forgotten all about the claw and the crab and helping you with your experiment at Omnigen."

"What's the catch?"

"The president placed a call to Colonel Travis. Put in a few good words on Mr. Bateman's behalf, enough to save his ass."

If Clayton had indeed intervened, Larry's future would remain intact. "I appreciate you stepping to bat for him."

"No reason to wreck a good man's career."

"If it's OK to ask, where's the crab now?"

"Your genetically enhanced crustacean has become classified property of the United States government. It's been transferred to a confidential location. A team of biochemists and geneticists from NIH have already begun examining it."

Maybe he was overly tired, but for some reason, the thought struck Allen funny. "Sort of like the alien who landed his spaceship in Roswell and got dissected at an Air Force base in Dayton."

Clayton grimaced. "Not that horseshit again."

"What about the therapeutic value of the crab's mutation — its ability to delay senescence? I guess the public never gets to see that."

"I already told you: policy-makers at the highest level firmly believe this country isn't ready for its entire population to suddenly start living to 150. We've already forecast the dire economic effects. What about the social impact? Over the course of an extended life span, a person might choose two or three careers, religions, even families. Would that be good or bad? Tough questions.

"And what happens when Methuselah gets into the wrong hands overseas? Balances of power could shift forever. Right here in America, what if only big money could afford the miracle of longer life? The poor lose out again, leaving political upheaval, maybe revolution, the only equalizer. Too chancy. Someday, a phased approach might work. But in the foreseeable future, nobody — absolutely nobody — gets the benefit of the Methuselah Gene."

To himself, Allen gloated, but to Clayton, who was dead wrong and might never know it, he merely smirked. "What about the tumor-suppressors?"

Clayton's lips traced a broad smile. "Different story. At this very moment, a team of scientists sequestered at Bethesda, including two of the country's top oncologists, are picking apart the crab's Chromosome 8 codon. They're analyzing the same sequencing data, incidentally, prepared by you and Dr. Miles. Preliminary word from the Bethesda think tank — Hope-1 works fast against a broad range of tumors. It's a winner."

"Great. So the world gets a sure-fire gene therapy to fight cancer, and I get to go to jail." In truth, he would serve time gladly, knowing he had fulfilled the most important promise he'd ever made to his son. "Before you take me into custody, might I spend a few minutes with my family. Jennifer knows nothing about you or BHERT, and I'd like to prepare her for what's coming."

Clayton's eyes opened into wide, incredulous circles, as if ogling at a creature from another planet, then burst into laughter so loud Allen was sure his neighbors heard.

"I fail to see what's so funny."

The major stumbled backward, off the walk, onto the stones. He pointed to Allen, and gasped, "You? Jail?" He broke into laughter again, this time popping his hand to his mouth, struggling to stifle his mirth.

Allen sneaked a timid glance at the house next door, waiting for his neighbor to walk outside and investigate the commotion.

Clayton's roars receded to intermittent chuckles. "You really think I'm here to arrest you?" Clayton looked like he might break into another fit of laughter. Mercifully, he held back. "Prison or not, you have 10 times more knowledge than Mr. Bateman of what went on this week in your quiet little hamlet by the Jersey shore. That's all the government needs. A loose canon, a reliable one, blabbing to anyone who'll listen about a giant mutant crab that evil Uncle Sam is unjustly concealing from his constituents? No way. I'm not here to arrest you. I'm here to make you a proposition."

So here came the rub. "And what might that be?"

"I trust when you get past what you did for David, you'll remember you still need to put food on the table."

Clayton was right. Omnigen and his job were no more. "What do you have in mind?"

"Well, you see, I have this really big problem. Lots of folks in the world, some good, some bad, have gotten their hands on recombinant DNA technology. Every month, more and more scientists try rearranging what natural selection has taken millions of years to achieve. BHERT makes sure all those smart folks playing God don't alter the scheme of life in a way that harms people or the environment, whether by accident or design."

"What's the problem? Your job sounds impressive, even exciting."

"Glad you feel that way." Clayton flashed a rascally grin. "You see, after a while, Colombian rain forests and Egyptian deserts get pretty old, especially when you have a beautiful wife and three kids who miss your butt something awful. Fact is, these days, a job with BHERT is a high-growth career opportunity. I can't handle the shit that comes in fast enough. You're as good an all-around geneticist as I've met, and you're already familiar with Methuselah, BHERT's number one secret."

"I take it you're offering me a job."

"I'd consider it a privilege if you'd join my team. Besides, with you aboard to lighten the load, my marriage might just be saved."

He had expected BHERT to drag him off in shackles. Instead, Clayton was recruiting him for the most sophisticated scientific intelligence organization in the country. He inhaled two deep breaths, probing for a reasoned response, then shook his head. "You sure know how to make an offer that's hard to refuse."

"I hope you won't."

"Can I discuss it with my wife?"

"Only if you accept."

"Fair enough."

Clayton reached inside his suit jacket and handed Allen a business card. "Leave a message at that number. When a young woman answers 'Dory's Florist,' don't worry. It's a cover."

"Of course."

Clayton looked up at the ashen sky shrouding Barnegat Bay. "I best be on my way. Got a lunch date with a very special lady. Break it, and my next call's to a divorce lawyer."

Allen extended his hand. "It's been a pleasure."

Clayton's grip was firm. "The pleasure's been mine. Hope to hear from you next week."

Sporting a satisfied smile, Clayton sauntered to his blue Buick and drove off.

Allen watched him disappear around the corner, then stood alone, whiffing the invigorating salt of the sea, wondering where life would lead him next — or better yet, where he would next lead life.

Saturday
July 4

40

A smooth ocean breeze cooled the evening sands of Island Beach, and the first stars of twilight twinkled in the purple sky over the dark Atlantic. Invisible under the shroud of night, the surf broke gently against the sand in a faint, barely perceptible rhythm.

Crossing the wide parking lot beside the beach, Jennifer held David's hand. "Sure you're up to this?"

David pulled away from his mother, obviously insulted at her suggestion he wasn't well enough to walk the distance. "Are you kidding? This is easy. I hiked a whole lot more with Dad last week, and that was when I felt really crummy."

"Good. After we trek all the way there and you poop out, don't ask me to carry you back."

"Don't worry, Mom. I feel great."

Jennifer looked askance at Allen, then rolled her eyes to the blackening heavens. "You're two of a kind. Always pushing. Never stopping."

Relishing the thought he and his son shared such an attractive quality, Allen beamed.

"Of course, with you as a father, I can't expect him to act any different." She swung around, facing a Mr. Goodtreat ice cream truck idling under a tall lamppost at the far end of the parking lot where the sand skimmed over the asphalt. About a dozen boys and girls, two baby strollers, and assorted moms and dads, lined up at the window of the shiny white truck, waiting to be served. "I'm buying myself a lemon Froze Cone," she said. "Any requests?"

David whined, "We can't stop. We'll miss the fireworks."

"We've got a 10-minute walk, young man, and I'm thirsty."

Allen intervened, "Your mom's right. The fireworks don't go off until nine. Even if they start sooner, we can see them while we're walking."

"All right," David said begrudgingly, "I want chocolate ice cream. In a cone, not a cup. And I don't like the soft kind. I want the hard kind, like we buy at Shop Rite."

"The magic word?" Allen said.

"Pleeease."

"Thank you." Allen looked wistfully at his wife. "I'll have chocolate. But make mine soft. You know, the kind you lick slowly from the top down, then finish off around the sides."

Jennifer smirked in a way he found enticing, the sort of smile that made Allen know sleep would be the second thing to come after they slipped under the covers that night.

"Pleeease," Allen said, slipping her a sly smile.

"Don't go anywhere," she said. "I'll be right back." Jennifer turned and dashed off to Mr. Goodtreat.

Allen's hungry eyes followed her.

David intruded on his fantasies. "So Dad, when do you start the new job?"

Allen's eyes lingered on his Jennifer. "What's that, David?"

A sharp tug on the back of his T-shirt jerked Allen from his cravings. He turned. "I'm sorry son. What did you say?"

"The new job. When do you start?"

Allen couldn't help but feel proud of what he had accomplished. David hadn't complained of a headache or dizzy spell in the 48 hours since the ribozyme vectors delivered the crab's potent tumor-suppressor genes to his brainstem. David's MRI yesterday afternoon indicated a 32 percent shrinkage in the tumor's mass, leaving Dr. Loman at a complete loss for words.

For all he'd risked to help his child, Allen knew he could not have performed the delicate gene transfer procedure without the wisdom and foresight of his slain colleague, Dr. Nathan Miles. When they'd last spoken, Tuesday in the lab, Miles vowed, "When it's time to help your son, I won't let you down." Miles kept his word, and thanks to Hope-1, the legacy of his fallen friend would live on in his boy.

Now, for the first time in a year, David's energy level exceeded his own. "I won't start my new job until the end of August. First, I'd like to spend time with you and mom. Catch up on some of the fun things we haven't been able to do."

"Like what?"

"Like a trip up to New York to see the Bronx Bombers in action. I also owe you a ride on Barnegat Bay."

His son giggled. "Yeah, when you get a new boat."

David still wore his Yankees cap, but Allen suspected by the time school started in September, he'd be wearing it by choice, not to ward off the stares. Allen had already spotted soft, downy fuzz growing on his son's scalp.

"Will we have to move when you start the new job?"

Allen's duties would require he venture far from his seashore sanctuary, sometimes for weeks at a time. But during those absences, his heart would remain sheltered in the embrace of his family. "We won't have to move, but I do have to travel."

David's arms circled Allen's waist. "I hope not too much. I'll miss you when you're gone."

Allen squeezed his son tight. "If the job keeps me away from you and mom too much, I'll quit. Traveling once in a while, I don't mind, but not all year. I've got a vested interest in sticking around to see you grow up."

"I'm glad we don't have to move. I like it here."

How fitting his son loved the sea, for the sea had spawned the miracle granting him his reprieve.

Arms wrapped secure around his father, David looked up. "This new kind of medicine you gave me. Do you really think it'll help me live as long as other kids?"

Allen stared into eyes a copy of his own. Never one to leave destiny to the vicissitudes of happenstance, Allen had taken all necessary precautions to assure his son would enjoy a full, healthy existence. Hope-1 would stave off cancer. For long life, the wondrous crab offered a different miracle.

"I have no doubt you'll live as long as other children." Allen grinned. "And who knows? Maybe a lot longer."